FADE TO BLACK

Mahala, city of contrasts. Sun and hope. Dark and despair. I love her, and I hate her too.

As a boy, I would look down, into the mesh of walkways that criss-crossed the gaps Under. Into the gloom of thousands of lives lived in near-darkness, all squashed together by the weight of Over above them. The weight of obedience.

Even at ten it rankled me, but my hate wouldn't fully harden for years yet. At ten, I knew little else except the stories Ma told us, and what the priests said in the little classroom behind the temple, or in their sermons.

But I was still a good boy, then, who believed what he was told. I believed what the priests said, that the new Archdeacon would make everything right if only we prayed hard enough, that the world was essentially a fair place and our father would come back to us.

I roll my eyes at the boy I was.

FADE TO BLACK

FRANCIS KNIGHT

www.orbitbooks.net

ORBIT

First published in Great Britain in 2013 by Orbit

A CIP catalogue record for this book is available
from the British Library.

ISBN 978-0-356-50166-6

Typeset in Garamond by M Rules
Printed and bound by CPI Group (UK) Ltd, Croydon, CR0 4YY

Papers used by Orbit are from well-managed forests
and other responsible sources.

MIX
Paper from
responsible sources
FSC® C104740
www.fsc.org

Orbit
An imprint of
Little, Brown Book Group
100 Victoria Embankment
London EC4Y 0DY

An Hachette UK Company
www.hachette.co.uk

www.orbitbooks.net

To Burtus, and afternoons of pendulous crunchalating.
Because Dwarves make perfect muses.

Chapter One

Chapter One

I forced the door, nice and quiet, with my ever-so-slightly-illegal pulse pistol at the ready. Magic wasn't usually on the agenda for runaways, but this little madam was exceptional: booby traps a speciality – I'd almost gone up in flames this morning. Twice. If it wasn't for the obscene amount of money her parents had offered me to find her, I'd have given it up as a bad job.

The room beyond the door was even more dingy and rubbish-strewn than the corridor, and that was saying something. Rainwater had driven through a broken window and the faint stench of synth drifted up from where it pooled. I sidestepped around it. You could catch a fatal dose and never know until it was too late. Residents hurried away behind me with a mutter of footfalls. One sight of me, a burly man in a subtly armoured, close-fitting all over with a flapping black coat, and the scavenge-rat teens that called this place home took to their heels. I dare say it looked too much like a Ministry Special's uniform with an added coat. Living this far down, a nose for trouble was essential.

I checked around carefully, trying to listen past the far rumble and thump of factories above us. A flash of movement off to my left, a hint of bright blue shirt. Lise, the girl I was after. With nothing to alarm me – yet – I made my careful way in. There it was again: a flicker of blue, floating in the gloom. I slid my fingers round the pistol's trigger and pointed it. It wouldn't kill her, but it would give me just enough of an edge. I didn't understand it myself because it's not my kind of magic, but the man who sold it to me had explained it as a way of interrupting thought processes, quite abruptly. An almost painless magical cosh, if you will. It would shut her down, at least for long enough for me to restrain her. Killing people wasn't my line of work, or my style. If I'd had a taste for it I'd have stayed with the guards or, Goddess forbid, gone into the Ministry Specials, but I hadn't liked the amount of paperwork, or the restrictions. I preferred the more freeform business I was in, where responsibility wasn't something I needed to worry about.

I slid forwards, making sure there were no nasty surprises waiting in the rubbish at my feet. She moved again and black hair whirled out as she ran down a short corridor. I followed with exaggerated care, in case she had any more tricks in store for me. She wasn't stupid. There had been those booby traps. Plus, she'd covered her tracks like a professional. It had taken me a week to find her, a length of time almost unheard of. I'd nearly had to resort to magic, and I never like to do that.

The information from her parents had shown me she was book-smart at least, a high-ranking fifteen-year-old student in alchemy. Bright enough to cover her tracks almost seamlessly; and ruthless, or desperate, enough to defend her retreat. Clever enough to come down here, on the border of Namrat's Armpit and Boundary, right where the people she normally mixed with wouldn't dream of coming. Where people minded their own business or else, and she had a hope of hiding without falling into the black hole we knew as Namrat's Armpit, or the 'Pit for short. I tried not to think of the alchemist's brew of toxic chemicals, residue of the synth disaster, just below the floor.

Rain rattled a broken window and a door snicked closed ahead of me. The little brat had led me a merry chase, but I had her now and the fat pay-purse was all but in my hand. She knew I was there though, and she'd proved resourceful so far. I decided not to trust the door, or the girl. Trust wasn't a luxury I could afford in this line of work. I had a small wooden baton attached to my belt and used it to push the handle down.

As I pushed, fat sparks bloomed from somewhere above and dripped down the doorframe. I leapt back just in time to avoid the blast. Heat seared the exposed skin of my face and hands and the stench of burning clothes choked me. I rolled until I was sure the flames were out.

Electricity was a new development, and not more than two or three of the really good alchemists had got a grip on it yet. Luckily. Yet she'd learned from my earlier care with her traps, wired the whole damn thing and rigged it up to black powder just as an added bonus in case I avoided the electricity. I was reluctantly impressed.

Runaways had never given me this much trouble before; it was the bounties that did that. This girl had a powerful desire not to go home. Having met her parents, I could sympathise, but a paying job is a paying job, and once I took one on it was hard not to follow through.

I slipped through the door with the pulse pistol held out in front of me. The room was dank and gloomy, lit with fifth-hand light bounced down from better areas far above. Among heaps of rubbish, a parade of small puddles rippled on the bare stone floor where rain leaked through two broken windows. The water gleamed with an oily glint – synth, almost certainly. A thin, filthy mattress contaminated the end of the room. A small light, a rend-nut-oil lamp with a glass cover, scented the air as it glowed next to the makeshift bed, casting a pool of warm light on the sodden blanket that was littered with food wrappers – pretend meat, fake gravy, the tarted-up processed vegetarian shit that was the only kind of tasteless junk available down here. Or pretty much anywhere under Trade.

The wavering light of the lamp made the room behind seem black as Namrat's heart. Namrat: tiger, stalker, winner

4

in the end. Death. If I was a religious man, I would have prayed to the nice Goddess that he wasn't stalking me today. As it was, I kept still and kept looking. She had to be in there somewhere.

My finger tightened on the trigger at a shadowy movement in the dark beyond the mattress, and something flew towards me. I leapt away, but not in time to completely avoid it. It smashed on the stone and let loose a rush of greenish gas. Streamers of it ballooned like smoke, sticking in my throat and blinding my stinging eyes. Oh, she was good, more than good. She was making me work for my money. That's nearly as bad as using magic.

Footsteps pattered on the concrete as she passed me and I aimed the pistol blindly. Pain leapt through me where the blade on the trigger bit my skin, not much but enough to give me some power to fire. The pistol let loose a buzzing pulse in a wild trajectory and I was rewarded with a snatch of a scream that ended with a heavy thump as she fell to the floor.

I took a few moments to drag myself away from the gas, wiping my streaming eyes and coughing it up. Finally it began to clear, helped by the breeze from the broken windows, and I could see her. She was stretched out in an ungainly pile, face-down in a puddle. Before I did anything else I cuffed her. She'd given me too much trouble already; I wasn't taking the chance of her escaping now, or maybe pulling something else out of her bag of tricks. I rolled her out of the puddle, saw to my bleeding thumb with a quick bandage from the stash in my coat, and had a look around as she came to.

It was, quite simply, a shithole. Walls crumbling where they hadn't been strengthened against the ravages of prolonged synth contact. No window intact. No direct light, not ever, not down this far, yet no Glow tubes to light the room. No nothing really, except that mattress and the oil lamp, something only the poorest of the poor ever used, because of the rancid smell. Even the people who lived in Boundary didn't live in this sort of place, unless they were seriously desperate. The rats weren't keen either, which was its only plus.

I had to wonder why she thought this was preferable to living with her very well-off parents, albeit an arrogant bully of a father, and a mother sneaky where he was blunt. Another three months, her sixteenth nameday, and she could have left them to themselves.

They were made for each other. He'd been a big man, fifty perhaps, had once been muscular by the looks but running a little to fat. Two streaks of grey sliced through his black hair like arrows and he had a way of walking as though he owned anywhere he was – or, perhaps, anyone. He'd given me the creeps, especially as there had been something so oddly familiar about him. Not the face as such – bland in a fleshy kind of way – but the way he held himself, the gestures of his hands. It had brought back long-buried memories, but I'd shrugged off that creepiness, told myself I was imagining the familiarity, when I'd seen how much he was willing to pay. I'll forget a lot for that much cash.

As he'd shouted and railed, threatening to have my licence withdrawn if I should even dare to think about refusing the job, his wife had winked and flirted and hinted at other methods of payment. She was perhaps ten years younger than him, carefully trim to the point of being haggard, with a shrewish mouth and watchful eyes. I'd been tempted to refuse them, just to see what would happen, but the money was good and I preferred the runaways to the bounties. They were easier to find, less likely to try to kill me, and I could pretend I was doing something towards setting the world right rather than souring my underdeveloped conscience by condemning some small-time fraudster or petty thief to twenty years or, worse, a one way trip to the 'Pit.

Well, runaways *had* been easier, until this one.

She groaned as she came back to herself and I stopped looking in the tatty cloth bag that probably held all her possessions. There was little enough in there, except for a large stack of money. I was a good boy for once, and kept my fingers away from shiny temptation. Daddy probably knew how much she had, down to the last copper penny.

"Come on, Lise, time to stop playing house and go home. For some reason your parents are looking forward to seeing you."

I hauled her up to her feet, not as gently as I could have; the wired door could have caused me a lot of pain, or worse, and she'd burned a hole in my best coat. She obviously hadn't been thinking clearly, didn't know I was a mage or didn't know that pain is a very good source of power for magic. Not many people do, because there aren't supposed to be any pain-mages any more, not since the Ministry took over. My pistol isn't the only possession of mine that is ever-so-slightly-illegal.

She wasn't very steady but I grabbed her bag and half pulled, half carried her back to the carriage. On the way she regained the use of her voice and I was treated to a stream of language I was sure a girl of her age and privileged background shouldn't know. By the time we reached the carriage and I had the door open ready to throw her in, she was kicking and biting and doing everything in her power to get me to let go. I was tempted once or twice to dump her as hard as I could on the floor, or maybe use the pistol on her again, but I held on to myself with all the restraint I could muster. Her screeches brought a gaggle of spectators to see us off, and I had a reputation to keep clean. In public anyway.

I dumped her in the back of the carriage, behind the metal grille I'd had installed for just this sort of thing. She tried to bite my hand when I threw in her bag and slammed the door in her face. I suppressed a smile as she shrieked with rage, and used my spare juice for a little more magic. If you know what you're about you can store it, for a while anyway. It didn't take much to mould my face into an approximation of her father's — one of my talents, my Minor, to change the way I look. Not for long, or very much, which makes it fairly useless most of the time, but handy for getting a rise out of people when I'm feeling, shall we say, less than well disposed towards them?

She spat through the grille. "You bloody bastard!"

"Technically, no. But I can understand why you might think so." I wiped the spit off my cheek and her father's face off mine. Moulding my features like that always gave me a banging headache, and I soon regretted using it to satisfy my little urge for revenge.

I fiddled with the valves and flicked the glass vial with the Glow in it. Should be enough left to get her home, and me home after without going to the expense of getting another. That wouldn't stop me charging her father for a new vial. I started up the engine with a yank on the frayed cord, wincing at the grind of metal as the gears mashed. I'd never quite got the hang of carriages, or getting them started anyway.

The Glow doesn't work as well as the synth did, not on carriage engines. The synth had been engineered for this sort of thing, brewed up in an alchemist's tubes to power the city, the factories, carriages, everything. Cheap and easy to make. A glorious achievement for Mahala and the Ministry which ran Alchemical Research along with everything else. Also a handy way to get rid of the mages who'd powered everything before, and had thus had way too much power for the Ministry's liking. Shame synth turned out to poison people too. Glow was the replacement: clean, just as cheap and not given to killing anyone. They said.

The newer carriages managed the switch from synth to Glow better of course, but this one was old when they stopped the synth, and the conversion from one fuel to another had been a rush job. It made for a clunky ride, not helped by the fact I was too stingy to sort out the springs in the suspension; the upholstery, which had long since got ripped out in the back there; and the general dents, gouges and what-not from unhappy passengers. Not much of a ride, my carriage, but at least there *was* a ride. I took us out into the choking flow of rattling, creaking traffic that surged through Boundary and on towards the more exalted areas where her parents lived.

"Why are you taking me back?" She'd settled down into a morose, accepting huddle.

"Because I was paid to." I thought about the electrified doorway. "Not for fun, I can assure you."

"I'll pay you," she said, and I wasn't surprised. It was a usual tactic.

I shook my head. "They're paying me more than a young girl with no income could afford to match."

"I'm shocked they even noticed I wasn't there." Her voice was quiet, suddenly sullen. All the fight had gone out of her. It usually did when they realised it was a lost cause, but the look on her face as I glanced backwards before I overtook a lumbering beer wagon made me pause in my standard responses. There was a panicked look to her, a thoughtful desperation behind her eyes. She turned away, maybe angry that she'd been caught feeling something.

10

"Your father was very concerned," I managed to lie; though I was pretty sure it was the fact that he wanted to avoid any gossip or scandal that had prompted his concern. I'd half expected him to say, "What will the neighbours think?", though he'd fallen just short of that.

"Concerned he won't have anyone to blame now," Lise said. "Concerned he's lost his personal punchbag and scapegoat. Concerned he's lost the money he paid to you."

It took a tricky bit of manoeuvring to get us on to the road through the slaughterhouse district, which these days had nothing much to slaughter, and on to the ramp that led up to No-Hope and beyond, past the thundering factories of Trade, up to where the sun actually shone on people, to Heights and Clouds and beyond. The slaughterhouse was almost empty of any animals, and full of people making use of the space anyway. You could no longer tell where you were from the waft of blood and the stench of the tannery's main consumable as you headed down Pigeon Shit Lane. Nothing much to slaughter meant nothing much to tan either.

Once we turned the corner on to the Spine, the twisting road that led from the rarefied heights of Top of the World right down to the sunless depths of Boundary, adverts shrieked from every shop, the little blinking Glow lights that powered them shining red and yellow against the planking. We got caught up in a snarl of wagons, carriages and walkers so I was pushed to find a way through. I managed by not caring about scraping the shit out of my carriage – it was too screwed to worry about, with every last scrap of decorative brass rubbed or gouged off years ago. Other people did care, and when they saw I wouldn't give way they usually made a hasty swerve to save their paintwork and the little brass icons of the Goddess, saints and martyrs that were so in fashion in these days. I took particular pleasure in knocking them off.

Glancing in the mirror, I saw what should have been obvious from the start. The fading yellow bruise, a sallower counterpoint to her dusky skin, all along the whole of the left side of her face, half covered by her dark swing of hair. She fiddled with her sleeves, ensuring they were pulled well down over her wrists, making me wonder what could be worse to see under the cloth than was apparent on her face. "Your mother?"

She laughed, a short snatch of cynical wretchedness. "She wouldn't notice if the world ended, as long as she could keep finding new boy toys to play with. She doesn't notice half the things *he* does, or if she does she doesn't care."

Somehow that didn't surprise me. These days, not much does. I miss it sometimes. "So, just wait three months, till you're sixteen, and then go. There won't be a damn thing they can do."

"I won't last that long. It was only luck that I managed to get away this time. He can make me stay, if he doesn't finish me off by then. There's a lot he can do. He's in the Ministry. If I don't stay, I'll end up in the 'Pit, dead first or not."

That made me suppress a shudder. The Ministry were sticklers for appearances, that everything should be seen to be perfect. They ran the guards, were experts in making people disappear, usually sending their corpses to the 'Pit to save their precious crime statistics, or so rumour had it. It would never be common knowledge: they ran the news-sheets too and guarded that privilege jealously. The Ministry ran *everything*, and had done since well before I was born, though Dendal says they didn't used to be as paranoid. That had started around the same time as the synthtox, when they began slowly and subtly drawing the strings ever tighter round us, till now you hardly dared breathe without permission.

I wasn't surprised that my background check into her father hadn't turned this Ministry connection up. It was standard practice among Ministry men to hide who they were, even when someone probed as thoroughly as I did. Secrecy was almost like a second religion for them.

I should take her home. My personal motto runs: Mine is not to do and die, mine is to find the warm body and take the money. Motto number two is: Don't mess with the Ministry, it's bad for your health.

We all have our off-days.

Maybe it was the soft pinging noise inside my head – Dendal trying to get hold of me. Maybe it was the name that accompanied the pinging, one I never wanted to hear again. Or maybe I have a rebellious streak a mile wide. Never fails to get me into trouble. I swung the carriage round with a crunch of gears and headed back down the ramp, making a dray almost crash into the back of me in a welter of swearing and skid marks. We headed for some of the less salubrious addresses, like mine. I liked the lower-rent places; it meant I could save more money for when I got out of this trade. Plus, people in those areas tended to mind their own business, if they liked their ears where they were. I wasn't about to lose the cash for this job, but, contrary to popular opinion, I'm not completely heartless – provided it doesn't cost me anything.

I glanced in the mirror again; Lise's eyes were wide and wet with surprise. I coaxed the Glow to churn faster, skittering the carriage round corners, turning always downwards, towards the workshop of the little man who had made my pulse pistol. Dwarf ran a business making outlandish, and ever-so-slightly-illegal, instruments for a hefty price. He could use an alchemy-student apprentice with a talent for booby traps. I slowed the carriage to a crawl as we passed his workshop. I couldn't afford to give up the cash for this job, and I really didn't want to piss off her Ministry dad by not taking her back, but I could make sure she had somewhere safe to run to next time.

"I've got no choice but to take you home. I don't mess with the Ministry, they don't break my door down and drag me off to the 'Pit. But a girl with your talents should be able to blow a damn big hole in her father's house to escape, right?"

She looked thoughtful, and I detected a hint of deviousness about the quick smile. Good – she was going to need it, but I reckoned she had the brains to figure it out.

"Next time you run away," I said. "Come here."

Chapter Two

By the time I reached the shabby little rooms in No-Hope that Dendal laughably called his offices, it was mid-afternoon. The brief minutes when real, actual daylight shone through the windows were long gone, and the tatty signs proclaiming our business looked forlorn in the almost perpetual half-light of dim Glow globes that had seen better days. Dendal's sign said MESSAGES SENT IN MAHALA, 6M. MESSAGES FURTHER AFIELD, 6M + 1M PER MILE. OTHER SERVICES ON REQUEST. He'd left out the part about magical services only after a long and detailed argument. Mainly about how I didn't want to be arrested for being a mage. It's the only argument I've ever won against him. My sign said simply, PEOPLE FOUND, REASONABLE DAILY RATES, DISCRETION GUARANTEED. Both the signs were rather incongruous, as Dendal had never got round to replacing the bright red flashing sign over the door that stated brazenly, MA'S KNOCKING SHOP,

CHEAP BUT CHEERFUL. We still got the occasional confused customer.

Still, in my rather shady line of work, an address to work from got you out of hired-thug territory and into the licensed-bounty-hunter area. There isn't much difference, I'll grant, except you tend not to get arrested so much in the second category. Being arrested was a somewhat permanent position in this city. Basically, it often meant you were dead. I didn't want to be dead. I still don't.

Dendal was happily absorbed in his work, surrounded by candles of every size and colour. Not to mention a few shapes that would make an acolyte blush. If he'd used his magic he could have lit the room up brighter than noon at Top of the World, that rarefied place at the pinnacle of the city that soaked up sunlight and blocked it for us lesser mortals. Unfortunately for him, and me, our magic wasn't something you spent lightly. Unless you were kinky that way. Instead, he was busy writing, probably a missive for someone who'd not learned their letters, which was most people down here. That's how he earns most of his cash. The magic is a sideline, and one we have to be both discreet and careful about using.

I handed the pay-purse to our secretary, Lastri, and considered asking her to make me some tea, but changed my mind. Lastri always answered the request with a look that seemed to intimate she'd rather stab me.

She raised a cool, dark eyebrow my way and the corner of her mouth slid up in that superior smile that always made me wonder why Dendal kept her on. She must be one of the few attractive women I've met that I've never tried to talk into bed. She'd eat me alive and spit out the bones to use as toothpicks.

"You have a message," she said with a pleased purr that I didn't like one little bit. "Several, actually."

I waited for her to carry on, but she pinched her lips together and wrinkled her nose. Not out of reluctance to share bad news, of that I was sure. Lastri had never quite approved of me. I felt a need to twist her a bit, make her say it when she so obviously wanted to string it out and make me squirm. "If you'd care to share?"

"Message number one is from Val." Ah, yes, the delectable but not exactly bright Val. Nice line in massages, great pair of legs and tonight's lucky lady. I had the whole thing planned, the food specially smuggled in from the takeaway down the road, the wine that was stronger than it appeared, even had a scented candle I'd pilfered from Dendal's collection. Not that I'd need those things, but you had to make it look right.

"It reads, 'Screw you'."

Ah. Well, not entirely unexpected. At least there was still Nirma—

"Message number two is from Nirmala." Lastri was trying hard not to grin by now. "It also reads, 'Screw you'."

Sela wouldn't let me down. Long-term girlfriend, for me that is: must be at least two weeks. Only Lastri looked insufferably smug. She calls me the Kiss of Death, and I am that to any fledgling relationship. Any hint of it taking wing, I kill it. Not intentionally, not even consciously, but I manage it just the same. My trouble isn't that I dislike women or enjoy messing them around. It's just I like them *all*, and the chance to flirt is one I can never pass up. Except with Lastri. I'm not irretrievably stupid or suicidal. "Message number three?"

"Message from Sela reads, 'Screw you sideways'. The PS reads, 'Hope you like how we decorated your rooms. I'm sure you'll like the abstract art. Blobs of red paint are very in this season, but may clash with the curtains'. Seems like your diary is suddenly free, Rojan." Lastri was openly grinning now.

"Anything else?" I kept myself as still as I could, given the circumstances. One hint of weakness and Lastri would never let me forget it. Besides, no point dwelling on it. Only I would, if I didn't do something to take my mind off them. All of them. How the fuck did they find out about each other? It didn't matter. What mattered was that my rooms were splattered in paint and lonely time stretched ahead with little to fill it but work. I was going to miss them. All of them.

I threw myself into my shabby chair behind the desk with no two legs the same length and a complicated system of books and pieces of folded paper trying to keep it level. I'd long since come to the secret conclusion that the desk was alive. I'd get it level, go home, come in the next day and it would be more uneven than ever. We'd come to an uneasy truce, me and desk. I stopped trying to make it flatter than a flatbread, and desk made sure it wasn't so tilted that my cup slid off when I wasn't looking. I'd taken to taping my pens to the surface, none the less.

I reached into one of the drawers, gingerly: we had yet to come to a truce about the springs that made the drawers snap back shut on unsuspecting fingers. My hand darted in, grabbed the bandage and was out again before desk knew what I was about. A small but satisfying victory.

I laid my right hand on the desk, palm up, and undid the hasty bandage from earlier. My finger throbbed with the release of pressure and a runnel of blood oozed out. Luckily, I was used to this sort of thing. It still hurt though. I used the old bandage to clean the wound up as much as I could and got a dollop of the thick green salve that Dendal swore by poised and ready. This was going to sting something chronic. You could etch steel with that salve, I was sure.

"Told you, shouldn't use the pistol."

Dendal's papery voice startled me and the salve dropped from my fingers and splatted on to the floor.

"Namrat's bloody balls, Dendal, you almost gave me an apoplexy."

He grinned at me in an absent-minded way, his thin, grey hair flying about him haphazardly. A spare sort of figure, quite a bit older than me, though I've no idea how much. He'd just always been around. He had thin, fleshless cheeks, a shy smile that could transform his face into a kindly grandfather's, and a sort of air that he should be meditating, or was. His thoughts were probably a thousand miles away, playing with fairies. He wasn't always very *here*, if you see what I mean. Too obsessed with his work. Lastri made sure he ate occasionally and didn't fall out of the window thinking it was the door or something. But Dendal wasn't just another absent-minded idiot with fly-away hair. When he managed to get his head out of his books he was sharper than the blade on my pistol and shrewder than ten rich traders. When he spoke, I listened. Well, mostly.

"Pistol's clumsy for someone like you, Rojan."

I looked up sharply. It wasn't often he could recall my name. "No, it's a pretty efficient way of producing pain. I promise you that."

Dendal hummed a tune under his breath and rocked back and forth on the balls of his feet. My thumb was forgotten as his eyes detached from the now. He linked his hands together and *twisted*, bringing a great crack from his hand and a breathless cry. Shit, I hated it when he did that.

His eyes flew wide and he began to babble, nonsense things at first, gradually becoming more coherent. One of his fingers stuck out at an odd angle. Dislocated. Double shit.

Lastri stood behind him, her usually bland face looking worried now as she mouthed something over his shoulder. Something about Dendal trying to contact me all morning. That explained the pinging noise in the carriage – I'd been too distracted by Lise at that point to answer.

The quality of Dendal's voice changed, became deeper, younger. A voice I knew and never wanted to hear again, channelled through Dendal, who would take any pain for his magic, to fulfil his gift and communicate.

"Rojan, at last!" Perak's voice was rasping and weak and I wondered what trouble I'd have to get him out of now. We hadn't spoken in almost eight years, and that was how I liked it.

"Perak." I tried to keep my voice steady as I swore in my head. My brother was trouble, always had been, and if I got involved I knew the trouble would end up being all mine while he waltzed off into another daydream, unaffected. He didn't have his head in the sand about life; it was so far down he could see bedrock.

"Rojan, you have to come." There was that rasping again, and a bubbling sound in his voice. He spoke so low I could barely hear him, but the panic was obvious as he rambled. He'd always seemed to float through life, never seeing or hearing any dangers, and this fear seemed so unlike him I sat up and really listened.

"I'm in the Sacred Goddess Hospital. They took her. They shot us and took her. You have to come, you have to help find her. That's what you do, isn't it? Find people? Please, you have to come." He trailed off and it was only then that I realised he was crying.

My teeth became islands in a mouth as dry as desert. "Find who?"

"Elsa's dead," he said, as though I hadn't spoken. "They killed my wife, they almost killed me, and they took my daughter. You'll come, won't you?"

21

I didn't hesitate. He'd caused me enough grief to last a life-time while he sailed through every calamity without scratch or punishment, left all of it for me, but I couldn't leave him with this. I hadn't even known he was married, never mind a father. Yet now his wife was dead and his daughter was missing. The years, and with them the animosity, rolled away. No matter how much I hated it, I was always going to be big brother. "I'll be there as soon as I can."

Dendal staggered to a chair and began the painful business of putting his finger back. At least he'd have enough power from that for a spell or two later, storing the pain, the power, in his muscles for a time until it leaked slowly away. One advantage of the dislocation over the cut, as he often told me, at infinite and tedious length. Pain dislocating and pain putting it back. Twice the pain, twice the power. Which is all very well, but I'd rather have as little pain as possible.

Seeing Perak again was going to be a different sort of painful. On my own personal scale of bad days, this was shaping up to be at least an 8.4.

Chapter Three

The Sacred Goddess Hospital was one of the plusher ones, up above Trade, and it took me most of the rest of the afternoon to negotiate my way up the ramp. Mahala's Spine they call it, the link between each layer from the depths of Boundary to the pinnacle of Top of the World. By the time I reached the right level, the sun was setting behind a rack of rainclouds. I stopped the wheezing carriage and watched for a while. It wasn't often I got up high enough to see the sun directly, normally relying on second- or third-hand light bounced from mirrors or seeping dimly through light-wells.

From here, I could see right out over one side of Trade, the huge, hulking factories that seemed to permanently shake the feet as they pounded out Mahala's lifeblood – the technology we invented and made so well. Behind them sat warehouses, black and squat and menacing. No buildings above the factories or warehouses – they'd have been shaken to pieces – so

I could see, far off and grey, the tops of the mountains that surrounded the city, that gave us our strength, and our weakness, the reason we built up rather than out. The reason we had to trade for food, because we had so little land left to farm.

Mahala was built to make you look up, and then up again. The other side of Trade, the merchant houses, shops, arcades, markets, showrooms and laboratories were all covered by more buildings, so that all I could make out in the lowering light were facings, flashing red Glow lights shouting out wares, and black chasms between. Walkways clung to them like spider's webs, as if they were spiders trying to spin a city. Above lay Heights, on graceful spires and spindles, then Clouds, giant platforms that I would never see except from underneath, full of gardens and rarer wonders, or so I'd heard.

Above everything, on a spire so thin it seemed it must break, with only the gossamer strand of the Spine reaching its dais, sat Top of the World. Heart of the Ministry, home of the Archdeacon, far off and impossible to reach. All the better to look down on us, mere mortals, unworthy of divine notice, or sun, at least once you got down past Trade. I supposed you couldn't see us from up there; Under-Trade, or the area they called the Buzz, was where rich men might come if they were feeling adventurous, but not too grubby. Down further into the murky depths where the sun was a rumour, buildings squashed together as though for comfort, was the area once called Hope City, now known as No-Hope Shitty, and, at the bottom, Boundary. The city used to go further, before the synth.

Ah yes. Synth. Hailed as the great invention to save mankind from pain-mages and from the city's reliance on the power they had, the way they could run all the machines in Trade, make us the city that everyone looked to. Only magic had its side effects: odd splurges that got out of control, weird fogs that choked and fumed; the pain-mages either falling into the black or going mad and blowing up portions of the city, or each other, on a fairly regular basis as the workload increased and the number of mages didn't, or not very fast. So when the Ministry discovered synth, they knew they could topple the King – a mage himself, with a habit of defending every mage's action even when they were blowing each other and the non-magical populace up. With a new power source behind them, the Ministry had banned us, for "the good of the city", introduced synth to run the machines, and all had been well. The Glorious Revolution had saved the city and of course, as the instigators, the Ministry had become the new government. Fair, even-handed – or they were to start with. Never stays like that, does it? But most importantly, they were *not magical*. The air cleared, no one blew anyone else up except the odd alchemist. All the same, it had taken them years to realise synth was killing people.

No one knew of the toxic properties of synth to start with, and it was only when a new and virulent form of disease had swept over the plains north of Mahala, and then raced through the lower layers of the city, before it ate its way through most of the rest of the continent, that they'd realised something was amiss. The synthtox. It seeped into every part of you, from the rain, the water you drank, the food you ate. In itself it wasn't harmful, but it did something to the body, made it retain all the toxins that should have been flushed out, until the system could take no more and the tox took over. It was a long, painful death, as I could attest. Watching my mother die of it over a period of ten years was the single most gruesome experience of my life.

We couldn't go back to pain magic: all the mages had either left, been sent to the 'Pit or been driven into hiding by the Ministry. The King they'd beheaded – the surest way to kill a pain-mage, because it's so quick – and shoved his body off the edge of his own palace in Top of the World and left him for the rats. Without him and his absolute authority to protect them, and with the sight of his headless body plunging a hundred levels or more imprinted in their minds, the mages had scattered.

Even if the Ministry hadn't got rid of all the mages, synth had been more powerful. Mahala had grown so much on the extra trade in the only way it could – up – that even if we'd had all the mages back they wouldn't have been able to power a tenth of the new machines. So the powers-that-be had panicked, and pulled together. Synth had been banned and the alchemists and priests had come up with a new fuel, Glow, one shrouded in mystery, not as powerful as synth but at least clean. Of course that's what they'd said about synth, but people would have believed anything at that point and maybe it was even true. No one has ever been known to die from Glow, but it's early days yet.

The lower places were the worst-infected by the synth, where the tainted water pooled. They'd cleared them out, sealed them off in Namrat's Armpit, cleaned the remaining water supplies Upside. Over the course of the next few years the synth levels had dropped dramatically, though those who had it in their bodies already couldn't get rid of it, and so they still died. Fewer each year, until now, almost fifteen years later, it was becoming a rarity except far down in Boundary.

If it was as bad as this, why didn't I leave? Why didn't we all? I could see those mountains, grey, mythical shapes. I knew they existed. Probably. I knew there had to be an Outside. I had yet to meet anyone who'd been there. For all any of us knew, it could be worse. According to the news-sheets it didn't even exist, not really, a story the Ministry stuck to despite all the evidence to the contrary.

Even if I'd been tempted, two very real things kept me here. One, getting Outside would take more money than I could blag in a lifetime. Oh, things went out, machines, inventions, all the little things that kept us in crappy vegetarian mush. *People* didn't, though. Maybe the occasional Special, the élite Ministry guards who escorted the merchandise out. But anyone else? If you weren't Ministry, forget it.

The general feeling Under-Trade was either that, given the lack of people who'd actually seen it, it was mythical, or you'd die trying to get out. Neither appealed. Besides, reason number two: Dendal. I owed the old bastard – quite a lot, and not money. Lastri would look after him if I went but . . . but I've abandoned a lot of people in my life. I just can't quite see myself abandoning Dendal. Not least because, if he wanted, I'd be a smear of blood on his carpet, the knowledge of which sharpens the mind wonderfully. Only idiots tried to get Outside, that was the crux of it, and they died, or got sent to the 'Pit. I kept telling myself that, and never failed to stop to look at the pale ghosts of mountains when I got the chance.

But I didn't stop to stare at the mythical Outside and the not-so-mythical but highly pungent Inside for long, because the view always left a bad taste in my mouth.

The Sacred Goddess Hospital was a great grey building, squashed between the outer boundary of Trade that supported its base and the more graceful area of Heights above.

I left the carriage and negotiated the clanking iron walkway that led out over the gap. I've said I prefer the lower-rent districts because it saves me money. It also saves my head. With one hand firmly on the handrail, I stepped out, eyes fixed ahead. *Just keep the hospital in view. Don't look down.* You'd think I'd be used to it after a lifetime in this city, but I've seen too many fallers who've missed the nets and bounced their way down twenty or thirty levels. Or rather, I've seen what was left of them once they reached Boundary.

The walkway swung alarmingly with all the people crossing, barging and pushing to get home before the sun went, but I managed to get across without screaming like a little girl. The hospital was new, scavenged from the guts of the old building that had stood here and refaced with a newer type of steel that shone faintly in the lights of the Glow globes hung around it. I made my way towards the larger glow of open doors. The Sacred Goddess Hospital never shut.

Inside was more traditional: lots of wooden panelling, floors that squeaked under my shoes and the scent of every hospital everywhere – disinfectant, boiled cabbage and death waiting to happen.

It didn't take long to find out that Perak was in one of the private rooms on the top floor, which made me raise my eyebrows, though not as much as the phalanx of hatchet-faced guards outside the door. They stood out like blood on a bandage with their bright red uniforms, red linen over pale body armour. Each of them had a gun at his hip, a new innovation. Mahala alchemists had used black powder for various things in our less salubrious past; the ability to use that powder to launch a piece of metal into someone's body was relatively recent. Luckily, that meant it was also too expensive for most people, especially the sort of small-time low-lives I dealt with on a daily basis. It should also be out of the reach of guards – the Ministry had yet to equip them with guns due to the cost – and the fact that it wasn't was unnerving.

I recognised one of them, Dench. He often gave me surreptitious tip-offs on bounties coming up in return for a small cut. He nodded almost imperceptibly to the other guards, murmured he knew who I was, and let me in.

It took a moment for my eyes to adjust to the dim interior. The room was small but well appointed, much more so than the open wards below. Instead of bare whitewashed walls, lush hangings in muted green and gold softened the square room. The Glow globes, while dimmed, were top-notch quality; and proper fruit, not reconstituted crap, sat on the side table in enough variety to shame all but the best grocers. Perak must have done well for himself, or had powerful friends.

He was asleep, the dark hair that we'd both inherited from our father mussed and clumped with blood. He'd always taken after our mother more than I had. His skin was lighter, a creamy brown like Ma's, his cheekbones somewhat broader than my own too-gaunt ones, the nose shorter. But that we were brothers showed in the rounding of our chins, the downward tilt to our eyes, the shape of our mouths.

A sheet covered him below the waist and blood spotted a large bandage that was wrapped tightly around one shoulder and over his chest. A doctor with a sharp, dark face leaned over him, his fingers registering Perak's pulse.

The doctor scowled at me. "No visitors, not yet."

I shrugged. Putting this off would be a relief, but Perak didn't have that luxury. "I'm his brother."

The doctor laid Perak's arm down and regarded me critically, maybe assessing the likeness. He seemed convinced. "Hmm. Well, when he wakes up again you've got two minutes. We managed to get one bullet out. The other's still in his chest somewhere." He shook his head so his hair flopped over his forehead. Suddenly he lost his arrogance and looked young and tired and pissed off. "This is only the third bullet case I've ever seen. The others were minor, but the potential for damage – the wounds are nothing like knife or sword wounds and we're still learning. That bullet might be fine, or it might kill him, and I haven't a clue which it will be. Whoever invented guns, I just hope Namrat takes the guy's soul *and* balls when he dies."

The doctor made for the door, trailing weariness in the slump of his shoulders. He turned at the doorway with an afterthought. "I haven't told him everything about his wife. He just knows she's dead. Perak said you find people for a living and you're going to find his daughter. If you think anything about the mother's death would help, come and find me after. Ask for Doctor Whelar."

The room was deathly quiet when he left, with only the bubble of Perak's breath to break the silence. I went over his words earlier, the way he'd sounded as though tears were choking every word. I'd never known Perak cry before. I'd rarely seen him any other way than in his own head, grinning at what went on there and occasionally trying it out in the real world, generally with disastrous consequences.

Of course the consequences had always been left for me to deal with, like that time he'd mixed together all the powders, liquids, bits of soap, paint and scraps of wood he could find with a thimbleful of black powder he'd found somewhere, and lit the resulting mess. Right near the guard's station. It was a clear area, he said, like that was an obvious place for an experiment. Well, yes, it was clear because no one went close if they could avoid it, so as not to get arrested for being alive. Which at least meant no one got hurt when it all exploded, but the station had a large hole in its side and the guards were seriously pissed off. Who did they chase? Oh yeah, me. Almost caught me too. I suppose it was inevitable that Perak would end up in Alchemy Research.

Still, he'd never meant any harm, which was part of the reason it rankled so much. Now real life had finally caught up with him.

I was just beginning to doze myself when Perak woke up. He struggled to sit and I helped him get settled on some pillows and tried not to see the way his eyes tracked me. When I sat back, he couldn't hold it in any more. Tears choked him until I thought he'd open up his wound with the wrenching sobs. Or maybe I just worried about that to take my mind off the misery that seeped into me. I was reminded just how much I loved him, even if he had almost got me thrown in jail at least four times, more than one of which would have meant a one-way trip to the 'Pit. I remembered what I'd made myself forget when I'd cut myself off from him: his generous heart, a complete faith that everything would work out; one I could never share. That faith was stretched to its limit now.

"She's only six," he kept saying. He couldn't seem to say anything else without it coming back to that. "Only six."

I didn't know what I could say to him that would help. In

the end there was only one thing I could do, the reason he had called me. "What happened? And since when have you been married?"

He managed to pull his sobs back into him, and gave me a ghost of his old smile. "Not long after I saw you last, when you—" He didn't need to finish that sentence.

The last time I'd seen him had been just after our mother's funeral, when it had seemed that I was going to be the only one responsible for him. As I'd been for so long growing up, since our father disappeared not long after Ma got sick, before we knew for sure what it was, that it would kill her. I was ten and all I really remembered of my father was his dark hair, his bitterness and his voice. I remembered the timbre of that voice, the way the rhythm of it seeped into your head and conjured pictures there. It stayed with me long after his face had become a blur, or I'd learned to hate him for leaving us. Leaving me. I'd been responsible for both Perak and Ma since then and when she died I'd wanted to be free of it, of responsibility, of people depending on me.

After the funeral, Perak and I had had words, you might say, although the words were all mine. I'd pretty much told him the only reason I'd put up with him that long was for Ma's sake. I hadn't meant it; her death had still been too raw then, and all the bitterness and despair of her long, slow decline had come spilling out in a black torrent of abuse. So I'd just spewed it all over him, watching the acid in my voice dissolve his smile till all I could see was a desperate, shocked hurt. I'd stopped looking at him so I couldn't see that hurt, but I couldn't stop the bile. I turned to face the wall and my words fell out of my mouth without thought. When I turned back he'd gone and I hadn't seen him since. If I was truthful, it was shame that had kept me from getting back in touch.

"So what happened?" I asked.

He shrugged as well as he could, his mouth dragging down into a grimace of pain. "We went out, for lunch. Left Amarie with a sitter, young girl from Under."

"Under where? Where are you living?"

"Clouds," he said, and I was frankly astonished. How had my daydreaming little brother managed to get a place in the rarefied air of Clouds? It seemed he almost read my mind. "I made a very lucrative discovery. They gave me a job in Alchemy Research."

Now I was speechless, and he smiled again at the look on my face. Alchemy Research was the single largest, and richest, arm of the Ministry, ever since the disaster with synth when the 'Pit had been sealed off, years ago. Given the way our mother had died, and the long-hidden alchemical poisoning that had caused it, it was a subject close to both our hearts.

"You were right, what you said about me," he said. "Took me a while to see it, but you were right. So I got my act together. Got myself a good job, a lovely wife, and Amarie. She was the pinnacle of everything I had." He blinked back fresh tears. "We'd used this sitter before, nice young girl,

34

Amarie liked her. We came home early – Elsa wasn't feeling so well – and when we got in ..."

"And when you got in, what?" I had to prompt him; he was lost in his thoughts again.

He blinked back to reality. "We must have disturbed something, someone. The sitter was dead on the living-room floor. Elsa screamed and ran for Amarie's room. I was frozen, just looking down at the body. There – there was blood everywhere. I couldn't believe it. Then there were shots from the bedroom. That's irony, isn't it? I worked out how to get black powder to launch bullets, I invented the concept of the gun and then – I ran in but Elsa was already dead. Amarie was there with two men, but she looked glazed, like they'd drugged her maybe. She tried to say something, but it was all slurred and—" He broke off again, and this time he couldn't stop the tears.

"And that's when they shot you and took her," I said, when it was clear talking was too difficult for him. He nodded.

This wasn't like any case I'd had before; I found runaways and bounty-hunted small-time thieves and embezzlers on the run, not kidnappers or anything that might turn too violent. I value my own arse too much and the responsibility of a life depending on me gives me the jitters. But the look on his face, and shame for the way I'd treated him, forced me to say what I did.

"I'll find her for you, if the guards don't first. You concentrate on getting well; when you are, I'll have her here." He looked so pathetically grateful that I had to turn away for a moment. "You have a picture?"

He nodded towards the locker by the side of his bed and I took out the slim wallet, noticing it was real leather, a rarity these days that made this wallet worth about as much as everything I owned. First thing I saw in there was a card giving his rank at Alchemy Research.

"You're a *cardinal?*" Cardinals were one step down from the Archdeacon, who ran everything like the spider at the centre of the web. The Mouth of the Goddess, who spoke her words to us for her. Supposedly. That was how he kept control, anyway. He spoke for the Goddess and everyone else jumped to obey, first the cardinals, who passed on orders to the bishops and down through the ranks. Everyone jumped, excepting maybe the Specials, but they swore to the Goddess herself, not the Archdeacon, so they had some leeway there. I couldn't remember the last time they'd used it – they were usually pretty forward about doing the Archdeacon's bidding.

Perak's smile was small, lonely and rather shame-faced. "An honorific one only, because I'm head of research. I've never even been to Top of the World, and I only met the Archdeacon once, when I got the promotion. Too busy with my work."

"What's he like?" Not a pertinent question perhaps, but the Archdeacon ran my life whether I wanted him to or not.

"What? Oh. Ordinary. Just . . . just like anyone else really. Nothing memorable about him. He shook my hand, gave me a funny look like he recognised me but couldn't remember where from, said well done and then he was gone. I couldn't pick him out in a crowd."

Same old daydreaming Perak – he met the man in charge of the city, the man who loomed large in every aspect of Mahala, and couldn't remember him bar he was ordinary. I went back to the wallet.

Behind the Alchemy Research card was a tatty and much-thumbed picture painted in oils, nicely done. I could imagine Perak showing it at every opportunity, to anyone who asked and anyone who didn't.

The thin scrap of paper showed a vibrantly pretty girl of about five, fair hair blowing under a pretend tiara and eyes shining as she waved and said, "Daddy, Daddy, look, I'm a princess!" A ten-second loop, a hideously expensive piece of tech and just the sort of thing a proud father would carry. A niece I had never met because of my own stubbornness. There was a picture of his wife there too, and I could see that Amarie took after her, the delicate prettiness, the intelligent eyes, the bright blonde hair.

"What did the men look like?"

He shrugged, and I had to stop myself asking why he couldn't pay attention to what was under his nose – it was obvious he'd thought of no one but his daughter.

"One tall and thin, scarred face – a cut across one eye," he managed eventually. "The other was younger, but they looked similar, brothers maybe. They were dressed oddly – I don't know, but not like I've seen anyone else dress. Lots of leather. I don't remember anything else."

Leather, which only the rich could afford, and even then only in small pieces. There weren't enough animals left to warrant killing them for their skin, though some got out when the few fattened ones were slaughtered for their equally expensive meat. Sometimes we got some leather in Trade, but its very rarity made it dearer than gold. Most of the farm animals had died of the tox and now it was more efficient to grow crops, which were more resistant to synth.

"You really think you can find her?" Perak asked, and for the first time he let a desperate, pleading hope into his voice.

"I'm sure I can," I lied. What else could I say?

At least there would be no angry girlfriends, or rather ex-girlfriends, waiting to launch another paint broadside.

It wasn't a whole lot of comfort, if I'm honest.

Perak's eyes were drooping and red-rimmed. I left him with a solemn promise to find Amarie and he promised he would sleep. I wasn't so sure either promise would be kept any time soon.

I slid out of the door and blinked at the brighter lights of the corridor. The guards either side of the doorway made me feel both that Perak was safer, and more in danger. Ministry paid the guards' wages. Perak, my daydreaming little brother, had invented the gun – that incident at the guards' station with the black powder now seemed prophetic – and now he'd been shot, his wife was dead and his daughter kidnapped. I caught Dench's eye and we didn't need to exchange words. I had to talk to him soon though, and from the worried pinch of the skin round his eyes he wanted to talk to me. He palmed me a piece of paper as I made my way past, and I took pains to hide it from the other guard.

The nurses' workstation was a blur of activity along the corridor and I read the note as I walked. *Beggar's Roost, midnight.* Dench's favourite pub, where the women were cheap and the beer cheaper, but only just. Well, it would be rude not to go, right? Besides, it wasn't like I'd had anything planned for that night, not now.

The nurses were efficient and scrubbed to shiny-cheeked perfection, their acolytes' robes brilliant white and stiff with starch. One of them – the name "Lilla" was embroidered on her robe – led me along corridors, down stairs, past wards that wafted the stench of synth at me so I hurried to get away, up another set of stairs and round till I was lost. I didn't mind too much: the nurse was pretty in a clean and clinical way and I flirted my best. Even got a promise of dinner at a later date. Nurses: clean on the outside but, in my plentiful experience, absolutely filthy in bed.

Finally, with a dimpled smile and a giggle that hinted at much naughtiness, she showed me through a door. The room I entered was, simply put, staggering. I'd expected a cramped office overflowing with charts and bits of doctorly paraphernalia with cut-away diagrams of ears and hearts and livers.

Maybe a skeleton grinning at people. What I got was a full-blown laboratory.

Glassware covered every surface of one half of the room, sadly not bubbling in a mad-scientist kind of way. I kind of hoped something green and seething would emit a whiff of gas that would give me visions, but no such luck. A half-dissected pig lay across a table, but that wasn't much of a consolation. Mainly due to the smell of shit, which made me think it might have still been alive when the good doctor started. Wait, wait. I backed up a bit.

A pig. A real live, er, dead pig. How much money did this hospital have? Pork was even more expensive than beef – pigs had suffered more than cows from the synth. And the skin: pigskin was worth more than gold – shit, more than diamonds, pound for pound. Altogether the pig was worth more than everything I owned *or* was ever likely to. Plus, I'd heard they tasted nice. I'd smelled bacon once, and I still dreamed of it sometimes. It smelled crispy and crunchy and a hundred, maybe a thousand times better than any of the processed slop that was all anyone from Under-Trade could usually afford to eat. And Whelar was cutting it up.

"Mr Dizon." Whelar appeared as if out of nowhere, though in reality it seemed his desk lurked behind a display of pickled organs and animals with more than the usual number of limbs. A three-headed cat stared at me gloopily through the thick preserving fluid and I tried not to stare back. "Is there anything I can help you with?"

It took a moment to regain my composure. That pig was unnerving me. So was the cat. "I, er, oh yes. Elsa Dizon. You said if I had any questions?"

He looked me up and down. I seemed to meet his approval, because he indicated a chair next to his desk. He sat in the desk chair and swung it to and fro, his hands elaborately loose in his lap, but his lips were pinched tight. Trying to look unconcerned and failing.

"So, what do you want to know?"

"I'm not sure. What can you tell me?"

One of his fingers twitched to life and tapped out a staccato rhythm on his thigh. "Not much. She died very quickly. Two shots, as with your brother. One was directly into the heart, the other shattered her jaw. Not pretty."

I shut my eyes briefly against the image of the delicate face in Perak's picture shattered by a lump of metal. Not pretty indeed. "What about the bullets?"

The finger stopped its tapping for half a heartbeat before it continued. "What about them?"

"I'd like to see them, if you have them."

Whelar's lips pinched just a fraction more, then he relaxed and gave a curt nod. "A moment, please."

He left and I took the opportunity to nose around. I kept away from the pig though; I didn't like the way it grinned at me, or the smell. There wasn't much else of interest, only instruments that I couldn't name and which seemed designed for torture, messy stacks of paperwork and a framed letter

41

from the Archdeacon thanking Whelar for his sterling work in medical research.

It didn't take long for Whelar to return; I guessed he'd only gone to order a subordinate to fetch the bullets.

"They won't be long," he said. "Is there anything else?"

I cast a sidelong glance at the pig. A neat little hole marred the skin by its neck. "The pig – seems a rather expensive thing to just chop up in a lab."

To my surprise he didn't become evasive or defensive, but instead grinned like a kid on his nameday. "Ah, yes, but it's important, you see. More important than money. Did you know that pig's flesh is more like ours than almost any other animal? One reason they succumbed as badly as us to the synth. So, very important in my research."

"And what are you researching here?"

Yes, there it was: now he closed in. His shoulders hunched slightly, as if to ward off a blow. "I – I'd rather not say. Superstition, you know. Us doctors like to keep it all close to our chest until we know we're right. It's all theory at the moment, though there might be a breakthrough soon."

"So that isn't a bullet hole there?"

He looked about to protest when a knock at the door interrupted him and Nurse Lilla hurried in with a covered dish. She dimpled prettily in my direction while handing the dish to Whelar and left with a wink and an implied promise.

I dragged my eyes back to Whelar and gave him my best smarmy smile. He pursed his lips in tacit disapproval but said nothing and shoved the dish my way. I took off the linen cover and peered at the two bullets rattling around in the bottom. I'd no idea what I was looking for: I'd never seen a bullet before – heck, I'd never seen a gun before today – but the request had made the good doctor fidget so I took them out and looked them over. One of them was so squashed I could hardly tell what it was, but the second still had a recognisable uniform shape and I peered closer. It was flattened on one side, but the other had a maker's mark. One I knew from long acquaintance.

"Thank you, Dr Whelar, you've been most illuminating." I only said it to make him squirm. OK, and to stop him seeing that I'd just palmed one of the bullets.

Chapter Four

It didn't look like much from the outside. A tatty lock-up on the wrong level of town, just under one of the towering factories of Trade. The hustling thump of machinery drifted concrete dust down to mingle with the rain that fell on the Over-Traders, and us too, once it had gathered enough dirt along the way. Drips bounced from building to building, across gaps and walkways, feeling their way down, until they reached my neck. I flipped the collar of my coat against them, and against the all-pervasive factory thump that shook the bones; it succeeded in stopping neither.

The tube that powered my scabby little carriage was the size of my hand, the shining element of yellowish-pink Glow a delicate filigree winding about inside. The ones that powered those factories above me were big as men, bigger, their elements twisted snakes as thick as my leg. Whole lines of them up there, side by side like monstrous fireflies lighting up the underside of Heights day and night, powering the power of Mahala – trade. The heart of our city has always been trade, ever since our sneaky-bastard warlord ancestor decided that this mountain pass was where he wanted to build a castle and strangle all the trade through it. Our strength, apart from the cunning position, is what we can invent and produce for the outside world, and we're damn good at it. Being the middle-man between two countries that loathe each other helps too.

So, just under Trade, beneath the factories that were the pumping heart of the city, their rumble echoing through every brick and girder and bone. This place wasn't a factory. It was a shack with graffiti that would make a whore blush painted over the shutter. It *looked* derelict, as though the only thing holding the place together was the neighbouring build-ings, to the sides, above and below. In the shuddering darkness, the shop hulked like a giant abandoned baby, unwanted, unloved. A classic case of appearances being deceiv-ing. Yet if you knew just where to look . . .

The bell-pull was disguised as a piece of chain that appeared to hold the door together. I made sure to avoid the myriad of traps that surrounded the shutter and doorway and gave the pull a yank.

It didn't take Dwarf long to answer. He wrenched open the door with a scowl that seemed to occupy his whole scrunched-up face.

"What the fuck do you want?" This was a pleasant greet-ing by Dwarf's standards. Then he saw who I was and dropped the act with a twisted grin that only served to make him look twice as ugly as the scowl. "Rojan, come in, come in."

I stepped through, ducking my head to avoid a string of cogs that Dwarf's head cleared with ease. He walked with his odd, rolling gait down the narrow aisle between boxes of springs jingling from the shaking of the factory above and a consignment of sulphur that made my nose itch.

Dwarf was well named. I'm pretty big, but he only came up to just above my elbow and was as wide as he was tall. His so-ugly-it-was-attractive-in-a-weird-way face was mobile, lips and eyebrows and even nose seeming to mould to his mood or thought, so he had to exert a lot of effort to appear uninterested. He tried, though he'd never be better at dissembling than a five-year-old trying to con a sweet off their parent.

We came to the main shop floor, a riot of bits of metal, odd gangly tools and chemicals I have no name for. Everything smelled of oil and sulphur and metal and – actually, I don't know. I only know that no other place in Mahala was quite like it. It smelled of ingenuity, something that seemed to ooze from Dwarf like other men oozed sweat.

Dwarf made himself comfortable in the tall chair behind his workbench and socketed a magnifying lens into his right eye. Something small and intricate lay in parts under a bright Glow globe. These bits alone in this place were perfectly still: while the factory rumble made everything else shiver, the workbench was one of Dwarf's masterpieces, and the surface stayed tranquil and motionless. He rubbed his fingers against his thumb, selected a minute screwdriver that looked even smaller in his fat, sausage fingers, and began to put whatever it was back together. "So, Rojan, what is it you're after? You don't like the pistol?"

"It works all too well. I don't like the pain, but that's by-the-by. I want to know who made this, and who for."

I dropped the bullet into the circle of light on the bench. Dwarf didn't move, still as stone for long heartbeats. Then his magnifying glass dropped out and he looked up at me beneath his beetling brows. "Rojan, you don't want to get mixed up in this shit. I know you, and I promise you this will cause you more pain than you've ever known. Wave the bounty on this goodbye. I tell you this as a friend. You follow this, you're going to find a lot of pain."

Not the best answer I could have had. "No bounty on this one. I need to know. Personal reasons. *Family* reasons."

He winced at that, his shoulders coming up as though to protect his neck. His rubbery face looked – well, it looked like an abused and incredibly ugly doll. But a scared one.

Dwarf licked his lips and stared down at the mass of cogs and springs and other less identifiable bits of metal that were tumbled around his desk. "You know I made the bullets, you saw the mark. Sometimes – ah shit, Rojan, sometimes you just have to take the job, you know? I've got rent to pay, same as you, and I'm quite fond of my legs being both this shape and attached to my body. I didn't ask what the bullets were going to be used for, I just made the damn things and was happy to have them out of my shop. This gun thing is Namrat's invention, to be sure. No finesse, no *style*."

This from a man who had once theorised about a hand-held device for castration from a dozen paces away. "Not Namrat's, my brother's. And now someone's abducted his daughter."

Dwarf stared down at his hard-bitten fingernails, but he said nothing. That was all I needed to know. Well, almost all.

"Which branch of the Ministry was it?" And why was the Ministry getting Dwarf to make the bullets when they had plenty of their own smiths?

He flicked me a look of absolute terror, one that made my balls shrivel. Dwarf wasn't afraid of anyone that I'd ever seen, and I've seen some bad, bad people in his shop.

"Rojan, I'm saying nothing. *Nothing*, you understand? I've got a family to—" He caught my eye and blushed, but he was still as stubborn, or as terrified, as ever. "OK, I got no family, I forgot who I was talking to, but I can't say anything. Not if I want to live. It's bad enough they'll know you were here, if they find out what you're after."

"All right, Dwarf. All right. I'll leave you to your cogs. But I want a favour."

He looked up, half terrified still, half relieved. "Of course, of course. If I can, that is. Without losing my legs or any other vital pieces."

"Maybe you will and maybe you won't. Depends whether the best – and most devious – alchemist I've ever seen comes to see you like I told her to. She's fifteen and she almost killed me three times in one day."

Dwarf perked up immediately. "Fifteen, eh? A looker?"

"You keep your hands to yourself, or I'll use my pistol on you. A lot. In a certain area between your legs."

Dwarf held up his hands and chuckled in the filthiest way imaginable. "No, no, she'll be safe with me. I like mine willing, and there's precious few who'll be that when they see my face. What did she use on you?"

"Electricity."

He went very still apart from his eyes, which darted to and fro like wild animals in a cage. "Electricity, oh my boy, the things we could do. Consider her safe. What's her name, so I'll know her?"

"Lise, and be sure to keep her secret till her birthday. Daddy is something high up, but he doesn't know how to look for people. I don't think he wants it broadcast that she keeps running away, so he won't use anything official to find her. Three months till she's sixteen. Deal?"

Dwarf nodded, slow and thoughtful. "You think she'll really come, and she's really that good?"

"I'm surprised she's not here already. And she's damn good. Look at the hole she made in my coat."

"Then I owe you, and not just keeping her safe. The 'Pit. The bullets I made went down to the 'Pit, and don't ask me how I know that, or tell anyone how you know."

The 'Pit? That was for corpses or those soon to be corpses.

It was on the tip of my tongue to ask, but I'd pushed Dwarf as far as he could go. I knew Lise would come in handy for something other than making my day more interesting and way too painful. "Deal."

I shook the rain from my coat and pushed open the door to the Beggar's Roost, thinking dark thoughts about the synth levels in the falling water, almost fifteen years on from sealing the 'Pit. They said it was back at safe levels, but who knew for sure when it was the Ministry talking? There were still cases of synthtox down at Boundary, where the rain pooled before it drained away through the 'Pit. Where it looked like I might be headed.

Synth: seeing Perak again had brought it all back, the way my, our, mother had died, when all I wanted to do was forget it. I concentrated on the task at hand instead and made for the bar, trying to ignore the dancers under the special Glow globes, lights more commonly known as Ten-Pinters, because they made the girls look as good as if you'd had that much to drink.

Dench was nursing a pint at the end of the bar and eyeing up the dancers. He was a thick-set man in his fifties with a drooping, care-worn face and equally drooping moustache that belied an easygoing manner, especially with information. Today he had the frazzled air of someone with fifty things to do and only the time to do five.

I took the seat next to him casually and he nodded, as

though to someone he'd never met before who just happened to be there. He didn't look at me after that, but stared vacantly at the dancers and mumbled over his glass like a drunk. I followed his lead and ran my eye over the girls.

A place like this, they were likely either riddled with pox or hooked on Rapture. Spotting the junkies was easy – they moved with a languid grace, as though the world revolved at a different pace for them. The faces were blank of emotion, the drug sucking all feeling from them as surely as a knife drew blood. That was the attraction, of course, especially for girls in their profession. Don't feel, don't care, only survive. Make a hideous existence possible. If Lise ran away again and didn't get under Dwarf's friendly umbrella, this was probably what she had to look forward to. I'd been firm with Dwarf because I couldn't leave anyone to that, even if they had tried to blow me up. The white and clammy underbelly of a pious city, where the shit falls to the bottom, quite literally.

And the Ministry, the offices of the gods who keep those in Top of the World in chains of piety, let it happen. Why? Never quite figured that out.

Of course, every now and again some starry-eyed acolyte will come down here to do Good Works and Save the Fallen. Most of them fall prey to a knife somewhere dark and fetid, followed by a judicious lifting of their purse. Some have such a crisis of faith, due to the fact that the Ministry haven't sent these people to the 'Pit already for such crimes against the Goddess that they never believed were permitted, that they go mad. Some succumb to the Rapture, especially the acolytes that go mad. Occasionally we actually get a good one, one who accepts things as they are and tries to help. They do some good too. And hey, guess what? The Ministry "promotes" them in order to stop it. The Ministry like us down here, wallowing in shit. I think it makes them feel better about themselves. More pious or something.

Maybe I should cheer up. Maybe tomorrow I'll be incredibly rich and handsome, but I doubt that'll happen either.

Dench straightened up a tad, drained his drink and nodded at the steward for more beer. Once he'd skimmed the froth by sucking it through his moustache, an act that always made me feel vaguely sick, he started talking, low, almost as though he was still mumbling to himself.

"I've got no leads to speak of. Been a few of these kidnappings lately, and I can never find who did it. You know what it's like. The only thing I did find out, I don't have time to follow it up. Won't lead to anything anyway. Never does, cases like this."

Code for "I'm not allowed to look into this too far" maybe. The Ministry paid his wages, and sometimes, just sometimes, they don't want people caught. Not *Ministry* people anyway.

"And just what was that only thing?" I mumbled over my own beer without looking at him. He spluttered at the bald question so I placated him as best I could. "All I want to do is help you out here. I can take a load off you. One less case for you to worry about."

52

He gave me a sour, disbelieving glare from under bushy grey eyebrows. "Two guys, similar to the description the husband gave. Stayed down in Boundary, night before she got taken. Boarding-house owner complained because they didn't pay up."

"Two guys who can afford to be dressed all in leather, they stay down there, and give themselves away because they don't pay? Doesn't that strike you as odd?"

His face became guarded and pinched. "Yes. And no."

Three words that spoke volumes to me. Told me – again – that the Ministry were wrapped up in this somehow and Dench didn't like it one little bit. And that was all I could get out of him.

I didn't bother going home. My rooms would be covered in paint, because Sela was a girl of her word, and I was too tired to clean up now. When I left the Beggar's Roost I threaded my way through the dark, rotting alleys and up dank stairwells towards the office. At least down here, a mere few storeys above the bottom of Boundary, the walkways didn't bother me so much. Besides, moonlight never made it down this far, sucked up by the godly folk above us, so I couldn't see how far it was to fall.

The little temple stood open as I passed, sandwiched between a brothel and an apothecary that only ever had two herbs in stock, and those were both best for cooking. The priest here was one of the better ones, but I ignored his call to join in prayers. Temples held no interest for me, not any more.

I watched the poor deluded fools going into a bland, white-washed box instead of the temples we used to have, before Ministry tightened the strings on our souls, before they got rid of anything remotely joyful. It had been a slow, insidious path from the glorious Ministry revolution, saving us from the corrupt mage King, to this. At first they'd been benevolent dictators. One little step at a time, but all those little steps over decades added up to total control of mind and body.

It had started when the synthtox came, when the Ministry knew it had fucked up and a slow wave of hatred had moved up from Boundary. They'd stamped on it, but made it seem like it was for our own good. It started with the banning of any song lyrics that weren't hymns, to protect people, to let them know only faith. Then the changes in the prayers. The proliferation of these soulless buildings that masqueraded as temples, robbed of the grandeur, the serenity, the *peace* they had once had, even when I was a boy. Before the synth ruined everything, scarred a generation with loss and grief, where most everyone under Trade had known and lost someone to the synth, or the sealing of the 'Pit. It had started with one little step, and ended with this.

They tried to keep up the pretence, but religious men in the Ministry now were few and far between. There was a flurry of activity in the temple, a poor and spartan thing compared to those I'd gone to as a child. No stained glass to strain the faint sun and paint rainbows on the floor. No incense, no choir, no pomp. No tranquillity.

I'd call the people entering "worshippers" for want of a better word – most of them only went in to get out of the rain. But they gave thanks, Goddess knows what for, poor bastards, and they gave alms. They never wondered, never thought that they were the ones who needed the alms. In the churches Over, no bastard gives a lousy coin. These fools gave because then they were better, weren't so low they couldn't afford a bit of charity. It was a piss-poor way to feel better about yourself, and I couldn't even bring myself to do that any more.

I made it on to the wider walkway that fronted the office, avoided the homeless man slumped in his usual spot outside the All Night Flash Fry Grill, spouting some claptrap about the end of the world, and unlocked the door. The office was lit, which seemed odd given that it was somewhere between midnight and dawn. Dendal sat at his desk, papers skewed across it every which way, scribbling something in crabbed handwriting that might as well be code. I shut the door quietly so as not to disturb him and padded across to my own desk.

We kept a large sofa behind it, jammed against the wall between the spare chair and a stuffed tiger that Dendal refused to throw away, even after moths had mauled it so badly you couldn't tell the colour any more. I took off my knee-length coat, eyed the new burn hole sourly, rolled it into a soggy ball for a pillow and lay down on the sofa with a sigh. It had been a long, extremely trying day and I had a lot to puzzle over before I could start seeing about finding Amarie. I needed sleep first, because exhaustion and beer were fuddling my brain. The sofa wasn't long enough to stretch out on, so I propped my feet on the tiger's head, wriggled my shoulders and shut my eyes.

"So, you're going to the 'Pit in the morning then." Dendal's voice was right by my ear; I'd never even heard him coming. I jumped half off the sofa before I realised it was him.

"Namrat take you for his bitch, Dendal. Don't *do* that."

He sat on the chair by my desk and gave me a wild grin. "But I like doing it. Take your great filthy feet off Griswald. Thank you. Now, you're going to the 'Pit, yes?"

"Maybe. And how do you know about it anyway?" Stupid question. Though he had other, more shadowy talents, the bulk of his magic – his Major – was communication and knowing things, just as my Major was finding people who didn't want to be found, with the occasional flare – my Minor – of making my face look different, though I don't use that part too often. It isn't especially useful except for pissing people off. "OK, wrong question. Why do you want to know?"

Dendal picked up a pen from the desk and began twirling it through his fingers, which generally meant he was going to try to be artful. It rarely worked, precisely because of the way his magic was. Communication – and truth. "Oh, no particular reason. But are you?"

"I don't know. My niece – you know that's who I'm looking for? I thought so. She's down there, that's what my gut is telling me. But there shouldn't *be* anyone down there. Except corpses, anyway. And what about the synth? Even if she is down there, how do *I* get down there? And what the fuck am I going to find when I get there?"

"Your gut? Tut-tut." Dendal shook his head, as though at a small child. "Have you tried your magic?"

"No." A cautious one-word answer seemed best, before Dendal started banging on about my potential and how I was wasting it. Truth was, not only do I not like pain, I didn't want to end up like Dendal, addicted to the magic, a slave to it, lost in my own head more often than not. I've had to pull him out of the black before, a thing I hate worse than using my magic, because it reminds me what I'm afraid of. And Dendal isn't a bumbler in there – no, he's big and bright in the darkness, and fucking powerful, and still the black is stronger than him. It rules him, I sometimes think.

Worse, if I use my magic, if I let that black into me, let it pull me, I could be sent stark raving mad by it. It's happened, quite often, before our brand of magic was banned. Pain magic – and the mages who use it – are far too unreliable. But at least it doesn't poison anyone but the mages. Much.

"It's about time you started believing in more than your gut, Rojan."

"You know me, Dendal: I believe in cash, and that men aren't made for monogamy, that there isn't a woman alive I can't get into bed if I try hard enough, and never cross the Ministry. Shit like that. I believe them like crazy."

"You have to believe that you're better."

"I think my ego's big enough, don't you?

Dendal pursed his lips. "At magic, Rojan. You never use it unless you have to, and not the way you were built to use it. You use cheap tricks and toys. You could be so *good*, if you just believed in it. You were made to use magic, and not just for playing about with."

I scowled at him, but he just grinned more. "No, I was made to be a bastard."

"It's time to start using it. And if she's in the 'Pit, I think I know how to get you down there. After that, you'll be on your own, unless I can call in a favour or two."

The pen had stopped whirling and Dendal was watching me, no smile on his usually cheerful face. It wasn't often he was both mentally present and serious, but when he was – when he was, I listened. Pain magic wasn't the only kind he could conjure.

I creaked to weary feet. "I'll get the knife."

"You will not. For this, no cutting corners, pun intended. Not for your niece, Rojan. Not for family."

I wanted to say I had no family, as I had when I'd taken this share of the office and Dendal had pretended to believe me with a sly, knowing smile. Instead I sat back down and stared at him for a while, trying to gather the will to resist him and cut myself instead, but nothing and no one could defy Dendal in one of these moods. I'm not sure whether it was the sharp shine of his eyes, or the reproach behind them that got me every time. Namrat himself would have a hard time defying that.

"Fine, fine," I muttered and fished in my pocket for the picture of Amarie, something to focus the spell on. "Fucking fine."

"Daddy, look at me, I'm a princess."

Brought out into the light, the picture began its short loop. A fair-haired little princess waving to her daddy. The room around me began to fade away as I gathered myself. The lights dimmed in my eyes; Griswald's smell no longer assaulted my nose; the rough fabric of the sofa no longer lumped under me when I shifted. The tiniest inklings of my magic, all I could use without an extra power source, without pain, tingled where the picture touched my fingers. Shit, I really did *not* want to do this.

"Daddy, look at me."

I had to, for Perak, and for the boys we both once were.

Down – she was down – and it was dark there. She was crying – awful, wrenching sobs for her father. For my brother. If I wanted to know more, if I wanted to help her out of there, I had to do it. I'd promised Perak. Fuck, I'd promised Ma too, to help Perak, keep him safe. A promise I'd failed in for too long.

I laid the picture on my knees and kept contact with the edge of one pinkie. The rest of that hand grabbed and twisted – and pain spun through me, over me, picked up the residue of my magic and thrust it into my head. Stars pulsed and beat in time to my heart, dazzling me, pulling me into the whirl, and then I was there, with Amarie. Two hundred and ... thirty ... four feet below me. Yes. Four hundred and two feet to my east. I can tell which way north is, easy as spitting, which Dendal always says is spooky, and not part of my magic, since I don't need to hurt myself to manage that part.

My magic though, that's something on top, the difference between knowing just by looking which way north is, and having a map drawn with all the details and fiddly lines on it. This time the map took me to a dark and airless chamber made of reconstituted stone, water dripping down the walls, the stench of synth everywhere. I tried to ignore the darkness around me, the pull of the magic, to go deeper, always deeper, lose myself in the black, be comforted by it, become it. *You want me, you need me.* A whimper cut through all that.

Amarie huddled in a corner, a small angular shape folded in on itself. Two bright eyes, wide with terror, peeped over her scabby knees. Behind me, off in the darkness, something growled. Something *big*. The sound bounced off the walls and seemed to grow rather than diminish: a growl from beyond history to prickle the neck, pump fear-quickness to legs and say, "Here is something that wants to eat me."

I wasn't even really there but I felt my eyes grow to mirror Amarie's. She couldn't see me, hear me, know I was there, but I crouched down beside her anyway. How could I not?

"I'm coming. Hold on, because I'm coming to take you home, to your daddy. Just you hold on for Uncle Rojan."

She couldn't hear me, couldn't have, but her eyes flicked round as though she had and her whimpers subsided.

Then I was back in the office, on my knees with Dendal holding me up. I threw up sour beer all over his shirt.

See, this is why I don't like other people relying on me, on responsibility. Because dislocating your own thumb to cast a spell really fucking hurts.

Chapter Five

So here I was, an hour later, in the arse end of the city, as far down as you can go without hitting the 'Pit, and in a far worse area than I'd found Lise. If I recalled correctly I was just yards from one of the ports where the 'Pit had been sealed, keeping the dead and dying from infecting everyone else. This was truly the bottom of the shit-pile, as evidenced by what I was trying not to step in.

I should have slept first, really. I'd been knackered before the spell and I was worse after. My thumb throbbed like buggery. But there was a girl down there, in that dank and awful place. My flesh and blood. Just a small girl, alone and afraid in a room with who-knew-what. If I was a religious man, I'd have prayed. Instead I told myself that sleep was for idiots and went where Dendal told me.

The walkways down this far were corroded and shaky, but it wasn't far to fall. In fact it was about six feet to the bottom of everything that was called Mahala. I didn't come down here often. Maybe I was just as snobby about what was below me as everyone in Heights or Clouds or Top of the World. Everyone likes to have someone to look down on. But if you hit this place, all you could look down on was rats – and not by much, because they were better-fed than the people round here.

Dendal had given me an address and a name. Someone who could help me get into the 'Pit, though how or why Dendal would know someone like that, who knew? I'd seen him leave the office precisely once in the three years I'd been working there, when Lastri was sick and he'd taken her some food.

I lurked somewhere out of the way, under a dripping overhang of crumbling concrete, and took a look around. The air was dull and gloomy, as it always was in Boundary. The sun was rising, peeking over the mountaintops to shine on the godly in Top of the World, but it probably never made a direct appearance this far down. The sun rarely got further than Trade, fifty or more levels above us, and the only lights here were the fitful beams of dirty yellow Glow globes that should have been replaced years ago. All they really lit up was the damp running down the walls.

When I finally moved, I walked warily and kept my hand on the butt of the pulse pistol in my pocket. I needn't have worried. The allover and coat that looked like a Specials uniform did its trick. In places like this, fear was better than any weapon. Especially when I was going to see a man who didn't show on the records, or at least on any record I could find. Tam Ratana. I'd never had to use his services before, but I'd heard of him in hushed whispers and Dendal had pointed me this way.

I reached the doorway I was after, a blank face in the pitted, dark body of the building. The windows to either side were crudely boarded up and decorated with some inventive language the scavenge-rat teens had undoubtedly thought highly amusing. I gave the door a solid knock. It was firmer than it looked, with a faint ring of reinforcing metal. After an age, and a couple more knocks, something clicked behind it. Someone must have seen something they liked, because there was an extensive scrape of locks and bolts before the door sprang open.

I couldn't see much in the dim light beyond but I could smell plenty, enough that I was glad I hadn't bothered with breakfast. I gripped my pistol tighter in my pocket and edged in. The door swung shut behind me and locks and bolts rattled home again. It was only when I turned that I saw the little man lurking behind the door. I put my back to the wall of the corridor, more from habit than any actual worry. He seemed spry enough, but the lines, droops and general sagginess of his dusky skin and the gnarled roots of fingers clubbed with rheumatism made me put his age at least eighty. He gave me a piercing look, but he didn't seem in the least bit frightened. I must have been losing my touch.

"Tam Ratana?"

He gave a bobbing nod, and I was reminded of the little birds you used to see in the upper parks, where the sun shines straight on to your skin and isn't second-hand, bounced off innumerable mirrors and concrete pillars before it reaches you. Of course you only got to see the birds, and the sun, briefly before the guards threw you out for being "from Under".

"What do you want?" Tam's voice was scratchy, like the rustle and scrunch of walking on gravel. It gave no hint of how he might feel about me being there, no anger or confusion or even curiosity. Muffled steps ran and petered out further down the corridor. He wasn't on his own in this place. I'd planned on getting some more information on just who this man was before I did anything else, but now I thought straightforward honesty might be the best policy.

"Dendal sent me. I'm looking for a kidnapped girl. My niece."

He smiled, completely unsurprised, his mouth wide and gummy. He crooked one knotty finger at me and headed off down the corridor, seemingly unaware of, or unconcerned by, the target his back made. I followed cautiously, past a dark opening on my left, full of the sound of someone trying not to be heard and failing. The person who had made those muffled steps earlier? I forced any nervousness from my face and carried on behind Tam but kept a discreet watch. No one fell into step behind me.

Then we were out of the dark, dank corridor and into a fuggy little room, full of old-fashioned, overstuffed chairs and bright rugs worn almost to rags underfoot. A musty, organic kind of smell, not unpleasant, assaulted me and I was reminded of a back-street shop my mother had taken me to when I was no more than five, before the 'Pit had been sealed. Before she got sick. A dark, secret kind of place where women had talked in whispers to the proprietor and swiftly hidden whatever little brown packets he had sold them.

Tam indicated I should sit. Bundles of dried plants – herbs, I thought with astonishment – hung from the ceiling to dry. My mother had always dried her own, but even when I was a child it was a rare practice. There was so little room to grow frivolities such as herbs and since then the synth had killed most of them.

Speaking of synth, its deadly tang underlay the sweet-smelling herbs. Not just a tang, but full-blown synthtox, there in the corner. A body reeking of it. A thin, frail body that could have been a man or woman. Not much hair to speak of, fluttering eyes big and black in a face that was drained of everything. I looked away.

As I sat, two girls, young, gangly teenagers from the look of them, hurried away in alarm into the darkness of an opening at the far end of the room. They had dusky skin and dark hair, but there was a pallor underneath that suggested that hadn't seen even so much as the little sun I got in a long time. Their eyes fixed on me and the younger seemed almost paralysed with fright, until the other dragged her away. I thought I saw a strange mark on the inside of her wrist, a tattoo of some sort maybe, and caution sprang up in me again. There were gangs around here that no one from above Boundary would survive meeting. Then they were gone, and Tam's watchful eyes were on me.

"Why have you come here?" There was a faint hint of accent, a flavour of somewhere that wasn't here.

"You're the man who knows how I can get to where I need to be," I said, carefully neutral in tone, mindful of who else might be here, watching and listening. I'd never met anyone from this far down that was worth knowing. I took out the picture and showed it to him. "I'm looking for this girl." Amarie said her little piece. By now it was starting to poke at my spine. "Daddy, look at me, I'm a princess."

He looked at the picture carefully, watching it through three times before he handed it back with a shrug. "Lots of girls go missing every day in a city this big. You should know that, Mr Dizon."

I wondered how he knew who I was, but then Dendal had surely told him I was coming. "I deal in runaways and boun-ties, not kidnappings. As far as I'm aware, there are few enough of them."

He smiled knowingly and the skin on my shoulders began to itch. "Used to be there were few of them. Lately, a lot more. Too many, and the guards won't, can't, touch them."

"Why not?" But I knew. Always the same answer to ques-tions like that.

The knowing smile pulled back into an unnerving grimace

that might have been intended as reassuring, but only succeeded in showing his gums and the small brown stubs that were all that was left of his teeth. "They take them to the 'Pit. Not a guard alive that will go down there, Mr Dizon. Unless they're Specials."

No wonder Dench didn't want anything to do with it. I'd have been off the job in a second if it hadn't been Perak's girl we were talking about. No, it wasn't that. That pretty girl in the picture, far from all the cynicism in me, far from pain or sadness or fear. The child I had been once, before life had its way, scored its lines into me with savage glee. Or she had been, and I had to hope she still was, inside. That it wasn't too late. A pretty girl who loved her father and now sat in a black box, sobbing. I felt a flicker of anger. Perak back in my life not five minutes and here I was, shouldering everything again.

I'd spent a lot of time and effort making sure that didn't happen. Runaways and bounties: little responsibility, lots of lovely cash. The runaways wanted to be gone and ninety-nine times out of a hundred they could take care of themselves as well as I could. If I didn't find them, they were just another kid turning adult, trying to make their way. The bounties – well, if I didn't catch them, tough luck for the guards. If I didn't take a job, or didn't see it through, they weren't my responsibility. But I couldn't walk away from this, and not just because Perak was my brother. I swore vividly in my head.

"Who takes them to the 'Pit?" I asked. "There's supposed

to be no one down there. They cleared it out before they sealed it."

Tam laughed, looking like a wrinkled gnome who's found he can make any wish come true with a wink of his eye. "That's what the Ministry say, but when do they ever tell the truth? They sealed a lot of them down there, the dregs they wanted to do without. They thought the synth would kill them soon enough, and they'd be rid of all those too undesirable, too feckless and faithless to live in their brave new clean pious city. Only it's not brave or clean, is it? They left them there to die, Mr Dizon. And when they didn't die, or not all of them, the Archdeacon found a use for them."

Left them there to die of the synth. I shook my head in shock, but it was likely true. In the 'Pit, who knew? It was sealed, but the tainted run-off from Upside was likely still filtering through: the water had to go somewhere. Now here was Tam, saying that people lived in that horror? The thought made me squirm. Not least because it looked like that was where I was headed.

"Why would they take girls down there?" I asked. "And how can I get her back?"

Tam grinned at me, but it wasn't a pleasant one. "I can get you down there, so you can look for your niece. Papers that will get you through the Ministry checks. I can give you a name once you're in there, a man who might help." His head bobbed up and down as though it were on a string. "For a price. And there's no one else can do that, excepting the Ministry."

There it was. He was right. For all my contacts, I'd never even known there was anyone down there, never mind how to get there, and Tam was offering me a way in. A chance, the only one I was likely to get.

"How much?"

In the end, it was easy. I should have known really. Tam got a young lad to show me where, and it was right under my nose, only more cleverly disguised than Dwarf's shop. Under a dripping stairwell that had been propped and patched so many times you couldn't see the original, a door lurked in the darkness. A maintenance door, it looked like, with a stout padlock and a small sign that said danger, alchemical storage and a picture of someone blowing themselves up. Hidden in plain view. It took the lad under a minute to pick the padlock and then I was in.

Right up to my neck.

Inside was a space about the size of a roomy coffin, which seemed appropriate. A dirty yellow Glow globe twitched on and off erratically with a highpitched whine that did nothing for my state of mind. Across from me stood another door.

Tam had told me what to expect and I didn't like the sound of it. At all. But needs must when Namrat has you by the balls and is ready to twist them off with a grin and a wink. There was a complicated button, lever and pulley arrangement by the door and I pushed it. While I waited, I fiddled with the false papers Tam had given me, along with a pin that I'd stuck to my coat. The pin was shaped like a tiger, with black stripes done in enamel. So they'd know I was Ministry, Tam had said.

The inner door ratcheted open, each clink and clank echoing damply and twisting my nerves to breaking. It was a long way down, and a long way down is something I try to avoid. I stepped into the compartment and tried not to think how far, or how this thing worked and whether it ever got any maintenance. Or whether whatever held it up was rusting, corroded by synth and ... *Stop it*. I took a deep, not quite steady breath and pushed the button/lever thing on the inside. The world fell away from my feet.

I was thrust downwards at what seemed to be an excessive speed that made my insides want to come out through my ears and had me thinking that maybe, just maybe, it would be nice to believe in a god or two so you could pray to them at times like this, when all you wanted to do was either cry or crap yourself.

The compartment finally shuddered to an abrupt halt that made my knees crumple. The door swished open and I pulled myself together enough to step out purposefully into a clammy chamber where dark liquid dripped down the walls and steamed sullenly in pools on the floor. Synth-tainted water. Stronger than I'd smelled it in years.

Two soldiers stood facing me, armoured and armed to the hilt, their eyes hidden by dark visors on their helmets. Ministry Specials, from their uniform and insignia, though the helmets were new. One stepped forward smartly and looked at my papers. I was immediately reassured that Tam had been worth the money. The soldier snapped off a salute so sharp you could have shaved with it, and there was a hungry awe in his voice when he spoke. "Any instructions, sir?"

I allowed myself a small smile and tried to look as arrogant as possible. "My first time here." I took in the badge on his shoulder. A reverend, on guard duty? Saluting *me*? Thank you, Tam. "I'm not really sure what I want as yet, reverend."

"Sir, the" – he licked his lips before he changed tack, as though he'd almost said something he shouldn't – "your department has special privileges, sir. I'll arrange transport immediately, sir." That was a heck of a lot of "sir"s.

The reverend was as good as his word. In less than two minutes I was led away by an unctuous individual called Kerd, a small, slimy little man with hair to match, dressed in a tatty holy-green robe, who didn't so much walk ahead as flow.

As we left the chamber behind, I could hear the heavy clank of chains, and almost swore out loud in surprise as a bulky cage appeared at the rim of the ledge in front of me. Kerd opened a battered gate and ushered me in. The floor was slick with the same fetid liquid as the chamber, and I tried not to wonder whether the soles of my boots were up to the challenge, or whether I'd just exposed myself to a lethal dose of synth. It took my mind off the long drop underneath me.

We rattled our way down through a shaft and after a moment or two of blackness there was the 'Pit, laid out below

me in all its gaudy decrepitude, glittering in a constant drizzle from the roof that refracted the light like prisms.

The buildings shone with light from rend-nut oil – which
was warmer than Glow light – and alleys swam with shadows.
There were no walkways clogging the air, but a series of cages
moved in a jerky dance around the sealed-off roots of Mahala.
As we descended I could hear the life of the city. Music! I
hadn't heard any real music in years: the Ministry disapproved, considering most lyrics to be seditious, so it was only
allowed on high days and holidays, and then it was bland and
vacuous hymns about how the Goddess was so lovely and nice.
They made me want to throw up.

Here, songs blared constantly from broken windows, the
old-fashioned music that had had a brief resurgence just before
the 'Pit was sealed, all heavy throbbing beats and wailing
words, a desperate outpouring of anger against the synth. It
still sounded as angry now, the rage of it pounding in my
veins. It made me want to laugh despite the gap between my
feet and solidity.

We clattered down smoothly, the clamour from all the
cages dulling to a soothing background noise that I soon
learned never stopped, along with the rain – run-off from
Upside that leaked through the only place it could, into the
'Pit. We neared the level of the street and the pulse of the city
surrounded us – shouts, screams, bursts of song. I'd never
heard anything like it.

Upside there were no streets as such, only walkways that

often swayed and bounced with the steps of shoppers, a few small parks and the tiny zoo that housed the few last horses, dogs and cats that had once numbered in millions; poor inbred things that bore little resemblance to those that had lived before. Upside, Over-Trade at least, people didn't want to get close enough to touch, unless they were behind closed doors. Under-Trade, people were too wary to touch, unless money changed hands. There was nothing up there like this, a pushing, shoving, good-natured, heaving humanity. It was glorious.

Below me was an endless parade of people, shuffling about their business on a solid street. On the *ground*. Men and women shouted out against the blasts of music, their heads covered with flamboyant hats against the constant drizzle. There were heady wafts of steamy, spicy food, and glittering lights from shops trying to tempt people in. I watched it all through the curtain of diamonds that the rain had become, aware of a vibrancy I'd never noticed Upside, as though the people here were prepared to wrench every last drop of blood out of life. Small groups of children wove their way through the giants above them. The only places children ran Upside were in the parts so bad that they ran with a gang and a lot of knives.

The cage ran down another shaft and into a heavily armoured compound. Two of the guards followed us and Kerd smiled at the look on my face as he let me out of the cage. "I'm sure you'll have time to sample all the delights the 'Pit can offer. Now, first, have that pin off, but be ready to show it when asked."

He led me through a small maze of buildings to a solid-iron gate five yards tall. Half a dozen sharp-looking guards stood with new guns ready as he opened the small doorway set into the gates and took me through. "Have to keep the port safe, we don't want any of these going Up, and you need to be careful where you go too, as a Ministry man. Too many places down here aren't very welcoming. Not surprising, all things considered, but best to be wary. If you leave the hotel at all – and I don't recommend it without guards – then keep to the main streets, and keep your wits about you. You aren't Upside any more."

Then I was in it, inside the animal of the crowd, and I was almost swept away before he took hold of my arm.

"This way, sir." He led me down a short alley lit with a kind of soft yellow light I'd never seen before that made all the shadows seem friendlier in the damp. Another cage, this time with a dark-haired boy in there, no older than ten. He gave us a sharp little nod and his hand flew round on a series of ratchets, and then we were up again, this time rattling along three yards above the ground. For once I wasn't bothered about the drop – I was too busy gawking.

Around us, hundreds of cages jerked their way in a complicated dance through alleys, across streets, around the ancient, giant towers that supported the upper reaches of Mahala, over smaller, cobbled-together buildings. Above us a web of cables strung themselves between turning discs. We hurtled towards one and I didn't even have time to wonder what the hell was going to happen before the mechanism that attached us to our wire swung around the disc, and with a flick of his wrist the boy sent us hurtling at right-angles to the way we had come.

Misty rain tingled against my face as we swooped through this garish, noisy, people-ridden, beautiful city. Boundary as it should have been. It was the most exhilarating ride I'd ever had, and I was sorry when we reached our destination. We were in a quieter area, but there was still a bustle on the streets, a never-ending choke of people. Kerd led me past more security, into a building that looked in good repair, and when we walked in and I saw the blue and gold of a vaulted roof, the thick carpets and the quiet, luxurious splendour, I silently thanked Tam once again.

With a quick salute and a knowing smile, Kerd and the guards left me to the devices of the hotel. A young boy, dressed in impeccable white and gold, led me away and handed me a numbered key. The lift was smooth-riding and bizarrely sumptuous, all brass icons of the Goddess, saints and martyrs, etched mirrors, thick carpet and soft scents. More like an old-fashioned temple than a lift, so it quite took my mind away from the drop under me.

When I tried the key in the properly numbered door, I found a huge room with carpets you could swim in and a bed almost the size of my room at home. A bath big enough for four dominated the next room, and when I tried the taps, hot water came in a torrent. I couldn't remember the last time I'd used a bath and not a shower. Maybe never. I had to shake myself.

I couldn't stay here. This was a hotel used by the Ministry, and whilst I had the pin, I'd be found out if I stayed too long. Still, maybe for tonight ... No, this wasn't what I'd come for. I gave myself a mental slap. I'd order some food because it was way past my breakfast time and I was famished, find out how to get where I was going, and go.

Before I could do anything else a discreet bell dinged at the door. I peeked through the spyhole and there was food, accompanied by the same young boy who'd given me the key. I raised my eyebrows but opened the door, my hand on the pulse pistol in my pocket just in case. The boy came in, dark-haired and -eyed, with a skin almost blue-white in its pallor, like most of the people I'd seen here. He quickly laid out the food on a table.

Steak. Steak! Where in hell did they get it from? Upside it couldn't be had for love nor money, but then this was the Ministry, and I supposed they had influence, and money, even here. Not just steak either, but real vegetables, not some reconstituted grey mush. Even the gravy was enough to have me salivating. I couldn't take my eyes off the food, and waited impatiently for him to be done and leave me to it. The boy didn't look at me as he set it out, and it was only when he went to leave that I saw who'd come with him.

One of the most stunning women I'd ever seen, a sultry brunette with eyes like black diamonds. Her silky dress slid over her legs as she walked, promising that her skin was as soft as the material that clung to every curve. I realised now why the bath and bed were so big, and why Ministry men came down to the 'Pit. Fact-finding missions, my arse. Up above, anywhere above Trade, there was too much damn piety for this. Under-Trade, too much pox. Here, it would seem, it was something they could indulge in without being caught, or catching anything in return. This was my kind of place. And this was most *definitely* my kind of woman.

Briefly, I couldn't decide which was more tantalising, the sight of her or the aroma of steak that drifted up behind me. I wasn't here for fun, I told myself sternly. I was here to find— She made for the bathroom, and with a wriggle of her shoulders the dress slid from her smooth skin to land in a puddle on the floor. I told myself I imagined her nervous smile, the odd way she looked at me, the little hints of something not quite right, when I heard the gush of water. Sod the steak, it could wait. I followed her into the bathroom. Well, it would be rude not to, wouldn't it?

In the end I let her have the steak, even though I couldn't remember the last time I'd had real meat. It was her blank-eyed look that stopped me from doing anything except let her soap my back. Don't get me wrong, I like women: they're a pleasing distraction from the grey grind of work, though I've never been tempted to make it more permanent. I've had more than my fair share of escorts, mistresses and flings. Often concurrently. I've even been paid in kind a time or two. But they'd all been willing participants. This girl had coercion stamped in subtle glowing lights behind her eyes. It was in the way she moved, the hesitant look to make sure I wasn't angry, the hint of a cringe when I moved too fast.

I like to think I have at least *some* standards, though I can think of plenty of women who might disagree with me there. But in my line of work I've seen a dozen beaten wives like this, two dozen beaten children. Was it any wonder I was such a cynic? And they all tried to hide it the same way as this girl, beneath lowered eyes and hesitant moves. None of them could help the look that was there if you wanted to see it – the same veiled, cowed look that made me want to choke.

The look of relief on her face when I handed her the soap and presented my back made me squirm in disgust. She hid it well enough that I'd come that close to not noticing, to just jumping in, and on her. I would have done, would have missed the subtle clues and thought no more of it, if I hadn't seen the mark on her wrists. The same mark I'd seen on the girls at Tam's place. Not tattoos, I saw now, but a swirling mark burned into the thin, tender flesh just under the thumbs. A brand, like they used to brand cattle back in the days when there were some, and maybe it meant the same thing. Ownership.

So I reined myself in for once, tried to hide my disgust,

which would only shame her worse, let her soap my back, fed her the steak and sent her on her way. She was so grateful, I didn't mind the loss of the meat and I made do with the vegetables and gravy. Even that was a treat, ten times better than anything I'd eaten for years.

I dressed quickly and tucked the pin inside a pocket, just in case. It wouldn't prove popular out there, I was sure. In other circumstances I'd have gone out and lost myself in the decadence around me, found a woman or two without brand marks and a bottle of something strong and had myself a damn good time. But I had a responsibility, people depending on me, maybe for their lives. Already it seemed to stifle me, and I'd barely begun.

Chapter Six

Three hours, and several wrong turns, later I was standing in a narrow alley between two shanty-built houses leaning out so far that they looked like two drunks supporting each other. Only a fitful oil lamp gave me any light to see by, but I was pretty sure that was a mercy, given the smell. Someone was dying of the synthtox somewhere close by. Rain dripped constantly from the roof far above, plastered my hair to my head and tingled on my face. I double-checked the address with the one Tam had given me and approached the small door, tucked away behind a stall selling some kind of food I couldn't recall having even smelled before.

The door was unlocked, as Tam had said it would be, but that didn't stop the hairs sticking up on the back of my neck. Under a feeble, swaying light – a rend-nut-oil lamp, not a Glow, the whole place reeked of rend-nut and poverty and synthtox – a set of wooden steps led upward, the treads splintered and broken in places. The bottom step groaned when I trod on it, but it took my weight and I advanced gingerly. Something chimed at my nerves, made me grip the pulse pistol hard inside my pocket; but, look as I might I couldn't see anything to alarm me.

Without warning a part of the wall came away and swung towards me. I lurched back, quickly enough to avoid the smack of the door, not nimble enough to avoid falling to one knee. Before I could bring up the pulse pistol, one of Perak's new guns was an inch from my nose, the muzzle quivering slightly. I hadn't seen one up close before, but there was no mistaking what it was. The face behind the dark eye of the barrel was in shadow as the light swung in a lazy arc above.

"What are you doing here, Ministry man?" he said, and a sharp fear vibrated in his voice. The finger on the trigger twitched. "Jake'll have something to say about that. You may end up as dish of the day on that stall down there. You'll probably taste better, too."

The only papers I'd dared bring down were the Ministry ones, in case I was searched before they let me in. Tam had warned me: among the general population, the Ministry were less than welcome, and they were dead if they left the approved areas. I was not in an approved area by a wide margin, and I suspected the Ministry were as welcome as snot in the bathtub. "Tam sent me."

The gun lowered a fraction, but I still couldn't see much of the guy's face except the hard line of his mouth. "Prove it."

Luckily, Tam had foreseen this. Mindful of the gun in my face, I slid a hand into a pocket and took out the picture Tam had given me. It had a bland scene of one of the plusher parts of Trade painted on it. The slip was snatched out of my hand. Gun Man gave it the briefest of looks and stood to one side, gesturing me upwards with the barrel.

"In there," he said, pointing to the doorway he'd come through. "Sit on the first chair, keep your hands on the armrests."

I resisted the instinctive reaction to tell him to go screw his mother, did as I was told and entered a small, spartan room. There were two rickety chairs, a bed with a threadbare blanket and a lumpy-looking pillow, and a small desk, neat, no papers. The floor was bare boards, worn to splinters with odd stains making weird patterns. Some pictures on the wall, but I couldn't make them out in the light from a guttering oil lamp. That was it. A room for sleeping in, working in. Not for living in. It was scrubbed so clean it could have been made yesterday, though the building that housed it was eaten away by the synth, almost to nothing in places.

I sat in the chair and put my hands on the armrests. Even without Tam's warnings about the dangers here, the jittery twitch of the man's finger on the trigger would have made me do it. Not just craven self-preservation: I needed to live to find Amarie. I told myself that and almost believed it.

I bit back a laugh when I saw the man who walked through the door. If I'd have seen his face before, I'd have had that gun out of his hand in two seconds flat. He was a few years younger than me, mid-twenties I guessed, though he still had the gangliness of youth and he looked scared half to death. He was dressed in tatty black, the arms of his old-fashioned cloth shirt pulled down fastidiously to his wrists, every crease in place, all buttons done up. In contrast, his dark, collar-length hair rumpled round a face that managed to give the impression of a small wizened monkey that's had its banana stolen. But he held the gun, even if his hand did tremble so much it was only pointing at my face half the time.

He stood and looked at me for a moment, his dark eyes ranging over my face uncomfortably before he relaxed, just a fraction. He took a look at the picture in his left hand and glanced my way again.

"You don't look much like a Ministry man," he said. "Too thin, not arrogant enough."

"I'm not Ministry."

"You're from Upside, though. Accent's wrong for a Downsider. You don't dress like one either, that allover, the coat. The only Upsiders in this place are Ministry. Which means I will take great pleasure in shooting you. No Specials here to guard your back, not this far out. This far out, they don't even care enough for that." His hand tightened on the gun and his face twisted, as though gearing himself up to do it.

"I'm looking for Pasha. I need his help," I snapped. I wanted to be back Upside, where I knew the rules, where I didn't need this kind of help, any help, where my life was contained to a nicety. I wanted to be in the bed of one of my girls, or drinking at home with barely a thought to the people I looked for, apart from the cash finding them would bring me. Where I could do as I pleased, within reason, and didn't have this duty weighing on my every thought. Or synth on my boots.

The name seemed to startle him out of shooting me. For a while, anyway. "Help with what?" He moved across to the bed and sat down, the gun still pointing my way. He seemed to have got his nerves under control, because it wasn't waving about any more. The picture flipped over and over in his other hand.

It was bad enough that I had to ask for help, but this was getting irritating. "For fuck's sake, are you Pasha? Yes or no? If yes, stop pissing about; if no, where is he? I haven't got time to dick around."

He gave me a shame-faced grin and laughed a little. "You don't sound much like a Ministry man, for all your accent. Let's see."

He reached down, still pointing the gun my way, and felt under the bed. When his hand returned he was holding what looked like a lamp, but the glass was black. He laid the picture on the covers of the bed and held the lamp over it, flicking a switch with his thumb. No light shone that I could see, but the picture changed in some indefinable way. He laid the gun on his leg, though he didn't take his hand off the butt, and grinned, making him look more monkey-like than ever. "I'm Pasha. What is it you want, Mr Dizon?"

I relaxed a little in the chair. "I'm looking for a girl."

He shrugged in a poor attempt at nonchalance. "Aren't we all? But I'm not a pimp."

I refused to give in to the sharp retort and kept my voice level. He had a point. "My niece. She was kidnapped. She's down here."

His raised his eyebrows. "From Upside? And the kidnappers? You're sure?"

I shut my eyes against Amarie's sobbing, the growl in the background. Then I lied a bit. Lying about my magic was second nature, and probably why I wasn't yet dead. "Tam seemed to think so, from the little descriptions we had."

"Which were?"

I ran through the brief details I'd found out: the scarred man and his lookalike companion, the way they were dressed, and how they'd disappeared. I didn't like the hard glint that leapt into Pasha's eye, at odds with his impish face, or the way he was chewing his lip. Or, indeed, the way his hand tightened on the trigger of the gun, because it was still pointing my way. "Why should I help you? What's one girl when all the 'Pit needs help?"

"Tam said you would. I'm happy to pay," I said, hoping he would refuse the money. I'd paid too much to Tam already.

"I don't need your money." His face flushed as though he was affronted by the offer. "Tam's never sent anyone down here before. What's so special about you, or this girl, that he'd risk it?"

"She's my niece. I want to get her back."

He gave me a pitying look but said nothing. My temper started to get the better of me but I resisted the urge to thump him. Tam had warned me this man was my only hope. I didn't stand a chance down here without him. I didn't quite manage the diplomacy I'd hoped for; the words fell out of my mouth before I could stop them. "How are you going to help anyway? You can barely even hold a gun straight."

He raised the gun and hefted it as though testing its weight, or its ability to blow my head clean off. He didn't look quite so monkey-like now. "You'll see."

Pasha splashed through the streets and I followed. It wasn't long before I was wishing I had a hat like everyone else, to keep the constant drizzle off. Every drop felt like another nail in my coffin. It might be laced with synth, might be working its way into my blood and bones right now. Which kind of offset the pleasure of being able to walk on solid ground and not have the niggle of a long drop to chew my nerves.

We passed through a large and thriving trade district, so different to Upside. The windows were full of things I hadn't seen in years, banned by the Ministry for being seditious: gramophones, both wind-up and powered by some mysterious source, and the records to go with them; instruments – brass, woodwind, even a twelve-string guitar. Music vibrated along the streets, blaring out of windows, songs and bands competing with each other, mingling together, but somehow it never became discordant.

Whole shops were devoted to books. I don't mean factual books – even the Ministry allows them, after they're vetted carefully for anything they don't like. I mean *stories*. The sort that my mother used to read to us, that make you think there's hope yet for people. That something better exists, even if it isn't here or you'll never experience it for yourself. Unicorns, dragons, myths and legends, noble warriors, dread mages, you know the sort of thing. I'd forgotten about those stories she'd read. I'd forgotten the sentiment too, and I itched to dive in among them, try to regain some of that wonder. It was probably a good thing I didn't, because I suspected any wonder in me was long gone.

Some of the goods hadn't been banned Upside but they might as well have been, considering how long it had been since I'd seen any. Big, fat pork chops, a brace of game-birds, beef enough to keep me stuffed for a week with prices so cheap any low-life in Boundary could have afforded at least one meat meal a week. We walked past a shop that baked and sold pies, and my stomach rumbled audibly at the aroma that wafted along the street.

There were other differences from Boundary and the rest of Upside too. I hadn't seen one Rapture addict, not a single working girl, or if I had they were being exceptionally discreet. Yet, for all their food and the apparent lack of the flaws

of Upside, there was an undercurrent, something raw and visceral that vibrated my bones almost as hard as the music.
Anger and hopelessness flowed through the crowds just as it
did in Boundary or anywhere below Trade. The only difference
was that here they hid it better, because it wasn't directed at
each other in brawls or knife fights. It was here, but I got the
feeling they kept it all inside, brewing, waiting to escape in
a violent explosion. It made me shiver and hurry after Pasha.

He led me further in, passing no comment and answering
none of my questions except with an offhand shrug. The
undercurrent was affecting him, I think. Once he'd stepped
outside his door, his shoulders had hunched into his jacket, his
mouth had hardened. He no longer looked like a little
monkey but like a vicious, if skinny, ape. I could be wrong –
I've only ever seen monkeys or apes in books when I was a boy.
However, putting on a different face when you step out of the
door, that I know.

Buildings towered over us, hemming us and our sightline
in. I was used to that, to the crumbling façades, the blank-
eyed windows. What I wasn't used to was the constant rain,
the occasional glimpse of someone half dead from synthtox, or
the thought that, no matter the time, I wouldn't get to see
even third-hand sunlight. It would always be dark down here.
The thought made me shove my hands further into my pockets and hunch away from the rain. So it wasn't until Pasha
stopped and said, "Here we are" that I noticed the building.

It wasn't like the others, didn't reach to the far-above Seal that divided the 'Pit from Upside. It alone looked pristine against the ravages of synth. Three storeys tall, that was all, faced with white stone and curved. If I could have seen it all, it'd probably be round. Lamps blazed from every barred window, lighting the streets and setting the shop windows into sparks and bright reflections. It looked like a temple – or a prison.

The streets were filled with people, all heading for the main entrance which opened like a dark mouth in the side of the building. Barkers wandered up and down the orderly lines shouting, "Tickets, best tickets for the match of the decade!"

"Match?" I asked Pasha. Upside there were occasional sporting events, especially in the winter. Chayl matches – a kind of organised brawl involving, at least nominally, a ball – were fun to watch and I tried to get to most of them, even if my team always lost whenever I showed up. The games were so popular, it was a wonder the Ministry hadn't banned them yet. Only I had the feeling this wasn't that sort of match. The people queuing looked too – not grim exactly. I'm pretty grim when I go to see a chayl match, because I'm always sure we'll lose and too often right. With these people, it was almost as though they came to pay homage, to give solemn thanks. They looked like temple-goers on holy days. Well, from what I remember of going to temple, anyway. It's been a while, but these people had an added something that rang familiar to me when talking about temple. An added – I don't know what; that brewing anger, perhaps, just waiting to explode, or be released somehow.

Pasha looked out over the crowd with me, but didn't seem to see anything he liked, if the way his lips thinned was anything to go by.

"Come on." He nodded his head to indicate where he wanted to go. "We can get in the other way, away from these carrion birds."

He pushed through the orderly crowds and I followed. There were one or two murmurs, but it seemed people knew who Pasha was because no one gave any trouble. Before long we'd skirted the round building and were at the back. No crowds here, though a knot of teenage girls, wearing not a whole hell of a lot, giggled across the street under the protection of a shop's awning. Pasha ignored them and led the way to a small door that was almost hidden in stone scrollwork and shadows.

He knocked, a patterned rapping that was obviously some sort of code. After a few heartbeats, the door cracked open. It was dark in the gap, and for a moment all I could see was an olive-skinned face and a black eye. When the opener saw Pasha, though, the door swung wide, revealing a man clad only in short breeches and a sword, which had the girls squealing with delight behind us. I was distracted from the door by the sight of one of them very nearly falling out of her top. Until the voice that felt like it shattered one of my eardrums.

"Pasha!" The behemoth of a man enveloped Pasha in a hug that might break ribs. Every muscle was sculpted to perfection, a stomach to die for, a flow of thick glossy black hair –

and a face with no more sense in it than a five-year-old's. But a five-year-old with a large sword at his waist, who looked like he could use it if someone stole his lollipop. He waved at me, happy to meet me, which was a new experience. I tried to act as if I was allergic to lollipops.

Pasha extricated himself from the hug and grinned up at Muscle Boy. "Hey, Dog. Got someone to see Jake. OK?"

Dog nodded with an exaggerated movement as though it was something he needed to think long and hard about. He stepped back to give us space and I found myself in the sort of room that typifies any sporting endeavour. Grey walls, the smell of sweat, abandoned socks and jockstraps, damp towels, and people – generally athletic men who made me briefly promise to exercise more – wandering around in their under-wear. In the background, a crowd roared and cheered and stamped, blowing off their anger in an outpouring of noise.

The difference in this arena was that the towels were spot-ted with blood and all the players had at least one sword somewhere about their person. I got the feeling that a "match" wasn't a friendly thing, a game to be played. It was serious. Yet the people were welcoming enough. Several men nodded at Pasha, one or two waved or called out.

Pasha ignored them and wove his way through a throng of people and the aroma of unwashed socks. He stopped by a nondescript door – grey wood with a cheap handle. The look he gave me, just a flick of the eyes and a small, twitching little grin that could easily be missed, made me think of someone who's about to get one over on someone else. The kind of look that I love to give out, but am not so keen to get.

The door wasn't locked and after that look Pasha went straight in, with me close behind. I was quite glad to have some wood between me and the bemuscled specimens of manhood in the hall, bristling with sharp things and making me feel inadequate.

The room inside wasn't at all what I'd expected – I'd thought a changing room or maybe a sparring area. Instead, I was met with functional, tasteful luxury. Thick carpet the colour of muted gold on the floor, two chairs upholstered in leather – real leather, I could tell by the smell. A sideboard along one wall was choked with bottles of all different colours and sizes. Booze for every taste and appetite. A rack of crystal glasses to drink it from. But that wasn't what made my jaw drop.

That was what I could see through the smoked glass that took up the whole of the far wall. Two men, two swords and a whole lot of muscles, sweat and blood. One of the men was big and beefy, blond hair rumpled and sweaty, stuck to a face that, whilst not handsome, was striking in its purposefulness, its intensity. The other was more like me: tall but not especially broad, dark skin, hair and eyes. Quicker than the blond, but not as strong, that was obvious from a glance.

Both had more than one slash across their chest or arm, blood soaking into their armour, dripping to the sand of the arena. I could see every bead of sweat that broke on the combatants' brows as they slashed and kicked and crunched. Two men in close-fitting leather armour, hacking away in a brutal ballet of swords. Not what I'd expected.

Around the two men, the cheers and howls of the crowd blocked out any other sound. Viewing-boxes like this one, with blackened one-way glass, almost surrounded the arena at ground level, leaving only an entrance ramp that sloped up to a stage. Above the boxes the stands shook to the stomp of ten thousand feet. It was primal: the fight, the noise, the crowd, the blood. I loved it and feared it all at the same time.

Pasha poured himself a stiff drink and swallowed it down in one. He didn't look at the fight. "Welcome to the death match." He poured another shot and knocked it back with a shudder and a grimace.

The blond aimed an overhand slice at the dark guy and the sword bit in. Blood streaked the window and the crowd screamed its approval. I turned to the sideboard, grabbed the first bottle that came to hand and poured. I don't know what it was, and it burned the shit out of my throat, but it was better than watching that.

"Why did you bring me here?"

Pasha stared straight ahead at the greyed plaster of the wall and ran a lazy finger around the edge of his glass. "Because. Because you need help, and Jake is the one who'll give it. Because matchers have power here, more than anyone who isn't Ministry, and you'll need that too. Because you needed to know what life Downside is, and this shows it better than anything. Ministry controlling from behind you, pretending to give the people what they want, and pretending it isn't them running it. But while they give with one hand, give blood to the bloodthirsty, sate the hunger, the anger of the crowd to keep them pliable – while you're watching them give, they take double the blood with the other hand behind your back. If you're lucky that other hand won't have a knife in it. But most of all, because Jake is like a god here, and you need all the damn help you can get."

"OK, that's the third time you've mentioned Jake. Who is he and what can he do to help?"

Pasha's low laugh made me shiver. "What can anyone do against the Ministry? But Jake will help. We both will, where we can and for our own reasons. Just don't ask what they are."

His eyes were fixed on a crack in the plaster but I got the feeling he wasn't seeing anything. His hand gripped his glass almost as though he was trying to choke it. But whatever his reasons were, frankly I didn't care. I didn't care if he thought I was made of cheese, as long as I got Amarie out of that damn hole. I could hear that growl as a subtle background to every thought, and Pasha's cryptic offer of help was sent from the gods I don't believe in.

"So what now?"

Pasha looked down blindly at his glass, seemed to realise it was empty again and sloshed a good slug of something blue into it. "First, we behave like good little Downsiders and watch."

He slumped into one of the leather-covered chairs just as

Blondie brought his sword down to rest on Dark Guy's throat, one foot casually keeping him on the ground. Dark Guy's sword lay on the other side of the arena. The match was over. The crowd went berserk, shouting, cheering, stomping. Money rained down into the sand and a young boy scampered round, picking it up. Some thumping music started and Blondie strutted round the arena, sword held over his head in victory as he lapped up the adoration. He didn't seem to notice the blood running down his upstretched arm.

"So this is a death match?" I asked. "How is it that the dark guy's still alive?"

Blondie swaggered up the ramp and two men hurried to help Dark Guy to his feet. They each took one arm over a shoulder and half helped, half carried him up the ramp.

Pasha kept his eyes on the arena, scanning the crowd with a curled lip. "Because if they died too often, we'd have no one left to stage the matches, and the Ministry would have nothing to offer the people who watch, no sop to keep the people quiet except religion – and that's not enough, not down here. People need somewhere to vent their anger, safely, not against the Ministry, and this is it. The matchers die often enough as it is, without anyone trying too hard. Gregor, the dark guy as you call him, may yet die from his injuries or infection. But it's mostly a sham, Mr Dizon. A pretence to feed the crowd what they want; that's what the men who run it say. The crowd think it's real, but they love a matcher who shows a bit of mercy. Though, as it's the Ministry that started it up, and say it's for the people, I don't believe this is for the crowd's benefit. Azama thought of it, and he's one devious bastard. There are other reasons, I'm sure of it. Azama never does anything for only one reason."

A couple more men were clearing the worst of the blood from the sand and the windows. A damp cloth squeaked on the glass and the streaks of blood disappeared. "And those reasons are?"

A wail of music drowned out the crowd for a moment and then a roar that made the previous chants seem like whispers almost deafened me. Pasha straightened in his seat.

The crowd calmed a little, but there was a buzz in the air as they waited for something, someone.

They didn't have to wait long. A shout went up as music started up properly. A heavy throb of it preceded the man who stepped down the ramp. He swung his sword flashily in time to the beat, his black leather-armoured allover gleaming, matching the hair slicked back into an oily ponytail and the eyes that flashed with life. There were scattered cheers but some of those at the front of the crowd spat on him as he paraded down to the ring. He seemed not to notice, his eyes sharp and focused on something internal. He looked ablaze with confidence, as though he couldn't imagine how anyone could ever seek to beat him.

"That's Jake?" I asked, though I couldn't see how it could be anyone else from what Pasha had said. I was surprised when he laughed.

"Oh no, that's not Jake. That's the Storad. He's just here for the one fight."

A Storad? They supposedly came from outside Mahala, from a hard country to the north, one that had no love for us, for the way Mahala controlled its trade through the mountain pass. How did he get into the city, let alone down here?

"Got some name no one can pronounce," Pasha went on. "He's the best from the north. Killed the last fifteen men in his fights. Three from poison, or so the rumour goes. He's come because he thinks he has a chance to beat Jake."

"Poison? They poison the blades?"

"Not here, no, and he's not supposed to where he's from either. But then, the Ministry doesn't run things there. They fight because they've always fought, because the mountain tribes think that's what they were born to do. Some religious thing, though luckily it's only a few small tribes, or Mahala would be in trouble." He shrugged, but there was a pinched look to his face. "Maybe he uses poison, maybe he doesn't, there's no way to know for sure. I'd plug your ears now if I were you: here comes Jake. Two hundred fights and not lost one of them, and never killed anyone, by accident or on purpose."

There was a blast of music again, more melodious yet just as loud as before. A figure appeared at the top of the ramp, and if I'd thought the crowd had been thunderous before, they were deafening now. Pasha said something and though he was right next to me as we watched, I couldn't hear any of what he said. And not just from the noise.

Jake stood for a moment before she descended the ramp, a lithe figure in black leather and steel with a shock of hair dyed cherry red pulled back from her face. Where the Storad had been confident and showy, she looked absolutely calm and collected, as though every movement was smoothly calculated. Her face showed nothing as she looked down at him and her eyes held only a wary reckoning. As the cheers and screams peaked she began a measured, graceful walk down the ramp; fluid, confident and sexy as all hell.

She reached the sand and the Storad gave her a small mocking bow before he raised his sword with both hands. It was almost as big as she was. She stood looking at him as the music tailed away, her eyes flicking between his face and the tip of his sword, then to his feet. The noise of the crowd above me subsided to a dull roar. He didn't wait for her to pull a weapon but attacked with a blinding thrust and a twist of his body.

Before I'd even realised she'd moved, she had a sword in each hand. She parried his thrust and made one of her own with her left hand, and they were away, into a world of their own. We didn't matter, I could see it in both of them. They weren't aware the crowd was there as they slashed and parried and danced around each other, Jake always that little bit quicker, more nimble than him.

When I tore myself away for a moment, Pasha's face was set in a grimace and the skin stretched over his knuckles as he grasped at the arm of his chair. He was breathing oddly, as though it was him that fought. A shout from the crowd drew me back into the fight.

I could see why she was so good, why the crowd loved her. She didn't just use her swords, she wasn't just fighting; she was entertaining. Every part of her was a weapon. The Storad seemed restricted to his blade, with little use for anything else, and if he hit with it he wouldn't *need* anything else. But she dodged every blow with a swirl of panache that made the crowd chant her name, and when she did he felt the smack of her elbow or a foot would come up and crunch into his knee before she spun out of his reach. It was almost as though she was toying with him, playing up to the howls of the crowd, giving them what they wanted. The bewilderment on his face was in stark contrast to the confident swagger of five minutes ago.

He threw out a sudden roar that made me jump and Pasha almost come out of his chair beside me, then the Storad was on the attack. His blade moved smoothly in a well-practised series of manoeuvres that I was sure would have taken the head off any other person in the place. Jake fell back before him, her swords glittering as she blocked and dodged, but she seemed beaten at last, her speed nothing before his power. I felt sure I imagined the little twitch at the corner of her mouth.

She hesitated a split second too long as his sword swept round at waist height. Pasha let out a panicked "Shit!" and dropped his glass. But she bent backwards at the waist, like a reed in water, just enough so the sword passed her. The Storad, sure he had her at last, was left off balance and she wasted no time now. She seemed to run up his body; a foot blasted into his groin followed by a straight-legged kick to his nose that spread it over his face before she flipped herself over and landed lightly, crouched on the sand.

He let out a bellow of rage, lost among the roar of the crowd, as he flew backwards, blood spraying, to land on his back, hand loose on his sword. A foot landed on his right arm with the slap of stiff leather on skin. Her other foot landed no more than half an inch from his head in a puff of sand. When he looked up through pain-filled eyes there were two sword-tips touching his cheeks. Jake's mouth was hooked up in a grin, her face alight with some emotion, pride maybe, or just the sheer rush of not being sliced to ribbons.

The Storad glared upwards and the muscles in his arms moved as though he would try to raise his weapon, but the tips of Jake's swords moved almost imperceptibly forwards, the points pricking his skin. Then she leapt up and brought both feet down on his right arm. Bone broke with a sick, wet crack and he lost his grip on his sword altogether. An instant later the blades rested on his skin again. One of them trailed its way down his cheek towards his unprotected throat, a silent, potent threat.

With a look of intense hatred and humiliation, and with what I could only assume was some curse in his native tongue, he held his good hand away from its sword. She looked down at him and from this close I could see a blank calculation, backlit with a little flame of that pride.

She spun away from him and the noise from the crowd rammed into my ears, vibrated in my bones until being shouted to death became a distinct possibility. Jake didn't parade in victory like Blondie had, just raised one arm briefly and held her bloodied sword aloft. It was only then that I saw what I'd missed in the rush of the fight. Blood trickled slowly down across her forehead from a gash among her hair. She held the arm by her side stiffly and there was a bloody rent in her armour. With a quick, blank glance at the box where Pasha and I sat and watched, she turned on her heel and stalked up the ramp, past a band that was setting up on the stage, and out of the arena.

Pasha sat back in his chair, shaking and sweaty, and murmured a few relieved swearwords. He got up and made his way to the drinks, poured himself a stiff shot and drank it down. The band started up a raucous tune that had the crowd stamping their feet in time and singing along.

"Must be tough," I said. "Watching your girlfriend do that."

Pasha shot me an alarmed look but another voice answered before he could say anything. A curious tone to it, half amused warmth, half deadly warning. "I don't do relationships. I don't do boyfriends. I don't do flings, or one-night stands. I don't do friends. I barely even manage acquaintances. Pasha is my employee, that's all. And if he doesn't stop snorting my booze we're going to have words." Pasha laughed and brought out another glass.

The singer in the arena wailed that he was suffer, he was smite, he was hope. I turned my head, very slowly. I didn't know about the singer, but the woman sliding a swordpoint towards my eye – well, she was at least two of those things. I couldn't be sure about the hope.

The sword stopped a scant half-inch from my eyelid and I kept very still. She looked me up and down without a flicker of interest and I regarded her carefully in return. Normally I'd have liked what I saw. Just slim enough while still going in and out in all the best places. In and outs all snugly cased in leather. Soft, slippery leather that made naughty thoughts appear like a rash in my imagination. A smooth face that might be pretty behind the blood.

I don't go for looks as a rule. Don't get me wrong, I like a pretty face as much as anyone. But it's the way they walk that always gets to me, the way they carry themselves. Jake walked as though she owned the place, with an unconscious grace that made me tingle. An ice queen, untouchable, just how I like them. A challenge, and there's normally such a volcano underneath. The only difference here was she looked like she meant it; the ice went all the way through.

So, she ticked all my boxes. Over eighteen, female, still breathing, a challenge. Unfortunately she ticked the "not on your fucking life" box too. Maybe it was the swords, or maybe it was her eyes. Those calm, dead eyes talked to me, told me she could slice me limb from limb and not worry about it, but there was something else, deeper, darker, and even now I couldn't tell you what it was. What I *can* tell you is that she scared the crap out of me. That I liked it and wasn't about to let that stop me. I was just going to have to be a bit more careful than usual.

Then she gave an easy grin that didn't quite warm up the deadness behind her eyes, flicked the sword away and dropped it and its twin on a table. Pasha handed her a shot of the liquor and she drained it. "What's the Upsider doing here?"

"Looking for someone, a girl gone missing," Pasha said, and gave me a look that meant "Let me do the talking". I was happy to leave him to it, because a stammer rarely comes across as professional.

Jake pulled off her gauntlets and peeled back the armour-clad allover down to her waist, revealing a sweat-soaked undershirt that clung to her and almost ensured I didn't see anything else for a while. I dragged my eyes away, to soft leather strips that wound around her hands and arms to her elbows. Her upper arms and shoulders, what I could see, were covered in a tracery of old scars, and a gash split the skin on her left arm near the shoulder.

She sank into a chair and grinned up at Pasha as he hurried over with a small medic kit.

"Any poison, do you think?" Pasha asked, his face scrunched and monkey-like again.

Jake looked my way and shrugged. "Who can tell? We'll

find out when I keel over, eh? So, Upsider, who are you look-ing for and how'd you get down here?"

I stared in horrified fascination as Pasha got out a needle, thread and tweezers. Without pausing for anything other than sterilising the needle in the flame of an oil lamp, he began stitching the wound in Jake's head. He seemed very careful not to touch her with anything other than the needle or tweezers. Jake barely flinched. By the looks of the scars, she'd been through this a fair few times before. Pasha opened his mouth to answer her question for me, but she waved his words away and asked me again.

"Tam sent me," I managed after a moment. "He said Pasha could help."

"And? There's thousands of girls missing down here. Why should we worry about finding one when we could be finding dozens?"

"She's my niece."

Her eyes stayed steady on mine and there was a hint of something there, deep down, too deep to know if it was really there or only my imagination, but her lips smiled sadly and I think she actually meant her words. "Sorry to hear that. Any proof you aren't Ministry?"

Pasha stopped his stitching a moment and fished out the picture that Tam had given me. Jake looked at it with a frown. "You checked this out, Pasha?"

"Of course. Right message. And an extra." Pasha finished with the gash on her head and moved down to her arm.

"An extra?" She hissed quietly as the needle dug in, but there was no doubt about the warmth in her voice. When she spoke to Pasha, anyway. "Careful, you great lug."

"Sorry. A possible name." Pasha's voice tightened and Jake gave him a wary look. Pasha kept his eyes on his stitching. "Azama. Tam's sure he's back."

Jake's arm jerked and pulled the stitches tight in her skin. She didn't seem to notice. Some meaningful look passed between them but it was difficult to say why, or even what sort of look. Weighing up whether to help me tackle someone they clearly knew something about, perhaps.

"You think you're the first person the Ministry's sent down here to try to find us, find out who it is keeps taking those girls back? Eh? Not the first, and probably not the last. The others didn't make it back." Her eyes and mouth were set hard now, and the way she glared at me almost robbed me of words.

"The Ministry didn't—"

Pasha interrupted me before I could go further, his voice low so I had to strain to catch the words. "If he is Ministry, he doesn't know it."

Jake flicked him a quick, surprised glance before she returned to looking at me, with a hard, thoughtful stare that made me quiver.

If I couldn't get her to help, her and Pasha, I had no hope, not down here where everything was arse about face. I knew nothing and nobody. I said the first thing that came into my head. "I can pay you."

Jake shot out of the chair, wrenching the thread from Pasha's hand. "You think all these girls going missing from down here don't have family too? People who love them? Parents, sisters, uncles? Do you think your niece is worth more than they are because you can *pay* to try and get her back?"

I flinched back in the chair, grateful that the swords were out of reach at least, although I doubted that would help much if she decided to go for me. I gripped the butt of the pulse pistol in my pocket. It didn't seem very reassuring. "No, that's not what I meant at all. I'm a bounty hunter, that's how it works Upside. Money is the grease on the squeaky wheel of life."

She slid back into the chair and looked at me levelly. "You aren't Upside any more."

I relaxed my grip on the pistol, gladder than I could ever remember that I didn't have to use it. I had my doubts it would work on her. "And don't I know it. Look, I need your help. I'll gladly help you in return, any way I can, pay you that way. But I have to find my niece. I can't go back to my brother and tell him I saw where she is, but couldn't rescue her. I need to get her out."

One red eyebrow raised and her look sharpened. "You saw her? How? Where she is now?"

"I, er—" Damn Namrat's fucking bollocks. I didn't usually have a problem talking to women. To anyone. But my magic, I don't like to talk about that. Not just because it could get me arrested and dead faster than you can say mage. It didn't seem I had much choice, though. "It's how I make my living, how I find people. I can see where they are. If I – er, if I use my magic."

Pasha dropped something which bounced across the floor with a tinkle. Jake sat up straighter. She looked very interested all of a sudden. "What sort of magic?"

Normally I'd have lied. A lot. Somehow, with that disturbing gimlet gaze on me, with that soft growling marauding around my head and Amarie's sobs a counterpoint, I couldn't. I wanted my life back, to be back where my worst worry was what mushy crap to have for dinner or which girlfriend to see tonight. I wanted to not give a shit again. Right at that moment, I would have given my left bollock to be an only child. I hated myself for that thought.

I gave myself a mental kick and looked her in the eye when I said it. "Pain magic."

That was the first real sign of disturbance in her – one hand flew to the other wrist and fluttered there, a strange gesture for a woman like her. She got herself under control quickly enough. More than I could say for Pasha. He looked younger than ever, his eyes wide and his mouth working as though he was trying not to – what? Cry? Shout? I was oddly disappointed in them, as though I'd hoped they'd understand. I hadn't consciously thought that, but maybe – yeah, maybe I'd hoped. A guy can dream, right?

"You – you don't ..." Her brow creased as she trailed off from voicing the thought. Pasha put a gentle hand on the chair, a hair's breadth from her shoulder.

"Only on myself. I swear, I keep to that code. I swear, just help me find her. Please." I left the rest unsaid. Please, because I couldn't bear to watch the pain on Perak's face otherwise. Couldn't live with myself if I fucked this up. Which might make more sense to my brain if I knew *why*. The emotional part of me said, *Because it's your brother and you promised Ma*, and the other part, the one I'd let fester and take hold and was now a part of me, said, *So what? You haven't given a fuck about anyone in years, and you did OK. Better than OK really. Why stop now? What's in it for you?*

When I looked up from the shoes I'd contemplated while I thought this, Jake was staring at me. I couldn't tell you what was behind that gaze. I never have been able to, not with Jake.

I expected . . . well, something angry, or disparaging. What I got was "Has today left you wanting a stiff drink?"

Normally I'm not one for serious drinking, but Namrat's balls, I needed one right then. Anything to rid my mind of the growl and the sudden resurgence of a conscience. "A whole bottle. Screw it, maybe two."

Jake stood up with a smile and shrugged her leather allover into place over the arm that was still bleeding. "I know just the place."

109

Chapter Seven

The bar was seedy, with a floor sticky enough to lose you a boot, and some very suspicious stains on the walls. On the tables too. It was also more upmarket than anything in Boundary. The clientele drank out of glasses rather than jugs or straight from the bottle, the doorman didn't look like an ape in a suit, none of the windows had any cracks and there weren't any working girls touting for business, or if there were, they were being discreet about it. However, the thing that struck me most was the smell.

By the time we'd walked through the door I was salivating. Unless you counted a few vegetable leftovers at the hotel, I hadn't eaten since – hey, since lunchtime the day before? Time was difficult to tell down here. But I didn't care about time, I cared about the smell of cooking beef.

This, Pasha said, was where the matchers hung out after a hard day slicing each other to ribbons, and it appeared matchers had the money. I tried to ignore the fact that I was in a room full of men with swords and the scars to match, where one wrong word could see my guts on the floor, and followed Pasha to a table. Padded benches all but surrounded it, making it a quiet haven from the more raucous of the drinkers in the bar. Jake slid in next to Pasha opposite me. He was more relaxed when she was around, I noticed, less jittery. They might not be lovers but there was something there, something I couldn't quite put my finger on. Some shared history, perhaps. I probed a little – it's always good to know as much as you can about the people you work with. Saves nasty surprises. Besides, I'm a nosy bastard and questions were my only defence, from long habit. Shame they didn't seem to go down so well. "So how long have you been doing these matches? It's not a normal kind of job. Why do you do it?"

Jake's smile froze for a moment before it came back, rather forced this time. She tried a nonchalant shrug but there was a tension in her shoulders that she couldn't hide. "Nothing else I'm good at. Besides, suicide is against my religion." She laughed but that deadness was behind her eyes again. Pasha hunched into his chair and chewed at a nail.

"But you two, known each other long? You seem to trust each other." I didn't know anyone I'd trust to stitch me up with no anaesthetic. Dendal was all thumbs and Lastri would take great pleasure in my discomfort, especially if she could make it worse.

111

Jake's smile melted away. "Long enough. You always ask so many questions?"

Pasha stared at me intently, a scared sort of look on his face, the mousy little monkey again, but he didn't say anything.

A waitress ignored everyone else in the bar, slipped out from behind the counter and came to take our order. I looked around; no one else had service like this, they all went to the counter for drinks. The waitress was a trim little thing, all dark eyes and long black hair framing a pert face. I couldn't conjure up a flirty smile, not even when she leaned over and gave me a flash of ample cleavage. I must have been sickening for something; and she was sitting right opposite me.

The waitress bobbed her head towards Jake. "Usual?"

Jake slid her gaze towards me and back again. "No, we'll take the whole bottle and three glasses. Have another bottle on ice for later."

We were silent until after the waitress came back with a bottle of something so green it almost took my eye out. She laid the glasses out on the table, gifted me a cheeky wink and left.

I squinted at the bottle. The liquid sloshed viscously as it settled. It looked dangerous. "What is that?"

"This? Oh, this is just booze," Jake said with a cultivated air of innocence belied by a crafty smile. "Big, strong man like you shouldn't be afraid of booze."

Pasha poured three generous glasses and didn't manage to hide a grin.

The stuff stank, an acrid, biting smell that promised more than just alcohol. It promised oblivion. I looked at Jake as she drank, grimacing the stuff down, her eyes blank of feeling. Pasha gripped his glass too tight, whitening the skin on his fingers, before he knocked it back in one hit. I wasn't the only one in need of a drink, but I didn't have mine just yet.

Jake poured herself another, her hand wobbling only slightly. She didn't take her eyes from the garish green that slithered in her glass, as though it was the only salvation she was likely to get. "So, Mr Dizon, no questions. You tell me all of it."

"You know it. My niece was kidnapped and brought down here. I've come to find her and take her home." I sniffed at the glass and almost choked on the fumes.

"That's not all though, is it?"

"What more do you want?"

She raised her eyes to mine. They were a soft blue, like the sky on a sunny day, from my few glimpses of it. In other circumstances those eyes might have seemed attractive or feminine. Right now all I was getting was a cold calculation regarding whether I was worth talking to, with an undercurrent of something that made me want to lean forward and kiss her. Luckily, I'm not *that* stupid.

"Ministry or not, do you think you're the first Upsider to come down here with a sad story, hoping to smoke out trouble? Tell me everything," she said. "All of it. Her, your magic, why you're really here. Why I should trust or help you. Everything."

I sneaked a look at Pasha, hoping for help. The booze oiled up and down his glass in time to the way his hand shook, ever so slightly. He didn't look at either of us and a brick-red flush crept up his neck. When I looked back, Jake's eyes locked on mine. This whole thing was giving me the creeps something fierce, but I had no choice. They knew things I couldn't know, people I couldn't know. They were my link, my – no, Amarie's – only hope.

I took a hesitant sip of the green stuff, choked it back over a tongue that wanted to reject it and felt it worm its way to my stomach. Almost immediately a warmth began to work its way out, seeping into me and soothing me. Telling me everything would be OK. I could see then why they drank it. It gave me the nerve to say it all.

So I told them, about Ma, about Perak and our estrangement, Amarie's kidnapping. About my magic and how it's not such a good thing to use Upside, not if you want to live. How I don't like using it, and don't unless I really have to.

Jake took it all in without a word or flicker of her eyes, without even a twitch of her face. Until I named the Goddess, when I mentioned the hospital and the doctor. She shut her eyes, just for a moment, scrunched them up as though warding off a blow. A heartbeat later it was as though nothing had happened.

Pasha kept clenching and unclenching his hand on his glass, but he said nothing either. So we sat in silence again for a while, until Dog came in. He stood in the doorway and waved his hand over his head. "Hey, Jake! I got something for you!" He was like that five-year-old again, one with sweets, or something secret to share.

Funny how her face changed. She went from wary and sharp to soft and smiling in a moment, stood up with a fluid grace and went to him.

"What's the problem, Pasha?" I asked when she was out of earshot.

His mouth stretched in a grin I didn't believe. "It's – it's difficult, Rojan. Down here, it's all different. Most of them don't know it, you know?"

"Know what?"

"What they are. Cows, that's what they are, we all are. Well-fed fucking cows, fattened up before they get slaughtered, and those that do know it can't do much about it. We try, but – it's hard. We get caught, we're dead, and so are the people we're trying to help." He shook his head sorrowfully. "Fattened up for the mages, and they don't even know it."

His hands trembled, making the booze roil in the glass. My own hands didn't feel much better.

"Pasha, I—"

"Girls, boys too sometimes, go missing every day. No one dare say a thing, because if they do, they disappear too. So they pretend it's not happening, except in the back of their brains, they know. Going from Upside too now, so you say. Well, don't expect a pity parade. A thousand. That's right, a thousand that we know of in the last year. Probably more,

getting worse every week. As many as that and we can't –
can't, you understand – give preference to one girl. No matter
who she is. But we'll try. If you can find her, there'll be others
there. You can be an asset, Rojan. A real help, if you can use
your magic like you say."

"Mages? But we're banned, there are none except me and
Dendal, far as I know. Why though, why are they doing it,
taking children? What for?"

But it seemed Pasha had said all he was going to, or maybe
all he was going to in front of Jake, because he clamped his
mouth shut and turned away just as she came back.

"So the girls, you rescue them," I said. "Why? It seems
you'd make a lot of enemies."

"Someone has to. No one else gives a shit," she snapped. I
was doing well on the insulting front, even if I wasn't sure
what the actual insult was. Several of the matchers turned to
look at me when Jake raised her voice. Dog took a step
towards us with a growl in his throat. Pasha shook his head
and Dog stepped back, but kept a wary eye on us all the same.
Maybe tact might be worth a try. I'd certainly live longer.

I looked back at Jake. She was all closed up. I'd said some-
thing, done something to stop her wanting to talk to me. But
I needed to know. "So what exactly do you do to help them?
Once you've found them, what do you do?"

Jake tapped her fingers on the table and scowled. Pasha
drained his glass and the girl was there instantly to top it up.
He set it down, laid his hand on the table just out of touching

distance from Jake's fingers, and waited for the girl to go before he spoke. I had trouble hearing him over the blaring music. What I did hear was that he didn't like talking about it; it was in the jerky way the words came out.

"We look after them. Most of them don't know where they came from, even their own names. They forget, because they have to, are told to, forced to. Even if they do remember, we can't send them back to their families."

"Why not?"

Pasha's mouth twitched sadly. "It's just how it is down here. I don't know about Upside, but down here, they catch a branded girl – the Ministry have smoked through rumours about them, about the brands. Brainwashed people, really, so they don't ask questions, hate who they're told to hate. They have to, have to pretend they don't notice all these kids going missing, because if they say anything, they go too. The kids aren't safe on the streets, or anywhere once anyone sees those brands, because if you're caught helping one, you're dead. So they believe the lies the Ministry tells them, the priests preach to them. Little Whores they call them, an affront to the Goddess. Had a case last month. Girl escaped, a while ago. Managed to hide it, found herself a guy who wanted to marry her. Until he found her brands. Throttled her on the spot."

I took a hasty glug of the drink and coughed a bit at the fumes. It beggared belief. "Why? It wasn't her fault."

Pasha shrugged and stared down into his drink. "Just the way it is down here. He felt she'd, I don't know, dishonoured him, dishonoured the Goddess? They all think that way down here, all but a few, because they believe what they're told. If it had been a woman found her out, she'd be just as dead. Little Whores."

Pasha played with his glass as he spoke, not looking up from the reflections that moved on its surface. Jake was staring at the other matchers as though she had no interest in what we were talking about. Which was pretty odd when you considered that she risked her life to save these girls on a regular basis. But then she risked her life in the matches often enough. Maybe she really didn't care about that, about living. Maybe she only cared about dying. "So why do you and Jake do it?"

"Wouldn't you, if you had to live here? We're not all animals, no matter what you Upsiders think."

"Most Upsiders don't know you exist. I didn't until Tam told me, right before I arrived. So what *do* you do with them?"

"You ever seen a cow, Mr Dizon?" It was Jake again, her voice low and measured, as though it was taking a lot of self-control not to lose her temper. Or maybe just to get the words out. Her fingers kept tap, tap, tapping on the table next to Pasha's hand, like she was nervous or not used to talking to people.

Seen a cow? What was I, Archdeacon? No one from the city ever saw a cow, except maybe him. I wasn't even sure there was one within a hundred miles. "Once or twice. In a book."

"I have, and not in a book," Pasha said.

Down here? Where in fuck could you keep a cow in this cesspit? And how could the 'Pit be richer in those things than Upside? My disbelief must have shown on my face because Pasha flushed a little. "I have! *Outside.*"

I sat there with the glass halfway to my lips. Outside was, was, well, almost mythical to anyone brought up in the city. It had to exist, of course, but only the super-rich even got to see it from their windows up in Clouds or Top of the World. All I could see from my apartment was a stretch of rubbish and a bunch of other buildings. You could catch a glimpse of mountains on a clear day from Trade, but they were just shadows, far-off and unreal. Up there, in the rarefied heights that only Ministry could afford, they said you could see the *real* Outside. Grass, trees, the mountain range that enclosed us, everything. Getting to go there was something that was a fabulous but unlikely dream. Like, I don't know, unicorns. "How? Where? How'd you get out?"

"How do you get anything? Money, and connections. One of the girls we found, we managed to find her parents and they weren't from in here. From Outside, where they don't see the girls the same. It's not the place they told you. Not at all. Their daughter was safe to go back – it's like another world out there. So Jake bought a piece of their land. And that's where we take them. Outside. We get them surgery to cover the brands, the scars, and that costs a lot, to have that surgeon on hand. We help them come to terms, get rid of the shadows. Some of the parents of the missing girls, they help us, hoping

119

that one day it'll be their girl coming in. And when the girls are ready, then we help them have a life. A good one, as good as it gets down here, like they might have had. Some of them stay and help us, but we don't have room for many. A few find places Outside, but they're pretty wary of new people so it's difficult. Most of them come back to the 'Pit. It's what they know. But we make sure they stay safe, set them up in a little business or find them a legitimate job. Takes a lot of money. We make some from the cows on the farm, the meat and leather, but it's not enough, not near enough. That's why Jake does the matches, because it's the best, almost the only, way to make any decent money down here. And that's where all the money goes."

I sat and stared at him, speechless, for a while and then the girl came back with three plates. "Thought you might be hungry."

She popped them down on the table and it was all I could do not to dribble on to the food. Real meat. Lots of it, and smelling so good there was a possibility I was dead and in heaven. I might have thought so, but I don't think they have bars like this in heaven. Shame, or I might start believing.

I restrained myself from wallowing my head in the gravy, instead eating as though meat was something I got on a regular basis, and returned to the topic at hand. Damn, though, that was tasty. "So, you'll help me find her?"

Pasha sighed. "I spend all my time trying to find these girls in any case. Finding just one, among all of them? I don't know if it can be done. But if we find her, we'll welcome any help getting her out, along with any others we find with her. I'll let you know. Now, do you need a place to stay? That Ministry place might be a little warm for you right now, if you really aren't one of theirs. You can stay at my place."

"There's not enough room there for two." There had been barely enough room for two people to sit, never mind lie down, in the room Tam had sent me to.

Pasha shrugged. "Oh, I've another place to stay. I'll get Dog to show you the way; he lives near by. I'll come find you when we're ready."

When Pasha turned up to fetch me, I was sitting bleary-eyed on top of the bedcovers. I hadn't bothered to undress or get under the damp blanket because I knew I wouldn't sleep much, no matter that I was knackered. Too many thoughts running round my head for that, though I'd managed a doze. Even that hadn't been much help because I kept seeing lost girls, teeming crowds of them, ghost-like and pleading, and every one had Amarie's face. I'd spent the night looking at the walls, at the pictures of different brands that Pasha had pinned there. Part of his job, no doubt, to know which brand meant ownership by which person, but it made my stomach twist and my heart burn. I suspected not all the girls in the pictures had been alive when they were made.

So I was pretty glad to be out of that room with its ghosts staring down at me. Pasha gave me a penetrating look, not unsympathetic, but said nothing and led me back to the bar. It was empty, either too late at night or too early in the morning. I couldn't tell – to my eyes morning and evening all looked the same here, and I didn't know how long Pasha had left me asleep. The girl who'd served us before kept a wide berth and wouldn't look at Pasha. A young boy brought us more food and Pasha picked at his. I didn't feel so much like eating myself.

He broke the silence first. "I think I may have found the men you're looking for." At last, the first bit of good news. "I've talked Jake into helping you too. You're going to need it. These guys you're looking for work for Azama, Tam was right about that. And she wants to catch him, wants to catch him something fierce."

"What's so special about him?"

He might have told me, but Jake came in and he clammed up again.

"You want to help, Mr Dizon?" She slid along the bench next to Pasha, her face hard and bright with savage hope. "Now's your chance."

"Now?"

"Now."

She let me eat first. I restrained myself from shoving it all in in one giant, bloody, gloriously meaty lump only with a great deal of effort. Instead I chewed through another steak that made my mouth think it had died and gone to heaven. Jake disappeared about halfway through, following Dog out into the dark street. Pasha stayed and watched me eat. The instant I was done, he stood and made to leave. I wiped hastily at my mouth, licked up a stray bit of gravy and followed.

"Where are we going?" I flipped up the collar of my coat, but it didn't do anything to stop the rain from dribbling down my neck and back.

Pasha shrugged on a high-collared coat of his own and slid on a floppy hat that would have made his monkey features comical if it weren't for the set, savage look he had. "To find some girls. The mages move them about, so it's not always easy to find them. Usually they're kept locked up tight, but maybe they're moving them somewhere, or resting them. Or maybe they've only just got them, haven't had a chance to spirit them away yet. Won't know until we get there, but when they do this, it's the only chance we have to get them out."

We slipped through dark streets, the lights dimmed now for the 'Pit's version of night-time. Chains rattled and clanked overhead, cages whizzed by, sometimes too close for comfort so I ducked instinctively. Lamp-lit rain fell, soft, insistent and with a faint hint of synth, beautiful and deadly. Music no longer blared but murmured. The bright shops were shuttered and the crowds had thinned, but new crowds were already coming out to replace them. Night people, same as you got Upside, a city's underclass, even lower on the scale than some-one like me. People to clean the streets, hawk forbidden wares, rob the unsuspecting. I could see some of them eyeing me up as a potential target, but then they'd catch sight of Pasha's face and slide back into the dark alleys to lurk and wait for someone else. I made sure to keep close to Pasha.

The ancient towering roots of Mahala surrounded us and pulled us in. Maybe it was a vain hope that they wouldn't spit me back out. Pasha led me away from the busier district of shops and arcades, out into a wilderness of dark stone buildings with darker synth gouge-lines swirling across their façades, split by midnight alleys where what I hoped were only rats scurried among the rubbish. The Seal was lost in darkness above us. The streets emptied and a pang of trepidation struck my gut. If Pasha wanted rid of me, here would be the perfect place. My hand never left the butt of the pulse pistol.

We rounded a corner and Pasha stopped, abruptly enough that I ran into him. He held a finger to his lips for quiet and crept on. The building ahead looked like all the rest. Synth had left its mark in line and crease and wrinkle. Chunks of brick and concrete had fallen from the walls and sat in little heaps of sodden dust. The doorway was a black mouth in a decayed face. Windows that had once seen the sun looked out blindly into perpetual night with only the fitful gleam of lamps two streets away to give me light enough to see. A shadow moved in the doorway and my grip on the pistol tightened. Pasha tensed and melted into a shaded recess so well that, if I hadn't known he was there, I wouldn't have seen him. I tried to do the same, with less success. A cage clanked overhead and I bit my lip to hold in a startled yelp.

The shadow in the doorway resolved into a muscle-bound man with a good-natured and what women would call an interesting face. Craggy where it should be smooth, a nose that had been broken one too many times, a silvery knife scar that ran down one cheek, and a snarling wariness behind his eyes when he saw me. A sword hung at his waist and I couldn't help but see the blood dripping from it.

"You're late, Pasha: we're pretty much done bar the clean-up. Who's the ponce?"

Pasha stepped out of his hiding place. "No one special. Find anything?"

Craggy Man grinned and it reminded me of Griswald the stuffed tiger, all teeth and menace. "Got a couple of the bastards' goons, and some girls. Got them before they took the girls too far. Some of them, anyway. Some of them ... well, you know." His mouth twisted bitterly.

Another cage rattled and Craggy Man waved an arm over his head. The cage lowered to the ground near the end of the street and Craggy left for it with a grim nod.

A quick glance told me this wasn't an ordinary cage. It was larger, and two women operated it rather than the usual men or boys. Another three women came out as it dropped to the ground, and a couple of men.

Pasha took my arm and led me into the building. I stopped at the doorway, pulling him up short. There were five men lying on the floor, bleeding from deep slashes. They moaned in pain, and one of them writhed as though a snake was winding its way through his gut.

Pasha called after Craggy. "The hole?"

Craggy nodded to the man writhing on the floor. I caught a glimpse of the inside of his belly and looked away. "He'll show you. Most of the girls are through there." He pointed to a dark doorway on the other side of the room. "They'll have to come out through here, there's no other way. But if they have to come out this way, make sure they see this lot."

Pasha gave a short little nod, and the man-square left.

"What the . . ." I couldn't say anything else. Men were bleeding from everywhere in front of me, a sight I'd never had to deal with before, not on this scale. Deep slashes to their muscles that exposed the occasional wet glint of bone or coiled rope of guts. I thought of the sword the big man had held, which dripped with blood, and I couldn't repress a shudder.

"Just goons," Pasha said when he caught sight of my face, misreading me it seemed. "Not mages. We aren't giving them any power."

That wasn't what had me open-mouthed in horror.

The two men from the cage came in and with a short greeting to Pasha they set about handcuffing the men on the floor. They offered nothing in the way of resistance but one man quietly begged and another prayed under his breath. Their words were ignored as the two men wrenched arms up behind backs, further than they had any right to go, adding a few thin screams to the noise. Their pain set my fingers tingling and I fisted my hands to try to stop it, try not to store any magic. Not from this.

I looked at Pasha and the weak, scared look was gone. He looked like a different man as he strode over and grabbed at the hair of the writher. The man screamed piteously, but Pasha looked at him as though he'd kill him on the spot for a lousy copper. I tried to speak but my mouth was as dry as ancient hills.

"Where is it?" Pasha said, his voice flat and hard.

"I don't—" the man began, but Pasha shook him by the hair, and a stream of hot blood splashed from his gut on to the floor. "Under the rug, behind me. Under the rug!"

"Tell them to start getting the girls out," Pasha said to one of the two men as he strode for the rug.

"What are you doing?" I found my voice at last. "This is torture. You're no better than they are, no better than the Ministry. At least Ministry just kill people, they don't see them in agony first."

Pasha stopped at my voice, and the gun was pointing at my face again. There was no quivering this time. "You think? Come and take a look."

I hesitated; I wanted nothing to do with this. Even if the mages were kidnapping girls, for whatever reason, I wasn't sure they deserved this. Prison, yes; long slow torture, no.

"Come *on*." He was glaring at me, his eyes hot and frantic with some emotion I could only guess at. One of the men to my side drew a gun from inside his jacket.

"Just say the word, Pasha. You can't trust an Upsider; they're the ones that keep the trade alive. Without them we wouldn't be doing this. He don't care about them, or us."

Pasha shook his head, bent down and rolled the rug back, revealing a thick, bolted door set into the floor. He kicked at the bolts till they came loose and his eyes never left mine. He was trying to tell me something, trying to will it into me through his burning eyes, and I couldn't for the life of me have said what it was. I only knew that his transformation from wizened, comical monkey to avenging angel was scaring me badly. He heaved the door open and a waft of fetid air rushed out, making him gag a little as he let the door clang open.

"This is the hole, where they put them when they're done, when they've used them up," he said, gesturing into the dark with his gun. "The girls here are ones they've finished with, mostly, which is why they're easy to find, because they don't care about them any more. A body can only take so much, then they hand them to the goons to take their pleasure in what's left. Look in."

I felt the prod of a gun barrel at my side. I had no choice, but I didn't want to look down there. I didn't want to see what had made this mouse of a man so ferocious, or why others thought torturing the people who owned it was of no consequence.

A collection of tiny gasps sounded to one side of me. The women from the cage had come in and gone through the doorway at the back of the room unnoticed by me. I turned my head that way now, and there they were, ushering twelve or fifteen girls through towards the cage. They were dressed in all manner of clothes, from rags for the smallest to silk and satin for the older. Every one of them had a cringe in her eye that rose to panic when she saw us. A brand on each wrist. I could see whip-marks across the shoulders of some, fresh bruises to faces and old wounds that had burned their mark into the skin, while others were seemingly untouched, but just as dead around the eyes. I searched their faces for Amarie, but she wasn't there. The women held tight on to them and ushered them forwards with soothing words.

There was one little girl at the front, no older than eight or nine. Her eyes were far too large in her face as she tried not to look at me. Scars ran down both arms, winding down around the brands, seeming almost alive, with the pink raised skin, the blood-red scabs of fresher wounds and the silvery marks of old ones. The fear in her eyes shamed me somehow, and then she stole a glance at the hole. When she saw it was open, her eyes rolled up in her head and she fainted. One of the women picked her up gently and carried on shooing the girls ahead, helped now by one of the older girls, who still couldn't have been more than twelve.

Pasha waited till they'd gone and then handed me a lamp. "Look," he said, and there was such a dead, defeated quality to his voice I could do nothing other than obey. Flesh thunked and thudded as the two men began hauling out the injured goons, making sure they hit the doorjamb on the way out.

I swallowed hard. I had a sudden knowledge of what I was going to see when I managed to aim the lamp into the dark mouth of the hole. The stench warned me, and I tried not to breathe as I looked down.

There was a drop of about two yards or so, and then it was just a pile of bodies. A tangle of stick-thin arms, purple-bruised legs, nests of dark hair. I couldn't seem to take it in, the smallness, frailness, the vulnerability of them, the realisation any one of these could have been Amarie, and even if they weren't . . . My thoughts became incoherent and I struggled to control myself, only to think how *satisfying* it would be to deliver a good hard kick that might finish off the last of the men that still lay on the floor behind me. I looked back down into the hole and wondered how deep it went, how deep the bodies went. Then one of the bodies moved.

"Pasha! One's still alive."

He stood next to me, and I knew what it was he'd been trying to tell me. That he would do anything, anything at all to stop this happening again. He looked down with me and caught the movement. Almost before I realised he'd moved, he was clambering down, finding some handholds in the wall to lower himself gently in amongst the bodies. One of them flinched and began to try piteously to crawl away from him. I heard him murmur something, and a hand flapped briefly, accompanied by a strangled moan of fear.

Then he had his arms round her and reached up for me to try to grab him.

I stuck my hand down, as eager now as him. I was almost falling into the hole myself before his hand gripped mine. I inched my way back slowly until I had enough leverage to pull him and the girl up. When they finally flopped on to the floor, Pasha was shivering and I couldn't see the girl breathing. I barely even noticed she was naked. "Is she alive?"

He nodded, too breathless maybe to talk, and got himself to his feet before bending down to pick her up again. I pretended not to see the tears that dripped on to her skin, or the way her face twisted in terror as he wrapped her in the rug with soothing, murmured words and took her out to the waiting women.

I was on my own. I could have walked out of the door and no one would have cared, and ten minutes earlier I would have done. But now all I could think of was whether there were more of them down there, alive.

I'd been jolted out of my comfortable existence, where I'd been peripherally aware that not everyone had my style of life but sure that, the Ministry notwithstanding, there had been a reverence for life; that something like this would not, could not go on. I knew the worst parts of Upside. It was part of my job to know the worst of it all up there, but whilst there was hot-blooded murder and cold-blooded assassination, and whilst you got the odd person whose views on girls were extreme – they don't last long as a rule – I'd never heard of anything approaching this. Not treating people as we used to treat cows, when we had any. And Amarie was here somewhere, maybe in a place just like this, and I had to get her back. I had to. I couldn't bear the thought of telling Perak what had happened to her if not.

By the time Pasha came back I was in the hole, in amongst the dead, looking for the dying.

Chapter Eight

Once they'd got all the girls out and into the cage, ready to be whisked off to wherever, Pasha took pity on me and led me back to his room. I don't remember much about the trip; my mind was too busy trying to block out the sight of that hole, the smell that seemed rammed into my nostrils, the pitiful efforts of that girl to escape her rescuers. I do remember Pasha buying a bottle of something on the way, because the first thing he did when we got there was open it and pour us a generous measure each.

I sat on the bed, barely aware of my surroundings at first, staring into the green depths of the booze as though it held some sort of answer.

"Takes you pretty bad the first time, doesn't it?" Pasha asked. "But it gets worse than that."

I looked up from the drink. Pasha was watching me carefully, with pity in the set of his mouth and a dull fury in the shine of his eyes.

"It gets worse?" I couldn't, didn't want to, imagine anything worse.

Pasha stood up and went to the desk. I noticed again the pictures pinned to the wall over it, now closely lit by a lamp. Pasha unpinned one and gave it to me. A forearm, with a mark branded into the wrist. I scanned the others: the same, except some of the marks were different. The one I held showed a swirling pattern, a stylised letter A. Others were spiky, hard shapes, or representations of other letters.

"Part of my employment with Jake. I try to track the girls, make sense of the different brands and what they mean. I record them, each new one I find. Whether the kid is alive or not. I have to, to try to make sense of who does what. Try to make sense of their pattern so we can break it."

A sick roiling in my stomach was alleviated by a slug of the drink.

"What worries me about your niece is she isn't in that pattern," Pasha went on. "Not at all. Why her? Why not take someone who wouldn't be missed? Why send the Jorrin brothers up that far when they could have found any number of girls closer, easier, less likely to bring trouble? Why *her*?"

A question I'd asked myself more than once, though not too closely because I was uncomfortable with the answers I'd got. "Maybe ... maybe to get at Perak? He invented that damned gun."

"Or maybe to get *you*. Odd, that you're a pain-mage and

you're the one to come down here after her, right to where pain-mages are needed, *wanted*."

That was the answer I didn't like. "No one knows I'm a mage, except Dendal." And I didn't see him having anyone shot just to make me use my magic properly. Lastri might, if the person being shot was me.

Pasha raised a suspicious eyebrow. "No one? Your brother, family?"

"He's the only family I've got, and no, he doesn't know. He just knows I find people, not how I do it. It doesn't pay to advertise, and we hadn't spoken in years anyway. Look, I don't care why, I just want her back. Now, how are we going to do that?"

Pasha frowned, like his question still bothered him, but he left it for now. "I can't track them like you do. That's not how my magic works." His mouth stretched into a predatory smile. "It's very good for other things though. Yet I can't ever have the power they do, because I won't use anyone else's pain, you see? They can, and will, and it makes them very powerful. That power is what you're up against, trying to find your niece. You might find her, if you're good, but can you get her out? Tonight we were lucky, like I said. The girls were ones they'd used up, finished with, and none of the mages was there. Relatively easy to take, once we know where it is. But the main factories, that's another matter entirely. You ever fought against a pain-mage with almost unlimited power?"

Not only had I not, I *really* didn't want to. It would be

tricky at best. The more you hurt them, the more power they get, unless you can tip them over into death quick smart. To do that generally means you end up physically weak yourself, because of the power you need to do it. Dendal was fond of telling tales of that sort of thing, before pain magic was banned Upside, when two mages would fight and almost the only thing that determined the outcome wasn't who was better, but who could hang on to life longer. I'm fairly sure Dendal only told me these stories because he knew what a coward I was for physical pain. Well, he calls it cowardice; I prefer the terms "sensible", "practical", "intelligent" or "not-stupidly-masochistic".

"It doesn't sound like the best plan," was what I actually said.

"Not the best plan, indeed. Which is why we haven't managed to rescue any from the factories. Occasionally the mages get a bit lax when the girls are resting, or the mages are gathering a group to take in, or like tonight when they've finished with them, but they've tightened up a lot lately. A *lot*. But first, you need to try to track her. If she's in a holding-house on her way to the factories, we'll have a chance, and we can rescue whoever else is there too."

And hope that wasn't exactly what someone wanted me to do. But who? I shook that thought away. It wasn't helping. I sat on the bed again, or slumped more like. The pictures swam in front of me, skin and brand blurring together. For a heartbeat they seemed to merge to form a sketch of Amarie's face, then melted, moulding to the faces of the girls tonight. Today. Whatever. I had no idea what time or even day it was; I only knew that it seemed like weeks since Pasha had woken me.

Pasha took the picture out of my hand. "It's been just over a day." He smiled at my startled look, a sad twitch of his lips. "Part of my magic. You can sleep here. You'll need your strength to find her. Drink the rest, it'll help. It's the only thing I've found that does."

His voice sounded muffled and far away but it seemed to make sense, so I drained the glass and didn't object when he took my coat off and draped it over a chair, pushed me so I lay down on the bed. I don't even remember my head hitting the pillow.

It seemed like I'd only closed my eyes for a second when someone shook my shoulder.

"Wasft?"

"Rojan, you've got to wake up."

"Snff," was all I could manage to that. My head was stuffed with something sticky that made my thoughts run like cold treacle.

"Rojan, will you wake *up*?"

A hand grabbed my shoulder and pulled me up. I squeezed my eyes even further shut, then opened them. Everything looked fuzzy. I blinked rapidly, and Pasha's urgent face swam into view.

"At last! Come on, you have to get out of here. There's Ministry men all over, looking for you."

"Ministry?"

"Yeah, trying to look like Downsiders. Not doing such a bad job either, but I can smell one a mile away. It's in their head, see? Anyway, not many people down here have guns, excepting me and one or two others – they're too expensive unless you steal one like I did. Besides, who else but Ministry would have a picture of you and be showing it around every last bar and shop?"

With one last hard blink and a scrub of my eyes with the heels of my hands, I was awake. Kind of. "How long did I sleep?"

Pasha looked apologetic. "A couple of hours. But it won't be long before someone says they saw you with me, and then this place will be crawling with Ministry. I don't want to be here when that happens."

"Neither do I." I rubbed a hand up my face and took the glass of water that Pasha proffered. If I concentrated I could barely taste the synth. At least it took the worst of the after-taste of green booze off my tongue and made me feel semi-alive again. "If not here, then where?"

"I know a place or two. Come on."

We slipped out into streets dim with night, slick with rain and peopled by shadows. Pasha kept a hand on his gun under his coat, and I did the same in my pocket with my pulse pistol. How in heck did the Ministry know someone had come down here, and especially, how did they know it was me? I had to trust that Dendal was all right, that they hadn't dragged it out of him one way or another, either one of which would be very painful. I had to trust that, because the alternative was too awful to contemplate.

We moved further out, into a neighbourhood that made Pasha's place look positively plush. More than one building was propped up with huge steel girders – not for the Downsiders' benefit, I assumed, because the rest of the place was such an unabashed shithole; no, it would be because someone important lived in a building far, far above, supported by this one. A thought that quickly gave rise to other thoughts, like – if I could find which building supported the Archdeacon's palace in Top of the World, I could change the face of the city with one well-calculated girder destruction. It was a very tempting thought, moderated only by the matching thought of all the people living between the girder down here and the Top of the World up there. Shame.

I shook the persuasive thoughts out of my head and concentrated on where we were, on the towers, surrounded by shanty-shacks and wreck-built houses, on the shadows and dark chasms between buildings, blank-faced windows and eyes that might be watching. Not many, it seemed. Even the rats appeared to have deserted the place, and we walked warily through quiet streets and silent alleys. Every now and again a blurred face would appear at a window or opening, a brief smudge against the darkness before it withdrew. I kept my head down. No knowing if the Ministry men had been this way, or would be here soon, and no sense showing my face to all and sundry.

At last Pasha stopped, at the entrance to an alley so narrow I might never have noticed it in the dark. A flick of his head indicated I should follow and we squeezed our way through the huge blocks of stone that held up who knew how many floors above us. A door sat at the end, a pathetic wooden thing that was half eaten away and hanging, just barely, by one creaking hinge. It looked like it would fall apart if I breathed too deeply.

"Where—"

Pasha stopped me with a raised hand and rapped on the doorframe, gently of necessity. I barely heard the rap, and I stood right next to him. Even so, a flake of stone above the door that had been hanging on for grim death lost its fight and fluttered to the ground. There was quiet for long moments, only broken by our breathing and the faraway beat of music.

A flash of metal whipped past me and a sword pinned Pasha to the door by his coat. Simultaneously, a boot hit me in the back and sent me face-first into the stone. I managed to get a hand out to avoid breaking my nose, but lost a fair bit of skin on my palm in the process, making me tingle with sudden magic.

"For fuck's sake, Pasha, what do you think you're doing? I could have killed you."

By the time I'd turned, hand on pulse pistol, Pasha was

grinning sheepishly, his hands in the air, the gun dangling from a finger by its trigger-guard. Jake was glaring at him.

"Sorry. Only there's Ministry men after him and—"

"And you thought bringing them right to *my* door was a good idea?"

"Where else could I take him? Besides, I think I know where the Jorrin brothers are."

Jake's mouth twitched with annoyance before she relented. "All right, you're here now."

The door opened straight into a room and, though it was much larger than Pasha's, this place looked like it was about to fall down. There were holes in the wooden floor, the reek of damp and a hint of synth. Green mould made a surreal pattern on one wall and there was a nest of something small and scuttling in one of the holes in the floor. Even fewer things than Pasha had in his room. Just a bed, a chair with a few shreds of linen that might be clothes draped over it, an odd contraption in the corner I couldn't name, and bare floor.

"I was right in the middle of practice." Jake moved over to the clothes draped on the chair, rummaged till she found a threadbare towel and began to rub sweat from around her face and neck. Her hair was tied back in a complicated knot, but a few tendrils had come free and were stuck to the back of her bare neck. I tried not to stare there, or at the sweat sticking the undershirt to her. It was quite hard, until she shot me a look that could have curdled milk. "All right, Pasha, what have you got? The Jorrin brothers?"

"Maybe. You know that old place of theirs, up on Ruby Street? Seems there's been movement the last week or so."

"Could be anyone. Could be squatters, or they sold it, any number of things." Jake finished rubbing herself down and walked over with the kind of easy grace that makes my knees go all funny. She wasn't looking at me though. She and Pasha seemed to be able to talk without talking, if that makes sense. Her eyes softened just so, the corner of his lip lifted a touch and she nodded. Something had been decided, but I hadn't a clue what.

"Azama is definitely back," Pasha said finally.

There was no doubt now, there was a heart behind that blank façade. Her hand twitched and she looked down sharply at the floor, but not before I saw a flash of fear. Pasha looked at a loss for words. He put his hand out as though to comfort her, then seemed to remember and snatched it back. And I thought *I* had a screwed-up love life.

"Mr Dizon." Jake turned to face me and moved subtly closer to Pasha, just far enough apart that they weren't touching. Employee–employer relationship, my arse. Disappointing for me, though. I blinked myself back to the subject at hand.

"Please, it's Rojan. All this 'mister' shit gives me a headache."

"Rojan, then. The best way to find your niece is for you to do your magic, try to track her. Or we can try this lead, which will take time – time your niece may not have – and may end nowhere. Your choice."

I tried to keep my face blank but a small grimace surfaced anyway. I didn't want to, Namrat knew I didn't want to. I'd been brought up to know my magic was wrong, and I did know it. Purposefully giving yourself pain was a stupid, stupid way to do things. Besides, we had a lead, one that didn't involve me hurting myself. But . . . But. I wished my conscience would shut up, because it was starting to annoy me.

I took a deep breath, slung my coat over the chair, took out the picture of Amarie with its little singsong voice and got to my knees. It's always better to be sitting down, because generally I fall down.

"Rojan—" Pasha began but I shook my head. Too much was crystallising in my brain. There was something else, some other reason I was here, I just didn't know what it was yet. But I didn't want to think about what Pasha had said, that maybe this wasn't chance, maybe someone *wanted* me here. That was secondary.

I let my eyes become unfocused so the cracks in the floor blurred and ran. A deep breath, another, and another, working up my nerve, narrowing it to a point where this – hurting myself – was not only possible, but a sensible thing to do given the alternatives. Lying to myself so I could bring myself to do it, in other words.

I found one big crack shaped like Griswald the tiger, and concentrated on it till I couldn't see anything else. Somehow I knew that dislocation wasn't going to be enough, not now, not against other mages who would be hiding her and others. They were bound to take precautions, especially if they knew I was here. Even before I'd done anything except breathe and concentrate on what I was up against, it was there at the back of my mind, what was trying to stop me.

A black wall of magic hovering over the 'Pit, like the sort of raincloud they'd never see down here. Now I could sense it, I knew what that edge was to the place, the one that had been jarring my teeth since I'd got here. The Ministry watched Upside, so you had to be careful where you stepped, but if you knew what you were about, you could step round them. Down here, it was this cloud that kept everyone's steps in check, whether they knew it or not. Moving round this, round a blackness that hovered over every man, woman and child, was not an option. They were all a part of it, unwitting, unknowing.

Concentration was key. So was the amount of pain I'd need, and it would be a lot to penetrate that cloud. Somebody said something, but all I heard was an insignificant mumble. Nothing mattered but the crack, the rasp of my breath, what I was trying to do. I punched at the floor, at Griswald, with everything I had.

Something snapped in my fist and pain shot through my hand and throbbed up my wrist. I swore out loud, and worse in my head. No fucking wonder people never used pain magic much. With my other hand I raised Amarie's picture. She seemed to float above it, more real than a child right there.

"Princess, Daddy." It wasn't enough. I could feel a tug, a nudge in my mind, the hint of something, something and then it was gone. Buried under a black tide of someone else's magic. I could feel it, pushing against me, pressing against my forehead and face, squeezing them till I thought my eyes might pop out.

Not enough. I needed to do more. My hand smashed into the floor again and I think I cried out that time. My knuckles were wet. Now I could see her, hear something, the sob of her voice maybe, it was hard to tell. So close, yet that black tide was there, blocking me, pushing me. They had power I could only dream of. I couldn't tell where she was, I can always tell, I couldn't tell. Not this time.

My knuckles hit the floor again, and that's when it came. Along with the hot silver agony came the sudden, brutal realisation that, if I wanted to track her, I'd have to half kill myself to get past whatever was around her. She was due west, that was all I knew, and I should have known exactly where she was long before now. My mangled hand fumbled for the pistol that was in the pocket of a coat I wasn't wearing. If I used it, properly for once, it might be enough. Or maybe the knife sewn into the coat lining in case of emergencies. Yes, that would do it. I got to my feet and tried to grab at the coat. A hand stopped me, another landing on my other arm.

"Enough, that's enough."

I shook them off. It wasn't enough. I owed Perak, I owed him a lot. For all the times he'd made me laugh when my nature made me want to wallow or spit feathers. For being there when Ma died. For always believing in me. And how had I repaid him? I had to do this, for him, and for a girl I'd never met, whose picture worked its way further into my heart every time I looked at it. A sweet little girl who, if I couldn't find her, would lose that childhood, for ever. I couldn't let that happen.

I'd said that aloud.

"Sometimes you have to." Jake's voice, full of knowing sympathy. "Sometimes your best isn't good enough, and you'll spend days, weeks, months wondering if you could have done better. I know, believe me, I know. But right now, this is enough. If you don't stop, you won't use that hand again."

I shrugged Pasha's hands off, angry at Jake for understanding. "So?"

Jake turned away, her mouth tight with feeling, and Pasha answered for her. "So with one hand you're going to be crapall use to anyone. So that's enough. It was always going to be a long shot, the way they protect the factories."

"I thought you said it might be useful, tracking them like this?"

"Yes, when a girl's only just gone missing, or they've done with her. I was hoping that's where your niece was, at a holding-house while they collect more, but if that's the kind of resistance you're getting, either she's at a factory or they know she's your niece. Neither of those things will help her, so if you can't track her your way, we'll have to try ours."

I stared down at my knuckles, at the blood dripping

146

through my fingers on to the floor. It didn't look out of place there; I had the feeling this room had seen a fair bit of Jake's blood, one way or another. "West. She's west somewhere, that's all I could make out. And – and it's dark, and, and there was something there with her."

Pasha's fingers gripped my arm. "I know. We'll find her, I promise. Come on, let's get that hand wrapped up."

It was a better class of neighbourhood. Which down here meant the buildings didn't look like they were about to collapse and there were awnings across the streets so that I was at least saved from worrying whether I was catching a fatal dose of synth with every drop of "rain". It was an education watching people move out of Jake's way. She didn't say or do anything that you might class as threatening, just walked along as though she owned the place, and people melted away. They whispered among themselves after she had passed and one or two called out her name. She nodded in their direction, coolly cordial but no more.

Pasha, on the other hand, was more jittery than ever. He kept fingering the gun in his pocket and his face was taut and twitching as he muttered under his breath. We reached a corner that looked like any other and paused for a moment. "You got a weapon?" Pasha asked.

"Do you think I'll need one?"

He smiled but it had a nasty edge to it. "Maybe, maybe not. But you might *want* one."

I thought of the girls in that hole. He was right, I might want to use one, and that was enough to give me pause. For all my faults, seriously hurting other people is never something I've done and I didn't know if I had it in me. I did know that I didn't want to find out. Only now, if we found anything like that hole again I wasn't sure I could keep to it, to not hurting someone as hard as I could. I'd want to take it out on them, give them back every inch of pain. I pulled the pulse pistol from my pocket. "I've got this."

Pasha frowned at it. "What is it? It doesn't look like mine."

"It isn't." I told him what it did and he smiled grimly.

"That might come in very handy. We want them alive, or we won't find out a thing. Your hand up to it?"

I shrugged, more offhand than I felt. "I've got another one."

Jake leaned up against the corner of a building and looked round, eyes taking in every detail, checking every window. Finally she seemed satisfied and pushed away from the wall. "They'll know I'm here. Can't go anyplace without being recognised. So we might as well shake them up a little. Which one's theirs?"

Pasha pointed towards a door daubed with red paint that was slowly being etched away by synth. "Fifth floor. There's a handy little back entrance too, but no other real ways out. I scoped it out last night."

She smiled, but it wasn't pleasant. "Good. You get round the back, make sure they don't rat it out of there. I'll give you ten minutes before I announce myself. And Pasha?"

"Yes?"

Another one of those moments, when words seemed to be spinning in the air around me, only I couldn't hear them. They were just for Jake and Pasha. She smiled up at him, and Namrat's balls, I wished she was smiling like that at me.

"It's not worth it, Pasha, OK? It won't help, won't make it any better or make it never have happened. Remember that, and take care." Without another word, Jake walked softly over to the door and slid into the shadows, waiting.

Pasha watched her go, his mouth twisted with something, then led the way round the back. I followed, not entirely convinced of the course of action but following their lead, hoping they knew these places as well as I knew Upside. At least we were doing something, anything.

We slipped down a tiny alley and Pasha eased open a door that looked like it was held together by splinters. I took a deep breath and followed him in, my stomach in knots at the thought of what we might find. What these two might do once we found the men we were after.

The corridor beyond was black as night and all I could see in the light from the door was a muted flash of metal as Pasha pulled his gun from his pocket. We made our careful way up splintered back stairs to the fifth floor. The stench was indescribable, for all this was the upmarket end of the 'Pit. Unwashed bodies, stale cooking oil and, above it all, the unmistakable, sharp smell of ground-in fear.

Pasha stopped, his ear to a door that appeared out of the

gloom. After a moment he opened it and slipped through, leaving it wide for me. A short scream greeted me, soon silenced, and when I got through the door a family cowered on the floor. The father shielded the children behind him, a knife in his hand. The mother moaned in fear. Pasha's pistol was pointed at the man's head while he checked their wrists. There were no brands and he lowered the gun without a word of apology.

"Which way through to the next apartment?" Pasha asked in a soft voice. The man's eyes never left his face as he stuttered an answer.

"That's Jake's friend isn't it, Mummy?" one of the children whispered, and the mother clapped a hand over the girl's mouth.

Pasha nodded shortly. "I am. I'd suggest a trip out somewhere. Just for a while."

The father trembled his thanks. "Those men next door, been some funny noises past week or so. Nothing I could put my finger on, but ... odd."

"Other people in there with them, you reckon?"

"I – I don't know. Whenever the noises start they turn their music up real loud."

"OK. Now out. Quick."

All four of them leapt to their feet and made for the door, the woman herding the children in front of her. They didn't even stop for coats. Pasha waited till they'd gone and made for the doorway the man had indicated. There was a flimsy bolt on this side that didn't look any stronger than the door. If needs be I could force it without breaking a sweat. Pasha beckoned me over and put his ear to the wood.

I followed his lead, but all I could hear was a faint rumble. I kept my voice low. "What are we listening for?"

Pasha grinned. "You'll know it when you hear it. Get ready to break through this door when you do. You're bigger than me."

All was quiet for a minute or two, but Pasha was right, I knew it when it happened. A crash reverberated through the door as though a platoon of troopers had battered a wall down, and then a scream hit me. Not a scream of shock or surprise, or children afraid or someone in pain. The sort of angry scream that could easily contain the word "fuck".

I launched my shoulder at the door and it was even flimsier than it had looked. I almost fell through the doorway into bloody murder. Jake stood over two prone men, her face a study of angry frustration. One of the men lay naked over the other on the bare boards of the floor, and both had deep cuts to their throat, almost through to the spine. The whole room was splattered with blood: on the rumpled, fetid beds, over a chair that lay in splinters, on the table that looked like a hasty hand had swiped everything into a ripe mess of food on the floor. The dingy walls, once whitewashed but now a grimy grey, had splashes of crimson all over. There'd been one heck of a struggle, that was plain. Namrat's balls, had she ... I hadn't thought she would, at most I thought they'd be like the other men, wounded but not dead. As Pasha had told me, taken away to some hellhole to live in pain and remorse for as long as possible.

Yet no blood stained her swords, and she hadn't had time for the mayhem in the room. The frustration was because the Jorrin brothers were dead, that became clear. Because they could no longer tell us where Azama was, or Amarie. Pasha swore violently behind me and walked over to the corpses. The gun shook in his hands, pointed at the head of the closest body. He swore again, a quiet steady stream of words, with a flat force that made chill bumps run up my back.

Then Jake was in front of him, between him and the bodies, talking softly so I couldn't hear the words. I recognised the rhythm though, the singsong tone of soothing, the melody of a mother gentling a child or one lover trying to comfort another. She put out a hesitant hand that didn't quite touch his shoulder. Finally he lowered his arm in jerky increments before he screwed up his face and threw the gun to the floor. He seemed to realise I was there, turned his head away so I couldn't see his face and leaned against a wall. His whole body trembled and jerked and his fist thumped into the wall in a staccato rhythm of anger. Jake looked after him, her hands fluttering as though she didn't know what to do with them. Then she took a sharp breath and turned to me, cool and collected on the instant. "Check everywhere, see what you can find."

What we found was a brace of fearful, hollow-eyed boys, shaking and filthy in a locked closet, branded on the wrist. And a scrap of paper, with a hectic spot of blood on the corner, with Perak's address and Amarie's name on it.

Chapter Nine

Four hours later found us back at the death matches. Jake had another fight and she refused to back out or delay. The money was vital, and so was her not pissing off the men who owned the arena – Ministry men. If she didn't show, she said, they'd *know* something was up rather than just guessing. At least they pretty much left the matchers to themselves, hardly came out of their little compound, just so long as everything ran smoothly.

The other Ministry men, the Specials trying to pass themselves off as Downsiders, were still asking around for me, but they didn't seem to have twigged that I'd joined up with Pasha and Jake, because no one was talking to them. So far.

So Pasha and I hid in the viewing room behind blacked-out one-way glass, and watched in silence the parade of fights before hers. Pasha had said nothing since we'd found Azama's men dead, and I'd no heart for talk either. Those children, young boys this time, haunted me. Their weak moans of fear, the scarred bodies, the brands on their wrists. I'd done what I could to help Jake with them but they were pathetically afraid of me, whimpering whenever I got close.

They seemed to know who she was though, whispered her name on lips stiff with terror and a faint "please, Goddess" kind of hope, reached hesitant hands out to try to touch her. She soothed them, and though she never touched anyone else that I'd seen, seemed to have a pathological hatred of it, she had no problem helping the boys, covering them and holding them though they flinched from her hands.

She'd found someone to pass a message and within minutes there were people there to help, two women who gathered the boys together and led them gently away. Jake had coaxed Pasha away from the bodies, away from the house, and brought us back here.

Now Pasha sat and watched blindly as a succession of men tried to murder each other in front of us for money, or at least pretend to. It looked all too real to me. I kept a glass topped up with drink for him, worried at the lack of anything that could be construed as emotion on his face. I'd thought he was used to it, or as used to it as anyone could be. But he sat and stared and drank until finally his eyes slid shut, and maybe that was a mercy for both of us. I took the glass from his limp hand and set it on the floor.

With him out, I took the scrap of paper out of my pocket.

I hadn't let either of them see it, unsure what it meant precisely. That Amarie was targeted, that was all. They'd taken her on purpose, this particular girl. Because of Perak? Or because of me?

Jake came out for her match to a thunderous reception from the crowd, which yanked me from my thoughts. The match was brief, almost perfunctory, and she disarmed the man in only a few minutes. Still, he managed to cut her a couple of times when he shouldn't have been able to touch her. Her mind wasn't on the match, that was clear, or on the pleasing of the crowd. My mind wasn't on it either, a succession of images parading through my mind relentlessly until I wished I had the luxury of drinking myself stupid like Pasha. But we had yet to find any clue as to Amarie's whereabouts except that she was west of Jake's place, and the whole situation chafed at me.

I contented myself with a couple of stiff shots until Jake came back and slumped into a chair. I took Pasha's place and poured her a drink. She took it gratefully and eyed Pasha. He lay back in his chair, alternately sweating and shivering in his sleep and muttering under his breath. The hard creases on his face made him seem both older than time and just a child. It seemed Jake could hardly bear to look at him. She turned her eyes away and stared at the floor.

"So what was it with him today?" I asked.

She jerked one shoulder and drained her glass, but she still wouldn't look at me. "Those two men – he knew them, from years ago. He had a personal score to settle, and he's pissed off someone beat him to it."

"Personal?"

"None of your business." She stood up and paced the floor. "But I'm glad he didn't get to pass the favour on to them. I think – I think it would have destroyed him, no matter that he had good cause. He wasn't made that way."

I had to agree with that. Pasha had courage, I'd no doubt – he'd never flinched from things that made me shudder – but to kill a man ... like Jake, I think it would have destroyed him. You only had to see the way he looked at Jake, at the children he'd helped, to know he had the softest of hearts. That he probably broke it every time he had to get a girl out of one of the holes he'd shown me.

I turned back to her. "Is that why you do it too?"

She stopped pacing and stared at me guardedly for a moment. "Something like that." The look on her face warned me not to ask any more.

A thin line of blood trickled down one cheek, and she'd been cut a couple of times in other places. Pasha was in no state to patch her up, so I cast around and found the kit he'd used on her before. A simple affair: needles, tweezers, thread, antiseptic, ampoules of something that wasn't labelled, though I could guess, and some dressings that were at least clean. "Where're you cut?"

She looked up at me and down at the kit, her shoulders stiff with indecision. Finally she nodded and I sat down next to her. She shrugged off the upper portion of her armoured allover and blood marked her undershirt on her shoulder where the man's sword had found a gap. I pulled at the ripped material, hoping that I could stitch the wound through the tear, although part of me thrilled to the thought of her without the shirt. There was something about her. The cool exterior, her very aloofness, the way she kept even Pasha at a physical distance. A challenge, the *chase*, that was what always thrilled me, and I soon got bored once I had them. It probably says something profound about me. Like I'm a total bastard when it comes to women, even if it is unintentional. Mostly.

But I felt in my bones that she would be the ultimate chase. I might never catch her, never know what it was behind that icy mask, what drove her, who she really *was*, underneath, and that was a heady thought, because I love a woman with a bit of mystery about her.

I calmed my fingers from their twitching impatience and picked a needle. Then my fingers trembled for a whole new reason. I'd never stitched anyone up before. I'd never needed to: there was always a hospital handy. How were you supposed to see through the constant seeping blood? I took my life in my hands and used a dressing to mop at the wound. Jake tensed away from me with a hiss but kept her hands mercifully away from the swords.

"I'm sorry, I've never done this before."

"Neither have I – have someone other than Pasha do it, I

mean. And he—" Her voice lowered to a whisper, as though she was ashamed to admit a weakness. "I don't like it when people touch me."

"So I've noticed," I said drily, but a little voice in my head was pleased that she had said it, confided in me. Shown me the smallest part of her, a little chink in her armour. "I'll do my best."

"Me too."

It took a while, and Jake was a solid block of suppressed tension by the time we'd finished, but I managed it without touching her with anything other than the needle and tweezers. Even so it was a bizarrely intimate moment, as though by allowing me into her closed little world she had exposed herself, afraid of doing it maybe, but that she trusted me enough made me feel strangely privileged.

Jake shrugged her allover back on to her shoulders and looked at me, as though maybe really seeing me for the first time. She hesitated with the material halfway up her arms, just a moment, nodded and gave me the hint of a smile, a good warm one, like she shared with Pasha. It was like being blessed by the Goddess: a unique experience in a man's lifetime.

After that she was all business again. "We'll leave Pasha here for now; he could do with the rest. Meantime, we've got a few people to talk to. Subtly. Which means you'll be doing all the talking, because subtle I am not. You manage that, you think?"

"I think I can cope. Who exactly are we talking to?"

"Oh don't worry, you're going to *love* this place." She laughed, a deep-throated sound that made a tingle thrill up my spine. Does the Goddess do double blessings?

Jake and I stood across the way from a nondescript house in a down and dirty area. Well, all right, downer and dirtier than was average down here. The building pressed up against the old castle wall that was the root of Mahala, the well we'd sprung from. The blocks of the castle were black with dirt, except where the synth had scoured grooves in them, little riverbeds of insidious poison. Hard up on the left was a crumbling archway that might once have been triumphal, with its eroded statues of warriors long dead, their faces blank now, forgotten heroes of another world. To the right of the ramshackle house, the cobbled street gleamed wetly as it squeezed between a butcher's, shut up for the night, and a bar that was no more than an open stall with a flapping awning keeping the worst of the rain from its solitary customer.

"Ask for Kersan, tell him I asked you to come. He'll know what you're there for – he talks to Pasha normally. He'll ask you a question, to make sure you're legit. The answer is Home. Home Farm. OK?"

"What sort of place is it?"

"Don't worry. Let's just say everyone does what they do from their own free will. If I go in, it'll give everything away. But this is where gentlemen of taste come to relax. Gentlemen who don't like their women branded."

"What, I—"

She flirted with the idea of smiling at me before she turned and, letting a "Have fun" drift over her shoulder, she walked away through the arch, instantly swallowed by shadows of warriors.

I took a deep breath. Jake had said this was our best chance of finding Azama, of discovering who had killed his henchmen, the Jorrin brothers. Of finding Amarie. This was Pasha's part of the usual information network, but he was in no fit state to talk to anyone. I fingered the pulse pistol, winced as my throbbing hand protested, and walked over to the door. Before I could knock, it opened on silent hinges.

The inside was a revelation. Clean, for starters. The door led into a large, square room draped in rich fabrics in a plush red. No one was visible and I stepped through. Candlelight flickered along the walls and gave off scents that worked on me subtly. My shoulders relaxed from a hunch I hadn't realised they'd been in.

A boy, maybe twelve, popped out from behind the door and bowed. His clothes were pristine and pressed to a knife-sharp crease. "Sir, what is your wish?"

Startled, I blurted out my answer. "Kersan."

The boy directed me to a plush settee before he darted off. I sat down, relaxed and tense at the same time, and considered the room, wondering what it could tell me about who lived here.

Something very studied about the way the velvet swooped

along the wall, draped over the settees. It was in the lines of the gilt frames on the paintings – all very arty nudes – and the low tables with their trays of delicacies, and in the careful scent from the candles that lit the room with flattering light. The scent reminded me of home, when I was a boy. Of my mother, though that was at right-angles to my thoughts on who lived, and worked, here.

I shook that thought away as another young lad came in. He was about fourteen or so, with sharp black eyes and what would have been dusky skin a similar shade to mine, if it weren't for the blue-white tones from lack of sun. He introduced himself in soft, musical tones. "I'm Kersan. You asked for me?"

"I did. Jake sent me, in Pasha's stead."

He frowned and looked me up and down discreetly. "Why hasn't Pasha come himself?"

"He's indisposed. I'm a friend of his."

"I see. He is well?"

I nodded. It wasn't that far from the truth. Physically he'd be fine once he slept it off. Mentally, maybe not so much.

"Then maybe I could ask a question?"

"Of course."

"Where is Pasha's favourite place?" He looked at me intently, watching my face and eyes, for any hint of hesitation I suppose.

"Home Farm," I said, and the answer made sense now. The farm that they took the girls, or rather the children, to.

Kersan relaxed a fraction, though his eyes stayed wary, and with good reason if half my suspicions about this place were correct. "Good. Would you like to come with me?"

I followed him down long corridors echoing with the soft sound of gentle music from behind discreet doors decorated in the same plush velvet as the walls, so you could hardly tell they were there until you were almost on them. The whole place was well kept, almost luxurious as the 'Pit went. He opened a door at the far end of the house and ushered me through.

I was not unduly surprised to see a young woman, a very attractive one as it happens, dressed in a silky, flowing green robe, split to the thigh, sitting on a large bed decked out in silk and velvet. The wooden bathtub, tall enough that it came up to my chest, and a softly upholstered settee were unusual though. Another low table covered in plates of tiny delicacies sat in front of a lounger. The girl stood up, came towards us and bowed. "Who is this gentleman?"

"A friend of Pasha's."

She looked sharply at Kersan, but the boy made a small gesture and she seemed reassured. "Any friend of Pasha's is a friend of this house."

Really? Pasha was a habitué of a brothel? Because there was no doubt in my mind that was what this was. That seemed completely at odds with everything else I'd seen of him. My surprise must have shown.

The woman laughed and indicated I should sit on the

lounger. She sat next to me, smoothed back the elegant coil of dark hair at the nape of her neck and crossed her legs in a silky manoeuvre that almost popped my eyes from my head when the robe fell away from her thigh. "Oh, he doesn't use our services. Except the massage, the hot tub, a friendly face or touch. He sleeps here often. Poor dear, can't abide to sleep in a place on his own. He shares with Kersan."

"Still, it seems a little odd . . ." I trailed off, unsure what this woman knew, or whether I should be revealing what Pasha and Jake did. They'd seemed pretty clear that most of the populace knew nothing about their lives after the matches, or what happened to the girls that went missing.

"That he comes to a place like this when he spends his time rescuing girls like me?"

Ah. "Well, yes, now that you mention it."

She leaned forwards and picked up a tray of the little sweet-meats. "Please, do try them. They're scrumptious." I picked one and chewed it thoughtfully as she carried on. She was right — it was glorious. "Pasha is why most of us are here, rather than with *them*."

"He got you away from them, and you do this?" It hardly seemed a fitting end to a rescue story.

She shrugged, a delicate action that seemed to hide a multitude of emotions. "For some of us it's too late, Mr — I'm sorry, Kersan didn't say your name. I'm Erlat."

"Rojan, just Rojan. Too late? I'm sorry, I don't catch your drift." Or I did, but I couldn't quite bring myself to believe it. Or maybe I wanted to be blind, so I didn't have to think about it. That sounded more like me.

"Are you an Upsider?"

"Yes, I am. I'm here to find my niece."

She turned her liquid brown gaze to the table, but not before I saw the flash of pity. "I'm sorry, truly I am. I hope that Pasha can find her in time, or that she gets a different mage instead of Azama. They each have their own favourite things to do, and Azama – it's almost all his girls here in this house. Because of what he preferred to do, and after a while . . . After a while it's all you know. Now at least I pick and choose my clients. I am not forced. I am cherished to a certain extent. It's the only way I can be. I know no other, I was taught too well." She licked her lips nervously, and drew up the long sleeve of her silky green robe. There was no brand, but a faint scar where one might have been once. I caught a movement as Kersan reached behind him for something.

I couldn't think of a word to say. I wanted to say I was sorry, but I didn't know her and it would be insincere, even if that'd never stopped me saying anything before. I wanted to say it didn't have to be that way for her, for any of them, if only because I had to hope that for Amarie. I wondered at myself for even thinking these thoughts, when I could be trying to jump her bones.

"I suppose – I don't – if you're content, then that's good." Kersan pulled his hand back and sighed. Had they thought I would hurt her? Of course, she must have done. Little

Whores, Pasha had said they were called, lowest of the low, a crime against the Goddess and to be treated as such.

Erlat smiled again, a little strained but it was a start, and tucked her legs under her in a curiously attractive way. I think it was because she put away her working persona, and became herself. A young girl chatting about the goings-on around her, the gossip. Of a sudden, she looked ten years younger – that is, she looked about eighteen. So young, with an elegant poise and a depth and knowing behind her eyes of a woman twice her age. A twist in me, for how she got that knowing, because she'd belonged to this Azama. I was starting to wonder just how big a bastard he was.

"So Rojan, why have you come to see me? Did Pasha recommend my services?"

"No! Er, no, nothing like that. Pasha is – unwell. We need to know about Azama, the Jorrin brothers. Jake seems to think you might help there."

She tilted her head, and reminded me of a mouse I'd had as a pet, many years ago. He used to look at me the same way when he wanted something. I doubted she wanted another kernel of corn.

"Kersan," she said, and the boy slipped silently out of the door. "We'll find what there is to find. We're so much more invisible than Pasha and especially Jake. Everyone knows them, so when they ask questions it gets noticed. Besides, men are so indiscreet in the bedroom, and do love to boast. Men like Azama don't even see us unless we try to hamper him, or we can be used. But the young girls are easier to control than those of us that managed to get out. While we wait, may I entertain you? A bath? A massage? Anything else?"

A flush crept up my neck. This was ridiculous. I was embarrassed, and I'm never that. Embarrassed that I'd thought of the girls I'd used, and yes, that included the girlfriends, as nothing more than warm flesh that I had to have. Interesting only as long as I didn't have them, and then ... there was always another to catch my fancy. Now I could see nothing else but those young girls we'd rescued from the hole, the boys that had cowered in the Jorrin brothers' flat. Erlat before Jake and Pasha had rescued her, young and hurting, and now knowing nothing else. People, with their own hurts, their own reasons for what they did. It shocked me to silence for a moment.

Erlat read my mood perfectly. She walked over to the tub and tested the water with a delicate hand. "Rojan, if you'd like to relax? Many of the matchers find our hot tubs are very good for unknotting muscles. I'll go and see about towels, so you'll have it to yourself." There was a mischievous glint in her eyes. "I promise not to take advantage of you when I get back."

She left the room, and me in a state of bewilderment. If she'd been one of those girls, if Azama had done what she'd hinted at, how could she joke about it? Nevertheless the thought of a bath was relaxing. There was nothing I could do now except wait, wait for Kersan or Erlat to come and tell me what they could find out. I stripped off and slid gingerly into the tub. The water was so hot, I thought it might actually slough the skin off my legs, but once I slid in to the neck, my injured hand dangling over the side, it was bliss. All the muscles in my back and neck relaxed slowly and untangled themselves. The steam fogged my eyes so I shut them, lay back and thought hard about Pasha and Jake.

I couldn't figure them out. Mousy little Pasha with the courage of a lion. Aggressive, blank-faced Jake with her tender looks at Pasha, her softness with those boys we'd found, the hints of emotion beneath her icy façade. The pair of them, and what went between them, were an enigma, but one I fully intended to solve. That they were only friends was true, at least in the physical sense; the way they avoided touching each other made that evident. But there was something else, something that held them together like invisible string. Which was a pain because I was very attracted to Jake, gods knew why.

I must have nodded off, because I woke with a start when Erlat and Kersan came back in. Erlat giggled and turned away when I got out of the tub, and Kersan handed me some towels and a robe.

Once I was dried off and decent, Erlat turned back; her face was more serious now. "I found out what I could, from some of the other girls. Big party in last night, and they do like to talk after a drink," she said. "Azama had his own men killed. Seems they were taking a liberty or two, and he's not one to take that lightly. So he took his price for them – and kept a watch on their place, just in case. And now Azama suspects it's been Jake and Pasha thwarting him all this time, rescuing the girls. He's taking the threat seriously – Pasha and Jake have been getting too close lately, I suspect, and there's talk that he's moving."

"Where to?"

"Where Jake and Pasha can't, or won't, follow him. Upside."

"Upside? But the guards, surely they'll—" Not unless Azama was Ministry. The only answer, the only hope he had Upside. The Ministry was behind this, behind Azama. Had to be: let's face it, the Ministry are behind everything, only— Fuck, even I'd not thought they were that bad. But the Ministry had banned mages, and being caught using magic Upside was still an execution offence. It didn't make a whole lot of sense. "Whereabouts Upside?"

Erlat waved the question away, as though we were talking of the moon or something equally remote, somewhere she had no hope or expectation of seeing, so why should any individual place there worry her? "Just Upside."

This could be good news. I *knew* Upside, and more importantly I knew how it worked. Knew every nook and cranny, every infested hole of it, at least anywhere further down than Heights. If Azama really was Ministry, I doubted even they would have the balls to hide him there, up among the rich boys and people who might actually give a crap. No, down somewhere low I reckoned. Somewhere where life, whilst not as cheap as in the 'Pit, was at least reasonably priced. If that's where he was headed, we had a chance to catch him.

"I don't think it likely myself," Erlat said. "All the machinery is down here, nice and hidden. That's the reason they sealed the 'Pit in the first place, to be totally secret. It'd take too much effort to move everything Upside, even if the scandal wouldn't ruin them."

"I'm not sure—"

Her eyebrows crinkled quizzically. "You do know what they're doing?"

"Not *totally* certain, no. Or maybe, more accurately, I don't know why." Pasha had been infuriatingly cryptic and Jake could hardly bear to talk about it.

Erlat clapped her hands in delight. "Oh, Rojan, it's so nice to have amusing company for a change."

Warmth crept up my cheeks and burned at my brow. Surely I wasn't blushing? I hadn't done that in years.

She patted my knee. "I'm sorry, I'm just playing. I know Upsiders don't know what's going on. All they know is their machines work. They don't stop to think how, as long as it isn't the synth."

Realisation began to dawn. This wasn't just some little pleasure palace down here, where they could throw off the yoke of piety and be as debauched as they pleased without anything getting out, or knock off the occasional criminal they wanted to get rid of.

No, it was much worse than that. "They banned pain

magic," I started, "too weak to power much if you abide by the rules, use only your own pain. Too open to abuse. That was all right because by then they had the synth to run every-thing—"

"—Only when the synth turned out to be toxic," Erlat car-ried on for me, "they had to do something. It was supposed to be temporary, just until they could find a synth replacement. A necessary evil. Only they never found one. So all of Mahala is run on this now. On pain magic. Glow."

I sat in shocked silence for long moments. Pasha had hinted, I knew the kids were being taken to mages, after all. I'd suspected, but hadn't *wanted* to think it. I'd not fully admitted it, not in one hit like this, what they were doing with them.

"But, but that would take hundreds of mages. Hundreds, and there aren't that many of us." In fact I could name four that I knew of, and that included me, Dendal and Pasha, and that poor drunk bastard who slumped outside our office every night, his mind blasted by the black. We have to keep hidden Upside, but even so.

"It would take hundreds if it was themselves they chan-nelled the pain from." She smiled, a sad, fragile thing, acknowledging the way the world worked and her part in it. Somehow that was the worst of all, the part that cracked my heart for her, that she accepted it. I had an old-fashioned urge to kiss her hand, anything. Something. Nothing would help.

"Which is why they built the factories down here," she

carried on. "You only need a few mages that way. Hundreds of people, oceans of pain. All gathered to make Glow, feed the never-satisfied monsters they call their trade."

Trade: what the city had been built on, had thrived on with not much else going for it except ingenuity and the ability to drive a hard bargain. Without trade Mahala was dead, and so was the population. So little land left to farm, so much destroyed by synth, we survived because the rest of the world beat a path to our door for our inventions. Without a way to run the thunderous machines in the Trade district, we'd have nothing to barter for food. We'd starve.

All the thousands and more of us.

Instead, Ministry was using the lowest, poorest people of society to make sure everyone else prospered, and handily clearing out the bits of the population they weren't so keen on, those likely to cause trouble or make their city a bit too grubby. Which left only one question.

If they were clearing the dregs, why did they take Amarie?

Chapter Ten

I had no way of finding Jake, and I wasn't sure I could make my way back to the matches without getting lost, or mugged, so I accepted Erlat's offer of a bed for the night. I didn't accept her offer of sharing it with me. I must be getting old or something.

Kersan led me to a dormitory he shared with the other boys who worked here. There were a few spare beds, shabby but with crisp, clean sheets and warm grey blankets, and I settled myself in. But no matter how much I wriggled and fought with the blanket, how many times I thumped the pillow, I couldn't sleep. Amarie was out there, somewhere. Cold, alone and afraid. I hadn't dared ask either of them what might have become of her, what the odds were that I could find her, and soon enough. I was afraid I knew.

Finally I sat up. Pasha was sitting on the bed next to mine, looking dishevelled and a little green around the gills. He

173

didn't say anything. He didn't have to; it was in his eyes. Time to go.

"Have you ever been Upside?" I asked.

He shrugged, eyes on the floor. "Yes. I remember it was grey."

"Grey, that pretty much describes a lot of it." To be honest, even though there was no sun down here, there was more life, more vibrancy than I'd ever experienced Upside. Now it came to it, I wasn't so sure I wanted to go back. I could get used to it down here, but it wasn't time for that yet. We didn't know for sure what Azama was planning, to make sure he was safe down here or to cut and run to Upside. I could hazard a guess. A magic factory, that wasn't a small undertaking from my limited understanding, and I didn't even want to *think* of what kind of machinery and such they'd have to move. Any interrupting the flow of Glow to Upside would be costly, maybe devastating to the trade Mahala relied on.

If Azama really was heading up there, he'd have to do a lot of preparation first. My mind began turning over all the places he might hide Upside, all the derelict warehouses in Boundary, abandoned when the synth came to town. Would they be big enough? Hard to say. Before synth, when all we'd had for power was pain magic, and no using other people's pain to run it, trade had been thinner. It had made us money all right, but nothing compared to what we could turn out with synth and then with Glow. Those old warehouses were pretty small. You could probably fit half a dozen into one of the minor new ones up there in Trade. The bigger, newer ones took up vast cubed acres. So, where else? And, more importantly, where was he moving them *from*?

"Do we have any idea where Azama is?" I asked. "Any idea at all?"

"In the castle somewhere, but it's immense, not to mention almost impenetrable. Every time we get close, he moves. Sometimes we get lucky: we got Erlat out from a holding-house, where she was being 'rested'. Once or twice we've come across a smaller factory, got thirty girls out of one, down in one of the outer parts of the old castle. But that's not much to him. A blip. A minor inconvenience. The main place – they've got most of the old castle to themselves. No one will live there anyway, excepting by the walls. The places that are open, well, it's tricky to get in, and if you get caught, guess where you end up? That leaves you only, what, fifty acres over each of four levels at least? Even if there was no one stopping us, no guards on the old castle walls, it'd take years to search it all. I've been in parts: there's corridors and rooms where you don't expect and hidden stairways and ... Years. It'd take years."

"But which part is due west of Jake's place?"

"What?"

"My tracking – the spell. Directly west, that's all I could make out. Which part of the castle is that?"

Pasha frowned for a moment. "I'm not sure. We can find out, though. Come on, it's time to go find Jake."

"Where is she?"

"Going to see a man about a cow."

We took one of the cages. Pasha waved down a boy and we climbed in. I held on tight to a support strut as we clanked off at far too great a speed for my liking. Especially when we were fifty or more feet in the air. The cage rattled along, bouncing round the junctions till I was sure I'd be sick.

Pasha stood thoughtfully, balanced and keen-eyed now he had something to focus on. The match arena passed under us, its bright lights piercing the mesh that formed the bottom of the cage, painting him in stripes of gold and black. He didn't look at the arena though; he was staring at the looming bulk of the old castle.

Pasha murmured at the boy and the cage changed direction abruptly at the next junction, almost doubling back on itself and causing me to hold tighter to the strut. Rain, sliced into tiny droplets by the surrounding mesh, settled into a film on my face and hands. "Why the change?" I asked, once I thought I could manage it without stammering.

Pasha grinned like that little monkey again. "How's your sense of direction?"

Not good when I'm dangling fifty feet above the ground, because the only direction I'm thinking about is down. However, what I said was "Pretty good, usually." It is too: I can tell which way north is with my eyes shut. No dislocations are required, it just happens.

"Then from up here might be a good way to see what's due west, right?"

"Right," I managed, and concentrated on not looking down.

It wasn't long before Pasha got the boy to stop the cage. I didn't recognise the area, but presumably Jake's place was down there somewhere. We were surrounded by the jutting bones of Mahala, old buildings made of solid blocks of dressed stone, great girders that held up the Seal. Not part of the original castle, but of the town that had grown up about it as it became more powerful. Down below us, houses, shops and other buildings, made of whatever could be scrounged together, jostled for position, squeezed in between the stone towers. Inside the old buildings, families camped out in rooms that had once maybe been warehouses or rich merchants' townhouses, later fortified and strengthened with stone or steel to support additions above. Narrow slit windows flickered with light. The lucky ones, living inside stone that had lasted a thousand years and looked strong enough to last a thousand more, instead of in shacks and shanties that were vulnerable to whatever synth was left.

Pasha had the boy move the cage on a few feet and peered down. I risked a look, and thought maybe I could see the narrow alley that led to Jake's door. I tried not to notice how far down it was.

"All right," Pasha said. "Which way?"

I shut my eyes – not without some relief – and tried to feel it. North was that way, which made west a quarter-turn to the left. My boots squeaked on the mesh as I moved to face the right way. When I opened my eyes I was staring straight at, not part of the castle but one of the buildings that had grown up around it. A warehouse originally perhaps. Music blared from it, grey washing fluttered at windows and a stunted ginger cat with patchy fur sneered at me before a chubby toddler grabbed it from the sill with a crow of delight. Too close, I knew that. I hadn't been able to tell much, but this tower was too close.

"Any idea what's directly behind that?" I asked.

Pasha stood beside me and stared out thoughtfully. "One way to find out. Boy, you get us the other side of that?"

He could, at rather more speed than was good for my nerves. The way the cage swung out round the junctions so my feet went sideways almost decorated the mesh in interesting colours. I just about held on to what was in my stomach and kept my eyes shut. It didn't really help, but at least I wasn't forced to see the ground too far away and at an odd angle.

Finally we rattled to a stop and Pasha's whispered "Oh shit" got my eyes open.

"Oh shit" was about right. The tower was behind us now, and due west – due west was the biggest, chunkiest building I'd ever seen, built of blocks of stone bigger than houses. The old castle barbican reared up before us, ahead of a wall. It was easily fifty feet high, and that was just the outer one. It spread left and right, disappearing into the gloom. Inside of that, past a flat space we couldn't see into from this height, was another taller wall. No cage wires crossed the walls, no clanking chains. Beyond, tier upon tier of stone, each one piled on the other till the eye reached the forbidding grey bulk of the keep, with a great, squat tower at the top. Mahala had always gone in for building up rather than out, it seemed, and this particular part – the tower, the very centre of the keep – was exactly due west of Jake's place.

I took a breath and looked down to scan the wall for entrances. There were none, except the bricked-up and impassable barbican. "How do you get in?"

Pasha looked sideways at me. "Into the main castle? You don't. Always been that way, since before they sealed us off. Even if you could, getting to the keep? We were pretty sure that's where Azama was basing himself, somewhere in the inner keep, but how to get in? We can get into some of the outer parts, guard towers and such, even found a few girls there, like I said, but no way to get further. Lots of corridors and doorways bricked up, others hidden. Of course there's a castle gate, but that was bricked up too, same time we got sealed. Even if we found a way – like I said, you could spend years searching and not find anything. We might have been able to get in, perhaps, but the problem was always where to go once we were there."

"And now Amarie is in there. Well, there must *be* a way. If they're really preparing to move, it's going to be a vast undertaking. We must be able to spot something, some sort of activity."

Pasha leaned his elbows on the cage railing, his eyes dark and unreadable. "Maybe. But he's a clever bastard, Azama. We aren't even sure he's going to move. He's jittery, *maybe*. That won't make him stupid. Or maybe he's put that rumour about to make us rush so we trip up. Come on, we need to find Jake. She had an idea about getting us in."

The cage clanked off over the houses, away from the intimidating bulk of the castle. If I was of a fanciful nature, I'd say it felt like it was watching me, but I'm not, so I'll just say it really gave me the fucking creeps.

The temple was small and shabby. The doors were hanging off, so I could make out the statues – the Goddess, the faithful, the martyrs. Namrat, though his face was covered with a black and gold striped cloth. Namrat the tiger, the stalking figure of Death.

Pasha seemed content to wait outside, leaning against a post that held up the roof of a little shop selling pastries. We hadn't waited long before Jake came out, diffident and awkward today. Her left hand was stained with the devotional – a black circle of ash, a red spot inside. The old prayers, not the new, sanitised ones. The red spot would be blood.

"I never took her for a religious person," I murmured before she got close enough to hear.

"Pretty much the only hope we have down here," Pasha said. "All we've got to look forward to. Why, aren't you?"

I snorted a laugh. "Not likely."

Pasha looked as though that made him pity me, and Jake's look was the same – she must have overheard, no matter how quiet I thought I was being. A serious, gentle pity that pissed me off something rotten. Maybe because I deserved it, I don't know.

"Don't you go to temple, Rojan?" Jake looked at me with a puzzled frown.

I kept a tight lid on my words. "I believe in one thing. I believe I know where Amarie is."

The soft little smile playing around her lips just made things worse, because she was smiling at me, damn it, and I would have admitted to being Namrat's bastard love-child if she'd do it some more. She shook her head, like I was a lost cause, and turned away to meet Pasha's gaze. There was that feeling again, that they were talking without talking, and a tingle in my hands. A little thrill of magic in the air.

"In the keep," Pasha said. His voice came out as a croak, but he coughed and tried again. "She's in the keep."

Jake fiddled with the hilt of one of her swords. "No surprise, we thought as much. We've just never known for sure, and not enough help to just go for it, no one to tell us *where* in the keep. Rojan, if we can get you in there, do you think you can find them, her? Exactly?"

I thought about how hard it had been, getting past whatever protection was on her just to find the due-west direction. It would be worse in there, the magic closer, more intense. My poor hand throbbed at the thought. So did my head, at the thought of how deep I might need to go into the black. Whether I'd make it back out again in one piece, with my mind still my own. *Princess, Daddy*.

"Yes, I can."

At about that point I found myself praying to the Goddess and had to tell myself not to be so fucking stupid.

Pasha's face scrunched up in amusement, the little monkey again. Maybe he really could see my thoughts. I experimented: *That Pasha is a right smug bastard. No wonder Jake won't touch him.* No doubt about it – he looked like I'd just slapped him.

Jake was oblivious. "Rojan, would you like to see something?"

"That depends on what it is."

Her smile blew all thoughts of Pasha away. "Something you've not seen for a long, long time. If ever."

Chapter Eleven

By the time the cage set us down on firm ground, I was ready to kiss the street, I was so glad to have solidity under me again. No walkway Upside was ever that bad. I might even have done it, if the stink of the place hadn't warned me. It smelled like shit. Literally.

My stomach rolled over. It hadn't recovered from the cage yet, and now I was being assaulted by a smell strong enough to make my eyes water. No wonder the street was empty. "Jake, what are we doing here?"

She looked around furtively, as though gathering her bearings, then made her way to a shop with boarded-up windows. "I came down earlier, trying to find out more about the Jorrin brothers and why Azama had them killed."

"Taking liberties, Erlat said."

Pasha brought up the rear, his face simian, but he seemed to have recovered from my mental blast.

With a gentle shove, one of the boards came away easily from a window and Jake peered into the darkness beyond. "Ah, yes, but what kind of liberties? Makes a difference."

Jake stepped over the low sill of the display window and held the board until Pasha and I followed, when she pushed it back into place.

"I don't see why."

As the board snicked back into place, total darkness descended, leaving me blind. I reached out and found Pasha's shoulder.

"Wait a few minutes for your night eyes to come in," he said. "Look, if they were going against Azama, it would maybe explain why they took your niece. One for themselves, not for him. But if her kidnap was on his orders and it was something else they did that pissed him off, then that's another matter entirely. How many girls have you seen on the street since you've been here?"

I opened my mouth to say, "Loads," then shut it with a snap. None, that was how many. I'd seen children, but now I came to think about it they were all boys. Not many of those either, compared to the number underfoot Upside.

"They're running out of children?"

My eyes began to adjust and I could make out a dark blob that was Pasha, another that was Jake and a wall with a darker space in it behind them. We picked a careful path to the doorway.

Pasha went through first. "We can get some light in a

minute. Can't risk it being seen from the street, see. Mind the steps. And yes, I think they're running out of children. Which still doesn't answer why your niece in particular."

I went down three steps into another open space. Pasha shut the door behind us and fumbled about with something on a wall. After a minute or so a light flared, dazzling my eyes so I was blinder than I had been in the dark. I squinted against it until I could see again. A plain, squalid room with a hole in the floor: stairs leading down. Down? I'd thought we were as far down as we could get.

Pasha led the way. His voice echoed off the stone stairwell, flat and unemotional, as though he had to distance himself from what he was saying. Or maybe not show me how much he disliked me. "And when they run out of children – well, they go to find some more. They're getting desperate enough that they're taking people off the streets, and not just children, anyone. No one says anything, no one *sees*. They daren't. Only, you know, it's a funny thing. There's only so much a person can take of what they do. They rest them in between sessions, but still . . . in the end, it's the mind that gives out, gives up. And it's the children that last longer, they figured that out long ago. If they get them young enough, they'll last a long time. You know why?"

No I didn't, and I didn't really want to know. The whole damn thing gave me the shudders. It looked like I was going to find out though, because Pasha carried on before I could protest. His voice cracked with suppressed anger.

"Because the mind is a strange thing. The children, they're told they've sinned against the Goddess, that this is to atone. They think they're doing the right thing by her. They're told, over and over, that the synth was a punishment from the Goddess, that being in the 'Pit is part of their castigation. Most of the temples down here preach much the same, so it's easy to take it further. That if they want to atone, become favoured again – the Goddess will love them if they do this, if they take what the mages do to them, they tell them that over and over, until they believe it. When a person believes in something, their mind, and body, will take such punishment you can't imagine. And a child will believe anything you tell them, until they discover it isn't true."

Jake was silent, except for a small, lonely sound behind me that might have been a moan, or a moue of disgust, or sympathy.

I thought back to Dendal, to the quiet devotion he had to his magic, his utter belief that he was doing the Goddess's work, and how he would suffer any pain to do it. Stupid, fabulous bastard. "People do the damnedest things in the name of belief."

Pasha stopped to peer at me under the lamp. "Do you really not believe in anything, Rojan? The Goddess? Namrat? Anything at all?"

I led the way down the stairs, mostly so I wouldn't have to look at him. "No, not really. I stopped believing in things I can't see or feel a long time ago. Doesn't do you any good, and can do a lot of harm. What you've just said proves it. Belief is as stupid as the people who believe and the things they believe in. I believe in cold, hard cash, keeping out of trouble and trying not to die. I believe the sun comes up because sometimes I get to see it, and I believe this is the only life we're likely to get, and that earning good-behaviour points for the next life is worse than stupid, it's downright ludicrous."

I pinched my lips shut because I could hear the bitterness in my own voice. So I didn't say the rest of it, except in my head, and maybe Pasha could hear that. There was no heaven or hell, or any place after death, fluffy and wonderful or full of pain. There was nothing. No divine beings to soothe us or condemn us. No gods or goddesses. Because no *sane* god would allow any of this to happen – the girls, the synth, the sheer ugly uselessness of death. No sane god would let a small girl get trapped in among a cesspit of bodies, let people just take them and, and – do whatever it was they were doing. Who let people live in a stinking shithole like this and only gave them a hallucination of niceness after they died for hope.

Or let my mother, a good and blameless woman, die after so much agony, after so much *faith*. Allow a death where the organs slowly dissolved but left every pain receptor intact. Where even the brain liquefied until there was nothing behind the eyes but pain. No recognition, no love, no emotion. Where finally you drowned in your own phlegm and the churning poison your body produced. And not in days, oh no. In *years*. No sane god would do that. And despite the evidence of my own eyes I don't believe in an insane god, even if I do swear by him often. Or, more accurately, swear *at* him.

An insane god might explain a lot, but if he was there, then to believe in him was to give him power. I had my own, hotly forged beliefs. This was it, all we got. There is no afterwards, the guy doesn't always get the girl and happy-ever-after is a crock of shit. Now is all we have and we might as well make the most of it. I'll admit I might have made more of it than some. What I actually said was, "The Ministry believe, and look what that's done for everyone. They believe like fucking crazy, and it's brought nothing but misery. That's what I believe."

Pasha fell silent; we reached the bottom of the stairs and a corridor that dripped with damp and skittered with rats among the rubbish. He raised the lamp and nodded at a door at the far end. He hesitated before he opened it, and gave me a look that shrivelled me. His eyes were very dark under the brightness of the lamp. "I feel sorry for you," was all he said before he turned away and opened the door.

It was like a kick in the stomach, the soft way he said it, the fact that here was a fucked-up individual if ever I'd met one, and *he* was sorry for *me*. Fuck him. Fuck everybody. I was just going to get Amarie and get the hell out of here, back to normality, to my crappy little life.

The stench of shit as Pasha opened the door robbed me of my answer, because it was hard enough to breathe, let alone talk. The room was vast: long, low-ceilinged and filthy, lit by lamps that gave off a strange glow reminiscent of your actual sunlight. But that didn't really matter, because of what was in the room.

Cows.

Not just one or two, but row upon row of them in iron stalls. Their great heads poked out and rooted around troughs in front of them. They were so *big*. I'd never realised. The rump of the nearest one came to my shoulder. It looked at me with blank eyes and shook its head with the weirdest groan I'd ever heard, a deep, bass sound that reverberated in my belly. I was more than glad the damn thing was chained to its stall, especially given the horns. It was nothing like the cows I'd seen in books when I was a child. They'd looked warm and cosy, probably with a name like Buttercup. This looked like a demon in disguise who would be at home being called Evil Git.

It snorted, a hot, heavy rush of air, and I took an involuntary step back. My boot landed in something soft and squishy. I hardly dared look. Shit. Greenish, stinking shit covered the floor, and now my boots. Fabulous.

Jake and Pasha moved past the row of black and brown backs, and I hurried to follow them, treading carefully so as not to slip. I did *not* want to end up face-down on this floor.

The room carried on and on, seeming endless, for long minutes. Finally the far wall came into view, along with a small wooden hutch that might have been an office. Beside it was a dark doorway, open, the smell of death on the other side. That may sound a bit fanciful, but I know blood when I smell it, and I remembered the smell of the slaughterhouse when I was a boy, when there were still animals to slaughter and meat enough for everyone.

I reached the office just as Jake opened the door and went in. Pasha and I followed. I wasn't sure what I expected, a man dripping in diamonds maybe, what with the price of meat and leather Upside. Instead there was a bald, fat blob, dressed in rags. The top might once have been knitted, and maybe it'd been green, but now it was grey with age and had unravelled in various places, giving him the look of a statue overrun with lichen. The grey pallor of his skin did nothing to dispel that idea. His face was blotchy and drooped down in two folds by his mouth. A statue of a depressed dog, that's what he looked like.

The jumper was tied on with pieces of its own unravelling, and another length of yarn held up what was left of his trousers, which were stained the same greenish-brown as the stuff on the floor. The only serviceable pieces of clothing he had on him were his boots, but, given the state of the floor, stout boots weren't too much of a surprise.

His grey face dappled into purply-blue when he saw Jake.

"I ain't done nothing, I ain't," were his first words. The words of the not-so-innocent everywhere when confronted with the truth, or someone likely to arrest them or make things painful. His left hand scrabbled for a drawer in his desk, but Jake slid a blade out of a scabbard, making sure it scraped nicely. The sound made the left hand stop abruptly and it dangled uselessly in mid-air. "I ain't done nothing. I *told* you."

Jake left the talking to Pasha. He perched on the edge of the desk, his little monkey face lit up with a smile that looked kind – until you saw his eyes. Then it looked like Namrat the tiger, all grinning teeth and waiting death. "I'm sure you haven't, Darin. Now, we've been friends awhile, yes? You've done us favours and we've done you favours. So why the sudden panic?"

Darin's eyes darted to and fro as he thought, but not for long. Jake was getting restless and the blade inched forwards. "It's changed now. It's that Azama. Oh, a cruel bastard, that one. Crueller than the rest of 'em put together. And he came back Down, and found out, about the favours I did you." He was pale and sweating now, the creases of his face more pronounced as he screwed himself up to say it. I wondered briefly who he was more afraid of, Jake or Azama, but came to the conclusion the answer to that was "whichever one was in front of him at the time".

"He found out?" Pasha licked his lips and he lost the smile, replacing it with a sudden frown. "How?"

"I don't know, I swear, I didn't tell him. But he knows. He ... he found that last lot of girls I sent out. Poor wee things are dead as this lot of cows come tomorrow."

Jake's sword moved in a blur, but a motion from Pasha stopped her. Pasha looked worse than Darin did, all pale skin and sweaty, shaking hands.

Darin squeaked at Jake's movement, then sagged back into his chair when Pasha stopped her. "Please, I can't do you no more favours. Wouldn't do you no good anyway: he'll catch them. They won't be safe, I'm sure of it."

"But you're still alive."

Darin hunched a shrug, making all his excess flesh wobble. "I promised him – I promised him I'd dob you in next time, let him know when there was girls coming so's he could catch you. Only I won't, not if you don't bring me no more girls to get out. You got to find some other way."

"There is no other way." Pasha reached down and grabbed at Darin's top. Threads came away in his hand, so he grabbed for the fleshy throat. "But that's not why we're here."

"It isn't?" Darin rasped.

"Not this time. This time we don't want out, we want in. Can you get us into the castle?"

"What? No! No, I can't, so don't you be asking me. I never been past the first gate, you know that."

"But your beef goes in there, doesn't it, Darin? Your meat goes everywhere. Best beef Downside and they pay a month's wages just for a mouthful Upside too. Then there's the leather. You must be a rich man, trading all that." Pasha let go and Darin dropped back into the chair, which squeaked in protest.

Darin's face bunched up in sudden spite and he waved his hands down over his top. "Do I look rich to you?" The wave moved to encompass the room behind us, the cows and the stink. "You think I've owned any of this for the last ten years

192

or more? I got bought out, and had no choice because it was stop trading or stop breathing. These cows are Ministry cows. All of them are. The only reason your farm is safe is because the Ministry don't reach outside Mahala, they got more sense out there. But everything that comes in, *everything*, becomes theirs, one way or another. Even you two belong to them, don't you? Jake fights in their matches, and she pays you to work for her. You're both Ministry as much as I am, as everyone is, whether they know it or not. And for a while they didn't search what was going out, because they thought it was all trade, things paid for. They checked, yes, but not too much, and the guards were easily bribed. Only the last trip, they found them, the girls." Darin looked down at his hands, which tapped out a sad little rhythm on the desk. "It weren't . . . I had no choice. No choice. They took them girls and killed two of my men doing it, and, and there ain't enough men in the whole of Downside to resist them. There ain't. We're all Ministry, all of us, even if we don't know it."

Pasha stared out at the cows, chained up and acquiescent, waiting for the death they didn't know was only a door away, and I wondered if he was thinking about what he'd told me – that everyone down here was a cow too, fattened up, kept satisfied and ignorant, or silent, before they were used. "You might be Ministry, Darin, but I'll be fucked if I am. When's your next delivery to the castle?"

"Now, I can't—" This time Pasha didn't stop Jake and the blade skittered over the desktop towards Darin's copious stomach. The point sliced another thread from the top, leaving the whole garment perilously close to falling off. Darin dared a look at Jake and his jowls wobbled. I can't say I blame him; I've met a few nasty bastards in my time, men and women who'd kill you without a backward glance, but I've never seen any of them with such a cold hardness about the eyes, or such a still way of standing, as though she was just waiting for the movement that would release her like a spring.

Pasha had his gun out and laid it casually on one leg, barrel pointed at Darin. The dull gleam of metal, made for dealing pain and death, was like a parallel of Jake. I almost felt sorry for Darin.

The fat man gathered his wits. "The slaughtermen are coming in first thing. Reckon we'll be ready to start taking the carcasses along mid-morning."

Pasha patted his hand. "Then we'll be here first thing too, and you can have a nice plan of where you drop off the meat, can't you?"

Darin bit his lip and nodded.

"Good. I think you can stop now, Jake."

She scraped the sword back across the desk, leaving a long gouge mark in the already scarred surface, and put it back in its scabbard. Her gaze never left Darin's face and he fidgeted under her glare.

"I'm sure you won't be telling anyone about this. Will you, Darin?" The gun was still lying on Pasha's lap and one finger stroked the trigger, as though it was a pet.

"No, no course not, Pasha. Course not. Could you, er, point that somewhere else?"

Pasha's eyebrows rose. "Oh, yes, of course. I forgot." The gun disappeared into a pocket. "For now."

We left the office and a shaky-looking Darin, and I picked my way among the shit back to the door.

"What are you planning on doing?" I asked as the smell receded, though it lingered on my boots. "If the castle is full of Ministry, then what the fuck can three people do in there?" Apart from get killed, obviously.

Pasha slid his gaze sideways to me. "Same thing we always do. Whatever we can."

"And now?"

"Now?" Pasha chuckled but it had a hard, nasty edge to it. "Now we make the most of what's probably our last night alive. Drink?"

Chapter Twelve

The bar was packed, but as soon as Jake walked in, a table was free as if by magic. I slid into the booth opposite Pasha and Jake and we sat in silence until the drinks came: the same green stuff as before. This time I wasn't hesitant; I needed that drink, because now I knew more about what I was up against, what I was going to face come tomorrow, and I wasn't at all sure I was up to the task. I slugged the booze back in one.

A whole fucking castle full of Ministry mages, ones who weren't limited by the fact that their power came from their own pain. They had plenty of people there to supply it, a whole bunch of human cows. Including Amarie, who, for some reason I couldn't quite fathom, had been specifically targeted. Perhaps to get me in there. *Perhaps*. And Pasha, Jake and I were just going to walk in. If that perhaps was right, we'd be doing just what they wanted. They'd be waiting for us. Hah! Last night alive.

Did I have a choice? Yes, yes I did. I could walk away. I could ignore what felt more and more like a summons, pull out that Ministry pin and haul my sorry arse back Upside, sit in my office and wait for a new job to come in. Wouldn't take long, there were always jobs available, and I'd be free of this stone around my neck, free of responsibility.

Only this stone had a name, and a father who was relying on me. If I got rid of the stone, there'd be another more weighty to take its place: guilt, an emotion I'm far too familiar with. The effort of keeping myself free from it was why I hated responsibility. Too late now, though. It was one or the other. Shit.

The booze worked its magic, sending warm waves of feel-good through me. I needed more of that. A lot more. I poured myself another and it slid down smooth as you like.

"Fucking family," I muttered, and went for the bottle again. "Fucking brothers, always getting into fucking trouble and expecting me to sort it out. Fucking pain magic, fucking Ministry, fucking *everything*."

Someone sat down opposite me, which was odd, because the seat could only hold two and Jake and Pasha were— I looked up. Jake and Pasha weren't there. The bar was almost empty, as was the bottle in front of me. And the face in front of me. Dog grinned like I'd just offered him a bag of sweets, and waved.

I looked round, found that everything was blurred and all the angles looked screwy, squinted and tried again. Everything was still blurry, but I was pretty sure I couldn't see Jake or Pasha anywhere. A slice of panic slid into my gut. On my own, down here where I knew far too little.

Fucking Downsiders.

I pushed on the table and got to my feet, which seemed to have no connection to the rest of me. I almost pitched head-first over the table, but Dog grabbed my arm and held me upright.

"Jake said I got to look after you. Have you been drinking the naughty stuff?"

I peered up, and up again, into his good-natured face and concentrated on not slurring. "Yes, the naughty stuff."

"It's OK. Pasha drinks too much of it sometimes. I know what to do."

He sounded unbearably proud, like a child who has finally learned how to tie his shoelaces.

"That's goo—" I began, and then Dog hefted me on one arm, swung me over his shoulder and left the bar. The door hit my arse as it swung shut.

"Dog, you can put me down." It would be a damn good idea anyway, because all the blood was rushing to my head and I felt confident I was going to throw up all over him any moment.

Dog hesitated. "Are you sure? Pasha always has trouble walking when he's drinking the green stuff. Jake said I had to look after you."

"You can help me, all right? Only your shoulder in my stomach is making me feel sick."

He slid me down and helped me find my feet. His arm was good and solid, just what I needed to help me keep straight. Shame the same couldn't be said for my head.

Dog watched me, an uncertain smile twitching across his face. Probably afraid he'd done something wrong. Shit, I've always been crap with kids, and there was no doubt Dog was just a big kid. He chewed at his lip and followed every move with worried eyes.

"It's all right," I said, trying for that reassuring, almost wheedling tone parents sometimes use with their young children. "You haven't done anything wrong. I just need to walk it off."

His shoulders sagged with relief and the smile was back, the big, sweet-eating one.

"So, where were you taking me?"

"To the match. Pasha said you needed to drink something out of you first."

To the match. The last place I wanted to go, to watch Jake risk her neck, watch her move with a deadly grace that would not be mine. To watch Pasha watch her and try to pretend it didn't matter. I don't know why it had got under my skin so much. She was an emotionally dead bitch who had a way with swords, and Pasha was a fucked-up little monkey with a good line in intimidation, when he had a gun to hand.

I didn't want to see them; I didn't want to be down here, being rained on with what was probably contaminated water, talking to a man who could snap me in half without breaking a sweat but who probably had trouble grasping any word over two syllables long. I didn't want to be in this dark, damp, rotten place any more, and I knew why, too, which was worse. And I even lied to myself about that.

Jealousy, I told myself, plain and simple. Not fear, no, not me. It was jealousy, of course it was. I'd fallen for Jake, bad. Worse, I liked Pasha, most of the time, and I knew damn well how he felt about her. It was in the way their hands never *quite* touched, the way they seemed to communicate without speaking. It was in Pasha's eyes and the twitch of Jake's mouth and I didn't want to have to see it. I'd rather go into the castle alone than see it. Well, maybe that was going too far, but I didn't want to go to the match. It had absolutely nothing to do with fear of being found wanting in the courage department.

"Dog, do you know where the Ministry men come down?"

He looked around quickly, as though afraid we'd be caught talking about it. "Yes, but Jake says I'm not allowed there. Bad men, she says. Bad men are looking for you too, all over. Have to keep you away, but they won't come in this far. Jake made sure."

I looked up at his earnest face, scrubbed and ruddy. Bad men. "Yes, they are, only that's my way home. I – I don't want to go to the match, Dog. I need somewhere to get my head straight, do you understand? Somewhere to think."

A smile split his face. "Dog knows just the place. Oh yes, a grand place for thinking. Come on."

For a moment I thought he was going to run, but he seemed to remember himself just before he took me off my feet and we made our way along the slippery cobbles, through rain that dazzled in the lights, dripped down my neck, cold as my heart. Dog chattered contentedly about the matches, and Jake, and how he'd once found a puppy and wanted to keep it. "And they said that puppy was with me just how I am with Jake. That's why I'm Dog. I like the name. It's mine. The puppy is called Freckles. She's my friend, and she's so fluffy and Jake said I could keep her if I fed her and looked after her, and I do . . ."

I let his words fade into the background and tried to concentrate on which way we were going. I thought I recognised a shop, then a corner. The match arena bulked behind the ramshackle rooftops, but we moved at an angle to it, so I was confident Dog wasn't leading me astray.

Right up to the point when he stopped outside a temple. Its whitewashed walls were a dingy grey, streaked from the rain. The door was open and Dog moved towards it, but I stopped him with a hand on his arm. "Not here."

Dog's brow furrowed. "Why not? Good place to think, nice and quiet. I come here all the time, to think. I think better in the temple. The Goddess helps me." He hulked over me and I could sense disapproval in the set of his rather large shoulders.

"Fine. It'll be quiet, as you say."

The doorway enveloped me in silky darkness punctuated by

a beam of light bringing sparks from dust particles. Dog had to bend almost double to get through the opening across the lobby. I followed, ducking somewhat less, and entered the temple. Instantly I was taken back to my boyhood. To hours spent kneeling next to my mother as she prayed, priests and acolytes gliding silently along the aisles, offering practical help and impractical prayer. The sounds, the velvety shushes as feet shuffled over the embroidered runner, the murmurs of a priest imparting advice, the mutter of someone's desperate prayer. The smell of the burning herbs, a mellow scent as if the herbs' sole purpose in growing was to be burned and smell sweet. The way the scent could stamp a picture in your heart when you smelled it again. The way light slanted through the dark from the old-fashioned flame lanterns, cunningly directed by covers to pick out the face of the Goddess on the mural, and the faces of the statues. The statues themselves, of the three martyrs and the four saints, whose feet I should kiss in turn, each with their own chant attached. Chant the chant, pray for their souls before I prayed for myself. Nican, patron saint of many things, including lost children, stared down at me with stony eyes. I stopped in front of him, wishing beyond wishing that I believed in him, that he could help me find Amarie. The words to his prayer that my mother had taught me came back, unbidden, unwanted, unbelieved in. *Nican, see me here at your feet, help me find what I have lost, both in my heart and soul and in my life. By losing you I have lost myself, and I would come back to you now.*

I turned away from his plaster face, the way his eyes seemed to accuse me; ignored the rest of the statues, to Dog's consternation; and made straight for a pew. My head was clearing, but that didn't help. Nothing helped, or was likely to. I looked ahead to the blocky altar and the painting that dominated the wall above. The Goddess, looking down on us.

All temples have a painting of her inside their domes, but this one was different from all those I'd seen growing up. Usually she's looking benign and a bit constipated, surrounded by flowers and birds and pretty things. In this one she was anything but benign, and there was nothing pretty about any of it. It was primal, raw. Maybe what the Goddess had stood for before the Ministry had sanitised her, I'm not sure. The story of the Goddess and the tiger. It had been one of Ma's favourites, but had fallen out of favour among the priests.

Sacrifice, that's what Ma always said the story was about. The Goddess sacrificed part of herself to the tiger to save us. Fed him her hand to appease him, to sate his hunger so he wouldn't hunt us. I never saw that; what I saw and heard was the guilt I was supposed to feel about it, drummed into me, into everyone. Besides, her hand didn't sate the tiger. He still stalks us, only now we call him Death, or Namrat. As a sacrifice, pretty useless. Why should I feel guilty, or grateful, that the Goddess had done it?

Ma's death had made it worse. I was too angry with the

Goddess to even glance at a temple as I passed. That death had changed my beliefs, the faith I'd been brought up with. Sacrifice became guilt, goodness became cupidity, faith became stupidity. It still was. Faith didn't stop bad things or help good things to happen. It was brainwashing, just as Azama was doing to those girls. If you believe, if you're good, never mind how crap this life is, you'll get a nice one after you die. It was a sop, a cosh to keep the underclasses manageable.

I stared at the painting a while longer, at the vivid colours, the look on the Goddess's face as the tiger bit off her hand. As a boy I'd always felt such guilt. Now all I felt was a dull fury, that this load of lies was used to keep people from seeing what was going on around them, that the Ministry used it to try to keep everyone in line. To ignore what was going on around them.

When people are satisfied things will improve, even if it's only after they're dead, they tend not to rebel as much. So the Ministry had changed the story, changed the message. The Goddess was no longer about sacrificing herself so our lives would be better, now religion was about behaving well so she'd greet you with a pat on the head after Namrat paid his call.

I stood up abruptly, banging my knees on part of the pew, and hurried outside. The temple had been a bad idea. It always was, always left a bitter taste of bile and betrayal in my mouth. Even the matches would be better than this. Besides, I had someplace to be.

The temple, the painting full of life and death and visceral pain, had decided me. Not for the Goddess, but for me, for Perak and the promise I'd made Ma to look after him. I could go back to a lifetime of gentle reproach in Dendal's face, to knowing I'd let my brother's daughter stay down here, but if I did, I'd be dead of drink pretty soon.

So I went to find Jake and Pasha. Braced myself to go into the castle and face magic, my own and others'. Not for goodness, or the Goddess, not even for Perak or Amarie or because it was the right thing to do.

I went for the sake of my liver.

I got Dog to lead the way to the arena. He wasn't happy with me, I could tell. The chatter had stopped and he wouldn't look at me. That was fine: I wasn't much in the mood for talking myself. Being backed into a corner will do that to me. The steady drip of rain, the black streets and Dog's sullen air suited my mood to perfection.

The thump and thud of the crowd stomping reverberated through my feet and chest long before we arrived. By the time we got there the noise was indescribable, even outside. Dog left me by Jake's door with a morose, pathetic look, like one of his heroes had just let him down, but it wasn't Dog I was here to save.

I didn't bother to knock but strode straight in, and wished I hadn't. I had clearly interrupted something. An argument by the look of things. Jake's jaw was clenched tight as she leaned on the sideboard that held the booze. She pinched her lips together and squeezed her eyes shut. My entrance cut Pasha off in mid-something. Not a tirade exactly, because his voice was soft. He stood behind her, one hand reaching for her shoulder. All I heard was "Jake, for the Goddess's sake, won't you just—" and then he saw me and snapped his mouth shut. By the time I was fully through the door, he'd thrown himself into a chair and was studying the fight through the glass with infinite and exaggerated care.

I took a hesitant step towards Jake, and tried not to feel satisfied that there was some sort of break, some chink in their relationship where I could insert myself. I kept my voice low, so Pasha couldn't hear the words, though he shot me a look that could have cut through steel just the same. "Are you all right?"

Jake took a deep breath and looked upwards, as though calling on the Goddess for strength. "Fine." But she didn't sound fine, and the way her lips twisted and she blinked rapidly, the way her hands gripped at the sideboard, she looked *far* from fine. She wiped her mouth on her sleeve, took a deep breath and grabbed for her swords. Her hands shook as she strapped them on, but her face was still now, as still as the Goddess in the painting, and as full of promised violence. She stalked past me and out of the door. Once she was gone, I let go a breath I hadn't realised I'd been holding. Because with her in the room, even angry and closed off, even with two swords at her waist, I wanted her. Not my usual sort of want either – I wanted to make it all right for her, better for her.

Pasha looked up at me from under hooded lids and he knew. Of course he did – his kind of magic. A subtle and invisible wall appeared between us. He sat up from his hunch, leaned forward on his knees and studied the arena, his eyes flicking back and forth as though seeking a weakness.

I don't know why, but I felt compelled to explain myself. "Pasha, I—"

He didn't look at me apart from a brief glance, but his hands were between his knees, twisting, pinching, hurting. I'd never seen him do it openly before, though he must have done something for those flashes of magic where he seemed to see inside my head.

"Don't," he said. "You don't know what the fuck you're getting into. You don't know her. You think you want her, love her. I've seen it before, in the eyes of other men, in their heads. They see the grace, see her pretend to smile and they think they know her. Think they want her. But they don't. I know men like you, Rojan. They want to say they have, that they were the one to get her, they were the one to get past her wall. We all have walls, don't we? You and your cynicism, her and her ice-queen act. A wall to keep everyone away, outside, so they won't see the fear. Those men, *you*, never see past that exterior; you want her not for her, but for yourselves. You think you love her, but you don't even know what that means. Would you do anything for her to be happy? What about letting her dice with death out there? Would you let her risk dying for her to be happy, or would you try to make her stop, and kill her inside in the process? Would you take her Upside, away from everything that's important to her, or would you stay down here, for ever? Would you forbear to—" He broke off with a shake of his head, as though he'd almost let something slip he shouldn't. "How far would you go?"

That's when he looked at me, with eyes dark and round with emotion, and I knew just how far he'd gone. Further than he wanted to, but not as far as he would go, if he had to. I didn't know how to answer. We both stared out at the sandy arena, stained and spotted with blood. Finally, because I sensed he really needed an answer, I said, "I don't know. Women have never been ... I've never been good partner material. I don't know if I have what it takes, or how good I'd be. Piss-poor on past performance. But she makes me want to try."

Pasha's head hung low over his knees, but his head bobbed in a nod. He seemed about to say something else, but the music changed. Jake's music. Pasha leapt to his feet and planted his hands on the glass. Purple welts criss-crossed his fingers – where he'd used his magic. "That's not right."

I got up and peered through the glass, at the crowd as they began to chant, to stomp their feet and generally behave as though they wanted to make the building collapse. "What isn't?"

Jake made her way down the ramp. Pasha was right, something was up. Gone was the easy grace, the carefully still face, the assessing eyes. She moved jerkily, like a puppet on a string. Her gaze flicked our way for a heartbeat and away again. She was trying her damnedest to keep her face still, but her wide, twitchy eyes gave her away. She was terrified.

"Pasha?"

He pressed himself against the window, as though he could help her just by wanting to, by passing it through the glass. "I – she comes down second. Always, she comes down second. Fuck, oh fuck. It's a Ministry job."

"A Ministry job? What do you mean?"

He spared me a withering glance. "I told you this was mostly sham, right? This is the bit that's not sham. One person out there is really going to die."

"What?" I pulled him away, but he shook my hand off and pressed his hands back on to the glass. The music changed again. The singer's voice was raw, wailing about a betrayer's kiss, of Namrat demanding a soul, and things much, much darker. It sent a shiver along my spine.

A figure appeared at the top of the ramp, a dishevelled, bruised-looking man. His clothes were ripped and bloodstained, his arms shackled in front of him. Someone unlocked them, shoved a sword in his hand and ran. The swordsman looked down at the blade and gave it a practice swish. A demonic grin spread from his lips, seemed to alter his whole face. Made him look as though he was the kind of guy who didn't give a shit what he had to do, he was going to do it, and probably enjoy it too.

"Pasha, just what—"

"A punishment," he said, so low I barely heard him. "Don't you have them Upside? What do they do when someone breaks the law?"

"The Ministry holds a trial. Sort of. The priests oversee it and supposedly pray for guidance. I can't remember the last time there was a not-guilty verdict. It's a crock of shit. You get arrested, you're guilty."

The rumpled man swaggered down the ramp, the demonic grin seeming the only part of him now, the only part I could see. I'd seen that sort of look before. Normally right before someone got their guts laid out on the floor of some seedy bar, or down a dark and lonely alley.

"And what happens to the guilty?" Pasha's eyes flicked between the two combatants as they sized each other up.

"Depends. Prison, mostly; sometimes they hang them. They say some of them end up down here, though I never believed that." I'd never been sure which was worse.

"Well, it's true. Some of them do, and we have some of our own. But we have no prison. No open trials. When they're found guilty, they disappear. To Azama, to the mages almost certainly." Pasha's breath fogged the glass. "A nice, easy, still-alive body that no one will miss. But sometimes, with the worst crimes, they want to 'set an example'. That's when they send them here. For public execution, in the name of the Goddess."

My stomach went cold. Public execution had been banned many years ago Upside, way before Downside was sealed, though it still happened behind closed doors. This – this was barbaric. Jake was peerless with a sword. The man would be cut to pieces in moments, no matter the way his face was twisted. I couldn't see why Pasha was worried.

"And this is a problem for Jake because . . .?"

His gaze slid towards me and it wasn't just withering this time. If looks could kill, I'd have both Jake's swords rammed somewhere very intimate. Pasha snorted, dismissing me. I didn't know this place, or her, like he did, that gesture told me.

The prisoner and Jake squared up against each other and waited for the signal: the music stopping. As the last bar faded away, the prisoner lunged for Jake. She parried with one sword and feinted with the other. Yet it was all half-hearted. Her blades didn't come within a foot of the prisoner. Whilst I'd seen her fight before, and had been seriously impressed, now it looked like she'd forgotten how to attack.

I wanted to ask Pasha, but was sure I'd only get a sneer in return. I thought back, and back. The first time I'd been here, Pasha had said Jake never killed anyone, accidentally or on purpose. Two hundred fights and no deaths, a score she was proud of. Only, would that matter now? Surely she'd done an execution before, if this was common?

"Never done a Ministry job," Pasha said, reading my mind. I saw how he was twisting one of his fingers, just enough to hurt, and I could almost feel him rummaging around in my head. "Never. This thing, her with her swords, it's all a sham, a fake, a bit of flash to look good, to cover up what's under-neath . . . her swords are the wall that she hides behind. She's good at looking good, at making it look real, but you think she could really beat all these guys? She was damned lucky against the Storad, but that's it – luck, flash, a bit of panache and a showy way with swords, with the crowd. She's not a fighter, she's a . . . I don't know. An acrobat, an entertainer, gives the crowd what they want, a bit of blood, a hint of danger, the chance to scream off their anger. Half these men could kill her in a heartbeat: too strong for her. She's quick, and smart, so it looks good. But it's flash, that's all. Besides, no killing, that's her thing. Even when we rescue the girls, no killing is the rule. She won't. She won't."

That last was a drawn-out moan. "They know, Azama knows we're on to him, that we might try for him, that we know where he is. No hope of keeping it secret after the Jorrin thing. He knows, and he's arranged this." Pasha shut his eyes and rested his head on the glass. "Only she might even do it. Orders of the Goddess, that's what a trial verdict is, the priests say so. She'll do anything to please the Goddess, anything, but . . ."

"And if she doesn't?"

"Then she'll die. That's the rule of the execution matches. Only one comes out alive." He smacked a hand on the window with enough force to make it shudder, and turned away. Glass rattled on glass behind me as he poured a drink, but I didn't take my eyes off the match, off Jake. She defended well enough, but still, her blade never came close to hitting the prisoner. What she thought she'd achieve, I don't know. Maybe time to think.

The prisoner's grin had got wider all the while; he knew, I could see by the look on his face. He was *gloating*. A crack sounded behind me, muffled and weak, but I knew what it was. I didn't turn.

"He's a plant," Pasha murmured. "Been offered a pardon if he kills her." Another crack, and this time Pasha let out a moan of pain. I still didn't turn – I knew what I'd see and I didn't want to be reminded that I had power to intervene and wasn't. Would the pulse pistol work through glass? I'd never tried. There were other things I could do, only – the sound of a glass breaking and a breathy scream – only they'd hurt. A lot. The black was there, waiting for me to sink into my magic, go too far, fall in so I couldn't come back. It was waiting for Pasha too, but he didn't care. I kind of admired that, in a horrified way. *How far would you go?*

Jake was on the back foot in the arena and the prisoner had got past her guard enough to slice a bloody rent in her allover. The crowd screamed its disapproval as her blood seeped out rhythmically, dripping down her side and on to the sand, mingling with the blood already there. With a glance in our direction, a look of apology in her eyes mixed with something like relief, Jake made a misstep, staggered off balance and fell

213

to one knee. Subtle, but unmistakable. Deliberate. The crowd howled as the prisoner pounced, his sword high, ready to slice her clean in two.

Just as the sword reached its apex, the prisoner stumbled, his eyes wide. The sword fell from his hand and his fingers reached up to his cheeks, scrabbled there as though someone had poured acid on him. Jake's eyes were round and horrified, her swords loose in her hands. The crowd fell disturbingly silent. The only noise was the prisoner's screams. Steam began to curl out of his nose and mouth.

"Pasha." I had to swallow past the lump in my throat. "Pasha, what did you do?"

I dragged my eyes away from the arena because the sick feeling in my stomach told me exactly what he'd done and I didn't want to see it play out. Pasha sat cross-legged on the floor, huddled over his twisted, bleeding hand. The glass he'd used to cut himself lay scattered around him. Behind me was a popping noise, and the sound of the crowd saying, "Ahhh" as one. A satisfied yet disgusted noise, like you hear in the temples when they make a sacrifice. However Pasha had done it, and I had my suspicions, the prisoner was dead.

Pasha looked up at me with sullen, sneering eyes, daring me to say I didn't understand. "I did what I had to, which is more than you did. Too afraid of your own magic. Too much of a fucking coward to use it unless you've no other choice, too fond of your own skin."

214

I moved over to him and crouched down. "You're probably right. Let's get that hand—"

I leaned over to look at the mess of his hand but he caught me by surprise and lashed out with a foot. It caught me on the ankle and I flailed backwards. Pasha was on me in a second, smacking me with his good hand. It was only then that I realised he was crying. I grabbed for his hand and caught it in my own, held it fast and tried to stop him. His shirtsleeve twisted away from his wrist, and I saw it. The brand mark, black jagged lines interlinking in an A.

I dropped his hand from nerveless fingers. I'd seen that brand before. Pasha saw what I was looking at and wrenched his arm away, smoothing down the sleeve so the brand was covered, then got up off my chest and turned away.

"Pasha, I—"

But Pasha wasn't about to be reasoned with, or stopped. He was too far gone for that. He whipped back round and his dark eyes bored into mine, his face hard with hate. "Shut up. Just shut up before you embarrass yourself with your ignorance. They wanted me to be one of them, all right? They wanted me to, to – to gather the power. By hurting others. Not just a little, either. The mages told those girls that pain was their redemption into the Goddess's blessedness, that they were only doing all of, of that, the pain, so the Goddess would love them again. That the mages did it because they *loved* them, and wanted them to be saved, and the girls believed them. Believed that the mages were saving them, that the mages loved them and this was how they showed it, how they showed love. They want you to, as well. That's why you're here, that's why they brought you with the lure of your niece. That's why her. And you'll do it too, I think."

Something seemed to break in him then, the hate dissolving into fear and shame and pity, his voice dropping so I could barely hear it. "Only I couldn't. Not that my magic couldn't, I couldn't, because I could see it all in their heads, could feel it with them. I was twelve, and my parents were so *proud*. I'm from Upside, just like you. We lived just under Clouds, close enough to see it and want it. My parents thought that for me to serve the Ministry was an honour. It might have been. But I could hear those girls, in my head all the time, could hear all their thoughts, how they all got twisted up till they believed what they were told was true. Normality is only a matter of what you're used to, and after a time it's normal to them. Not as much time as you'd think, either. That's the worst part. They think it's normal. I couldn't do it, and when I couldn't, the mages, they, they ... Jake saved me. She saved me from Azama and the Jorrin brothers and I'd do anything to see her safe."

"Even use your magic to kill someone?"

He scraped at his face to scrub away tears and his eyes became cold. "Yes, oh yes. My Major, see, in the brain. See it all, feel it all, if I want, even if I don't want. I can make it grow in them too, make it build up enough till ... I'd do worse. Much, much worse. *Anything*. You have no idea what

216

she saved me from. No idea, and I'd kill every last person I found, if I had to, if I could save her in return. Only she won't let me."

We sat and stared at each other for what seemed like long, long minutes. I couldn't imagine being beholden to someone for something that big, or ever wanting to be. Yet Pasha seemed proud of it.

When the door banged open, we both jumped. Jake strode in, blood-splattered and seriously pissed off. I could tell by the way the swords weren't sheathed but pointed at me. It isn't a good feeling, being at the end of a sword and knowing that the person on the other end could beat you in their sleep, and despite Pasha's protestations that her talent was all show, all flash, she was damned well better than me. It feels even worse when you haven't got a sword of your own, only a weapon you loathe using and is non-lethal anyway. I slid my hand into my pocket – gingerly, because it was still pretty fucked up from thumping Jake's floor – just in case.

The swords hovered an inch from my nose as Jake looked me up and down. She cast a spare glance at Pasha, looked away and then back, staring down at his bleeding hand like she'd never seen one before. Everything seemed to drain from her face – emotion, blood, you name it. The swords dropped down to her sides.

"It was you?" She shook her head, as though trying to shake reality from her, to deny it was possible. Her lips twisted with words that couldn't seem to make themselves heard. She seemed to gather herself then, and the swords came back up, pointing at Pasha this time. "You killed him. It was you."

Pasha's face scrunched up, more monkey-like than ever. His eyes were dark with a sort of pleading, as though willing her to understand, but when the swords came up so did his temper. "I did it for you! He was going to kill you and you were going to let him. Well, I wouldn't let him. And I won't let you kill yourself like that. I can't; you've asked it of me too long, and I can't watch it, watch you killing yourself. Not any more."

He staggered to his feet and took a step forward, so that Jake's swords were just touching his shirt. She wouldn't look at him but kept her eyes on the shaking points of her blades.

That seemed to incense Pasha even more. "I know why you do these matches. Do you know how much it *burns* me to know?" He barked a bitter laugh when she flinched at that. "You think I wouldn't see it, know it? That you go into every match hoping this is the one that will kill you, only you're too fucking proud to just let someone beat you? That the only reason you don't just take your sword to your own throat is because the Goddess says it's a sin? You're good at hiding it, oh yes. But you can't hide from me, Jake. Not from me. And you might just as well stick that fucking sword straight through me rather than expect me to sit back and let it happen when you won't kill a man sent to murder you because of some fucked-up notion of what the Goddess wants from you."

By the time he'd done, his chest was heaving with the venom in his voice or the emotion behind it. He'd kept those dark, sparking eyes on her the whole time, but bar one flinch she hadn't moved. She didn't look up at him, or even acknowledge his words. The only reaction was a tiny trembling of her swords' tips and the tightness of her mouth. Until he went to move around the swords to reach for her, to touch her.

In a heartbeat one blade was flat against his throat and the other hovered between his legs.

"Best you went." If there was a tremor in her voice I didn't hear it. She was all ice. "Right now."

"Jake—"

She looked at him finally, but there was nothing behind her eyes, none of the warmth that had been there before when they'd spoken. "Right. Now."

Pasha's jaw jutted defiantly but he moved back, soft and slow, until he was at the door. She lowered the swords, but not by much.

"Please, won't you just—"

She turned her back on him, on his words and the look on his face, the way it crumpled when he realised she really meant it. He flicked his gaze my way, but all I could do was shrug sympathetically – and that was pretty much a lie. He knew her better than me, right? Obviously not. It was hard not to be the tiniest bit smug. I think he knew it too; his hand would still be hurting him, so if he wanted to know what I was thinking, it wouldn't be a problem. With a last, despairing look at Jake's back, he left, slamming the door as he went.

As soon as the door was shut, Jake dropped her swords. They clanged against the floor. I couldn't see her face, but her hands splayed out across the glass that looked on to the arena where another fight was already under way, to the crowd's noisy delight. She was standing in just the spot Pasha had been and her fingers caressed the smudge-marks his hands had made.

"Jake, I—"

"Shut up." Her voice was small and soft, almost inaudible over the roar of the crowd above. "Please, Rojan, just shut up."

I took my life in my hands but I had no idea what to do or say, other than try to get her back to normal. Well, what normal was for her anyway. "I will, just as soon as you sit down so I can stitch that cut. You're losing a fair bit of blood."

She looked at me over her shoulder, surprised, and gave me a wan smile. "Not yet. Azama is going to be pissed off that I'm not dead. He had every reason to believe I would be, and I'd rather not be anywhere obvious for him to find me, us. I'm surprised he's not here already, but maybe I caught him off guard. He almost certainly knows you're with me – he'll have been watching who comes in and out of the arena – which means the Ministry men looking for you know too. They'll be crawling all over this place soon enough, and I shouldn't have taken the time to—" She cut herself off with a grimace. "We need to go. Now. So first we need to find somewhere safe to hole up."

She had a point, so I grabbed Pasha's little box of sutures and dressings, she gathered all she needed and we left, being careful that no one saw us, or at least followed us.

Where we ended up was possibly the shittiest part of the 'Pit I'd seen yet.

"Alley" was too good a word for the passageway she led me down. A wall had caved in and timbers fallen, leaving a tented gap that I only just managed to squeeze through. There was no door at the other end, just a blank hole into what I suppose I must call a room. It had some crumbling walls and most of a roof, and the floor was still there, in places at least. Jake lit a small lamp, and I wished she hadn't. A pile of gently mouldering mats lay in the corner, stinking the place up. The stains were possibly blood, or possibly weren't.

"Nice place."

Jake managed a tight smile but her eyes were full of bewildered hurt that she tried to cover with a breezy manner. "You think? I think it's a shit pit, but they won't find us here."

She hung the lamp from a jutting piece of roof and found a rotting box to sit on, so I could reach the wound. She fumbled with the bindings for her allover, but got it finally and slid the leather down over her undershirt. The stitches I'd put in previously stood proud, but at least the cut seemed to be healing nicely. Finally she had the allover down to her waist and leaned forwards, her arms with their covering of soft leather windings dangling between her knees.

The wound ripped along her ribs and gouged a line along the side of her torso underneath. "I'll have to cut your shirt to get at it," I warned.

All I got in return was a terse nod, but that was enough. After a rummage through Pasha's box, I found a pair of scissors and cut away the blood-soaked linen so I could reach the wound. I was careful not to touch her at all.

The wound was starting to clot, though it still oozed blood. Jake laid her head on her forearms as I swabbed the area clear but she didn't flinch. I kept my silence until I had the needle and suture ready. To be frank, it was a wonder I'd managed to keep quiet till now. There were too many questions whizzing around my head, though the oddly intimate nature of what I was doing kind of distracted me for a while. When it came to actually stitching, though . . .

Jake hissed in a breath when I pushed the needle through, but didn't flinch.

To take my mind off what I was doing, and because I had a sudden pang of guilt, I said, "Pasha was just—"

Her jerk almost pulled the needle out of my hands. Her head came up off her arms and she looked me square in the eye. "Pasha betrayed me. He interfered, he betrayed the Goddess and my – *our* beliefs. He betrayed everything our friendship was based on. Everything."

Her eyes were red-rimmed but dry, and full of an icy anger. I looked back down at the needle when I answered.

"He did it because he didn't want you to die. That man was

sent to kill you. Azama arranged it, Pasha said. I'd have done what Pasha did too, if I'd had the guts."

"Everyone tries to kill me in the arena! The matches are sham, true. But they try anyway. They all want to be the one to beat me, to get past my guard. If I'm good at one thing, it's not letting anyone kill me. It's not lack of guts for you to do the right thing, or to let me handle things my way. I let Pasha off easy, because it was him, and he knows it."

I forbore to tell her what Pasha had said, about her just being flashy, that her swords were her wall against the world, against Pasha and everyone who tried to reach her. It didn't seem prudent. But maybe by this point I had a death wish, because the next words that fell out of my mouth were "Is it true what he said, about you wanting to die?"

Luckily she didn't go for her sword, though her tone was as sharp. "What's it to you?"

Maybe everything. I didn't want her to die. I wanted to make it so she wanted to live. With me. I would have rather died myself than say that out loud, so instead I said, "Because if you're still coming with me to the castle, I'd like to know you aren't going to take any stupid risks."

I was another three stitches along, and waiting for the inevitable explosion, before she answered.

"I won't take any stupid risks. I want to stop Azama. I can't do that if I'm dead."

"Glad to hear it. But if you won't kill him, or let me kill him, how will you stop him?"

Her mouth curved up in a cat-like smile, as though Azama was the unsuspecting mouse she had in her sights. "Oh, there's plenty of ways to stop him without him being dead. Death's too quick and easy for a bastard like that anyway. I've got plans for Azama."

Chapter Thirteen

It took me about for ever to fall asleep. Not just because of the rancid smell of the mattress either, but from too many questions crowding my brain. If Pasha had been right, how did Azama know we were planning something? Because he'd been watching the Jorrin brothers' place? Why had he warned us he knew by sending the prisoner to kill Jake rather than just getting us all? Was he bringing me here to use me, was that why he'd targeted Amarie? Were we about to walk straight into a trap? And just why the fuck had Jake threatened Pasha for saving her life? I didn't have any answers, but the questions kept my brain fizzing long after my body begged for sleep.

The rhythmic tap and swish of Jake's feet on the stone floor as she went through her sword practice finally soothed me. And her: all the tension seemed to run from her muscles until her face was calm, the still mask I'd come to know. I wondered

if I'd ever really know what lay behind it. I watched her practice with lazy, half-lidded eyes. Fluid as a cat, no hint of
favouring her wounds, rhythmic and hypnotic. Beautiful and
deadly.

Next thing I knew, Jake was prodding at my shoulder with
one of her scabbards. I don't think she'd slept; her eyes were
bloodshot and her cherry-red hair, normally impeccably
bound back, now curled in loose tendrils around her face. I sat
up with a grimace and scrubbed at my eyes to try to get them
to open properly.

"Time to go." She nodded at the floor beside me, to a plate
piled with, oh Goddess, with *bacon*. The fat, crispy smell of it
woke me fully. It was get up and eat or drown in my own
drool. I got up.

Jake tapped her foot and fidgeted with her swords while I
shoved the bacon in as fast as I could. I doubt the Goddess's
tits could have tasted better. The instant the last bite had
passed my lips Jake was off, and I ran to catch her.

She called a cage once we were outside and we rattled off
over the housetops, the chains weaving between towers and
raindrops. Instead of looking down, I kept my eyes on her. She
seemed to have shrunk somehow. Not in height, in personal-
ity. Before, her sheer presence was enough to stun a man
stupid. Now she seemed . . . I don't know, younger. Unsure of
herself, almost like part of her was missing. She looked help-
less. I wanted to tell her it would be all right, put a
comforting arm across her shoulders.

226

I was a good boy and kept my hands to myself. Mainly because I'm quite fond of all my bits being in the places they're meant to be rather than on the floor, unattached and messy with blood. So instead I said, "Are you sure just the two of us will—"

"Yes." A dark look from under her brows, a tightening of her lips, made me think pushing it was a bad idea.

"OK. So, we have a plan?"

"We have a plan; didn't I say? The mages eat well, and they make sure the girls do too, they make sure everyone does down here. So the girls last longer, see? And everyone else thinks everything is all right. Carcasses from the slaughterhouse, some of them go straight up to the castle. Today, you and I are slaughtermen. We take the carcasses to the duly appointed place and hand them over. Then we don't return with the others, but follow. There's a way in. There has to be, and that's the best way I can think of to find where it is."

"Then what?" I didn't like the sound of this, but what option was there?

Jake frowned up at me like I was stupid. "Then you use your magic to find where your niece is. We can go from there."

Fabulous. My hand was still throbbing from last time and I hadn't felt my index finger for a while. Maybe I should try somewhere else to hurt myself, but where? I wanted to keep my legs ready to run. "Just how sure are you that Amarie is anywhere near Azama?"

"P— he said that you knew she was in the main keep, in the tower. Makes sense that's where Azama'd be. It's still a big area to look through. I was hoping – well, I was hoping maybe you could track magic, seeing as you're the only magic user we have now."

Other words seemed to form ghosts on her lips so I could almost hear them. "Because that's what Pasha was going to try to do." But the words stayed unsaid.

"I can try," I said. "Have to be really close for it to work, though, within feet. It's not like tracking people." Like I'd ever actually done it before. I mean, I know the *theory*, kind of. But I've never traced magic. At least partly because, again in theory, there shouldn't be anyone Upside using magic to trace. Except me and Dendal and the drunkard who slept outside the office, and my once-a-year-or-less-if-I-could-get-away-with-it habit didn't really count.

"Exactly. That's why we could never try before. Without a tracker, it would have taken months to scour the whole castle, get close enough to trace, and months without getting caught. Too risky, for everyone. But if we find Amarie, then he shouldn't be too far. He keeps them close, mostly."

I knew we were nearly there because of the smell of shit. The cage jolted to a stop and the boy lowered us to the street. Odd, this time I barely noticed the drop.

Jake led the way in silence down through the boarded-up shop and dark corridor to the slaughterhouse. I tried not to think that going via a death-house was an omen.

Darin wasn't happy to see us, and I can't say I blame him. He bustled us past his real stockmen and into his office, where he provided us both with the protective suits the men were wearing. They had a rubbery sort of coating that felt odd under my fingers.

"Keeps the blood out," Darin said.

Nice.

Jake managed to find a way to stash her swords in the baggy suit so they weren't too obtrusive, and with a few quick twists her hair was up and bundled under a floppy hat. At a swift glance, she was just a stock boy. My pulse pistol went into an inside pocket. Jake looked at it with avid curiosity, but she didn't ask and I didn't say.

Darin took us through the dark door and into the stink of death. The room stood empty, but at Darin's quick nod one of the stock boys, with a suspicious glance at us, went to fetch in the first of the cows.

The next hour or so, I kept to the back of the room and tried not to look. Or hear. Or smell. The bacon swirled in my stomach, maybe in protest at what was happening to its bovine brethren. The first few cows were reluctant but not overly so. Yet, even though the stockmen knew what they were doing, and did it as quickly and humanely as possible, the rest of the cows knew. The whole thing descended into shit and blood and bawling animals. Even Jake found it easier not to look, at least until the beasts were dead. Once the noise had died away she pitched in to help gut and dress the carcasses. Me, I've never been good with blades. Especially after that incident with the angry husband and the bastard sword. So I kept out of the way and in short order all was ready.

Jake came to find me and looked me over with a critical eye. She appeared more like a stockman than ever at first glance, the splash of blood lending her an authenticity that she took pains to reproduce on my protective suit.

Another doorway led out the back, into a cobbled yard surrounded on three sides by stock pens, each groaning with cows and a few pigs. How was it so little of this meat made it Upside? Or maybe it did, if you could afford it. If you could afford it, you probably kept quiet about it.

We loaded the carcasses on to an open-backed cart and jumped on after them, settling on the benches that ran along each side. The driver – one of the mages' goons, Darin had whispered – fired up the cantankerous engine after a lot of cursing and shot out into the quiet of a street that wasn't awake yet. The only other person in sight was a drunk slumped in a doorway with a bottle just about to fall out of his limp hand.

We spluttered down the road, the cart's engine coughing like an old man with pneumonia. The springs had gone, so we jounced over the cobbles and potholes, jarring bones and bruising backsides. Once we turned off the main street, Jake sat up straight, her eyes sharp as she kept track of our route. From what I could make out, Darin and his stockmen kept this secret with their lives, until now. It still might cost them that if we were caught.

I'd thought we'd make for some part of the wall that surrounded the castle, but the driver turned off the street before we could see it properly past the towers. Jake stood up, frowning as we bounced along an alley so narrow that I'd have lost fingers if I put them between the cart and the wall. The driver pulled to a squealing stop as the alley ended in a wall faced with dressed stone. One of the stockmen gestured to Jake to sit, but other than that they all pretended we weren't there.

The driver leaned forward and rummaged under the board that held the controls and then tossed a black bundle back to us. Hoods. The other stockmen hurried to put them over their heads, and at an urgent, whispered word we followed suit. Something metal ground along rust by the sounds of it, and the driver moved the cart forwards. I braced for the impact, but when a gruff voice said we could take the hoods off, the alley was gone and a deep blackness had taken its place, punctuated by Glow globes set far apart so everything was flickering shadows and pools of brightness.

"What the—"

Again, a gesture from one of the stockmen, indicating rather urgently that I should stay quiet. I shut up and kept alert as we moved along a tunnel. It was old, I could tell that. The stones it was dressed with were worn smooth, the same size and composition as the ones in the castle's curtain wall. I thought back hard to the stories Ma used to tell us – well, me. Perak never actually listened. Even then, such stories were frowned upon by the Ministry, which is probably why Ma liked to tell them.

Among the tales of derring-do, of the castle and the warlord who'd built the city out of nothing but holding a handy pass between two rich nations that hated each other, of his sons and grandsons who'd been cleverer and craftier, I recalled a story of a siege. The two neighbouring nations had decided that Mahala was making too much money as their middleman, and secretly made a trade agreement. Yet they couldn't pass the mountains except in range of the walls of the castle. Again in secret, they amassed what armies they could from nations more used to hunting, farming and trade. As one marched from the south, so the other came from the north. The castle was trapped between two armies, or so it seemed. But what the foreigners hadn't understood was the basic nature of our people, at least as it was then, before the Ministry toppled the mage King and set its regimentation over everything, turned us into traders just like the rest. Even thirty years ago, a man couldn't properly call himself man unless he'd served his stint in the army, learned bow and sword and horse.

Back in the days of the warlord and his sons and grandsons, the way of the blade was every man's right, and his duty too. To protect the city and the small, high pastures that fed it – pastures that we'd later built on in our arrogance. Yet then, to fight for it, with it, to be part of it was a thing every man aspired to. But not to fight stupidly, or without forethought. No, that wasn't our way. As the warlord had once famously said, "The Goddess gave us arms that we might wield a blade, legs that we might steer our horse. But she gave us brains so that we might stab the enemy in the back before it comes to outright war."

Brains are our birthright. And not just any brains, but the ability to be fucking sneaky. That's what won us our power then, and brains are what get us our power now. The same kind of brains: how to twist something until we find out what its best use is, and then use it till it bleeds. These days it's the ability to invent things the rest of the world wants, even if it means stealing the idea, snuffing out the competition and stiffing your customers for as much money as you can.

Back then, being a sneaky bastard meant you had tunnels that led right from your keep that weren't only well hidden, they were nigh-on impossible to find. And incidentally led to the rear of exactly where any army stupid enough to try and besiege you would pitch its camp. Even then, the warlord hadn't gone straight there and attacked. Oh no. "Sneaky bastard" wasn't an apt description for him. "Sneaky, devious and downright underhand bastard" was more like it.

I always loved the stories about him. This was one that had stayed with me, all this time. Because when the two armies had camped and sent forward their negotiators, the warlord said only, "If siege is what you want, siege is what you shall have, if you can bear it. The high valleys you now camp in are those we use for our tests of manhood. A boy must withstand the terrors that lurk there for seven nights, alive and sane. If you can do the same, if you can become men to our customs, we'll treat with you."

The negotiators went away well pleased, and left an even more pleased warlord behind. Every night a dozen of his best assassins went through the tunnels, slipping through the openings hidden among the numerous caves for which the castle is named. Every night they would creep, silent and hidden, around the campfires. They'd sneak up on the sentries, slit the throats of at least twenty men each, before they made such an inhuman wailing as to wake the entire camp. Then, when the hunt was on, they'd fade away, back to the tunnels and their warlord's appreciation. More than one noble house found its estate through the endeavour.

Each night, the number of men hunting the assassins grew less and the murmurs of the armies – simple, superstitious men, mostly farmers – grew louder. By the fifth day, more than half the armies had deserted. By the seventh, when the negotiators returned, full of bluster and blowhardiness, all that was left of the armies was their standing soldiers, and not even all of them. The warlord sent them packing with a well-placed regiment or six, and Mahala never faltered in its duty as middleman thereafter.

All of which meant that we'd found a tunnel, one that most likely led straight into the heart of the castle. The cart rumbled on, out of the cramped initial tunnel and into something far grander. Smoothly dressed flagstones kept the floor level and we jounced less. The roof vaulted away from us, up into darkness and the secret rustle of bats. For all this was a tunnel, not meant to be used by the general population, vast carvings decorated the walls. It took a minute or two, but then I began to make them out in the dim light of the Glow globes. A history, not of the castle or the warlord but of warriors, his élite assassins. Men trained to use their pain magic to defend the city, defend the Goddess who protected it and us – with their lives, if called upon.

On one wall that training was depicted, going from battle-hardened veteran back through to pre-pubescent novices as we neared the castle. On the other, scenes for which the assassins were justly famous until the Ministry began its insidious campaign, casting pain magic as something sent not by the Goddess but by Namrat. A thing of evil, to be feared and, above all, reported so that its practitioners could be "saved". Even before they deposed the King, pain magic had been mistrusted by anyone who wasn't a mage, only abided because it powered the machines that were our livelihood and, of course, because the King had a habit of using extreme prejudice and decapitation against anyone who said a damn thing against it. Not many would – it was our power, a necessary evil, and one that the Ministry had got rid of just as soon as they could, replacing it with something even worse, the synth.

Jake studied the battle scenes with interest until the way ahead lightened, a hundred Glow globes arrayed across the way like so many fireflies. I didn't like the look of what they illuminated, not one little bit. The tunnel closed off, not suddenly but a gradual rounding and narrowing of the carvings until it drew down to one small, hard point. A passageway, unlit, dark and ominous, so narrow that a man would have trouble swinging anything bigger than a letter-knife. High on the walls of the passageway slits had been cut into the stone, just wide enough for arrows. Other, larger openings might have been a better way in, if it weren't for the boulders that balanced on their lips.

Worse was the welcome party arrayed at this end of the passage. A dozen men, all in Specials uniforms, which, now I came to think of it, bore a distinct resemblance to the uniforms the assassins had used. Black high-collared allovers in smooth leather leaving nothing for an assailant to grab, decorated only with dark blue paint in discreet swirling designs. Long gauntlets up to the elbow designed especially for close work, with flexible palms and fingers and steel plates inserted along the arm bones, used to block a knife or even sword attack. Along the underside, the hilts of throwing-knives peeped out shyly, overshadowed by the subtle but nasty-looking metal lumps on the knuckles. Boots meant for silent movement, soft-soled but reinforced with steel from ankle to knee.

Specials, the face, sword and swift knife in the back of the Ministry, and unturnable, unbribable, even by Ministry, or so rumour went. They swore to the Goddess, not any man.

While in *theory* that made them of and for the people, in practice, because the Archdeacon was the mouth of said Goddess, it made them the Ministry's hunting-dogs. Not to be messed with if you like all your bits and pieces attached. On the meaner streets of Upside the merest hint of a Specials uniform could create a mass panic. Even in Clouds or Heights, the appearance of a Special might cause sweaty palms and clenching hearts.

The uniforms weren't the worst part, the part that made my balls shrivel, my heart stutter and my mind go utterly blank in panic. Most of these were shabby replicas, covering men who from their pallor were obviously Downsiders, hired thugs pretending they were somebody. No, the thing that really made me want to panic was the one genuine uniform, and the face of the man wearing it.

Dench, my Upside informant in the guards. There was no mistaking that drooping face or moustache. What was he doing down here? More specifically, what was he doing in the Specials? Maybe he was the one who'd known I'd come down here, had brought the Ministry on my tail and a prisoner to murder Jake. Maybe. It didn't really matter. The Ministry knew I was down here, and what I was after. If any one of those men knew an Upsider was here, I was dead. Actually, worse than dead. Yes, there are things that are worse. I did not want to be Azama's new source of power for his pain magic. Nuh-uh.

I shuffled on the bench and lowered my head so that the

guy sitting next to me partially obscured my face. I should have brought a hat. Or been sensible and not come down here in the first place, or not let my hormones get the better of me when I let Jake talk me into this damn fool idea or ... The cart rattled to a stop.

Dench and one of the fake Specials stepped forward and I huddled down, hiding my face with my benchmate. It wasn't going to be enough. Dench had the driver bring the cart forward under the brighter lights by the entrance to the passageway.

"Get down, one at a time," Dench snapped at the stockmen. They began to file out of the cart and drop to the flagstones where Dench got each of them under a brighter Glow light and inspected their faces. With each one, he gave a curt nod once satisfied. Azama, or the Ministry – and I couldn't be sure whether they were the same or not – was taking no chances, but checking everyone trying to gain access to the castle.

Oh shit, oh shit, oh *shit*. It wasn't just me I had to worry about either: Jake had one of the most recognisable faces Downside, and someone was going to know it was her just as soon as she got under that light. As for me, I was surprised Dench hadn't picked me out already. The cart was almost empty of men. My turn soon. It was now or never.

I grabbed for my left hand, the one still swollen and bruised from trying to track Amarie, gripped the index and middle fingers and twisted hard. The fingers came out of their sockets with a pair of crackling pops that sent shudders of pain up my arm, into my brain. I couldn't keep it all behind my clenched teeth and a hiss escaped. It might be enough, I hoped to fuck that it would be, because I hardly ever used my Minor, the one thing my father had given me, a talent for disguise. In fact, I'd used it less than a dozen times all told, mostly when drunk or trying to piss someone off, and one of those times I'd almost popped an eyeball.

With the pain came the power, swelling up through me like a malignant tumour, forcing every thought that wasn't about the spell out of my head. I let it grow and spread further than I ever had before, let it take me till it wasn't pain any more but sweet, delicious magic. Until I saw why Dendal lived for it, why he loved it, why I'd always been afraid to use it, afraid I'd want it too much. It was everything, *I* was everything.

The pain, the magic, began to fade. Just a little. The world flapped at the edges of me, and a last fragment of sanity made a determined bid to keep me alive. I didn't have long, only seconds. It'd have to be a makeshift job. Just enough so they wouldn't recognise us, that was all.

I shut my eyes, took the thing in my head and squeezed. Not too hard, just right. Lengthen the nose, lighten the skin, compress the line of the jaw into a narrower shape. It would have to do. The magic faded, bleeding out of me, leaving me drained. I needed more: Jake, I had to do Jake too.

I held my breath and twisted the fingers again, shoving

239

them back into their sockets. I fought against the urge to sink into the pain, to let the magic take over and make me forget it, make me forget fear and sweat and blood and kidnapped girls, and concentrated. Somewhere out there, back in the real world, Jake swore, vicious words that were nothing to what was inside me. Her cherry-red hair; that was the first give-away. I deepened it to a dark nut brown with a thought, a silver spike through the blackness in my brain. Now the face: dull the cheekbones, spread the nose, thin the lips.

The magic drained again, and seemed to take a part of me with it, strength leaking out through every pore. The urge to feel that again, to fill myself with magic, to let go of my fear, had my good hand on my bad, ready to twist my fingers again, and again if I had to. It wasn't the pain I was afraid of, it never really had been. It was the feeling that the magic con-trolled me rather than the other way around, the thought of wanting something so badly I'd be prepared to give myself who knew what pain to get it. Now I'd delved in properly, now I knew the insistent knock in the brain of my magic trying to take me over, telling me how easy it would be to know it again, whenever I wanted, I wasn't afraid. I was fuck-ing shit-scared.

The worst part of it was, the black was everything you didn't want in your life, gone, poof, just like that. Whatever it was about your life you hated the most, in the black it didn't exist. For me, in the black there is no fear, and that was the part that called to me, the part that scared me the most, because I wanted it the most. A day without fear would be all the heaven I'd ever need.

"Hey, you, get off the fucking cart."

I raised my head and looked around blearily. Dench beckoned me, a scowling sneer twisting his drooping moustache into an odd shape. Someone was next to me but when I looked it wasn't anyone I knew, just some ugly boy. Only – it was Jake. No mistaking those eyes, the swift calculation behind them, nor the subtle tilt of her lips when she spoke.

"I don't know what the fuck you've done," she whispered, "but you've got to get up."

"I don't think I can." My whole body felt rubbery, as though my bones had been taken out. My hand throbbed like a bastard, and all I could think was, if I did it again, everything would fade away into the blackness in me. I couldn't do that, I had Amarie to find, Jake to win over – fuck, I had a life to live. If I let myself be tempted, I'd be lost for ever. But I wanted to, more than I'd ever wanted anything. I took a deep, shuddering breath. "I need a minute."

"We don't have a minute."

"Hey." Dench stepped up on to the footboard at the back of the cart. "You two, out. Now. Or we come in."

"We're coming." Jake called, then quieter, to me, "You have to, or you're dead."

I tried. I did. But the effects of magic don't go away quickly. I got to my feet and stumbled, almost falling on to the bench opposite. Only Jake's hand on my arm stopped me.

She got me upright and helped me to the step. "You owe me."

When I glanced her way her face was twisted into a grimace, and the moment I was down off the cart she let go and wiped her hand on her blood-splattered suit. Luckily, by then some strength had come back to my legs and I managed to stand, although I needed to steady myself with my good hand on the cart.

Dench peered at me, a little too carefully for comfort. His moustache was really quite impressive up close. "What's the matter with you?"

"Felt a bit faint."

"Well get your arse over here so I can look at you."

I managed to get to where he wanted me without falling over. Dench grabbed my chin and tilted my face into the light, all but blinding me. It seemed to take years of bone-aching tension before he let go and I blinked away the dark splotches from my vision.

When I could see properly again, he was grabbing for Jake's chin. She jerked away from him and her hand reflexively went for where she usually kept her sword. *No, Jake, don't. Don't.* I wished I could do what Pasha did – read minds, maybe send thoughts. I knew she didn't like to be touched, that even Pasha was careful not to touch her, how she flinched away if anyone looked like they'd brush against her, even her grimace of distaste and that wipe of the hand when she'd helped me on the cart. Now that would be a disaster.

Dench didn't miss a beat. His hand shot out and gripped her chin hard enough that her mouth scrunched into a puckered O. Her eyes flew wide and her hands fluttered uselessly. For only the second time, I saw real fear in her. There was something about the way she stood, the way she cringed her body away from Dench, together with the few things I knew about her just from watching, that made me think it wasn't the situation that had her scared. Not the fact that if discovered, we'd likely be dead. She didn't care, Pasha was right about that. It was that Dench had laid his hand on her, as though that was the worst thing that could happen to her.

She tried to pull away, but Dench gripped harder, his fingers digging in. For a second, I thought she'd kill him right there, the way her eyes were, all wide and staring above his fingers. The way her hands clenched by her sides ready to punch, and I didn't doubt she was as good at that as she was with her swords.

Then he let her go with a gruff nod, though he cast me a curious look. "I'm watching you," that look said; "I know there's something odd about you."

"All right, start unloading," Dench said, and all the stockmen leapt to obey. Jake staggered back until she hit the wall, her chest heaving and her face grey and slick with sweat. I caught her eye but she looked away swiftly, maybe embarrassed, and hurried to help.

I turned back to the cart, my strength returning now, though the urge to fall into the black remained. A half-carcass of cow over my shoulder was enough to make me stagger under the weight but I got it centred and it wasn't too bad as we made our way down the dark passageway. The weight was minor compared to the way Dench watched me and Jake, or the threat of Specials, however fake. They still had guns.

The passage was barely wide enough to get down with a cow on my shoulder, but I got to the end well enough and stepped through.

Into what I can only describe as Namrat's kingdom.

By the time we'd offloaded all the carcasses, I'd managed to get myself under control. Just about. At least I hadn't done anything totally stupid to give us away. I clenched my good hand into a fist in an attempt to stop the shaking. Not fear, not this time. This time it was anger and a raging pity that threatened my sanity. Jake wasn't much better, a grim and even more silent than usual figure hunched in the baggy suit.

Beyond the passageway, after an alley lined with houses that leaned towards each other drunkenly over the way, lay a square that was evidently a meeting point of sorts, with the surrounding houses serving as barracks. The buildings all had a squashed look to them, as though the weight of the city above was too much, and everything seemed crammed in too close. Doorways too narrow, winding alleys that seemed no wider than a cat. Fake Specials strutted along the ancient streets, incongruous with the new-fangled guns that the officers wore, their pretend uniforms looking shabby and false next to Dench.

The carcasses now lay in a heap in a squat stone-faced building on one corner of the square, the quartermaster's office, pantry and butchery. Already, two young men were jointing the meat and laying the different pieces on an array of shelves in a cold store. So far, so – well, not normal, but un-alarming, except for those guns and the fact that our disguise wouldn't last much longer. At least Dench was still at the other end of the passage.

No, none of that was what was bothering me. The problem was what faced us when we'd found a way through, out of the square and where the other stock boys never went, through a tangle of alleys so tortuous I half felt like I was following some demented worm. The fake Specials were pretty lax in here – I suppose we'd got past where they thought they needed to be vigilant – so it wasn't too hard. What we found the other side was.

The face of a girl in an upstairs window of a house that looked like it should have been demolished a few centuries ago, windows broken, beams drooping, tiles missing, reveal-ing mould and synth-eaten struts. The girl was only there a moment, a brief flash of a tiny face marred with shadowy bruises before she disappeared. Even that might have been OK, if I hadn't seen with my own eyes that room outside the castle and the state of the girls there, and the black horror of the hole. If the hideous, shrill screams hadn't reverberated around this tiny square of hell. If any of the men had even looked up from what they were doing. If the screams hadn't ended with the sound of flesh hitting flesh and the tingle inside me. Even I was getting some power, from this far away, not even touching her. Worse, she wasn't alone. Not by a long stretch.

Other moans and cries, some more muffled than others, crowded my brain. Other tingles worked their way along my fingers. A long-drawn-out scream of torture from one side, from a house that had once been smart and well-to-do but was now not much more than a gently rotting shell. The scream ended in a babble of prayer, that now the Goddess would love her, would forgive her, wouldn't she? A more rhythmic noise from across the square and, Goddess preserve me, I knew what that was. Goddess knew I loved my women, even if I couldn't hold on to one for more than five minutes without cocking it up. But I loved them, or at least the idea of them, because they were entirely willing.

This was something else. This was an affront to the Goddess, even if I didn't believe in her. This was an affront to people, to the city and all its teeming crowds of men and women just trying to get by. Yet the people here, the fake Specials, the quartermaster, other men haunting the slick cobbles of the square, never even flinched. To them, this was normal.

These men weren't even pain-magicians. It brought them no benefit.

Pain magic. Power from pain, and it need not be your own.

It crawled over my skin, burrowed in like woodworms in oak. It made me want to use it, to raze this squalid place to the ground, to twist my hand to shreds bringing this castle down stone by stone. I hung by a thread. Now I'd dug the depths, now it knew me, all my fears came true. It called to me, sang my name in sweet black tones, a lover, a goddess, a pleading girl. To give in would be to die, unless I could master it. Dendal was always banging on about mastery. I'd never really listened, and now I struggled to remember the lessons.

All I could recall were the tales of before the synth, when pain magic was all the power we had, what set Mahala apart from the hordes at either side. What gave us the edge. Yet that edge came at a price. More than three in ten mages were destroyed by the magic, fell into it until they couldn't think any more, couldn't feel, knew only that they had to hurt themselves more and more to keep the pain at bay, to feel the surge they craved – a never-ending circle that would kill them if they let it.

Even that was preferable to this. That was voluntary; this was . . . this was *inhuman*. I took refuge in my only protection. "Fuck this for a game of patooty. Let's go. Please?"

Jake's bowed head snapped up. Her eyes were hollow, shrunken things that couldn't even seem to conjure anger. She shut them with a look of pained control and nodded jerkily.

We watched from our hidey-hole in a narrow alley that pinched my shoulders while the other stockmen back in the square moved towards the passage, ready for the ride home. I followed Jake through a doorway half hidden in a corner. She shut the door behind us and leaned against it. Her breathing was halting, stilted somehow, so I thought she couldn't be getting enough air in her lungs. Surely she'd faint, but when I held out a hand she slapped it away. I couldn't tell what it was with her, whether it was anger and pity, like me, whether it was disgust or what. All I knew was that she wasn't the same woman who'd started out on this, who'd been so adamant we'd come here, that we'd do this. The wall of protection – the swords, the flashy pretence at violence, Pasha's acceptance, his presence – it had all come tumbling down, and now she was just a girl, younger than I'd first thought, up to her eyebrows and sinking.

She wouldn't take the comfort of a hand so I said, "Are you OK?" A peace offering, but she didn't take it.

The slightest shake of her head in return, the grip of her hands on the door handle, as though that was all that kept her upright. Then a deep breath, rasping in and out, a few determined, muttered words. When she raised her head, she was Jake again. Cool, calculating, eyes flat and chill, full of cold grace. Her wall was back, but it was shiny and slick with fakery, brittle as glass, so it might take just the wrong word to break it and lay a bleeding soul bare. She stepped forward in a smooth movement belied by the grit of her teeth and pulled off the protective suit. With a nod she indicated I should do the same.

"Where to now?" I asked.

She avoided my eyes and got her swords arranged to her

satisfaction. She concentrated on that rather than look at me when she spoke. "To the keep. Any way we can. You ready?"

She looked up at that, and I saw it there. Maybe it was the magic leaking into me from what was going on around. Maybe it was just obvious, but I was sure that she was regretting it being me and not Pasha. They'd planned this long ago, waiting for the opportunity. Planned it and yet, when they got the chance, one of them wasn't here. All she had was me instead, and I was a poor consolation. That look was a slice to the stomach from one of her swords. Well, I'd show her, show her I was worth two of him when it came to it.

"I'm ready. Are you?"

She fielded my question with a contemptuous look and headed to the far end of the room we found ourselves in, towards a door that looked semi-solid. "This way. I don't know how we'll get there, but the keep's this way. We'd best get going before the Specials notice they're two short."

I asked the irritating tingle that was numbing my arm, and the pull of Amarie raised my hand a touch in the direction Jake was headed. Lessened the tingle too, an added bonus. The thought of how the ability came to me made my balls itch. I wanted it to stop. I wanted it all to stop, the power leakage, the screams. All of it. The only way that was going to happen was through me and Jake. If we were incredibly lucky and didn't get ourselves killed first.

I followed her through the door and out into the twisting back-streets.

Chapter Fourteen

Jake was a natural at moving silently. Me, not so much. I'd never in my life felt this much ambient magic, this much raw power, and this was just leakage. The thought of how much power was milling around, how much must be making it into the Glow vials, gave me the creeps. By the time the keep loomed over us, only two crumbling streets away, every nerve-ending was stretched tight, every muscle vibrated with it, every hair stood straight out from my body. It was all I could do not to sink into it. Or maybe, rather than wallow, take out this whole place in one glorious blast, me and Jake and Amarie with it. Anything to be rid of the power that stalked my bones.

I was beginning to think I could actually do it, blow the whole place. But then the city would fall too. This castle, this keep, was its main root, the tap that everything had sprung from. I might be a bastard, but even I'm not up for genocide, so I kept a tight lid on it and hoped for something else to earth my magic on.

Jake motioned me to stay where I was and edged forward to check the street that crossed our path. We'd managed to keep out of the way of the people roaming about, though a ruckus behind us told me they knew we were missing by now. They'd be looking, and they were bound to have someone like me, a tracker. It was only a matter of time before they found us.

More to release some of the power than from any thought of actually helping, I clenched my fists and sank, very briefly, into the black, just a skim across the surface. I didn't dare go further, but it was enough. When I looked again, Jake waved me forwards and started to step into the street. Bad idea. Bad, *bad* idea, because I knew what she didn't. That there was a fake Special not two steps away, hidden in a dilapidated door-way. His gun was cocked and ready, but he didn't know we were here. Yet.

Instinct took over. I grabbed her arm, slapped a hand over her mouth and yanked her back into the alley and against the wall. I knew right away that my idea might be as bad as hers. She went still as stone, her eyes bright above my hand. I thought she'd struggle, that she'd at least try to kick me in the nuts. She didn't do anything except stand there and stare at me in horror.

I couldn't seem to move, or think. I could only look at her. At the way a tendril of her hair had fallen free from its binding and curled around her cheek. The little flecks of brown in her blue eyes that were no longer calculating but radiated some deep, inner terror. We were pressed up tight against the alley wall. Where I wanted her at last, and she wasn't fighting me. I took that as encouragement, but I didn't talk. Instead I slid my hand down from her mouth and replaced it with my lips. Just a touch, a taste. Not exactly the optimum moment, maybe, but it could be my best chance.

She tasted sweet yet tart and she trembled against me at that first touch. My hand found hers and twined in it, her cold fingers in mine. I leaned in, tasting her, drawing in the scent of her, of leather, clean hair, oil and a hint underneath of her, really her.

She didn't move, not to return the kiss or to pull away. My cynicism is what keeps me sane, false though it may be, and the last person to see beneath it had been Ma all that time ago. I'd slough it off like dead skin in a heartbeat. For her, because her shell was harder and more brittle than mine and probably forged in hotter places. I hurt for her, because I'd seen what softness could lurk underneath. All of that I'd tried to communicate with one brief, butterfly touch of the lips. Mainly because the thought of having to say it brought me out in a rash.

She slid out from beneath me, all trembling and strange. I signed for her to be quiet and pointed, and got a nod in return. But there was something odd about her. Not like a woman who's been kissed by someone she likes, which was bad. Not even like a woman who's been kissed by someone she doesn't like, which was better. More like a woman who had previously had no idea what a kiss was like. Her mouth opened and closed before she turned away with a wipe to her lips. She kept quiet, but her hand shook hard enough on the doorframe it rested on that I began to worry the wood might give way.

That was when everything turned to shit.

Something smacked me in the back and I smashed face-first into the wall, hard enough that I tasted blood. My first thought was that the Special had seen Jake, or had heard our movement, but he wouldn't have hit me, he'd have shot me; and besides, it had come from the wrong direction.

I whirled round and tried to ignore what the pain was doing to my thoughts, the surge of power through me. Whoever it was, they had no idea about fighting a pain-magician. Don't hit, kill, because the more you hit, the more powerful they get. I wiped blood from my mouth and nose and came face to face with Pasha.

Only this wasn't Pasha, mild-mannered, monkey-like and a bit timid, or Pasha putting on a front to scare a farmer into helping us. This wasn't even Pasha killing a man to protect Jake. This was a Pasha with hard eyes and a scornful sneer, twisting his fingers further than they had any right to go, and for no reason other than he wanted me to suffer. This was Pasha without the heart that had made him who he was, a man pushed to the edge by what he'd just seen. What I'd just done.

There was a possibility I was completely fucked.

Before I could speak or move, his good hand shot out and clamped round my throat. Power surged along his fingers, thick enough I could watch it wriggle along his arm like black snakes. I managed a brief, mangled thought, that he could pick up on the stray power here too, and then it hit me.

The snakes leapt and I could no longer breathe. I don't mean I had trouble drawing breath, I mean my throat was completely shut off. No air. Not a single puff. My hands instinctively scrabbled at my throat, trying to rid myself of whatever had me in its noose, but all I found was my own skin. I sank down to the cobbles and tried to think. Tried not to give in to the blackness in my head that was tempting me, telling me I could do it, could kill Pasha and live. That the pain in my throat and lungs was enough to light up half the city with fire, if I could only work out how, and work up the nerve to do it.

Pasha turned his back, done with me it seemed, and faced Jake as she stood thunderstruck. His face didn't soften as it once might have done. His voice didn't hold the tender tones he used to use with her. Everything about him was hate, from the set of his mouth to the way he stood.

"That was all it took, was it?" He grabbed her arm and in the instant had her up against the wall, much as I had, only his hand grasped her wrist tight enough that her fingers went white. "All it took was some random Upsider with a slick manner. If only I'd known. Was this it, what you wanted? Like this?" He shook her, his face twisted and I would have sworn there were tears in his eyes, but my vision was hazy by now. Purple splotches ranged across the world and then blackness fell with a thump. All I knew was what I could hear, and that I was going to die if I didn't think of something. I focused on his voice.

"Was it? Like this? Is this all I had to do, be a prick like him instead of looking after you?"

Scuffed steps on stone. Jake, in a voice that wasn't hers, saying, "Please, not you, please. You were the only one who didn't. Please, Pasha, you're scaring me."

A halting sob, surely not hers. Leather squeaking in friction, a pained gasp. A murmured "I only ever wanted to—"

A separate sound: a metallic click. The Special with his gun, alerted by the noise. Little white lights spun in my head. Pain, bringing up the black, making it swell through me, giving me the means to stop this. I couldn't hear anything now; my world was reduced to the pain in my lungs, the useless working of my throat and my magic, a sick tide through me. All I could do was use it, yet in using it I might lose myself, who I was. There was no choice. It wasn't just me. If it was I might have just lain back and died, anything rather than what awaited if the magic took me. Not just me, it was Jake and Amarie, and yes, even Pasha.

I let the black in. Then I let it out again, pushed it through every pore in one big, disorganised rush. Not fire, no; even so far gone, I knew that for a mistake. Not fire but the air I couldn't breathe, a storm of it, a hurricane. I was in no state for finesse, even if I knew how. Fuck, I wasn't even sure how I managed the hurricane, because it wasn't my kind of magic, not really. This level of power was alien to me; I'd only dabbled before, because I was afraid, and rightly so. But now wasn't the time for fear, now was the time to try to live.

It all blew out of me and my mind – and my breath – were my own again. I heaved myself on to my front and pushed up on shaking arms before I retched the meagre contents of my stomach up on to the cobbles. There was nothing left in my head, no tingle, no black, no nothing. I stayed on all fours for a few heartbeats, and hoped I wasn't the only one completely fucked. Or that, if everyone else felt like I did, I'd recover first.

The wall was a handy climbing-frame to help get me upright. When I looked round, I almost fell to my knees again. There wasn't much left of the alley. The walls were still fairly solid; there was a reason they'd stood the test of a thousand years. The rest was . . . gone. All the rubbish in the alley lay piled up at the end, twisted into a mangled mess. Jake lay half in and half out of it, with blood running from a cut to her temple. I staggered over, crouched down beside her and ran a hand over her cheek. Still breathing, thank anyone who might be listening, I hadn't killed her. Yet another reason not to use my magic; when things got out of control, other people got hurt.

I looked around for the other two. A trail of bloody footprints led away, but I couldn't know whose, whether they belonged to the guard or Pasha, and I had no power, or inclination, to use any magic for quite some time. That took care of one of them, but what about—

Click.

A cold, round hardness at the side of my neck, a shadow looming over me. I kept very still and risked a sideways glance.

"Stay right there. Don't move or your head will be a big mess."

Not Pasha. My only advantage: not another mage. Probably. I was in no shape for this, no shape at all. I wanted sleep, preferably with some booze first. I wanted my own bed and a friendly girl to share it with. I wanted to be out of this hellhole and home, where I knew how it all worked and I didn't have to do this shit any more. I wanted to forget my magic.

"Stand up. Slowly, hands out."

I stood, slowly as asked, my hands out, palms up. The Special moved round in front of me, but the gun stayed planted firmly in my neck. His face was hard to read beneath the blood from a cut to his cheek and a rapidly darkening bruise around his jaw. His eyes were steady as he looked me over, and then his mouth lifted in a grim little smile.

"I think Azama will be very pleased to see what I bring him."

I tried to keep my eyes on him as the rubbish moved to our

side, tried to keep him distracted, cover the noise with my voice. "Not so pleased when I blow his sorry arse up."

The smile turned to a grin and the Special jabbed the gun harder into my neck. "You think people haven't tried before? Turn around and put your hands on the wall. Good. Now stay there while I deal with the matcher." He said that last with a kind of relish, as though he looked forward to it. Maybe so he could boast to his friends about the day he killed one. "I want you in one piece if I can, but one move and I'll blow your brains out."

I did what he said. There wasn't anything else for it, because I could hardly keep my feet for exhaustion. The gun left my neck and I turned, not sure what I was going to do, if there was anything I *could* do. Just in time to see Jake take him across the face with one sword while the other hovered near his stomach.

The Special staggered back into me with a scream and his gun went off, the shot wild but not wild enough. The bullet punched straight through Jake's upper arm in a spray of blood and the force knocked her back into the wall. The weight of the Special was enough to bring me to my knees, but I had just enough presence of mind to grab the gun and smack him with it, right in the wound Jake had made. He slumped to the cobbles, unconscious, his face a bloody mess. I turned away, sick to my stomach and glad I'd already brought it all up so I wouldn't vomit again with Jake to see.

She had her hand clamped over the wound in her arm, but

blood seeped freely between her fingers. Her face was deathly pale, her mouth agape as she looked at what she'd done to the Special's face, none of her cool composure left. I could almost see the way her whole world was falling apart, everything she'd known and trusted slipping away, with only me to replace it. Fat lot of good I was doing her, too.

I took a step towards her but she backed away with a shake of her head. Her hair had come completely free and straggled over her shoulders and face as she hunkered down. Her legs gave way before she could sit and she sprawled forward on her knees, trailing blood.

I took another step and she snapped, "Haven't you done enough?"

I winced at that. "No, not yet, because I haven't found Amarie, and I haven't set things right."

She stared round at the alley, the ruined cobbles, the rubbish piled in one corner by the wind I'd made, the chunks of stone that had come loose from one of the walls. "How did you *do* that? I've never seen or heard of a mage that could do half of that. What are you?"

I crouched down next to her, careful, because she was skittish, on the edge of something – her sanity maybe – and she still had those swords. "Just a guy, that's all, looking for his niece and finding too much else. Just a guy who hates using magic because of what it does to you. And now I've used it, I've gone too deep and it's started."

Her eyes narrowed, calculating again, but she still had a

jittery air to her as she sat back up and tried to bring herself under control. "What's started?"

I rocked back on my heels, reluctant to put it into words, because that would make it real. But I owed her that much, the truth, as much of it as I knew myself. "I'm falling into the black." Her blank look prompted me further. "Pain-mages, if they aren't careful . . . well, they don't use magic. It uses them, drags them into the black and in time crushes them. I used it when I shouldn't, and went too deep. Further than I've gone before, way too far. I think Pasha's doing the same, worse than me. I think he's not in charge of Pasha any more."

She looked round wildly, as if noticing for the first time that Pasha wasn't here. I picked up the Special's gun, but without bullets it was useless. Jake's gaze stopped on the trail of blood, splotches of it blooming on the shattered cobbles like red flowers, leading away. To the keep.

The room was a dark and fetid mess, full of rat droppings and odd rustles in the shadows, but it was secret and no one followed us there that we could see. We holed up for a time, while Jake sorted out the wound to her arm by the light of a candle she found in a cupboard and I tried to sort out the mess in my head.

I'd always sworn it wouldn't happen to me. I wasn't ever going to use my magic past the superficial stuff: a quick track here, a subtle alteration to my face there. I think I'd worked out what maybe I'd always known instinctively, and Dendal had hinted at. It wasn't the magic, as such, that was the danger. It was using it out of emotion. Jealousy, hatred, love. Fear. The magic mingled with the feeling, each magnifying the other. So I'd kept myself apart – hadn't I? – and not even realised why, not anywhere except at the back of my mind, where even I fear to tread. There are nasty things back there.

Jake found some tattered cloth, grimy with Goddess-knew-what. I don't think she noticed. I don't think she cared either. Her face was set into rigid planes as she tried to keep her cool, tried for the same level of control that had so impressed me when I'd first met her. An ice queen, I'd thought then, with hopes of a volcano underneath.

A volcano that seemed on the verge of eruption now. She wouldn't talk, she didn't seem to hear anything I said to her. Her eyes were turned inward on to some private hell, her face harsh with lines beyond her years. Finally, she was done with the bandage and eased the sleeve of the allover back on, over old scars and newer stitches.

She looked out of the small window, streaked with grime, that opened on to a view of the castle keep, the tower squat and forbidding. It was a long time before she moved or spoke, but I let her be, even though we didn't have the time. Everything that I was and knew was sloughing away, just like it was for her. I didn't want to be the prick that Pasha thought me, not around her. I didn't want to be the cynic any more. So I watched her, and realised that it was her that had driven me to the magic. Not Amarie, and I dare say I'll be damned to

Namrat's hell for that. Not Pasha, or the hell around me, or the hope I saw in faces like Dog's, in Dendal, even in Pasha before he'd gone into the black.

I'd done it for Jake, because she had a powerful need to do this, because I wanted it to be me that made it possible for her. Amarie was in there too, don't get me wrong. I wanted to stop this for her, for the girls I'd seen in the hole. For Erlat, so she needn't be ashamed of what she'd been. I wanted to stop it because it made me sick to my stomach. But mostly it was for Jake, for the way she'd smiled at me and let me in, however briefly.

Her head dipped from the smeared view of the castle. "Rojan." She halted, her voice rasping, but caught herself and carried on. "Why did you? Why did he?"

She didn't say what she meant, but I knew. I stood behind her and resisted the urge to lay a hand on her shoulder or run a finger along her neck. With a sudden, blinding clarity I saw what Pasha had meant. Would I forgo touching her? He had, and then I'd blundered in with my hoofing great feet and smashed it all for him.

Her back was straight and stiff, proud, with a hint of fear in the tremble of the shoulders.

"You don't know?"

Deep breaths shuddered the contours of her allover and she shook her head. "No, no I don't. It – I never—" She broke off and hunched over her crossed arms. "I don't know anything since you got here. You changed everything, and not for the better. Pasha said you were all right, he talked me into it, into letting you help, and now – I wish you'd never come."

"So do I. But the reason I'm here hasn't changed. Amarie is still in there. I still need to find her. I still need your help."

"No, your niece needs my help, and so does Pasha. Which way?"

"Jake, I don't——" I cut myself off. If I went in again, into the blackness inside, I might not come out. It was pulling me even now, a subtle ache of every muscle, a constant niggle in the brain. It wanted me. I wanted it. This wasn't going to end well, but I had no choice. The remembrance of Amarie cold and alone, hunched into herself in the same posture as Jake now. The knowledge that I could help her. Maybe help them both, if only I had the guts.

I turned away from the window, from Jake and her request. It could be the end. It was all I could do to help. Shit, I hate when I have to stop pretending to be a cynic.

It didn't take much. My hand was still swollen and I was fairly sure my nose was broken where Pasha had smacked me into the wall. Together with the leakage, the pain that throbbed through the whole place and made my head itch, it would be enough. I pulled out the picture of Amarie. It was tatty now, worn at the edges from the amount of times I'd run my thumb over the image, listened to the words. *Princess, Daddy*. Every time I thought I could quit, could go back Upside and pretend this never happened, that little voice piped up. I couldn't look at it any more. I shut my eyes and held the picture tight.

It came easier this time, slipped into me far faster than it had before. It knew the way, I'd shown it. It slid in as though it'd always been there. I suppose it had been, biding its time, waiting for when I was weak enough or desperate enough to give in. I couldn't work out whether I'd been stupid, to use it like that, or whether I'd been a brave little boy. A fucking stupid little boy seemed about right. Too late now, though.

Not in the room any more, no guttering candle or the furtive rustle of rats on the make, no Jake at the window. There was no window. There was darkness, alleviated only by the chink of light from under a door. It didn't matter. I wasn't using my eyes.

The black blew through me like a midnight gale, streaming from my eyes, nose, mouth. It piled up in my head, wanting, needing, *pleading* to be used. I clamped down on it as hard as I could. A small bundle lay in the corner, a pile of rags that stirred gently then sat up. I drifted over to it.

"Are you there again?" Her voice was small, cracked from thirst or maybe fear. Odd, how she knew I was there when she shouldn't be able to see me. "Have you come to take me home?"

"We're close now. Very close. Hold on, Amarie. You hold on for Uncle Rojan." She didn't look hurt that I could see, and I took heart from that.

"I'll try," she whispered, and I knew then why this little

scrap had wormed her way into my heart. Not just because she was Perak's daughter, my blood. She was a brave little thing, and she reminded me so much of Ma, who'd borne so much. I couldn't save Ma, but I sure as shit was going to save Amarie, no matter what.

Something stirred behind me, and a growl oozed around the walls. Amarie huddled into the rags she used for blankets. One pale hand sneaked out and reached for mine but the fingers passed through my hand, leaving only the trace of a touch, like the waft of silk on skin. Footsteps sounded outside the door, accompanied by a rumble of voices.

"I have to go now, but I'll be here, for real, soon. I promise."

Amarie managed a nod. "If I pray to the Goddess, she'll look after me, won't she? I've been praying lots."

"I'm sure she looks after her own." Not really a lie. Just because I thought she was a mass hallucination didn't mean I was right. I wasn't going to tell Amarie my religious theories.

A key shot home in the lock and grated round. I willed myself back, away from the magic. It was harder than ever, maybe the hardest thing I've ever done, made worse because I had to leave Amarie alone. The heartbeat before I landed in my own body, the door opened and two men came in. The shock of who they were snapped me back with a slap to the brain.

I gingerly opened my eyes to the sound of Jake's voice. She was prodding my shoulder with the end of one scabbard.

"Rojan, wake up, or stop casting or whatever it is you do."

"Wzzft?" My mouth didn't seem to want to work properly. All the muscles in my arms and legs shook as though I'd just sprinted a dozen miles. Every part of me throbbed with pain, my hand leading the orchestra with my nose as percussion. My brain didn't want to be here, it informed me. If I just twisted my hand a little, I could fall back into the black and all would be blessedly numb, gloriously exhilarating, free of fear. It was tempting, so very tempting.

"Rojan!"

"Yes." Agreeing seemed the best option.

"Goddess, Rojan, I thought you, I thought . . . I thought you weren't coming back." Jake twisted the scabbard in both hands, first one way, then back again. It didn't seem a nervous thing, more like she was trying very hard not to be violent.

I picked my words with care, and was pleased when they came out ungarbled. "Sadly for us both, that is not the case." I sat up and couldn't quite bite back a groan. Surely fingers weren't supposed to be purple with blue blotches? "Anyway, I wasn't gone that long."

Jake snorted a bitter laugh. "Not long? Look at that." She pointed at the candle that lit our hidey-hole.

It was a good three inches shorter than it had been. I scrubbed my good hand up my face and tried to wake myself up properly. It didn't matter, not really, though normally the thought that I'd been out three hours when it seemed like ten minutes would have meant I needed a clean allover and a thorough scrub with disinfectant. What mattered was who I'd seen.

"Jake, this Azama, what does he look like?"

Her cheek twitched and she swallowed, hard. Her words come out in clumps. "Big, like you. Dark hair, er, and eyes. He has a way of twisting his mouth when he talks, like you're something bad he ate. His hands . . . he has big, bony hands, but it's his voice, his voice is the worst. He . . . he . . ." She trailed off with a pinched mouth and troubled eyes.

"Is that his real name?"

She looked bewildered. "No, of course not. No one down here uses their real name. You saw him?"

Shit. Because the first of the two men was someone I knew from Upside, a dead ringer for her description. Someone who'd hired me to find his runaway-alchemy-genius daughter, Lise. A blustering, pompous idiot I'd thought him, and when Lise had shown me the bruises I'd added bully to the list. A Ministry man. One who'd looked creepily familiar, though I was sure I hadn't known him before. Seeing him made it all start to come into focus. Why Amarie, why *her* instead of some other girl. It was me they were after, and I shuddered to think why – because they wanted me like they'd wanted Pasha, perhaps. Maybe Azama wanted me down here with him, making pain, and brought me the best way, tracking someone, knowing I wouldn't refuse the job because she was family. We'd assumed that all those Ministry men looking for me were looking to kill me too, or I had. But that Special hadn't shot me when he'd had the chance, had said he was going to bring me to Azama, in one piece. No, maybe they weren't looking to kill me, but just looking *for* me. A possible new recruit who'd disappeared from the hotel they'd put him in.

Maybe. The only problem with that scenario was how he'd known Perak was my brother, how he'd known I was a mage in the first place, because only Perak and I knew the first, and only Dendal and I knew the second. Maybe Azama just wanted to shoot me personally, or maybe he'd had Amarie taken for other reasons I couldn't guess at.

That wasn't the worst, though. No, not the worst, and I wasn't sure I could tell her. I had to. I stared at the guttering candle instead of her face, coward that I am.

"Pasha was with him. They seemed friendly. Very friendly indeed."

When I chanced a look, her lips had thinned and she took a step back, her hands twisting the scabbard harder. "That's not possible."

"It's not only possible, it's true."

She turned away and stared out of the window. The creak of her scabbard as she twisted was the only sound. I let her be. Let the enormity of it sink in. Pasha knew what we were about, and now Azama would have all the details. He'd know how we'd got in, how we planned to find Amarie. We were screwed and so was Amarie, so I didn't let Jake have long.

I managed to pull myself to my feet using a handy chair. "We have to get going. I think they're moving Amarie, and the longer we leave it, the further away she might be. The better protected she's going to be."

Jake nodded and turned around. I took a step her way, a hand outstretched. I caught myself when her gaze found mine, and instead I coughed awkwardly. "We have to go. Now."

"I hope the Goddess sends you straight to Namrat so you can get eaten alive on a daily basis." Her voice had no emotion in it, no hatred. She seemed completely calm, drained of everything. "I hope you fall into the black, and it consumes you. I hope you know the hell you've forced Pasha into. I hope you get it too, but not till we're done."

Guilt made me snap my reply. "I wasn't the one who sent him away because he wanted to save you."

"No, you were the one who overstepped the bounds and kissed me." Her free hand shot out and smacked me in the cheek. It was like being hit with a bag of rivets. "Why, why did you do that?"

Every pretence at composure cracked then, and she came at me with both fists. She got three good punches in before anger got the better of her and she swung wilder. I managed to grab one wrist and her eyes flew wide as she tried to yank out of my grasp. I got hold of the other wrist, clumsy with my swollen hand, as she panicked. Touch again. She hated it. Her foot lashed out and caught me on the knee. She pulled away from my momentarily weakened grip and stood back, shaking with rage and fear.

"Don't you ever touch me again. Not ever. Understand? Or I'll fucking leave you to Azama. Now let's go, before I change my mind and break your knees. I swear I will, by the Goddess, if you touch me one more time."

She made for the door, her steps unsteady. She was coming apart at the seams, and I couldn't quite understand why.

This was a record. *Well done, Rojan. Didn't even get further than a first kiss this time, and you've fucked it up*. Only this time was different. Maybe because this time I actually wanted to do something other than get in her knickers. As new experiences went, it sucked.

The flash of understanding came from nowhere, making me wonder how I could have missed it. Why she and Pasha had the affinity they did, how he understood her, why she hated to be touched. Why she wore those leather strips around her wrists – not as extra armour, as I'd thought, or support for the joints when she fought. Why she hated Azama so much.

"Are your brands the same as Pasha's?"

Her hand stopped on the door handle. "Fuck you, Rojan." A whisper, barely heard, then she whirled to face me, pale and furious and ashamed. "What do you want to know? Yes, they're the same. Azama owned us both, and he killed me, the life I should have had, the person I would have been. He killed me but didn't have the decency to make sure I was dead. All he left me was two brands, and shame and anger – and Pasha.

Now I don't even have him. I'm not like Erlat, not as sensible perhaps, not as forgiven by the Goddess. I can't just accept it. I have to fight it, him, all of them."

"How can you fight him? How can I?"

"I don't know, I don't care. All I know is a life lived in fear is less than nothing, and I refuse to live that way. Everyone is cruel; men were made for it, each in their own way. No one is without it. Him and his brands, Pasha and his betrayal, the priests with all their talk, with the hope, a cruel hope for me because I'll never see it. You and, and – everyone's cruel, life's cruel, and so is death and so am I, and I intend to find out just how cruel I can be. So fuck you, Rojan, fuck you. Now show me which way it is, so I can do to Azama what he did to me."

Chapter Fifteen

"Are you sure it's this way?" Jake spoke for the first time since we'd left the room. There was something about the way she held herself that was like hearing steel scraped down stone. Something that shivered my insides, made me want to shove my hands over my ears and at the same time hold her, pull her back from the brink she was clearly on.

I restrained myself and double-checked. The tingle was back, stronger than ever, not so much a tingle as a pulse, an aching throb. I was sure it was because we were getting nearer the source, but it was getting difficult to think. The call was getting stronger. Just sink in, it said, just lie back, twist a finger and all will be well. *Fuck that*, I said back. My hand was screwed enough as it was, and if I did that Amarie would end her days down here. It didn't matter why Azama had taken her, only that he had. Now this thing had gone beyond responding because I thought I should, because of guilt, because of what I'd promised Ma about looking after Perak. This was about a little girl who might become like all those girls in the hole, like Erlat, like Jake, if I didn't hurry up.

"Yes, I'm sure." I'd never been more sure of anything in my life. The tingle was a thrum, a buzz in my head. I barely even needed to ask: it was a red-hot brand in my mind. "Left at the next turning."

I knew why Jake was asking though. The path led us away from the front of the main keep, from the fancy parts where the Ministry would be holed up. We'd caught glimpses of velvet and marble and whiffs of the rich, slightly bloody hint of cooking steak. But our path led us along narrow stairways meant for servants, through cobwebs, dust and piles of dirt, past skittering rats and the debris of decades, centuries even. Away from opulence and decadence into must and disrepair. Our path led to the rear of the keep.

The throb got worse; it ran through me like Lise's electric booby trap. I held out a hand to the wall, and received a jolt of power strong enough to send me to my knees. Strong enough to make me crave the black, make it the loudest voice in my head. Sweat popped out on my forehead and ran down my face in streams, in rivers. I wasn't strong enough to resist the call.

An open-handed slap across the jaw rocked my head to one side and brought me back to the blurry now.

"Don't you dare."

I blinked up at Jake and was shocked by the hate that radiated from her.

273

"Don't you *dare*. Not now, not when we're this close. I need your help, and I'm getting it if I have to kick you the whole fucking way."

I staggered to my feet and tried to will it back, to concentrate on Amarie. She was close, so close. She was depending on me. I could sink as far as I liked, just as soon as I got her back to her father. I managed a nod to Jake and we went on.

It was odd. We hadn't met anyone on the way here, caught only brief, far-off glimpses of people scurrying about in the main halls. They knew we were coming, they must do. Azama would know I could track, from Pasha. We were close enough that I could almost touch Amarie, and yet there was no one here, no one stopping us. Even the black tide of magic that had stopped me tracking her before had vanished, dissolved like smoke. My brain was too mangled to think on it before, but now it was obvious. Azama wanted me here.

"Jake," I whispered. "Don't you think—"

She ignored me and took the left turn. A short corridor ended in a door with a shut grille in it.

"Jake, will you listen?" I grabbed at her arm as she went to open the door. I instantly regretted it when her elbow smacked my cheek into the wall. Namrat's balls, she was stubborn.

"I told you not to touch me."

"Fine, all right, just walk in there with who-knows-what waiting for us. They know we're coming. They're waiting for us, sure as I'm a bastard. And if they've got pain-mages, then

274

just hurting them won't work. You'll only end up fuelling them. We have to think this through."

I got closer to her, blocking her path and making her back up against the wall as she tried to avoid touching me. Her eyes were wild; the last part of her shell had dissolved and under it I could see nothing more than shrinking, abject fear. Maybe that was what it was about her – the fear we shared. I've always been afraid, every day, since I was ten and my father left me to watch Ma die.

She shoved at me, but I dug in my heels and stayed where I was. We needed to get in and get Amarie. It wouldn't help her if we died two seconds later because Jake had lost any semblance of self-control.

"I'm done thinking," Jake whispered. "I've been thinking about this too long. It's all I *ever* think about. I don't care what happens after, I don't care if I fuel his mages. I don't care if he blows this whole place up and me with it. Just so long as he'll never do this again, not him and not any of his cronies. It stops. Today." The edge of her sword appeared by my throat. "Now get the fuck out of my way."

I didn't move. Not an inch, not a muscle. I am not a brave man, I think we've established that. But this I could not allow. "No, I won't; because I *do* care. I won't let you kill yourself, and me with you, and Amarie and who knows how many girls. And Pasha, don't you care what happens to him?"

Her eyes filled with sudden tears that she struggled not to shed. The sword slid along my skin and the first trickle of blood ran into my collar. "No. Not any more. He – no. He can rot with Namrat and I hope he does. For him I'd make an exception. Him I'd kill."

She made to kick at my knee, but I was ready for that and swivelled out of the way, getting my neck away from the sword at the same time. It was all I could do not to draw on the magic that was pulsing through me, do something desperate. And stupid. She tried to push past me again, using her swords as a barrier to keep me away, but I wasn't having it. Not now.

I shoved her back against the wall and leaned in, making good use of my extra height and weight. I hated myself for doing it, thinking I knew what it would do to her, but I needed her help. Above all I needed someone with a clear head because mine was full of clouds, black and tempting. Her mind might be full of remembered pain and newer anger, but she was all I had. She cringed back from me, and now the fear was because of me, and that cut me to the quick. It didn't matter. I had to do what was necessary, no matter the cost, and at that moment I really was the bastard I always pretended to be.

"Jake, you have to listen. I need you to help me. I need you to be sensible. To be – well, the Jake you were, when I met you. In control. The last thing I need is you going off half cocked and getting us all killed. They're waiting for us, don't you see that? They know we're coming, they know what we're after, and maybe they *want* us to come even, and that gives

them every kind of advantage. They don't have to come looking for us any more because they know we're coming and they
want us to, so we need to be devious or we're dead. I don't care
if you want to be dead or not, but I don't. Pasha didn't want
that prisoner to kill you, because he loves you. So he did the
only thing he could other than watch you die, and you sent
him away. And I—"

I clamped my mouth shut out of instinct. These were words
I hadn't uttered to a living soul since Ma died. Part of me
sneered at myself for even wanting to say them. "And I love
you. I love you, fuck only knows why, and I know that you
want your revenge on Azama, and I know why, and I understand. I want you to get that revenge, for it to make you
happy. But I won't let that blind me to the fact that if you go
in there like this, Amarie is dead. All those girls, the ones you
say you'll do anything to help, they'll be dead too. You may
want to be dead, but they don't, so you will pull yourself
together, and you *will* help me."

She shrank back, her eyes wide and searching mine for long
heartbeats. I stood away, ashamed now for using her fear
against her, no matter how necessary it was. But then she
stood straight, pulled herself together. Her hands still trembled, but she had a solid grip on her swords – her last, only,
shred of her wall – and on herself. I have never admired
anyone more.

"So what are we going to do?" she asked and her voice was
cool again, controlled.

I really wished I didn't have to say this. "*We're* doing nothing. I'm going to try something. You are going to stay there and make sure no one kills me while I'm gone. All right?"

Her nod was terse but determined. "All right."

It wasn't going to take much – power was all but dripping down the walls. The call was too strong, and I couldn't be sure if I was trying this because it was sensible, or because I was too weak to resist. I leaned back against the wall and tried to close my poor swollen hand, and that was enough.

Amarie wasn't alone, not any more, and they weren't protecting her with magic either. They *wanted* me to know where she was, to try to get her, and they had done all along. Now they'd moved her, and she had company. Dwarf lay in a corner of the room, both his legs twisted unnaturally, his ugly-attractive face a bruised and battered mess. Lise was there too, holding Amarie on her lap and crooning a lullaby. That was a comfort to more than Amarie. So was the look on Lise's face when she saw me.

Amarie should never have been able to see me, know I was there even, but she had, the first time I looked for her. Each time, she saw me, she heard me when I spoke. Each time, she tried to grab my hand. The first had met nothing but air, but that last time – I'd felt her touch, soft as silk. That last time, I'd thought if I could just push hard enough, stretch far enough . . . It shouldn't be possible. It shouldn't but maybe it was. I was in uncharted territory now, at least for me. Maybe Dendal would have understood what was happening with me, with my magic, but I sure as shit didn't. Yet it didn't matter whether I understood it, as long as I could use it. Except, of course, it could send me mad or kill me. Sometimes you just have to say screw the ever-present fear and do it, or lose every hidden particle of self-respect.

Lise stared at me as though I was a ghost, and when I looked down I could see the faint outline of my hands. I was here, almost. Here and elsewhere too, because a tiny part of my brain was back in a corridor with Jake watching me, pacing up and down, muttering to herself and holding her swords like they were the only things that were keeping her this side of sane.

I could push it, I could go deeper, I could be here with Amarie and then do it all in reverse and take her away. If I did, I'd be lost. The black was calling now, a sweet song of temptation, a blaze of lust. I wanted it like I'd never wanted anything before. I could taste it on my tongue. Maybe Amarie was the excuse. It didn't matter.

All that mattered was that I had the power to do something, to save her, like Pasha had saved Jake, and I'd not had the guts to help. Then Lise was on her feet, her arms clasping Amarie to her, looking over my shoulder and shouting something, words I couldn't make out. I tried to turn, but the lust, the *wanting* made me clumsy.

I turned straight into a smack in the face, a face that shouldn't have felt a damn thing because it was only half there.

*

279

When I woke up, I was numb. Not just bits of me – not being able to feel the mess of my hand was a relief – but *all* of me. I fumbled my fingers over my cheeks and couldn't feel them, or indeed my fingers. I tried to sit up into the blank darkness. Finally I managed it, but it was no better. I couldn't feel what I was sitting on, not even the pressure of backside against wood. No tingle in my arms, no sensation of magic in the air. I've never been quite so terrified in my life. With the numbness came powerlessness. No pain, no gain. I was ordinary, I was useless. Funny how you loathe it till it's gone and then you miss it.

The door to wherever I was banged open, letting in flickering light and two shadows in the shape of men. One of them hurried towards me, and I caught a glimpse of his face. The good Doctor Whelar, patcher-up of Perak in the Sacred Goddess Hospital and cutter-up of pigs, now with a big syringe glinting in his hand.

"Experiments worked, then," I said. Or tried to. Not being able to feel your tongue or lips makes it hard. He seemed to get the gist though, because he blushed as he pushed the syringe in.

The other shadow came in. Pasha, looking kind of lost and dishevelled, his normally pin-neat clothes awry, his shirt buttoned up wrong, his brands clear at his wrists where he'd shoved up the sleeves, like he didn't care who knew any more. His hair was no longer rumpled round his face but stuck out in clumps and his eyes seemed blurred, as though he looked out on a different reality. I was pretty sure I knew what he was seeing, and feeling, and it was black. "Come on." Even his voice was distorted, muzzed at the edges. "Something to show you."

He turned away, his feet stumbling over themselves so he didn't so much walk as stutter with his legs, like they belonged to someone else. Whelar got his hand under my arm and helped me up. Surprising how hard it is to walk like that – my feet couldn't work out when they'd hit the floor. When I got through the door, I forgot about numbness, forgot about magic or the call of the black and how I missed it, wanted it, craved it.

The room was vast, towering high above me, receding off into a far distance. Not into shadow though, because the place was lit up like the sun. Glow tubes, everywhere, from tiny things the size of my pinkie to great tubes five times the size of a man. Every one of them glowed with the bright, pinkish-yellow light that Upside had come to rely on. Glow powered everything Upside, from lights to carriages to the great factories of Trade. Glow had saved us from synth, from a long, slow death.

Glow was pain magic stored, and it was only now I saw, now that Glow covered every available surface in a great, shining sea of fizzing tubes, that I really believed it, and believed that mages were farming Downsiders for pain, for Glow.

I could hear them, far across the room, out of sight. A faint shout, a weak scream, and each time another tube glowed brighter, fizzed with energy, with pain. The air vibrated with it, a constant hum in the bones that even my numbness could sense. This room held enough pain to fill the world. I couldn't seem to get my head round it.

"Pasha, what—"

"He promised me." Pasha swayed next to me, twitching at each new scream. His voice was a low moan stretching into words. "Azama promised me he wouldn't hurt Jake, not if I helped him. He promised. I can't let her hurt any more. Not any more. I can hear them, in my head. All of them. He promised. They scream in my head. They *pray*, that this time is the last, that the Goddess will forgive them. I – I –" He blinked and his mouth opened and closed, but nothing else came out. It was enough.

He staggered away, swaying so hard I thought he had to fall, but he managed to keep upright. I wanted to be sick, to fall to my knees and throw up everything, the whole black mess inside of me. I'd been a party to this all along, everyone had, whether they knew it or not. We'd moaned about the price of Glow, that it made the older machines clunky, that Glow globes for light didn't last long, and a hundred other things. Done what people always did, and complained when things weren't perfect. It had never occurred to anyone just how imperfect, how sickening it was, just as long as our carriages ran, our homes were light and warm, our food was on the table. We were blind because we wanted to be, and now I couldn't be blind any more, not with that light swarming over me.

Whelar pushed me after Pasha, out of the Glow room, away from the screams, into what looked like an office, of sorts. A desk, chairs, paperwork scattered all over. Some piping ran up one wall, making the occasional hissing grunt of badly maintained heating. Pictures on the wall: a faded one of a dark-haired man very much like Whelar grinning in his laboratory, other people, doctors or alchemists by their lab coats, patting him on the back as he held up a crude version of a Glow tube. A nicely done oil of a young woman, dark-eyed and with a hopeful look, as though all her life were spread out in front of her. Sunlight framed her face, made her ethereal and delicate, and hauntingly familiar.

"So here he is at last." A new voice that made me look away. Azama. Still creepingly familiar, he looked different now, not the arrogant bully intent on finding his wayward daughter. The daughter who sat hunched in a chair beside him. Lise looked at me from behind a tangled fall of hair and mouthed, "I'm sorry. He made me."

Azama smiled and nodded for all the world like this was a social occasion. I half expected him to say, "Pleased to meet you," or something. Instead he said, "It's been quite an effort to get you here. Didn't expect you to go missing once you got Downside, though that brought its own little benefits. But you're here now. The question is, what will you do?"

Jake had been right; his mouth did twist like I tasted bad. And where *was* Jake? I stole a glance at Pasha – no help there. Poor bastard was lost in it, and I envied him that, the expanse of my black where there is no fear, because I was full of it. Pasha's eyes were blank and far away, a faint twitching smile on his lips as he wrenched his fingers. He didn't seem to realise he was doing it, dislocating them, shoving them back in. New scars tangled round his hands and wrists, red scabby vines twining over his skin.

"It's a shame about Pasha," Azama said, and I faced him again rather than watch Pasha in his torment. "I had high hopes for him. The magic is strong, but the mind, the spirit ... Weak men are little use to me. I can use him to channel into the tubes for a little while, I suppose, until his mind goes completely. Then there will be other uses for him. You don't need much of a mind to feel pain." He shrugged, an offhand gesture that dismissed Pasha as beneath notice. Disposable.

I didn't like the way this was going and mangled a few words out. "Where's Amarie?"

Azama beamed and stretched his hands expansively to encompass the Glow room outside, proud of himself. "Safe, and she'll stay safe as long as you cooperate. Really, it's taken far too long to get you here. You were *supposed* to stay in the hotel until I came. That girl should have kept you there long enough. But there, an added bonus that you helped us see that it was Jake and Pasha stealing my girls. I've been searching for you for quite some time, especially since Perak came to my notice again, and watching you since I found you in that office with Dendal. Oh, the Ministry knows all about him," he said when I opened my mouth to speak. "He's no good for us. Too soft in the head, like Pasha here. Now you, Rojan, are a very different prospect from Pasha."

It was all too much of a whirl to process properly. "I am?"

"Oh, you are. Stronger in the head than young Pasha. Too clever to use your magic much, but powerful, very powerful; I knew that as soon as you caught Lise. That's when I knew I had to get you down here: the strength you showed then, the power of your magic."

It was on the tip of my tongue to say that wasn't me, that power was the pulse pistol, but I clamped down on the words just in time. No sense telling him I was weaker than he thought. He'd find out soon enough, it looked like.

He seemed to misconstrue my lack of answer. "Afraid of it perhaps? I think so, but a wise man bewares what can destroy him, and that care will save him. It feels good though, doesn't it? The flow of it in the air? The call of it in your bones?" His voice took on an odd timbre, somehow hypnotic.

The way Azama shut his eyes, the almost sexual purse of his lips, made me want to puke. The more so because he was right. It did feel good, more than good, and I wanted it back. He knew it too, because he came and stood right in front of me, eye to eye, like we were co-conspirators. The only two people who could know this thing, feel it. I still wanted to puke. Preferably on his shoes.

"We need it, Rojan. Not you and me, the *city* needs it, and there are so few of us capable of this. Without the Glow, what would happen? No machines, no factories, no trade. Without trade we'd starve. Almost every last ounce of food we eat comes in payment for what we make. We have little land left to farm, little way of producing our own. We grew too big on synth, trapped by the mountains that made us. The Glow is a necessary evil, I'm sure you can see that, the lesser of two terrible things. Without the Glow, it's starve – or back to the synth. Thousands dying a cruel and needless death. And you don't want that, do you?"

I stared at him in horror. He made it sound so necessary, so *normal*, when it was anything but. "So you kidnapped my niece to get me to help you?"

"How else would we have got you to come of your own free will? Besides, I wanted to see my only grandchild."

"Your *what*?"

Only then I saw it, because he let me. The nose shortened, the cheeks hollowed, the voice . . . the voice I'd remembered long after I'd forgotten his face, etching itself into my head, showing me pictures. The face that was now, piece by piece, becoming his own again, with the talent that he'd given me. The only thing I had of him, my Minor, my talent for disguising myself. I looked up at the picture of the woman on the wall – hopeful, and I hadn't seen her that way for decades. My mother, before she got sick, before she withered away in front of me.

I looked back again at Azama, and knew him now, and wished I didn't. My father.

I thought back barely minutes, to when I'd used my presence to scare the crap out of Jake, used her fear against her to make her do what I wanted, because I had to. A necessary evil. Puking was becoming a real possibility. I wasn't like him, I wouldn't be like him. Would I?

"You had Perak shot." It was all I could think of to say – he'd had his own son shot, for this, but at least now I knew how they'd known Perak was my brother.

"I did it all for you, Roji," he said and I winced at the pet name, which I only remembered Ma calling me. "I did it because now you don't need to hide any more. You can get out of that shitty little place of Dendal's, doing shitty work for no money. You can be here with me, like you were always meant to. Perak being shot – that was a mistake, but it didn't matter. It's you I needed, you who were always so much like me. I knew you'd have the magic. I always knew it would be you."

He moved forward and I had to work at not flinching back, no matter my watery muscles. He was pleading now, needing me to see, but all I could see was the sickness in his head.

"I made the Glow for you, for your mother, so no one else would die of the synth. I did it for you, Roji. And it is your free will, your choice. To help us, or not. Only if you don't ..." his gaze slid towards the poor wretched figure of Pasha, whimpering with every crack of his joints, "you might find it not so enjoyable. I'll leave you to decide, but I know my boy. I know that you're a part of me, that you're strong enough in the head to know what needs to be done, what's necessary."

I wanted to leap up and strangle him, throttle the life out of the smug bastard, but I could barely stand up on my own. So Azama – my father, for fuck's sake – left without me killing him, Pasha trailing behind like a slack-jawed ghost.

Lise scurried to follow, but she stopped for a bare moment to say, "He made me, he made us all. I'm sorry. I keep trying to tell him about—" Her – my, *our* – father's abrupt call cut her off and she ran after him. I couldn't help but notice the brands on her wrists, the fresh bruises on her face. Even his own daughter wasn't safe.

No one was safe.

They left me on my own for a while, stirring it all in my head. Alone except for Whelar, who prodded at me every so often and jabbed me with the syringe when he thought his whatever-it-was had begun to wear off. I was starting to develop a serious dislike for Whelar, but was too numb to do anything about it. In fact I was pretty sure that if I tried to stand up I'd land flat on my face, the only consolation being that it wouldn't hurt. So I thought, because that was all I had left.

None of it made much sense. My father had brought me here to help him. All those goons looking for me hadn't been trying to kill me, but to *find* me. Lise had apologised, but I wasn't sure for what. I'd caught her with the pistol, and then Amarie had been kidnapped, by my father, to bring me here. I couldn't see how that was connected, except maybe Lise was scoping me out, maybe told him how I'd caught her and how much magic the pulse pistol shoved out. And what was Dwarf doing here, and Dench? My father, Namrat's balls, my father. And just where the fuck was *Jake*?

That last question was answered by a commotion outside the door. A man screamed, briefly, before the sound cut off into a gurgle, making Whelar leap to his feet in alarm. A loud bang followed and something, a bullet perhaps, smashed into the door and ripped part of the flimsy wood away. Then a sound I knew: the buzzing throb of my pulse pistol. A body hit the door and slid down.

When the door opened, Dench was holding the pulse pistol at Jake's head, but he didn't need it. She was spark-out, flopped on the floor like a raggedy doll. With a word to the guards outside – "I'll take it from here, off you go" – Dench shoved the pistol in his pocket, grabbed her swords, threw them back into the Glow room, and pulled Jake into the office, quickly cuffing her hands behind her back. Wise man – she was going to be pissed as hell when she woke up.

"Nice weapon," Dench said when he straightened up. He dabbed at the cut along his thumb with a grubby cloth. "Bit flashy, but does the job. Dwarf's a sodding genius."

"You're a pain-mage too?" I'd never even had so much as a hint of it from him.

He shrugged, offhand and casual. Not the usual Dench. "Little bit. Not like you. Just a little something that helps me through my day. Like all the Specials."

All this time I'd known him – damn, been friends with him, gone drinking and womanising with him – and I'd never known. Not even a sniff. I wasn't sure what was worse – that he was a mage too and I'd not noticed, or that he was a Special. It was a hard thing to believe, especially of someone like him, who'd always seemed so dedicated to helping the victims of the crimes he investigated, who always seemed to care. One of the good guys in a world full of arseholes. Now he was just another bastard.

It was getting to the point that if the Goddess turned up in a blaze of light and glory, I wouldn't have been too surprised.

On the floor, Jake blinked her groggy way back to consciousness. Her first action was to wriggle on to her back and aim a sodding great kick at Dench's arse, sending him sprawling to the floor. I'd anticipated that – well, anticipated she'd be pissed off and likely to hit the closest target anyway – and used it. Whelar watched open-mouthed as Dench hit the floor and I staggered to my feet and knocked the doctor down. I'd like to say it was with a fantastic punch, but I still couldn't feel anything, and when I stood up I fell into him. The effect was much the same – I was a fair bit bigger than him and I squashed him nicely, getting particular pleasure from the squeak he made as my elbow landed in his groin with all my weight behind it.

When I looked up, Jake had managed to get her handcuffed hands in front of her and was intent on hitting Dench with a double-fisted punch, right to the face. Dench wasn't out yet though – he blocked the blow with one arm. The other hand scrabbled in his pocket where he'd stowed the pulse pistol.

I managed to scramble to my knees, left Dr Whelar wheezing and dry-heaving behind me, and crawled towards them. Dench threw an elbow into Jake's face that sent her reeling on to her back, and in a heartbeat he was on her, pinning her with ease, no matter her frantic struggles. He dragged the pulse pistol out of his pocket and aimed.

My stumble unbalanced him, just for a moment but it was enough to knock him off Jake. The pulse pistol skittered across the floor, out of my reach, but Jake saw what it was and leapt after it. Not quite fast enough – Dench almost flattened her, but she got her hand round it and slid it across the floor to me. My fingers were clumsy on the handle. I almost dropped it twice, as Dench forgot about Jake and came for me, hands outstretched for the pistol.

He needn't have worried. I pulled the trigger and all I got was a dry click. No pain, no magic, no pulse. Fuck. Then Dench was on me, his fist pounding into my face with a precise finesse I would never have believed. Of course, he'd forgotten what I had forgotten. I never felt a damn thing, but I did manage to pull off one rough, wildly inaccurate punch that got me my only bit of luck that day. He pulled away from me, avoiding the blow, straight into the path of the chair Jake was bringing down over his back.

The silence was beautiful. All that broke it was breathing – my panting, Jake's harsh breath, Dench's battered snore, Whelar's almost inaudible squeak.

"The pistol," I said when I got my breath back. "Put it in Dench's hand."

Jake's frown showed a deep distrust of what I was saying, but she did it.

"Now point it at Whelar's head."

She grinned at that, a wild, heartbreakingly free smile that lit her up like a Glow tube. The buzz of the pistol was loud in the quiet, and Whelar slumped unconscious.

Jake rifled through Dench's pockets and came up with the key to her cuffs. I dropped the damned thing three times trying to get them unlocked but finally we had it. So had Dench and Whelar, because we handcuffed them to the heating pipe in the corner, locking one man on each side.

Jake sat back on her haunches and gave me a thoughtful stare. "So, now what? What happened to you? You were there one minute and not the next."

"Now what is, we're pretty screwed. And I'm not sure. I just knew how to be somewhere else? I was going to grab Amarie and bring her back, if I could. It was worth a try. Probably would have worked too, but I think I may have gone the teensiest bit mad in the process."

Her mouth hooked into a smile. "Then you can get us where we need to be, and no need to worry about being seen on the way."

"There's a slight hitch to that. Would you, um, mind helping me up?"

She only made a slight moue of disgust when she pulled on my arm, and finally I was back on my feet. A bit wobbly, because I couldn't feel my toes for balance, but the wall helped.

"What's the matter with you?" she asked.

"Long story. Short version: no magic. We need to get out of here, quick as we can before my father gets back. I may need you to help me walk."

She took a shaky step back, her hand groping for a sword, a reassurance that wasn't there any more. "Your father?"

I swore under my breath – why had I let that out? Because the very fact that it was him was still stunning my brain, I don't doubt, but it had been a stupid thing to do. "I had no idea, I swe—"

"You bastard. I believed you, I *trusted* you." Jake kept stepping back towards the door, her hands grasping uselessly at air. "You were working with him the whole time – I should have known. Not the first Upsider to try to get us, oh no, but Pasha said, he said you really believed that your niece had been kidnapped."

"She was, I swear it." I stumbled forward, and fell to one knee. Fuck Whelar's experiment and my numb legs, I needed to get up, needed to stop her before she did anything stupid. "I didn't know who by."

"But you led him straight to us just the same. I believed

you, and now you've killed us both, Pasha and me, and all the girls we could have got out. And Pasha, what you did to him . . . I – no, we – we *believed* you. We thought you'd help, not kill us."

It was that last that cut me the hardest, the cruellest words I'd ever heard said to me, in a hush of a whisper, barely heard. I tried to say it wasn't true, tried to say I wanted him dead as much as she did, but my numb lips couldn't form the words. For once I couldn't lie. Because, meaning to or not, I *had* led my father to her and Pasha, the same as if I'd pointed a big arrow over the top of them and shouted, "Hey, over here," and he'd maybe known I'd do it. All I could say, pathetic as it was, was this. "I'm sorry. I believed me too, and I should know better."

She staggered back into the door and fumbled it open. The look she gave me will stay with me for ever. I'd taken what little life she had left, the smallest things that meant everything to her, taken them and smashed them at her feet. Smashed her whole world, and left her reeling. *Nice job, Rojan, very nice. Kiss of Death, my arse, more like Angel of Death, Namrat's bastard love-child.*

Then she was gone, out of the door and lost in the brightness of the Glow, leaving me alone. Alone and ashamed, and scared out of my wits at what was waiting for me when Azama got back.

Not half as alone as she was, not half as dead as she'd be once Azama or his goons got hold of her, and she hadn't a hope of escaping them, not on her own. Especially as she wasn't thinking clearly, I'd seen that.

I stumbled to the door, squinted out into light brighter than any sun, and followed her.

Chapter Sixteen

She got further than she had any right to. The brightness of
the Glow, growing with every passing heartbeat, with every
whimper, scream and prayer that bounced around the chamber, burned my eyes and made tears stream down my cheeks.

Whelar's injection had begun to wear off and I could feel
my feet, which helped. Sensation came gradually back to my
hands and face, and with it the tingle. Goddess help me, I
almost didn't care where it came from, almost gave in to it
there and then, I was so relieved to have it back. It also meant
I didn't need to see, because Jake was a blast of force when I
asked it, a yanking tug on my innards telling me which way
she'd gone.

It also told me she was headed in exactly the wrong direction, straight towards a knot of goons, and Azama. Or maybe
that was the right direction, for her. I staggered after her, out
of the Glow chamber into a corridor that was black as

Namrat's heart in comparison. I couldn't see, but I didn't have to – she was right there in front of me.

I grabbed for her, missed her and tried again. This time I got her arm and yanked her back. She came, but not quietly, with nails and teeth and knees. I got my hand over her mouth and was rewarded with a palmful of teeth. In the end I had to use brute strength, what little I had left, but at least she wasn't biting me any more.

"I didn't know. I didn't, I swear." I kept saying it, quiet as I could, over and over, but I don't think she believed me. "Stop it, stop, or you'll get us all killed."

As soon as she quietened I let her go, ready for her to come at me again. I couldn't really blame her – we had precious few choices left anyway. I still couldn't see properly, but shapes were just becoming visible in the blotchy gloom.

"So what are you going to do then, Rojan?" Her voice was wet with tears, but steady enough. Maybe going for me had taken some of the recklessness out of her. "Turn me over to your father, like you did with Pasha? Or are you going to let me go, and let me do what I came to do?"

The voice came out of the dark, silencing us both. A voice of sanity in an insane world, a voice of order and calm and normality. "Now that's a very good question. So, Roji, what are you going to do? Who are you going to save, the worthless few or the worthy many?"

At Azama's word, Glow globes snapped on and I could see. I wished I couldn't. The face of the Goddess loomed above me, twisted beyond anything I'd seen before. There was no benignity here, no soft features, not even the staunch look of the mural in the Downside temple I'd seen. Here she was fury, she was loathing, she was contempt, she was hope, pain, suffering, an avenging goddess with a whip in her one hand and a bloody sneer on her lips. And a tiger at her feet. Not a mural, or a painting. A real tiger, and an explanation for the growling. Namrat, pacing up and down, eyes bright and fierce.

Jake moaned beside me and fell to her knees with her head in her hands. Her whispered prayers, more like pleadings, rattled along my spine and chilled my soul. So did the altar beneath the mural, a flat stone soaked with dark, ground-in stains. Jake's swords lay atop it, crossed and bloody. And he stood next to it with a smug, quizzical look about him, as though he'd enquired after my health, not asked me who to condemn. Azama.

He stepped towards us and Jake raised her head, as though against her will, to stare at him with dull, useless hatred. Then her gaze shifted and the rage drained away with her mouthed word. "Pasha."

Pasha huddled by the side of the altar, blank-eyed and twitching. A splash of blood smudged one cheek and his hands twisted, always twisted as he kept himself in the black.

Jake struggled to her feet and lurched towards him, but a nod from Azama brought one of his goons out of the dark to grab her. The instant his hand touched her arm she turned on him like a wild thing, like the snarling tiger that snaked around the Goddess's legs. The sheer ferocity took the goon by surprise — no doubt he was more used to the young girls and their subservience — and before I could even raise a hand to help Jake, to pull him off her, protect her, his face was bloody from where she'd raked her nails down over one eye and cheek.

Flash, Pasha had called it, her way of fighting. Not really a fighter, an acrobat, a show, an act — yet now it came to it, I still wouldn't have liked to take her on. She'd have killed me.

I don't think she really saw anything — her eyes were as wild as her movements. Every veneer was gone, every last bit of varnish over her soul, and all that was left was as she'd said — fear and anger, and this goon got the lot. He just about managed to raise an arm against the onslaught, to grope for the gun in a pocket, and then it was over, at a word.

"Stop." The voice, the sane, smooth, rational voice of reason. Azama's Voice. It had always been my father's Major, the way he could use it to command, to cajole, to conjure images to dance in your head. Yet either he'd never shown me its true power when I was a boy, or it had grown beyond all reason. That one word — "Stop" — and Jake froze in mid-swipe. The goon lay like a felled tree, hand still halfway to the gun. I halted in mid-step. The Voice was everything.

Azama's lip curled up in a sneer as he looked at Jake, then me. "See how easy it is? You, hold her this time and don't let go."

The goon stood up and grabbed at Jake, his hands rough as he yanked her to her feet with a whimper. "You'll pay for that, bitch," he whispered in her ear. "For a long time. Azama can use you to power a whole factory, all on your own. I wonder how long you'll last?"

His whisper seemed to break her free of Azama's spell and she writhed silently in the goon's grasp, trying with everything she had, but he had her now. I fingered the pulse pistol in my pocket, and wondered how many more goons lurked in the dark edges of the temple. Too many, almost certainly, and mages too without a doubt. Azama wasn't stupid. I'd have gone for it anyway, anything to help her, to stop that goon pawing at her. At that moment I'd have killed any man in front of me to help her, save her from what I knew was coming, but the Voice turned on me, caught me.

"Shall I assume that Dr Whelar and my guards are dead? I'll take that as a no for your answer then, Rojan? Shame: I was hoping you'd follow in the family trade."

Jake stopped fighting at that reminder of who I was, and Azama piled in, piled it all on to her in a voice like treacle. "Don't tell me he didn't say? I'm very proud of my son. Or I was. He did a splendid job flushing you and Pasha out, don't you think? Ah, my favourite blasphemous little bitch, Jake. Did you think a change of name and dyeing your hair would mean I don't recognise you? You always screamed so prettily, begged for atonement so pleasingly. I know you'll do so again, because I'm very sure you need to atone to the Goddess, and we know how to do that. Don't we?" His voice was soothing, smooth as skin, soft as pillows.

He walked towards her, slow and steady, his eyes not leaving hers. I expected her to lash out, kick him in the nuts. *Some*thing. But she stood there in the goon's grasp, unmoving except for a tremor that shuddered through her at intervals. She seemed pinned to the spot, powerless before his voice.

As I seemed to be. I tried to summon the will to move, to pull all the magic into me and blow it out of his big, fat head and save Jake from her worst nightmare. It all narrowed down to that, to Jake, to getting the goon's hands off her before she dissolved completely. That thought was what made the power come, flowing blessedly through me like a stiff shot of the green stuff, warming me, making my mind buzz with it. Only, try as I would to push it out, to turn Azama into nothing more than a pile of goo, all I could hear was his voice, and I wanted so badly to believe him. I wanted him to be the father I remembered.

His words bounced oddly round my head. They seemed to enter my ears as a vile, insidious outpouring, but by the time they reached my brain they made complete sense. I tried remembering what it had been like when my father had left, how much I'd hated the bastard for abandoning us, and all I could summon was the wish to keep hearing his voice, to see the pictures it made in my mind, to wallow in its reassurance. My father's voice had always meant safety to me when I was young. His voice had been warmth and reason and comfort. Hearing it again made everything between then and now seem irrelevant, a shallow experience not worth thinking about. I was safe with the voice of my childhood, and all the years of terror and reproach between were nothing.

Azama strolled towards Jake, and even when he signalled the goon to let her go, still she didn't move. When he lifted a hand to stroke her cheek, she jerked back, but not for long. He had her with his voice, with his words, no matter the real sense of them.

"I do it because I love you, because I want the Goddess to love you, forgive you. You know that. It was always because we love you and we want you to be in the Goddess's favour."

Jake's mouth worked, but no words came out. The Voice was right, and rational, sane in an insane world. We were safe in the Voice.

"Maybe I'll be even more generous and assign you to Pasha. You'd like that, hmm?"

I glanced at Pasha, and he was fighting it, every step, every word. Sweat poured from him, soaked his shirt, dripped from his brow with every twitch and tremor. He tried to speak, but only a moan came out. It took me long moments to work out why he fought, when the Voice was so right, when it rolled with such richness in my head. How could it be wrong, that voice of childhood, which always knew the answer to everything my young mind could ask? Then Pasha managed to come out of whatever nightmare he was in, just for a few brief moments. He looked up at me, and I felt him in my head. *Please, Rojan, please for the Goddess's sake, not again. Please. For Jake — it'll break her.*

Please, Rojan. Please, because I can't, I want to but I can't, we *can't, not against him . . .*

His voice echoed weirdly, at odds with Azama's power. It seemed that was the last of Pasha's strength, his fight, because his eyes rolled up into his head and he slid to the floor. The sound of him hitting the ground, the muffled, meaty thud, gave me a glimpse, a hope. Azama's voice was so right, so very right . . . and so wrong. Pasha twitched and moaned, fallen in for good now, into the black. I could feel him drawing away from me.

"Pain is the only salvation any of us has, the only atonement we can make to our Goddess," Azama said in a seductive whisper. So true, so very true.

I kept my eyes on Pasha, on the fading movements, the whispering breath, the thought that he'd spent his last ounce of energy on trying to save Jake, through me. Sacrifice, the Goddess and the tiger. Pain was my only salvation, the only salvation, the only chance of atonement or redemption any of us had. Azama was right, so right.

He turned the Voice on me, his eyes full of hope. "You'll join me, Roji. Become what you were always meant to. You can't turn me down now, not when I made sure no one else need die like your mother. We'll keep Mahala running, you and I, keep her people fed. The right people, of course. The faithless, the dissolute, the feckless all end up down here in the end. They're worth nothing, except the means to power Mahala, to save the righteous from starvation."

I wrapped my fingers around the pulse pistol. The Voice told me to trust it, that it knew what was best and that was pain, to atone for my sins, to make the Goddess love me despite them, despite my hatred of her.

"You can help save them all, Roji, save them from Namrat, from damnation. You can save a whole city of people, just by saving these girls down here, making them atone through the searing brightness of pain. When we hurt is when we're closest to the Goddess."

Pasha was almost gone now, fading away from me. If I had to track him, soon all I'd get would be a blur, a slick black place where he once was.

"You can be a great hero, save them all, and save the city too. You will save everyone, if you join me. You're so very much like me."

I yanked my gaze away from Pasha and back to Azama, to his sneering lips, his honeyed, hypnotic words that made such *sense*, even while I still wanted to puke all over his shoes.

"I think I'll save you first." I pulled out the pulse pistol and got him right between the eyes. Azama seemed to want me to be a priest. I didn't want to be one, though: priests never get the hot chicks.

Chapter Seventeen

The *thunk* of Azama hitting the floor made my lips curl. The goon holding Jake let go of her to go for his gun, and she staggered to the altar, to Pasha. A bullet zinged off the floor next to me and I looked up to see half a dozen of the fake Specials advance on us, all with guns drawn.

A clatter of metal to the side and then Jake had her swords, her wall and comfort, and the ice queen was back, as though the poor wretched girl of minutes ago was a dream. She stood in front of Pasha, shielding him, her swords ready and a lunatic grin pasted across her face, as though this was what she'd lived for all this time, why she'd survived. This was the moment Pasha said she hoped for, prayed for.

Her glance flicked up to the image of the Goddess hanging before us, stern, cruel and commanding, no hint of the sympathy her images usually held. With a whispered prayer that I only just caught – "Let it be today" – she went for the goons.

The next few minutes were a jumble of swords and bullets and swearwords, of magic pulling at me, pushing me, twisting inside my head, inside my gut till I was sick again. All over Azama's shoes, which made me feel a little better.

The men weren't mages, at least. Just goons, pretend Specials, or Jake and I would almost certainly have died right there. I'd have died anyway if not for Jake, of that I'm quite sure.

I had no doubt the mages wouldn't be long either. When I'd stopped throwing up, I did a quick stocktake. Pain: present. All too present. Whoopee, situation normal, hand completely screwed. Goons: down and out. Two were unconscious – mine. Four were on the floor in various states of bloody distress – Jake's. Flash, my arse. When her back was to the wall, she was more vicious than any tiger. Speaking of which, the last goon had got too close to the tiger chained at the bottom of the mural and was regretting it in a very vocal and splashy fashion. Bullets that had hit home: none, except one that had pinged from a wall and taken Azama's ear off. I wasn't too worried about that one. Fathers I had fucked over: one, even if it felt good and simultaneously a betrayal. Painted goddesses with painted whips in their hand, glaring at me like I was on the cusp of hell as they stood over a bloody, accusing altar that screwed with my gut: one, but it was a pretty bad one, mainly because I agreed with her. I was on the cusp of a hell worse than Namrat's kingdom. Dying Pashas: one. Jakes shaking me and telling me to "Do something, just fucking *do* something! Please, Rojan": one.

I staggered up and flopped against the wall. I wasn't sure what I'd done in the last few minutes, but I did know it had screwed me. Parts of my brain seemed to be missing, were black when I tried to look in. But they also seemed to be growing, sidling their way into my thoughts, taking them over, pulling me in, leaving only little pictures of the world that seemed like fake cut-outs.

A hand in mine, pulling at me, linked me back to here and now. Jake, her face wet with tears, saying, "Please, Rojan . . ." I couldn't seem to grasp what she meant, until she reached up on tiptoe and kissed me. It wasn't much, a cold pressing of the lips with a plea inside it, but hell, I've never knowingly missed a kiss.

The lights were bright suddenly, lighting up the dark parts of my brain and telling them to shut the fuck up and get the fuck out. Reality hit me with a good left hook. Pain in my hand, the tingle of magic, the smell of blood from the goons and beyond, from the altar under its forbidding Goddess. It was the blood on the altar that did it. I may not believe in all that religion shit, but this, in her name . . . Dendal had been right about one thing: it was about time I started believing in something, and that something was putting this right, one step at a time, no matter the cost. Like, me being lynched when everyone started starving to death. I didn't care about that. I didn't care about anything but stopping what he'd started, about making Jake not afraid any more, and about not being my father.

Jake's voice was vague behind me. The knowledge that very soon mages would be here, mages better than I was, stronger, was a mere afterthought. Pasha lay slumped on the floor, the sketch of him in my mind almost too weak, too dark to see. One step at a time, and I would start with him. For Jake, because she'd kissed me, because she was crying and I couldn't bear it. And for Pasha, because he was one of those kids once, and because he had helped me and all I'd done in return was fuck him over.

Another noise, this time one that penetrated.

"Holy Goddess, Rojan. I never thought you'd do it." I looked up into the surprised and careworn eyes of Dench. The gun in his hand was loosely pointing my way, but drooped as he took in the rest of the room. "Oh, we are in *big* shit."

I couldn't seem to grasp how he was there, and if he was, why he wasn't shooting me. I had more important things to worry about, such as what Azama might try once the pulse wore off.

"I need whatever Whelar had in that syringe." I don't know who I was saying it to, but Jake lifted her head from where she bent over Pasha's still form.

"Pasha, I have to—" She looked at him, slumped on the floor. I never thought I'd ever see her cry, but she was, great silent tears that she scrubbed away with a vicious hand. I wasn't sure Pasha was breathing any more, could barely feel the trace of him. I needed to get her away, get her mind on something, anything else while my own mind raced over what I could do.

"Azama first. Quick, before he comes to." Just in case, I ripped off a part of my jacket and shoved it in his mouth. At least I wouldn't be able to hear that voice, those vile words making sense, trying to tell me I was like him. "Once I've dealt with him, I can help Pasha, but if he comes round I can't do a damned thing."

She dithered for long moments, but in the end she stood up. "Be careful," Jake said. "Other mages, more of Azama's men." With a last, despairing glance at Pasha, Jake ran. Then I had Dench on his own, without Jake to hear what I needed to ask him, needed to know.

Dench paced up and down thoughtfully, watching the face of the Goddess. He cast me a sharp look, and then it all came out.

"Didn't think I might have more than one key for the cuffs, did you? You'd have made a really crap Special, Rojan, if that helps."

"A bit. You going to tell me what the fuck you're up to?" I mentally checked Pasha again. Slipping further and further away. We had to do something, and quickly. Or rather *I* did, but I needed to know too.

"I had to see which way you'd go. Thought you'd probably end up on your father's side. They all do, in the end. Or almost all. Fuck, Rojan, you just shot the Archdeacon! We are in so much shit, I'm surprised we haven't drowned in it. We still might. Ministry are on their way, and they'll be here any minute, and then you're dead. We all are."

It seemed like a couple of years before Jake got back, but it couldn't have been longer than a minute. Azama was just starting to groan his way back to wakefulness, and the words "you just shot the Archdeacon" were swimming round my head, pursued by sharks, but that wasn't at the forefront.

Jake handed me the syringe and a vial. I filled the syringe with clumsy hands and slid it under the skin of Azama's elbow. The way he struggled, the wide stare of his eyes, was more satisfaction than I ever thought I'd get out of bed.

"We're not in as much shit as we're going to be, Dench. And I still want an explanation. But first things first. Pasha needs a doctor, and Whelar will do." He needed more than a doctor, but I wasn't going to say that in front of Jake.

"You get Pasha there, and I'll see what I can do to hold everything off. This uniform is good for that." Dench strode off into the darkness, and I held back a twinge of misgiving. I had no idea whether he was Azama's man or not. Specials swore to the Goddess, not any man, but the Archdeacon was the mouth of the Goddess, and Azama was Archdeacon, if Dench was telling the truth. He *was* the Ministry. But I was too fucked up to stop Dench, or even demand any answers. He was gone, we were alone and that was the best I could hope for. A chance to get out, get everyone out. Maybe.

First Pasha. I had to get him somewhere safer, because mages, goons, Ministry men, everyone was going to be here very soon. It was a struggle, but I managed to pick him up without my hand screaming too hard. When I had him, he seemed too light, too insubstantial. I led the way back to the room where the good doctor was still cuffed to the pipe. Dench didn't trust him either then. Good. The doctor might come in handy. In the meantime, Jake didn't need to see this.

"Jake, find all the girls you can, get them all out, all right?"

"But—"

"No buts, that's the deal. You find them, as many as you can, and get them back to where we were, that secret room outside the keep. Find Amarie for me, and Lise. All of them, and get them out as fast as you can."

I don't know whether she answered, because I was already sinking, flowing after Pasha. Into the black.

I've said that the black is different for all of us, that it relieves you of what you most want to be rid of. For me, the black has no fear in it. I am not afraid there, except of it, of falling further than I can dig myself out of, of it persuading me to stay. For Pasha it was different. His black was silence, the dead quiet of no overheard words or thoughts, no screams or cries of pain, no desperate prayers.

When I'd skimmed the surface of Dendal's black before, to pull him out when he went on one of his little trips, he'd been a bright, brilliant presence. Even in my own personal heaven and hell of it, I could see my own light. Pasha was just a flicker, a tiny shining thread leading through a quietness that unnerved me. I tried to call out, to call Pasha back like I did with Dendal, but no sound came out; my words were dead in my mouth.

This was more than a skim of the surface, this was a visit to the worst reaches of another man's mind, and the thought of that made the flesh creep almost off my back. I tried again, tried to call out while I followed the thread, and there he was, a sad, fading light huddled at the bottom of a vast ocean of silence.

I'd never been this far in, not even in my own black, and my mind flailed around, trying to work out what to do, how to pull him back. In the end, instinct – fear – took over and I pulled at him with hands that didn't exist, talked to him with words even I couldn't hear. I had to, for him, but more for Jake. I was doing this for her, because I wanted her to be happy and screw everything else. At that moment, it was all I cared about.

The silence pressed in on me, muffled my thoughts as well as my tongue, and panic was a sour taste in my mouth as I wondered whether it was possible to get lost in another mage's black. Panic brought with it its own danger – my own magic, fighting to break free, fighting to *do* . . . and I wasn't strong enough, because I let it.

The next I knew, I was hunched over Pasha on the floor, something light and fragile caged in my hand. Without knowing what I was doing, or why, I pressed it into Pasha's chest and sat back, drained of all thought or feeling.

When I raised my head, Jake, Whelar and Dench were staring at me as though I was a ghost, or maybe just something really weird that had dropped out of their nose.

"What *are* you?" Dench's voice was barely a murmur. Not the first time I'd been asked that today, and I still didn't have an answer.

"My son, finding out just how powerful he is, how powerful he could be if he stopped this and joined me. When he sees that it's necessary," Azama said behind me. There was no power to his voice now, still recovering from the numbness, though the memory of it made me itch.

"Shut the fuck up," I said, but without much force. Pasha's eyelids flickered as he came back to the now, to the here. His breathing was laboured, and he'd begun to twitch again, but he managed a puzzled look my way.

I wish I knew, I thought at him, and I did. Something was happening to me, something twisting and changing inside, and it was scaring the crap out of me. But I was going to use it.

"He needs a doctor." Stating the obvious, but my brain wasn't up for much more. "Whelar?"

To give him some credit, Whelar never hesitated but pulled the cuff chain as far as he could from the pipe and began to look Pasha over.

I struggled to think logically, and turned to Jake. I really wished she hadn't seen that, because it seemed to have shaken her, badly. Her lips were white and trembling, her hands flexing into fists and then splaying helplessly. I had to help her, get her mind away. Besides, I needed *her* help. "You were going to get everyone out?"

She barely looked up from hovering over Pasha, and her voice was faint and trembling when it finally came. "Not on my own. There's too many, of them and his goons, his mages. I can't."

"Yes you can, you have to. And quickly. Don't try to take out all his men, just get the girls, get them out somewhere safe." The only way I could think of to get her out, to get *her* safe, by making it about the girls she'd spent all this time trying to find and save. She'd never leave otherwise, and I needed her to. Selfish thought, but if I got nothing else from this day, I wanted her and Amarie safe. They were part of every thought. I wanted, very badly, to hold on to her and tell her it would be all right, and maybe convince myself that I'd be all right too. I knew that for a bad idea, so this was all I could do, for her and myself both.

Jake rocked back on her heels, her hands rubbing at her wrists, harder now, almost scrubbing at them as though trying to get rid of some filth. She didn't seem to notice what she was doing as she glared a flat, dead stare at my father. I couldn't even look in his direction.

"I'll help." The last voice I expected to chime in. Dench.

I ground the heel of my good hand into an eye, to see if that helped make more sense of everything. "I don't think so."

"I do. I've been a Special a long time, Rojan, longer than I've known you. I never told you because — well, Specials are about as welcome as a fart in a temple. More feared than pain-mages even, because people know we exist. But it's changing.

I can remember what we used to be, what we *should* be. I'm not the only one, either. We swore to the Goddess, every last one of us. We swore to serve her, not the Ministry. Mostly everyone thinks it's the same thing, and mostly they're right, but like I say, some of us remember. We've been guarding the entrances here for years, ever since it was sealed, but we didn't know what was going on. They never let us in, they just told us this was where they made the Glow, so we had to keep it safe. And we did, and we didn't question it much, though there's some of us been feeling uneasy about it, about them. So we watched and waited. Until you came down here. I knew there was something up then, for you to risk your arse like that. So I followed, and I'm not sure if I'm glad I did or not."

Dench's gaze ran over Azama with a sneer. "In the name of the Goddess. This isn't what I swore to, or all my fathers before me, back to when Mahala was just a castle and the Specials were the warlord's sworn assassins."

I still couldn't look at my father, because I was pretty sure I'd punch him stupid, so I didn't see the look on his face when he spoke. The words were bad enough. "You swore to protect the city too, and that's what I'm doing. Protecting the people, making sure they don't starve. Or would you go back to the synth? Would you, Rojan? Go back to people dying in the thousands? I left because I couldn't watch your mother die, not like that, and I had to find a different way. And I did. I saved who knows how many people. I saved the city, Roji, and you and Perak. I saved everyone."

I shut my eyes and pinched at the bridge of my nose. This was all too fucked up for words, because even without his magic powering his voice, I knew he was right. He *had* saved people from an evil, nasty death that I wouldn't wish on anyone, even him. But. "You couldn't watch her die. I didn't want to either, but I did, and you weren't there."

"And you'll condemn people to that, because I left, for your own selfish reasons? How many more will die like that, if we go back to synth?"

The question hung in the air like a bad smell.

Dench saved me from having to answer it, his voice low and urgent. "Rojan, look at me. I've known you for years. We're all but trapped here now. Ministry men all over, Downsiders all through the keep. I don't know how or why—"

"I told Dog where we were going, and how we planned to get here." Jake's voice, a whisper of what it had once been. "Told him that if we weren't back by matchtime we wouldn't *be* back, and to stick with Gregor – one of the other matchers. I had to tell Dog something. He's just a big kid, and I couldn't let him not know where we'd gone, that we might not be back, I had to make sure he'd be OK . . ."

Dench looked at her with pity in his eyes, and the set of his moustache. "More than OK, I think. There's Ministry men everywhere, but without Azama they're panicking. Downsiders running riot outside the castle, not just matchers but ordinary men and women. Matchtime was hours ago. I don't know what you told Dog, or what he told everyone else, but they're going crazy. And my Specials – I called them down, thinking to help, but they've got their hands full with that lot. There's blood all over, and it's not just those girls either. Look, Rojan, I can help you, help Jake get these kids out, I can find a way, or get my Specials to make a damn way. Now." He pulled his gun out of a pocket I hadn't even thought to search. I really would have made a crap Special. "I could have killed her, or you, any time. But I didn't. I used your pistol on her to keep her from getting shot by his goons, because I wanted to see what you'd do, which way you'd go. Rojan, *look at me*."

This time I did, watched the drooping moustache, the care-worn eyes, and thought about all the times he'd helped me. I slid a look at Jake and back to Dench and he got my meaning perfectly. "All right then. Jake, I need you to show me where to find all the girls we can," he said. "It's going to be bloody, it's going to be hard and we can't take Pasha."

Jake tried to protest, but Dench cut her off with a slash of the hand holding the gun. "If we try carrying him, we won't make it. There's still plenty of mages down here and until – unless I can get things under control, inside and out of the castle, we can only take those who can move on their own. If we take him, we can't take anyone else, see?"

"I'll take him," I said. Dench looked away at that, as though I'd let him down. "I can certainly make sure the Ministry aren't concentrating on you. I can do both at the same time, if I'm lucky."

"What are you going to do?"

"No fucking idea. But I'll think of something. I've got him to consider too." I nodded at Azama who, perhaps wisely, was staying quiet, for which I was thankful.

Dench considered for a few moments, until a gunshot at close range brought us all up sharp. After that, Dench was all business.

"I don't know if I'll make it back to you, Rojan. I'll try, that's all I can promise, but we'll get the girls. Jake, you and me, we'll find everyone we can and get them out. I know an extra exit or two that can get us Upside nice and quick, behind the Ministry men."

Jake looked up from where she still hovered over Pasha. "But what—"

"Rojan will bring him when he's done. Come *on*, I need you to show me where to find everyone. Or did you want this all to be for nothing?"

Jake was in no state to resist his bustling efficiency, but she cast me a pleading look as they left.

"I promise," I said. "You just get them all out."

When they were gone I heaved a big breath to try to calm myself. I had no idea what I was going to do, but I didn't want her seeing it.

Whelar looked up from where he was tending to Pasha, his voice and face matter-of-fact, as though tending a patient while cuffed to a pipe was a usual occurrence. "He needs a hospital."

"He'll get one. You're very concerned, considering."

"I'm a doctor first. I stop people dying. It's what we're for. And it's why you should listen to Azama."

Finally I looked down at my father, slumped against the wall. I prodded at him, the same as Whelar had done to me. He still seemed a bit numb, but I gave him some more of the stuff in the syringe, just to be on the safe side.

"So what are you going to do, Roji?"

"Stop calling me that. And I don't know yet. Come on, you're coming with me. Whelar, you keep Pasha alive, if *you* want to stay alive. I'll be back for him."

I pulled Azama to his feet and we went out to the room with the Glow, echoing to the sound of far-off gunshots. Downsiders perhaps, come to try for the factory, for the Ministry. For Jake and Pasha, because matchtime was hours ago and they hadn't come back.

It would all be for nothing, if Azama got away, if the Archdeacon stayed on his pedestal. It would probably be all for nothing anyway – the Ministry men, the fake Specials wouldn't shirk, would delight in stopping them.

Glow was all around us, making us shadowless and bright. The glass of the tubes was slick and cool under my fingers, no tingle of magic, no hint of what was actually making the Glow.

"How many?" I asked.

"How many what?" My father pretended nonchalant igno-rance, and I resisted the urge to let him drop to the floor in a crumpled heap.

"People, children, whoever you use. How many?"

"Not as many as the synth killed. Not even a tenth of the number synth killed in one year. And why do you care, Roji? They're all from down here, the very worst of the city. The 'Pit always was full of people worth nothing, or less – the faithless, the feckless. An affront to the Goddess! Now they're doing something useful. Someone has to, Roji. We have to have the Glow, all of us, if we want to eat. Even the children Upside, if that's what's sticking in your throat. Save these down here and those up there will starve, and it'll be you that killed them."

A man-sized tube pulsed against my hand, the Glow growing, brightening. So pretty, from such ugliness. I watched it rather than him, fascinated, repulsed by the swirl and throb of it. I let go of him, pressed my good hand into the glass, and for a heartbeat I felt it soften, mould around my fingers. "Are they worth more, then? The ones Upside. Are they worth more just because of who they are? Is Amarie worth more than the others down here because she's my niece?"

"Roji, we've no choice but—"

"Stop calling me that! All right then, answer this. How is it I can do this?"

The glass was still glass, still cool and slick and solid under my fingers – around my fingers – around my wrist. I wriggled my hand inside the tube, trying to still the surge up my arm from the contact with raw Glow.

You need me, you want to use me, you want the black, you want to let it all blow through you and fall in, where there is no fear.

"Yes," I whispered, and pulled my hand free. The echoes of the Glow lingered in my brain, lit by the leakage that made the room seem to sparkle in my head. "And no."

My father smiled at me, as though what I'd done was something he'd made. "You can do that because you've got talents you don't know about, that you've always been too afraid to use. You always thought it was your Minor, didn't you? Rearranging your face to suit you, to suit the situation. Rearranging, that's how you can do that, making things move to your will. It's not your Minor, it never was. You can do almost anything with a talent like that, a power that big, and I saw how much power when you caught Lise. You only need to channel it, train it. Why do you think I brought you? That's why we need you down here, helping us. We need you, Roji. The Ministry needs you, the *city* needs you."

Rearranging. Sounds so simple when you put it like that, doesn't it? It didn't feel simple, and neither did the choice. Save one lot of people, condemn more. Let people starve, or help the Ministry farm humans for Glow. It wasn't much of a choice, but then I've never been much of a decision maker.

My father was still talking behind me, but it was a buzzing drone next to what was inside me. I was black inside, I always had been black inside, not with magic, black with fear. Fear of pain, fear of magic, fear of being responsible, of having anyone rely on me because I would always let them down. Fear of being with someone, fear of being alone.

I realised that Jake had been right – all these kids probably had families, people who loved them, wanted them back
even if they were too afraid to say anything against the
Ministry. Amarie wasn't worth more than any of them just
because she was my niece. Just because it was my father doing
this. Somehow we had to stop this. For good.

Then my role in history could go down as the person who
starved a whole city. At least I'd *have* a role in history.

In the end, one thing decided me. Not Amarie, not my
father, not the thought of all the hundreds of thousands,
maybe millions of people Upside who'd starve, or all the girls
down here who were worth as much as anyone else. It was
Pasha's black, the utter silence of it. That it was silence he
craved because he'd heard and felt too much, more than any
one person should have to, and I was going to save him from
having to hear it any more. For her. Always it came back to
her.

I shut my eyes and stroked at the glass, sucked up all the
tingle around me, and pushed my hand into the tube. It got
easier each time I tried this rearranging. Easier but harder,
more painful. Closer to the edge. Maybe too close, because
even when I opened my eyes I could see the black flapping on
the edge of my vision, hear it calling across the void to me.

*You need me, you want to use me, you want the black, you want
to let it all blow through you and fall in, where there is no fear. You
need me. You want me.*

Maybe one girl isn't worth more than another, even if she

is my niece. But every kid down here was worth blowing this room sky-fucking-high for, and Namrat's balls to the consequences. But in the end, I did it for one person. For Pasha – so that Jake could try to be happy, they both could. Because he was worth more to her. Shit, I'm getting soppy in my old age.

You want me, you want to use me, become me.

"Yes, oh yes." My voice was barely even a whisper. I fell into it, and let the warm arms of the black wrap me in fearless power.

Chapter Eighteen

I wish I could tell you about what happened next in clearer detail, but whilst I was there, I also wasn't. My father screamed as the first tube smashed, I remember that, and I remember grinning at the sound, at the sheer impotent rage of it. Then, as the Glow burst over me, through me, my brain simultaneously lit up like the day and became black as night. Tubes around me smashed, melted, exploded into a million sparking dots. Glow ran everywhere, flashed through the air like Lise's electricity, ran about my feet like thick, hot blood, seeped into every part of me, became me. I may have screamed myself, I'm not sure, but it wasn't with impotence. It was with knowing that now, finally, I had found something to believe in. Not the Goddess, not Namrat or any of the gods, not magic, not other people. Me.

When it finally stopped, when the last tinkle of shattered glass had finished echoing around the chamber and the last remnant of Glow had disappeared into nothingness and the only light was coming through the door from the lamps in the office, I was on my knees. Not sick this time. No, this time I had lightning for bones, electricity for blood. I staggered to my feet, looking for, hoping for someone, *anyone*, to come against me.

There was no one. Except my father, who slumped on the floor and looked at me with a sick, stunned amazement. "What did you do?"

I wished people would stop asking that because I didn't know, not exactly, not yet. I yanked him to his feet, and had to resist the urge to throttle the life out of him one inch at a time. Everything was becoming clear to me now. "No, the question is, what did *you* do? I know why. Why you did this, and it wasn't to save the city, or anyone from starving or dying of synth, was it? No, it was so you could feel like this, because you were greedy and you wanted to feel like the Goddess flowed through your veins and anything was worth that, even torture and murder. Am I right?"

"No, Roji, I—"

"I told you not to call me that. Ma called me that, not you, and you left because you didn't have the guts to stay. Didn't have the guts for anything, without it. Without this."

I could see how to do it, in my head. All too clear, and tempting, to rearrange *him*. My fingers started to sink into his skin and it took an effort of will, a conscious pulling back, to stop them. I didn't want to be like him, and maybe there wasn't much choice about that, but not now. Not yet. "I was like that too. No guts. Like you, afraid without it, but I was afraid *of* it too. Not any more. I am not like you any more."

And there it was. I wasn't like him, or afraid, any more. Dendal might have banged on about mastery a bit too much and I hadn't listened, but maybe some had sunk in. Now I could see how he managed to skim the black, barring a few accidents. I'd accepted, as he had, that the black was part of me, the sum of my fears, my dreads, my nightmares, and now it was a part of all of me, not feared but accepted, not a separate place in my head I tried to keep out of, and I could stretch further than I'd ever thought possible.

I was the black and the black was me.

I dropped Azama and wiped my hand on my chest, like he was something dirty. Fuck, he was the dirtiest of all, and he was part of me too, but not a part I was willing to follow. He lay on the floor, looking up at me as though I'd betrayed him. Maybe I had.

He tried the Voice, one last time. "Rojan, you've killed everyone, but you'll be the first to die, you know that? Not by me: by the Ministry, or maybe by the people Upside, when they find out what you've done. Give up, give in, help me make the Glow again, and you can live. You can atone to the Goddess for what you've done."

Oh, he was good; I'll give him that. The Voice dragged up deeply buried memories, pulled at long-forgotten strings in my soul. To be someone my father was proud of, to be someone he wouldn't leave. That wasn't enough, not any more. Not for my new faith in me.

"I don't believe in the Goddess, and even if I did, I don't think she'd want me to atone for this. I used to believe in cash and that men aren't made for monogamy, that there isn't a woman alive I can't get into bed if I try hard enough, shit like that. I *used* to believe them like crazy. Now I believe that, sometimes, one person is worth more than another. That these people down here, these poor shits you've been farming for Glow, are worth any amount of you, or me. Just one of them is worth ten of you, or your Glow. That's what I believe in."

A crunch behind me, boots on broken glass. Dench. He looked around him with wide-eyed wonder, turning and turning, looking up and down at what was now just a huge room with a floor full of glass. No magic, no Glow, no vibrant energy. No pain either.

Finally he pulled himself together. Azama tried to speak, to use the Voice on him no doubt, but I leaned down and clamped my hand over his mouth. "Keep quiet, before I make silence a permanent thing for you. I can do that now, you know. If I have to thank you for anything, it's that."

"Shit, Rojan." Dench stared at us both, his face grey under the astonishment. "They'll kill you. Ministry – you'll be dead as last week's news."

The last vestige of the Glow ran from me then: the lightning left my bones, the electricity drained from my blood, and all I felt was tired, stupid and utterly heartsick. I found I didn't really care whether the Ministry killed me or not. I'd had the feeling for some time now, since before we'd got into the castle, that Amarie wasn't why I was here, that I was here for another reason. Well, I'd found it all right, and now I'd done it, I didn't have the energy to care about much else, except one thing: "Did you find them all? Is she safe?"

"I think we got them all. Got some of my lads from Upside scouring the place too. Found a bunch of mages – trying to run, though that concoction of Whelar's came in very handy. And Jake's safe enough for now."

"I sense a 'but' in this."

Dench's lips lifted at the corners in what might have been a tired smile. "But Ministry are coming, between us and the exits. I can get by all right, and so can my men, I can talk us out of this. Following orders is a wonderful thing. But you need to get out quick – your name is going to be mud just as soon as they realise what you've done, and they are going to know it's you. This little shit," he kicked at Azama, "told everyone to leave you be, kept you alive, but now . . . now you are dead meat. You didn't kill all his goons in the temple, and they're talking like it's the last thing they'll do. I've sent all the kids Up with some of my men, and Jake, though she fought me tooth and nail, but there's you and Pasha . . . I can't get you out, Rojan. Not past Ministry, not yet. Maybe not at all. They're killing everyone they can find that isn't Ministry. And they'll be looking for you in particular when they see this. Your face is quite well known –

your father's been flashing your picture everywhere, trying to find you."

Sudden exhaustion dragged me to the floor. Pasha – I'd promised Jake I'd get Pasha out. But Azama – I wasn't leaving him for his Ministry friends to find. That way we could never be sure he wouldn't just start up again, in the time-honoured manner of Mahalian sneaky bastards. And while there was a glimmer of hope I could get one out other than me, two was beyond me. I flexed my crumpled hand and smiled at the tingle, the surge. Two was beyond me, but there was something I could do. With a grunt, I staggered to my feet.

"Do what you can, all right? As many as you can. And if this doesn't work – you look after Jake for me, for us. She'll need it."

Azama was a heavy weight against me, but I managed to drag him over to the office, where Pasha lay, Whelar hovering over him with an anxious frown.

"Rojan, what are you going to do?"

"Get out of here, Dench," I muttered. "You can talk your way back Upside. Take Whelar, because doctors might come in handy. I'll deal with this."

A short nod, a moment to undo Whelar's cuffs and drag him away protesting, and then it was just us three.

Pain came through my hand, my arm, pulsed through my shoulder as I flexed my fingers again. Not enough. It wouldn't be enough, nothing would be, not now I'd got rid of the Glow.

This was just the start of how I'd fucked it for everyone. That didn't matter. I'd promised, and whilst previously my promises were made of nothing but air and quickly forgotten intentions, I intended to keep this one.

"Bet you wish you'd still got it, don't you?" Azama whispered. "Bet you wish you'd not destroyed it all, all that power, all that glorious want in your head."

I glanced at him, at his hot, dark eyes, the vicious glee. "Bet you're glad that concoction of Whelar's started to wear off, aren't you? Not for long."

I punched him, hard as I could, straight in the face. My fingers, abused, bruised, broken and ready to give up, screamed at me, but that didn't matter either. In fact it was good, it was right, it was what I needed. That and what I could suck from Azama's pain. In fact, it felt so good that I did it again. Pain was a memory, a bright light on the edge of the black of my mind. It might be enough. I hoped to fuck it was, because I was going to be my father's son, just the once.

First, Azama. A quick jolt from the syringe to stop him undoing what I was going to do, and then I concentrated on his face. A small rearrangement. It didn't take much – we'd always looked alike. Then I was looking in a mirror, at my own eyes, my own face. A little ragged at the edges just now, but not bad-looking, if I say so myself. Not for long though, because just as soon as all the Ministry men saw what I'd done to the Glow, they'd be looking for a face just like this one. A last touch, as I'd threatened, a tweak of his vocal cords so that anything much past a hiss would be beyond him. No worming his way out with the Voice.

More gunshots, closer now. Other voices, swearing when they found the Glow room a maze of broken glass, calling out, ordering. A voice above the others, strident and used to being obeyed, shouting, "If you find the bastard, kill him. You've all got a picture, and you've seen what he's done. Azama was clear: if he won't join us, we kill him. No fucking about, bullet to the head, a second to make sure."

Sweat popped out on Azama's forehead as he realised what I'd done. I patted his cheek. "The face won't last long. But long enough, I think. A necessary evil. I bet you're glad I'm as much a bastard as you are, aren't you?"

He tried to talk, and I think it was "Kill you too," but it was hard to tell.

"Probably," I said. "But I think it'll be worth it."

Pasha's face was grey and wan, slicked with cold sweat. He was barely holding on, but it was all right, because I was going to save him. I shut my eyes and concentrated on Perak, on Dendal and Upside and all that I thought I'd known before, filled my mind with the thought of being there, back in the office with the smell of Griswald and a cantankerous desk and a lonely diary with no women to fill it. I listened to the black, to the sweet song that told me what to do, and with no further thought to consequences, I let it do what it would.

Chapter Nineteen

When I woke up it was dark, and not just because it was night either. For a head-spinning moment, I couldn't decide where I was, even who I was. No Glow globes lighting the room, or the walkways outside the window. A candle set on the bed-side table was the only light, and someone moved in the flickering shadows. A cool hand on my wrist, another on my forehead.

"About time you woke up." A cool voice to go with the hands. When my eyes adjusted, I saw it was the nurse. The one who, what seemed like several years ago, had flirted while she took me to see Dr Whelar and let me promise her dinner. Not flirting now, but she had kind eyes and a soft manner that was just what I needed.

"It was a long and very trying day." I flexed my broken hand, and winced at the throb, at the pull of splints and stitches that obscured my fingers.

The smile was kind too, when it came. "That wasn't today. Or yesterday either, for that matter."

I sat up and found I was in a bed, but not one I knew. The room was bare, blank of any decoration, unless you count bars on the windows. Or Dench leaning against a wall. Not very decorative, but a welcome sight just the same.

He pushed himself off the wall, away from the window where he'd been contemplating the view. "You're looking pretty good, considering you're dead. I was quite surprised when the news came in, that the Ministry had found and shot you, since you were already in the hospital."

"Ah, yes, well—"

"Mind you, it stopped a lot of the talk about having you executed. Seems the Archdeacon went missing too, which helped. Funny, that." He raised an eyebrow my way and I licked at dry lips. "But maybe not all that surprising, considering. Lots of people went missing Downside the last day or two. Might take us months to work it all out."

The nurse glared at him and made a show of inspecting the splints on my hand. Dench paid no attention to her, but came and sat in the single chair next to the bed. His face was more careworn than ever, but the moustache bristled nicely. I think he was pleased, but trying not to show it.

"You want to tell me what happened?" he asked.

The nurse stopped fiddling with the splints, but she kept close by. I got the feeling she disapproved of Dench, or maybe of his Specials uniform. An unexpected ally. I got up, a bit

shaky on my feet, and went to look out of the window. Cold
air ghosted across my bare back and chill bumps rippled down
my arms. No Glow anywhere, not even at Top of the World.
No lights, no carriages chuntering along the Spine, no glaring advertisements, no distant thump and rumble of the
factories. No lights, no noise, no life. Just the glint of moonlight on a dark and dying city. I laid my forehead on the glass.
The Kiss of Death. Way to go, Rojan. Dench might be
pleased, but I couldn't bring myself to feel anything other
than disappointment, in myself and everyone. Talking further
than trivialities seemed beyond me, because there was too
much else I wanted to let out, and didn't dare. "Not really.
You want to tell *me* what happened? Amarie?"

"Safe and with her father, who's on the mend. Pasha's doing
as well as can be expected." The nurse muttered something at
that, but Dench ignored her.

I stared back out of the window, not wanting to ask, but
needing to know. "Jake?"

"Jittery thing, isn't she? With Pasha – where else? That
isn't what you want to know."

The cool hand on mine again, the nurse murmuring that I
should get back to bed, that I might still lose the hand, had
lost a lot of blood.

"Did I stop it?"

A pause full of something; perhaps caution, maybe regret.
Maybe something else. "Yes. No more Glow. What's left up
here has been ordered to be saved for emergencies. Special

announcement by the Ministry. Along with the news that they're deliberating which cardinal gets to be the acting archdeacon, and that Alchemy Research is working flat-out to try to find a replacement. No official news on what the Glow was, but Downsiders are everywhere. It won't take long. My Specials are busy, along with the guards. Looting, rioting, you know the sort of thing. We need a new archdeacon fast, and a new power source faster."

I turned back from the window, from the darkness I'd made, and let the nurse sit me on the bed. "Can I see them?"

"Who?" Dench looked sympathetic, but there was a steely bent to the way he held himself that didn't bode well.

"All of them. Perak, Amarie – I never actually met her, you know? And Pasha, Dendal. Jake." Especially Jake.

"Rojan, you're dead. Officially dead; I identified the body myself. No, you're here until we can work out what to do with you. Right now, we've got bigger things to worry about. Like getting people food and warmth and light. Once we've got that done, most of the problems will fade away. Perak's working on it, and there's a good chance he might make Archdeacon, in which case we might be all right. Better than a lot of the alternatives. Dendal's helping him, but until they figure something out we're screwed. Royally. And so are you. Make your face someone else's, slide out into obscurity. I can get you Outside; maybe you can find another city, somewhere else to live."

When I looked up there was something like sympathy in

his eyes, but I knew he couldn't give in to it. I'd screwed with his city – and his Goddess too, probably. I couldn't find anything to say, and he left without another word. I couldn't work out whether he hated me, hence the bars on the windows, or was pleased at what I'd done, hence the fact I was still alive. Everything was a whirl inside me.

The nurse huffed about the room after Dench left, checking my pulse and my temperature with her cool hand. I remembered her name through the haze: Lilla.

When her hand rested on my forehead again, I pulled it away and held it in mine. Her eyes, the kindness in them, were all I had to hang on to, the only vestige of my former life. I needed something and I didn't know what. "Does the hospital have a temple?"

Lilla tilted her head, and I had to look away from her eyes, from the cool pity.

"I'll help you get dressed," she said, but I shook my head, oddly ashamed, and managed by myself.

The windows were barred, but the door wasn't locked. I soon found out why, but I took Dench's advice and changed my face, just a bit. The hallway was as dark as the room, and lined with Specials. I kept my head down and followed Lilla, past dim doorways and silent wards, past the nurses' station, a small haven of candlelight, starched uniforms and brisk efficiency. Past sidelong stares, knowing looks and whispers behind hands – and doors with grilles on them and heavy locks. Not the Sacred Goddess Hospital.

Lilla stopped by a door like half a dozen others we'd passed. The interior was dim, as everywhere else, but a candle had been set on the altar, and the moving shadows on the mural made the Goddess look alive. Lilla went to turn away, but I grabbed for her hand. Before I'd always, consciously or unconsciously, tried to stay apart, alone, even when I feared that same aloneness. Now it was the last thing I wanted. "Stay?"

She hesitated with a frown, but in the end we walked to the altar together, past the saints and martyrs and their blind, plaster eyes. The mural was one of the pretty ones, all flowers and sodding birds and the Goddess looking sweet and a bit constipated as she offered her hand to the tiger. Guilt and sacrifice.

I looked down at the splints over my fingers. Still guilt and sacrifice, and now I couldn't look at the mural, couldn't look at her face without seeing the other one, down in the 'Pit, all blood and violence and contempt.

"Rojan?" Lilla's voice was small in the space before the altar. "Rojan, forget Dench. You did the right thing. For everyone."

"I didn't do it because it needed to be done, or because it was right, or wrong, or for the Goddess. I did it because I was afraid." I flexed the fingers and thrilled at the run of magic when they hurt, at the memory of it all pouring through me and knowing that I wouldn't do it, wouldn't be like him, even though I was. That I'd made a choice, for good or ill, and could only hope it was the right one. The words tumbled out, but I wasn't talking to Lilla. "I've always been afraid, of my magic, of what it'll do to me, afraid since I was ten and he left us on our own. Mostly I was afraid I'd be like him. I always took after him more than I did Ma. So I made sure I couldn't be, and became like him while I did it. I did it because I was afraid, and I'm still like him. I did the necessary evil, and made sure he died, even if I didn't kill him myself."

Lilla squeezed my good hand. She probably had no idea what I was talking about, but she didn't let it show. "You got rid of it, you stopped it. You did the right thing."

"Is it? Was it right? All these people, no Glow, I—"

Lilla cut me off with a stern nurse-in-charge-of-patient look. "You weren't the one to get Pasha patched up, or those kids. You didn't see . . ." She shook her head with a pained look to her eyes. "I don't care about the rest, not yet. The Ministry have plenty of Glow stored, I'm sure. And plenty of everything else. Bet my boots *they've* got enough food for months."

"But—"

"Enough. Sod Dench and his 'you're dead'. Come and see." The smile was as dimpled as I remembered, and did nothing to me except make me want to sit here for ever, where it was quiet and no one knew who I was or what I'd done. No one except Lilla.

She led me out of the temple, and I had no strength to resist. I was sure I could feel the Goddess's eyes on my back. Great: eyed up by a figment of my imagination. Lilla stopped at the first door and nodded her head towards the ward. A dozen beds, each with three or four small bodies curled up under blankets. Two Specials stood silent and watchful just inside the door. As we watched, one of the kids whimpered in their sleep, and another curled into them, a soft hand comforting, understanding what only they could know, what they never should have known.

"You did that," Lilla said. "If you hadn't done what you did, they'd still be there."

Because they were worth more, to me. Because *Jake* was worth more and no one should ever have to go through what she and Pasha had. Yet all these people Upside, hundreds of thousands, more maybe, without Glow, without trade or any way to make a living . . . were they worth less?

"Come on, you need to get back to bed." Lilla pulled at me and I followed her, not a little bewildered and still feeling oddly floaty, as though I was no longer part of the world around me. The only solid anchor I had was Lilla's hand in mine and I hung on to it, bizarrely afraid I might fly away otherwise.

The moon shone through the windows of the corridors she led me along, ridiculously beautiful when it was unimpeded. Its silver light fell unhampered across Trade, lit all the factories and made even their silent, blocky bulk seem delicate. No buildings above Trade to shield the moonlight, no Glow to compete with it, to blind me to it.

Something was waiting for me on the bed. My pulse pistol, with a note in Dendal's writing. *I thought you might want this back. Maybe it does have its uses, after all.*

How did Dendal know I was still alive? Then again, how did Dendal know anything? I picked up the pulse pistol, and it felt oddly heavy.

Lilla looked at it curiously and I told her what it was.

"How does it work?"

"What? I don't know." I stared down at it, at maybe the very thing that had started this whole chain of events: me chasing Lise, and using the pistol on her. The last time things had been normal, when a cut on the thumb for magic had been a big deal and the black was to be feared, rather than just another part of me that I didn't want. *No more fear, Rojan, remember?* Easier said than done.

The pistol. The fucking pistol – the answer staring me in the face. "Where's Dwarf? And Lise?"

"Rojan, the doctor said – and Dench—"

I grabbed at her shoulders, wincing as the splints twisted on my fingers, and relishing it too. Also relishing the new hope surging through me. I could make it up, to everyone. "Lilla, this is it. The answer, maybe. I know how to get Trade up and running. I just have to get it to Dwarf. Please."

She looked up at me, her dark eyes worried, but in the end she nodded. "I'll see what I can do."

"Yes, but how does it work?" I waited impatiently for Dwarf to think it through. His broken legs had been set, and Lise – my *sister*, I had to keep reminding myself – had fussed round him worse than a new mother with her first baby. Until I turned up, and now they were both lost in concentration, considering what I'd asked. "Can you use that?"

Lilla had worked a miracle – found Dwarf a floor below me, behind the same sort of bars. Not the Sacred Goddess Hospital, she finally agreed when I'd asked. A secret place, for the Ministry. Run by Specials. A prison of sorts, for all those people who were just too awkward to have around but whom the Ministry, for whatever reason, didn't want dead just yet.

I'd changed my face again, but I had trouble with the voice, so at least Dwarf recognised me when I spoke. His attention was all on the pistol though.

"Well, I expect so," Dwarf said in the end. "But it's going to take some time to set up. And money."

"Of course we can do it," Lise countered. She looked up at me, a bit shy at first. "The pistol converts magic to energy, the same principle they used to run the factories before synth, only better, much better. Besides, the Ministry's got lots of money."

"But this mechanism magnifies magic?" A small cut on the thumb gave enough of a burst to knock someone out, using more power than it should rightfully have. Azama had known about my magic, thought it very powerful, because I'd used this. Particularly powerful I probably wasn't, but the pistol had magnified it.

"Oh, yes. It's very clever." Lise looked over at Dwarf, admiration in every quiver of her body. Dwarf blushed. It made him look almost human.

"So you could make one bigger, that does the same? Or maybe just some more of them, to start with?"

"What do you want to do, Rojan?" Dwarf was looking at me like I'd gone a bit mad. Maybe he was right, but it had to be worth a go.

"I want to get the factories running again. We have to replace the Glow with something. Maybe we can replace it with what it actually is – pain magic. Only no using anyone else. It failed before because Mahala got too big, too much of a drain on the mages. But if we magnify it?"

Lise's eyes snapped wide. "Or better. Eddin, electricity, the generator you've been working on. Couldn't we use that?"

"Eddin?" I raised an eyebrow at Dwarf.

"It's my name, you want to make something of it?" The blush was now a deep red and curling round his ears. "And maybe, Lise. But it'll take time. That brother of yours, Rojan, he can help. In the meantime, I've got another two of these at my lock-up. It might be enough to get some things started. It'll take a heck of a lot out of anyone, though. The amount of factories . . ."

"We can start with a few, until we get going. How long to make more?"

"A couple of days, once I get out of this bed. Or you can get someone to bring the workings here. I could manage something. Probably an enhancement or two."

I nodded my agreement and left them to their incomprehensible jargon as they discussed ways of improving the mechanism. Lise kept talking about electricity, and maybe that would be a way forward eventually, if she could get it to work.

It was Lilla that got the message to Dendal, and Perak.

And it was the news of what the pistol might be able to do that got Perak the archdeaconship. And me free.

I asked Lilla to find someone to get Dwarf's things, and snuck down to the nurses' desk. Dwarf hadn't been in the forefront of who I needed to see. I didn't want to, but I needed to.

As I entered the room, a shadow at the window turned. Jake's hair was a darker red in that light, her eyes shining. They clouded slightly when she didn't recognise me, and her hand went to the bed – to Pasha, dozing and pale, propped up on pillows. Such a small thing, that she touched his shoulder to wake him, but it told me everything I needed to know, and made my heart twist.

I let my face bleed back into its normal planes and her face lit up. It was almost worth it all just for that.

"They told us you were dead!"

"Not yet, sorry to disappoint. You like the view, then."

Her smile was timid, so unlike her it jarred me for a moment. "I never realised it was so beautiful."

"The moon?" I moved to stand next to her, keeping a careful distance because I was still tempted. To just touch her, run a hand over her cheek, across the back of her neck. Kiss her again. She wasn't mine and never would be. Like the moon, I suppose. Maybe that's why moonlight always looks so sad.

She shook her head and looked back out of the window. "The city. The *sky*. I never saw the sky before."

Her shoulders twitched and she kept her face carefully turned away from mine. "I did it for you," I wanted to say. *I did it all for you*. But I still wasn't quite fear-free enough to say it.

Pasha sat up on the bed, looking gaunt and hollow. He didn't speak, but he didn't really need to. We stared at each other for a while, not saying anything, and I wondered if he could hear what was going through my head. Maybe not – Lilla had said they'd doped him with painkillers pretty hard. Love and sacrifice, that was what was running through my head. What the Goddess had always been trying to say, I think, that she had done it willingly, for everyone. Jake had shown it to me, and Pasha, in what they'd done, every day. No life but the matches to earn money to fund what they really did: save children, with no expectation of thanks or reward. Pasha willing to kill for her, to die for her, because she'd saved him. Because he loved her in a way I never could.

Typical really, and Pasha had been right all along. I'd fallen in love, for the first time ever and against my better, or maybe just more cynical, judgement. And I'd fallen for a cipher, a bit of flash and wind, not the real her. I'd fallen for who I wanted her to be, not who she was. That, what lay underneath all the show, behind the wall of her swords, was Pasha's, through and through. I couldn't really begrudge him that. Bastard.

I couldn't look at him any more, or even at Jake, so I stared out of the window instead. That wasn't much better — the stillness, the silence, the waiting hunger — but I thought I might have an answer. Not a "for good" answer, but a "good enough for now" answer.

Pasha came and stood next to us, stared out over a city that he probably barely remembered. "I was going to go earlier, but the Specials wouldn't let me, us. It's like another kind of prison, only you get to see what you've lost."

"Go where?"

Pasha reached out to stroke the glass, and my eyes were drawn again to the brand, to the scars old and new. "Anywhere. I don't know."

Something about him was hypnotic, the dreamy way he stroked the glass, the faraway look in his eye, the twitch in his shoulder as he spoke. I pulled myself together.

"I thought you were going to join him," he said.

"So did I, for a moment."

"So why didn't you?" He looked up at me, a brief, puzzled glance.

"What, join in all that religion shit? No thanks." Then, because it was about time I started being honest, even if only with myself, I thought at him, *You were right. You know her better, love her better. I wanted her to have that. You two were worth more than any amount of people up here. To me, anyway.*

Some of it must have got through, because a smile twitched his face. "Rojan, thank—"

"Please, leave me a shred of dignity, all right? I can't have

345

anyone finding out I'm not a total prick. I've got a reputation to uphold."

He laughed at that, a small shadow of a thing but he was back to being the monkey again. Almost. "All right. But what now?"

"Now, I need you to help me. We're going to use our magic the old-fashioned way, with a little extra help from Dwarf and my pulse pistol. I took away the Glow, I've got to replace it with something. Or rather, *we* have. You, me and Dendal, we're going to power up what we can of the factories until we can figure something else out. Here he is."

Lilla escorted Dendal as he blinked his way into the room, looked around as though he was lost and only belatedly noticed us at the window. "Ah! There you are. Dench said it was urgent, so I came. Rearranging? Goddess, what we could do with that. Your father was always quite good at it, if I recall, in a limited way. As a Major, well, you could run half of Trade and not even think about it. Look, I've been working it out."

He shoved a sheaf of papers under my nose, but I couldn't make sense of any of the little squiggles. Lilla bit her lip and put a hand to her mouth and I was hard pressed not to laugh myself. I almost hugged the old fairy-brain, I was so glad to see him. I wanted to tell him everything and listen – properly this time – when he told me how I'd got it all wrong and what I should be doing, how I should be mastering myself and my magic. I wanted to tell him I'd found something to believe in, even if it wasn't his Goddess, and I wanted my feet up on Griswald while I did it.

"So, have you thought what you're going to do with it, Perak?" Dendal's anxious, not-quite-all-there face peered up at me hopefully.

"Rojan, Dendal. My name's Rojan."

"Is it? Oh, yes. But the question, what are you going to do with it?"

Lilla smiled at me from the doorway, cool and kind and dimpled, safe and normal. I wondered if dinner was still an option. My mind was only half on my words. "Fire up the factories, if we can. Start with the ones we need the most, maybe get some light back. It's going to hurt, but it's *our* hurt, not anyone else's."

Pasha nodded thoughtfully. "I can manage that."

Lilla walked off down the corridor and I admired the swing of her uniform, the memory of her kind eyes and cool hands. Dendal wouldn't want to hear it, but I also wondered if rearranging her knickers, as in arranging for them to be on my bedroom floor, might be somewhere in the future. I wasn't sure, but it'd be a whole lot of fun finding out.

Acknowledgements

Where to start? Tricky. Let's start at the beginning. My family, for ceaseless encouragement and putting up with the fact I spend as much time in my own head as I do with them. Absolute Write, for educating me about writing, publishing, and for the friendships it's brought me. Thanks, Mac! Special thanks to JCD and Quicklime. Smutty thoughts to Scarlett, like she needs them, for helping me when things got dark. The T-Party writers' group, for the unstinting ability to tell me where I've gone wrong, writerly camaraderie and curry. Deb, who taught me more about writing than I care to admit. Alex Field for his boundless enthusiasm. Devi and Anna for their illuminating comments, suggestions, sterling editorial manner and patience with a newb. And last, but by no means least, Bettie-Lee Turner, Luke Walker and Sarah Ellender, for reading my draft and telling me what you really thought!

Thanks, guys. I owe you all a pint. Except Luke, who gets half a mild and a packet of pork scratchings.

extras

www.orbitbooks.net

about the author

Francis Knight was born and lives in Sussex, UK. She has held a variety of jobs from being a groom in the Balearics, where she punched a policeman and got away with it, to an IT administrator. When not living in her own head, she enjoys SFF geekery, WWE geekery, teaching her children *Monty Python* quotes and boldly going and seeking out new civilisations.

Find out more about Francis Knight and other Orbit authors by registering for the free monthly newsletter at www.orbitbooks.net

interview

Have you always known that you wanted to be a writer?
No, I can't say that I have, probably because it never occurred to me to write down all the stories in my head. I've always read, and always made up little stories but it was only when I was struck down with ME that I started to write – I was housebound, and it was almost a defence against daytime TV. So I wrote one of my little stories and found I was addicted to writing.

Did the idea for the Rojan Dizon books come to you fully realised or did you have one particular starting point from which it grew?
As with most of my ideas, it came a piece at a time, each piece from a different direction. The idea really takes hold when they gang up on me. The theme came from one direction, Jake from another, whereas Rojan came as I was writing. He was kind of an experiment – I'd never written in first

person before, and he is the polar opposite to me in many areas (though we do share a trait or two), so he was almost a challenge I set myself, to see if I could do it. I splurged out fifty thousand words in a month – at this stage it was a future dystopian world, but then my writers' group pointed out, quite fairly, that I am horrible at making up future tech. One member suggested "Why not make it a dark fantasy?", which kind of fed into a separate idea I'd had for a world where magic lived with technology. I dabbled a bit then left it on my hard drive for a few years, tinkering with it every now and again in between other projects. It was only when I decided to actually knuckle down and do something with it, when I started with the idea of pain magic in fact, that it really came to life. It was waiting for me to have the right idea to make it work, I think.

What inspired you in your creation of the city of Mahala?
Again, not just one thing though I suspect that *Bladerunner* and *Sin City* had their influence! The city hives from some of Dan Abnett's Warhammer books were always interesting to me as well. Mostly it was something that happened as I was writing the story. It grew with the telling.

Which level of the city could you imagine yourself living on?
Well, I'd like to live in Clouds, because it's nice there and there's sun, but like Rojan, I suspect I'd end up somewhere

less salubrious. To me, the underbelly is more interesting. If not as pleasant.

How extensively do you plot your novels before you start writing them? Do you plot the entire trilogy/series before you start writing or do you prefer to let the story roam where it will?

Hardly at all. Generally I start with a character, in a situation. I have an idea of the tone or atmosphere I want to create, and the type of emotional response I'm aiming to invoke – happy, dark, bittersweet, nostalgic, etc. I have a vague idea of what might be the ending (which usually changes a lot). Other than that, it could go anywhere!

Where did the idea for pain magic come from?

I can trace that back directly – to Thomas Convenant. At one point he broke his ankle and a healer fixed it, but to do so she had to take the pain and injury on herself. I've always been drawn by the idea of consequences to magic (as there are consequences to everything), especially what might make it a less than desirable thing to have. If it's all reading and waggling fingers and cool fireballs, well that's fine but a magic that you *really* don't want to use unless you have to . . . that became very interesting.

Who could you imagine playing Rojan in a film adaptation of the book? And how about Jake?

Oh, now that's tricky. I use photos of real people, sometimes actors, sometimes not, on my wall as I write for inspiration. I kind of had Christian Bale in mind for a while (because of a photo of him with one brow raised, as though questioning everything, very Rojan) but I'd have to go with Adam Beach. Jake, well Jake was based on several very varied influences, but I recall having a photo of Deadly Little Miho from *Sin City* up on my wall as I wrote the scenes where Jake fights, so Devon Aoki would suit very well.

Do you have any particular favourite authors who have influenced your work?

Too many to mention! C. J. Cherryh really kick-started my desire to write; such complicated and very real characters. Terry Pratchett is phenomenal, but I wouldn't even attempt to go there . . . he's done it so well. Jim Butcher's the Dresden files for sure, Philip K. Dick, Ursula Le Guin, Lois McMaster Bujold, the list goes on. There's plenty outside the genre that I think have influenced me too – as a kid I devoured Dick Francis and Ruth Rendell novels, and lately Robert Low's Oathsworn series left me slack-jawed in admiration. Probably every book I've loved has influenced me in some way.

Do you have a set writing routine and if so, what is it?

Not as such. I work odd shifts, so it's a matter of writing when I can. When I started, I also had two small children, so that was an extra challenge. Now I just write when I get the opportunity of an hour or two free! I have been known to tell the husband to "just go to the pub, dammit" in order to get some writing time in. He rarely complains.

If you had a superpower, what would it be?
I'd love to be able to fly – I have a secret hankering to be Storm. Lightning bolts an added bonus!

if you enjoyed

FADE TO BLACK

look out for

ECHO CITY

by

Tim Lebbon

Prologue

As it left the city, the thing did not once look back. It walked with heavy steps, looked forward with rheumy eyes, and its misted breath soon dispersed in the air. It did not look back, because its purpose was ahead, and large though this thing was, its brain was small and simple, its reason for being very precise. It moved away from the world and out into the Bonelands, and it would never return.

Darkness concealed the start of its journey. It was aware of people in the buildings and ruins around it, but Skulk Canton was a place whose residents would keep to themselves. If they did not, its maker had instructed it to force their attention away. In its rudimentary mind, the idea of violence was little different from the process of placing one foot in front of the other, or breathing, or blinking its eyes to clear them of sand.

For a while as it started across the desert, the ground still bore signs of Echo City. Rubble from tumbled walls marred its path, and it had to step aside or climb over. One spread of land was scarred with the evidence of digging, the reason and results long since lost to time. And here and there it saw the remains of a body.

The moon's pale crescent lit its way. Beyond the moon, countless stars speckled the clear, cold night. The thing had no concept of what moon and stars were, because they bore no connection to its purpose. But it looked up at them with curiosity nonetheless. Its maker had granted it that, at least.

Soon it was away from the outer limits of the city. It walked as it had been instructed, avoiding places where the sands looked thin and loose and keeping to harder, easier surfaces. No plants existed out here, and no animals – nothing but sand and rock and the dry, heavy air it breathed.

Sometimes a gentle breeze whispered a skein of sand across its path, and it held its breath as it passed through the brief, scouring cloud.

Its body was clothed in heavy leathers. It had watched its maker constructing this suit, stitching together the garments of many normal people to create something expansive enough to cover its huge torso. The suit was tied around its bulky thighs, upper arms, and neck, and the exposed surfaces of its arms and legs had been sprayed with a thick dark lotion to ward off the desert's inimical influence. Woven into the layers of leather were fluid sacs, in a network of narrow tubes that merged eventually beneath a thin, hollow bone straw protruding beneath its chin. It took frequent sips of water, and it was not long before the sips were tainted by the salty taste of its own perspiration.

Its shoes were tied leather folded many times, spiked with iron studs to give grip. It carried no weapons. It bore no pack. The prints it left behind were wide, long, and deep, and they would command awe were they noticed in the days following. But by then the thing would be dead, and it would never hear the myths of its passing.

As dawn set the eastern desert aflame, the thing marched on. It glanced to its left only once, experiencing a brief flare of wonder and awe. Somewhere deep down basked shadows of memories that were not its own, in which the view of such sunrises was interrupted by the silhouettes of spires and walls, towers and roofs. Such a natural, unhindered view as this was something all but unique, but the giant creature was not here to pontificate. It was here only to walk.

The desert stretched before it. To the south, a low range of hills buckled the horizon. They were perhaps a day's journey distant, though distance here was difficult to judge, and there were no maps of the Bonelands. It focused on the hills as it walked. By the time the sun had passed its zenith and begun its fall to the west, the hills seemed no closer, and it had to reassess its estimate of the time it would take to reach them. Beyond the hills, so every story said, there was only more poisoned desert. They were a meaningless marker at best. It might reach them ... but probably not. Already it could feel the rot.

It paused to eat. Sitting on its huge haunches, the reduced weight of Echo City now many miles to the rear, it felt the rumbling, gnawing processes inside. There was a little pain, but it could compare the sensation only to the shimmering heat haze hanging above the desert far to the west – an insubstantial thing that would vanish as soon as it closed its eyes.

It closed its eyes, and the pain was warmth.

When it stood and started walking again, it looked down at its bare, sprayed legs. The skin was peeling, revealing a dark red rawness beneath. Its feet were blistered and swollen, and several of the tight leather straps had burst. It kicked off one of the folded leather shoes, and it flapped on the desert floor as the folds unwrapped. And then the shoe was still, and there it would stay forever.

A while later the creature removed the other shoe, because wearing only one had been swinging it slowly around in a great arc across the sands. It corrected its direction of travel and set off once more.

It had passed several bodies on its walk, but just as the sun touched the western horizon it came across the first of the ruined transports. It was a rusted, rotten hulk, its wheels skeletons of metal wrapped in the brittle remains of parched wood. The creature walked close and touched one of the wheels, curiosity lighting a small flame in its limited mind. The wood came apart under its clumsy stroke, drifting to the ground in a cloud of dust and splinters. A gentle breeze that the creature had not even felt carried some of the wooden shards away, and they added themselves to the desert.

Before the ruined vehicle lay two great skeletons of the things that had pulled it this far. Pelts were draped across their bones in places, and within the stark confines of rib cages were the scattered remains of insides not yet burned to nothing by the relentless sun. Their horns were long and graceful, pitted now from the effects of the desert air.

Here and there it saw the mummified remains of human beings. They had been riding the wagon, and perhaps when their beasts succumbed to the desert's toxic influence, they had walked on until they all lay down together to die. The creature did not like to look at them. Though its maker had made it unique, somehow they reminded it of itself.

So it walked on and stared at that undulating horizon, and

sometimes the texture of the ground beneath it changed. But it did not look down.

When dusk began to fall, it guessed that Echo City would now be out of sight behind it. But still it did not look back. The future lay before it – too far away to see, beyond its ability to feel – and as it considered what might come, the thing it carried inside seemed excited at the prospect.

It walked through the freezing night. Its motion kept it warm, but all the while it felt itself sickening. The desert's lethal, toxic influence was making itself felt upon the creature's flesh and bones, its blood and fluids, and though built strong it was now becoming weak. Darkness was its friend, though under the silvery sheen of moonlight it could still witness some of its flesh's demise. It was not worried, because it had not been made that way. But it did pause and stare up at the moon, and it realized that come dawn it would never see this sight again.

Sad, unsure what sadness was, it walked on.

When dawn broke on that second day, the creature realized just where the Markoshi Desert had gained its more common name.

The hills were still distant, and speckling the surface of the desert before them lay thousands of bones. There were skulls, some still bearing the leathery remnants of scalp and hair, and a few wearing the wrinkled skin of their hopeful, desperate owners. Beneath and around the skulls lay the skeletons.

Older remains were all but buried by drifts, but more-recent escapees from Echo City lay atop the sand. Many of them were still clothed in the outfits they had believed would protect them from the desert's terrible actions, and beneath these, leathered skin was scarred with the rot. Most remains were whole, because not even carrion creatures could survive the Bonelands' poisons. Some had been scattered, however, and here and there the creature saw evidence of violence having been wrought. It knew that the only living things out here to perpetrate such acts would have been other people.

Their equipment lay around them where it had fallen. Bags, water skins, weapons, clothing, an occasional sled or wheeled vehicle, all had been heated by the relentless sun and cooled by the fearsome desert nights, and successive heatings and coolings had destroyed much. There was nothing here to aid the creature in its progress, and after a while it no longer paid heed to the strewn remnants of desperation and hope. It focused on the hills it would never reach, sucked water from the bone straw, and felt the thing inside it rolling and gnawing, making itself strong for the time to come.

It could feel itself weakening, but purpose drove it on. Flesh sloughed from its exposed limbs, and blood speckled the sand beneath it. Its large feet had spread since shedding the shoes, and had it looked back it would have seen the trail of bloody footprints. Sand worked its way into wounds, and the creature felt pain despite the way it had been made, and taught, and given life. It howled, but there was no one to hear.

Eventually it came to a stop among the bones and rocks and hot sands, sinking slowly onto its side and then its back, turning its head so that it could look across the desert at the low hills. They had drawn much closer, it thought, especially in the past few hours when it had been walking with the sun sinking to its right. It felt a sense of accomplishment and hoped its maker was pleased.

Its movements ceased, its eyes grew pale and dry, and its limited awareness of surroundings and purpose drifted away like dust on the breeze. Its only thought as things grew dark was that it had done its very best.

Hearing was the last to go, and the sound that accompanied it down into death was something tearing, and something wet.

The thing emerged from the giant corpse. It had been made with hooked claws and toes with which to rip, and it tore its way out through the weakened flesh. It had also been formed with a sharp ridge running down its forehead to the bridge of its nose, and it used this to saw and snap at the thick ribs that encircled its host's upper half. As it emerged, a bloody violent birth, it also ate and drank. The meat was warm and the blood thick, and strength coursed through its body.

Free of its confines, it remained there for a while as it grew accustomed to its surroundings. It had filled itself with its mother's flesh and blood, but already it could feel this desert's rot.

Its maker had warned it of this. Time was passing, the desert was exerting its poisonous influence, and it knew it had far to go.

Standing naked beneath the sinking sun, it looked to the sky and felt a sense of release that it could not accurately identify or understand. It had little to do with being away from the body now lying beneath and around it, because it thought of that only as meat. It had nothing to do with being able to stretch its arms and flex its clawed fingers at the glittering points of light. Looking back across the desert, marking the bloody prints stretching off into the dusk, it saw a smudge of light low on the horizon. Freedom, release ... it thought it had something to do with leaving whatever that light represented.

Yet it knew that its destination lay in the opposite direction. It gathered folds of leather around its naked body, filled rough pockets with handfuls of meat from the thing that had birthed it, and started walking.

Daylight came, and night once more, and when it saw the sunrise for the second time it realized that there were no longer bones. The last set of remains it had passed had been wrapped in several layers of thick leather, a chain-mail body shell, and something that resembled the chitinous outer layers of a beetle. The mummified corpse had been lying with its right hand stretched out and finger pointing southward, as if indicating the place it wanted to be. Its mouth had been wide, and it had carried three obsidian teeth. On the corpse's skin, the creature had made out the dark smears of strange markings, and it wondered what that meant.

It had memories of something called Echo City, but they were very old, and they belonged somewhere else. It did not consider the strangeness of carrying such old memories when it had been born for only two days. It had a maker, and that maker's voice was the sole loud, clear thing in its fresh mind. *Walk,* that voice said, *avoid dangers, look south, and travel as far as you can.* It spoke in suggestion rather than words. The creature obeyed.

Though nothing lived in the desert, there were dangers. Around noon of that third day, it entered an area where great holes breathed dark fumes of gas and nightmare. Drawing in these fumes for the first time, the thing fell to its knees as its immature brain was racked with onslaughts of images dredged from some past it did not know. It saw faces and death, madness and war, and the release of an appalling disease that made it open its eyes again to look down upon its own body. It could not see its face to make out whether it resembled those in its nightmare, but its body was the same – and the abuse it suffered clothed it in the same sadness. Skin was weakening, flesh was rotting, and its insides churned as something sought release.

Father, its maker's voice said, hardly audible through the nightmares. The creature stood and ran, ignoring the staggering pain that pummeled up from its legs as weakening bones crumbled. When they finally snapped, it crawled instead, hauling itself out of that region of holes and ventings, giving it the chance to breathe air that seemed clearer. Its mind settled, leaving it with the idea of its maker.

By dusk on that third day it could crawl no farther. Its fingers had worn away, and whatever ills the desert carried had turned its eyes to mush, its flesh to rotten stuff. It lay still as it birthed the thing it had been made to carry, and the maker had created it so that the pain was only slight.

As darkness came, it tried to imagine the maker saying, *Good*.

The smaller creature crawled from the remains of its mother. It had four legs and a hugely distended stomach, but the legs were long enough to lift it from contact with the sands and strong enough to carry it across the desert at startling speed.

It passed over a low range of hills, negotiating a dry ravine on the other side and continuing into the desert that lay beyond. Nothing lived here but it, though it did not find that strange. It carried vague and distant memories of life and plenty, but it did not suffer loneliness, because the maker was always there. It listened to the maker's songs, poems, and words of wisdom and humor, and though it could not respond, it knew that the maker was pleased. It ran fast and far, avoiding patches of lighter-colored sand, which would have sucked it down to unknown depths, and places where flames twisted across the landscape in defiance of the breeze.

At last night came, and in the deceptive shadows of dusk the thing tripped over a rock and broke one of its legs.

It lay quietly as death approached, feeling the desert's deadly influences now that it was down. It listened to the maker in memories, and even as its rounded stomach split and gushed forth innards, it did not feel the pain.

The thing that rose from the gore and steam walked on.

A day later, as noon scorched the sands and something slumped to the ground to die, the journey came to an end.

As the creature edged toward death, its legs fell apart and revealed the moist heart of itself. It growled as it obeyed what the maker had instructed it to do, defying the sun and the desert, the heat and the air, the dust and the winds. It felt its flesh withered and diseased, but it pushed harder as it birthed its son and willed itself to die, comforted that it was not the desert that had taken it in the end.

The child mewled as it squirmed in the sand. It poked strong fingers through the translucent film that enveloped it and blinked wet, intelligent eyes at the heat and sunlight that rushed in to bathe its soft skin. It tried to stand, but its legs were still shaky. It looked around, seeing only endless sand and sky.

And it imagined its maker growing sad, because there truly was nothing beyond the Bonelands.

Later, perhaps only hours before the child would have died, a shadow fell across it.